RAISING THE STAKES

Softly, Abbey said: "You promised me I'd learn how Vitt died." In the midst of this great disaster, she still felt her own life, her own hopes, surge. They might mean nothing if the world was to end. But her thoughts clung to these hopes like flotsam in a flood.

"I promised nothing. But you have already proven yourself to me by confronting the round-faced man. He should have played. He should have died. But now you have found the Leap Point despite him. Now you must enter it."

She spit out her words, one at a time: "You don't get it. I'm in this for my daughter. I've always been in this for her."

Jaguar advanced on her, his eyes hard as fists. "And your people? One daughter for your whole people?"

Standing her ground, Abbey threw back, "She is my people! The last of my people!"

His sneer deepened. "Listen well: when the migration is complete, your people will serve the Hhso. The heat of your world oppresses them, therefore they will sleep much and work little. Your people's fate will be the opposite. Opposite."

Also by Kay Kenyon

The Seeds of Time

Available from Bantam Spectra Books

LEAP POINT

Kay Kenyon

BANTAM BOOKS
NEW YORK TORONTO
LONDON SYDNEY
AUCKLAND

LEAP POINT
A Bantam Spectra Book / March 1998

SPECTRA and the portrayal of a boxed "s" are trademarks of
Bantam Books,
a division of Bantam Doubleday Dell Publishing Group, Inc.

ISBN 0-553-57682-8

Published simultaneously in the United States and Canada

Bantam Books are published by Bantam Books, a division of
Bantam Doubleday Dell Publishing Group, Inc. Its trademark,
consisting of the words "Bantam Books" and the portrayal of a
rooster, is Registered in U.S. Patent and Trademark Office and in
other countries. Marca Registrada. Bantam Books, 1540
Broadway, New York, New York 10036.

PRINTED IN THE UNITED STATES OF AMERICA

OPM   10 9 8 7 6 5 4 3 2 1

This book is dedicated with gratitude to my parents, Catherine and Jerry Kenyon, in life and in loving memory.

Acknowledgments

Thanks to my readers and fellow writers Karen Mac-Leod, Leslie Adkins, and Veronica Weikel, who cheered me on, kept me company, and kept me writing. My appreciation to Donald Maass, whose counsel always inspires better stories, and to Anne Lesley Groell for her infectious enthusiasm and keen insight. I am indebted to my husband, Thomas: trusted advisor, scientific resource, healthy skeptic . . . and always, my foremost supporter.

They chose Medicine Falls for the Leap Point because it was average and unremarkable in every way—except for being just a little desperate. At the same time the town was isolated, twenty-five kilometers from the closest node of civilization.

Gazing up at the starry night sky, a typical citizen might remark how the stars were like diamonds sprinkled on velvet, or how bright the Milky Way was, far from city lights. Or a few odd ones might wonder if the sun was a twinkle in someone else's night sky at that moment. As, of course, it was. A signal fire. What some might call a lighthouse beacon.

But Medicine Falls didn't look up very often. Folks were preoccupied with alfalfa to be baled and shopping to be done. And at night most people gave themselves up to vids and the Net, never looking up.

Except for Rachel.

At the moment she was gazing up into the recesses of the station's ceiling far above, where a flaw in the roof metered out a slow plunk, plunk of melting snow.

Zachariah Smith followed her gaze upward, seeing more, immeasurably more, than the cracked and abandoned roof of the Lowell Street Rail Station. In his mind's eye he saw a bustling tide of shoppers and travelers under the brilliant station lights. The glory days of Medicine Falls revisited. The glory days of Zachariah Smith—lightning rod to the city's new jolt of life.

It wasn't the kind of life that most folks probably had in mind, but they were about to get it anyway.

"Can't you tell me what it is?" Rachel asked for the dozenth time. Her voice reverberated in the empty mall hall, with its row of dead viewscreen storefronts.

"It's a secret. Like I said." He kept his voice low, but the echo swooped out like a long, velvety tongue to snap up the remains of Rachel's question. The only other sound was the slap of their boots through the oily, tie-dyed water.

A spray of light bulged into human shape in front of them. "Say, neighbor," the promo holo said, causing Rachel to nearly climb up Zachariah's arm. "Does your cyberware compare?" The female image was wearing a short gel-fit, with tiny fish swimming through its transparent depths. She turned her forearm to display the glittering band of light nodes from her high-fashion cuff computer.

As the holo disintegrated, Rachel pushed at her hair, trying to force it back under her woolen cap. "My hair is crashed," she said, pressing for some compliment, perhaps. Poor dummy, to worry about her hair at a time like this, trying to compete with a holo, to trivialize what was about to happen. They passed the sagging remains of a food-o-mat, with its boxes full of desiccated pie and long-dead mildew. It wasn't *the* smell, but it was bad enough. He hurried her along.

Leaving the retail corridor, they entered the central rotunda. Here, the great domed ceiling loomed over them, with a few meter-long icicles marking the roof's slow leaks.

Rachel looked up at them dubiously, as though one might pick this very moment to come stabbing down.

Like most folks, she didn't know much of anything. But then, he had to admit, there was plenty he didn't understand, either. Like what they *did* with his donations. He succeeded in keeping that curiosity at bay, tucking it away in a little box to open later, if need be.

When, for instance, it was time to come back here.

Behind them in the mall area, another promo holo strobed in and out of life. For a fleeting moment it festooned their shadows out in front of them, across the glistening pond and up the far wall. Ghosts, Zachariah thought, the station is filled with ghosts. Ghosts of other Rachels, ghosts of past glory, the bustle of commerce, the piercing whistles of trains coming, trains going: Minneapolis, Duluth, Madison, Great Falls, Jackson Hole, Sioux City, and points beyond.

"Zachy . . ." Her voice wheedled at him. . . .

He sighed and turned to face her. "Rachel, if you want to go home, just say so." He threw in a snappish edge to his best, creamy deep voice.

Her eyes turned flinty. "This place stinks," she said. "What if there's freakers here? What's so damn important, anyway?"

"Well, you won't find out unless you come look, will you?"

Another glance up at the toothy dome. "How far is it?"

Rolling his eyes, Zachariah took her by the arm, sloshing ahead. "The longer we stand under those things, the better chance there is of becoming a kabob."

"Zachy!" she giggled, in feigned delicacy.

If she called him that again, he'd slap her silly. Unwillingly, the image bobbed into his mind, of shutting up that high-pitched shred of a voice . . . an image he quickly subfiled out of sight. Violence was not his way. He was a healer, a Server. In truth, it wasn't Rachel that set him on edge. It was the smell.

And here it was again.

They entered a corridor leading out to the eastbound-train platforms. In this darker and more confining space, he felt Rachel stiffen slightly as he kept his hand on her upper arm. With a quicker step now, he pulled her along, their boots clicking on the tiles as they left behind the orange pond in the rotunda.

"What's that smell?" Rachel asked, stopping and planting her feet solidly.

"Could be a cat died or something." In fact, the smell was so thick he could *taste* it, as though he'd licked something foul. But Rachel was the sort who looked to others for validation of her own senses. "Guess you never smelled a dead cat before, eh Rachel?" he said, and she started on again.

Halfway down the concourse he stopped at a door, a door like all the others. "This is it. We'll just stay a second."

She placed her hand on the doorknob, and looked back at Zachariah irritably. "Are you coming?"

Well, no. Not that he was afraid. Ordinary people feared new things. That was the difference between them and him, between Rachel and him. He was pretty sure she'd throw a fit—probably fry her motherboard—in that room. No spirit of adventure, at all.

Rachel looked at him, and he nodded his encouragement.

She opened the door.

In that instant he shoved his hand into her back, just hard enough that she staggered forward into the room. Quickly, he slammed the door shut behind her, holding the doorknob firmly as Rachel banged on it from the other side.

"Zacheeee!" she wailed. Then: "Please Zachy," her voice soft and close, through the crack next to the door-frame. "It *stinks* in here."

Her uncanny, normal voice sent a little shiver over his scalp as he gripped the door handle, now twisting slowly first in one direction, then the other. For a few seconds he heard the sound of shuffling, and the soft scrape of her clothing against the door. Then:

"Oh . . ." Her voice broke into a surprised crack, and began ratcheting up in pitch. "Oh. Oh. Ohhh . . ."

He would have plugged his ears but the door needed holding shut, so he squeezed his eyes closed. But still he heard several rhythmic gulps of air, which might be Rachel, filling her lungs to accuse him . . . and then a thumping sound, and a brief, soft buzzing, like an insect incinerated in fire.

After a few moments the room grew quiet, and he opened his eyes.

Head pressed against the door, he was forced to pull that hot stench into his lungs while fighting to distill some oxygen. He pried his fingers loose from the molten door handle and waited for a semblance of calm. Then he slowly pried the door open and looked into the room.

A glint of light from the hallway struck the shattered faces of built-in computer wall displays. He stepped into the room, leaving white tracings in the fine dusting of ash as he walked. On the ceiling, a scorch the size of a tire surrounded the cracked globe of the overhead light.

Rachel was gone.

In the center of the floor lay a heap of oblong packets coated with long, waving tendrils that snapped as he touched them. He fumbled the packets into his knapsack. Then, looking up, he saw it, lying in a pile of glass near the wall: Rachel's wool cap, with a thread of steam rising from it. . . . Zachariah crammed the last few packets into the sack and stood swaying in place, eyes riveted on the hat.

"I'm sorry, Rachel," he said finally. Then the stench really did get to him, and he stumbled backward from the room, slamming the door and sprinting down the hall. At the main doors he sidled through the hole he'd cut, staggering out onto the old train platform, inhaling great gulps of searingly cold, sweet air.

Chapter 1

~1~

Abbey McCrae cradled the World War I Fokker triplane in her hands. Its real balsa wood frame was in nearly mint condition after seventy years, a relic from the days when kids played with real things instead of the electronic bits. She carefully placed it back on the shelf next to a plastic-encased pamphlet entitled "You and the Atomic Bomb" and amid a thousand other twentieth-century acquisitions here in the storeroom of Abbey's Anteeks. She set her cup of morning tea on the typewriter stand next to the faux leopard multilounger, electronically dead but otherwise still damn comfortable, and breathed in the aroma of decades of dust, rusting metal, and the attar of desiccated sachet bags. Wonderful.

Among the golden-era favorites, inventory from the mid-twenty-first century dotted the shelves like poor cousins among royalty. The more sophisticated, the more electronic, people got, the less they were rooted to life in real,

honest-to-gosh stuff: behemoth pink ashtrays flecked with
gold, Avon automobile-cologne bottles, and framed post-
ers of Martin, Bobby, and John.

She held up a twenty-year-old velvet painting of Len-
non, Cobain, and Garcia. Not bad.

Renalda clambered down the stairs from the upstairs
apartment, followed closely by their dog, Harley, his huge
neck graced by a large-gauge chain collar that Renalda
had recently chromed for his sixth birthday.

"Hola!" A sharp spike of perfume hit Abbey's nostrils
like spilled pop on a shag carpet. Her roommate was
dressed to kill, long hair curled and the Sex/Mex earrings
dangling beside her rouged cheeks.

"Let me guess, a date?"

"Well, Monday's a slow day." She pirouetted on four-
inch high heels, a feat only Renalda, with a couple decades of experience in trying to be taller, could
accomplish.

"Monday's shelf day, so you can work, same as me."

"Come on, Abbey! I got people to do, things to see."
As proof, she flashed her wrist mobes, fringed with lace
and alive with calls-waiting.

"If you're in love again, I think I'm going to scream,"
Abbey said. Even at thirty-two, Renalda believed each
love affair was The One, not so different from her old
high-school buddy, Abbey herself.

"This guy's different." Their eyes locked for a moment.
Renalda backed off first. "And turn up the heat, its cold."

"It's almost April!"

"I don't care if it's July, it's fucking freezing in here."
Harley sat transfixed as Renalda roughed up his face and
ears with her fingernails, long as gangplanks.

As Abbey edged by, arms piled high with inventory,
Renalda tossed her hair back, highlighting the Sex/Mexes.
In the earring displays, Abbey saw a high-resolution
graphic of herself copulating with a Ken doll.

"You ought to stop that, it looks cheap."

Renalda followed her into the front store. "Somebody's gotta do the marketing! Here, I programmed lots

more." She grabbed a cigar box from the counter, rattling the earrings inside. "Come on, they sell great!"

Everything Renalda said came out with a little too much force. Everything was fun or wry or exciting. Well, she was in love. Abbey could remember being in love like that. Especially in winter, when the work dried up, and men went hunting for a warm bed—and free rent—until the growing season brought field-hand jobs. But, make no mistake, come spring they'd rather stand in lines at the gates of farms and shoot the shit with the guys than stick it out with a woman.

She nestled another Barbie doll on the shelf among her prize collection, each doll outfitted for a different dream: ski trips, horseback riding, proms, safaris, beauty pageants and astronaut adventures, and the greatest dream of all, that 36–18–34 figure. Abbey checked out her butt in the store mirror, glad that the size-ten jeans still fit, even if they were tight. Her breath clouded in front of her, endorsing her roommate's gripe.

"Store," she ordered, "kick it up to sixty-five."

Harley was whimpering at the mini fridge. Relenting, Renalda spread out a leftover bean taco for him on the floor.

"So. Who's the new boyfriend?" Abbey asked, charging back to the storage room for another load.

"DeVries."

"What kind of a name is that?" Behind the Smith-Corona typewriter, still in its hard case and bannered with a JERK DICK bumper sticker, she spied an avocado-colored bread box buried just far enough behind newer inventory to be all but forgotten. Wasn't it just last week some lady came in looking for fifties kitchen stuff?

"Help me with this, would you?" She pulled out the typewriter, handing it off to Renalda. Abbey hauled the bread box forward. Across the roller door a rooster strutted, red crest held high, and surrounded by hearts, as though he were the symbol of romance.

Abbey slid up the roller door, which grated and clunked into place.

Inside, a small, dark mass. Perhaps a *very* moldy piece

of bread. Something gleamed. She reached inside and drew out a black leatherette book with a metal, locking clasp and on the front, something written in script.

"What is it?" Renalda asked.

Abbey turned the book back and forth to catch the right angle of light to read the inscription. Finally, the words, *My Diary*, flickered to life. "Oh God," she heard herself whisper.

Renalda reached forward and grabbed the book out of Abbey's hand, tugging at the clasp. "Looks like a diary."

Abbey stared at the little book, forgetting to breathe. "It's Vittoria's, isn't it?" She looked into Renalda's eyes as though across the ocean. Too far to throw the rope.

"I never knew Vitt kept a diary," her roommate said, scanning the cover as she spoke. "She wasn't the type to keep a diary, do you think?"

"It is Vittoria's, isn't it?" Abbey asked, her mind stuck in the groove like an old 45 rpm record.

Renalda backed up a pace, clasping the diary behind her back. "Yeah, OK, it has her initials on the front," she answered. "And you know what we're gonna do? We're gonna put it right back where it came from and close that cute little rooster door, and shove it way to the back."

A diary. A window into the oh-so-personal world of the person you knew best and least . . . your own child. Abbey thrust out her hand for the book.

"No! No frigging diary! No more long goddamn nights with you obsessing about what's dead and gone, talking until I drop dead asleep, and I'm *still* hearing you, in my dreams!"

"If it was your child, you'd read it."

"I loved her too! I love both of you, God help me."

Even in her present state of mind, Abbey had to admit the truth of that, of Renalda's faithful friendship, through the times with Vitt and the times without. But still: "Hand it over," she said.

"Ever think that people's diaries are, like, *private*?" Backing up another step, her roommate tossed her head, swaying her earrings and bringing on an orgy of activity in the displays. "I can't do this anymore, can you hear me? I can't stand Vitt's dying anymore, night after night. I will go crazy." At the pitch of their voices, Harley slunk to the doorway, and parked himself on the threshold, looking like he was to blame.

Abbey conjured up a reasonable smile. It was either that or deck Renalda right here and now. "I'm over that now. Just give me the diary." But even to herself she sounded like a vampire saying, Just bare your neck.

"You're over it! I'm going to gag. When's the last date you ever had? Two years. When's the last new clothes you ever bought? Two years. When's the last time we went looking for some guys on a Saturday night? Huh?"

Abbey nodded, yes, yes. But not hearing.

"Huh? You gonna answer?"

Something clicked. Abbey's hands flew wide, her cascade of hair crackling. "Two years! Two years, OK? Think you're the only one that's counting?" She whirled around and slammed the bread box door down with a resounding clunk. The scratch of Harley's toenails on the steps receded toward the apartment. She swung back around.

Renalda looked at her a long while. "Let the dead rest, for Godsakes," she said softly.

Abbey reached for the book. The front doorbell rang. As Renalda let go of the book a moment too early, it slipped from Abbey's fingers and fell to the floor on the clasp end, breaking the lock into two pieces.

She stared at the splayed binding on the floor. "It's a sign," she said, "that I should read it."

Her roommate shook her head. "It's a sin. And you shouldn't." She went to the door to deal with their visitor, then turned back. "It's a sin to read someone else's diary, you know?"

Abbey raised an eyebrow at this pitiful tactic. "It's a *sin*?"

Renalda's face crumpled under that hot, hazel gaze. "OK. It's bad luck, then." She left the storeroom, scowling.

Abbey crouched down and picked up the book, as Vitt's voice crawled through her mind: *Just bury it. Dig a hole and bury it.* Abbey considered this for a split second, then opened the book at random, seeing the familiar scrawl, reading the oddly jarring words: *"Zachariah knows things. I don't know if he really hears voices from people passed over . . ."* A small tremor lilted across her hands, and she carefully closed the book. No, Vitt *wasn't* the type to keep a diary. But everyone has a few secrets, don't they?

When Renalda came back, she was shaking her head. "Just outers begging." She threw her arms wide, mobes sparkling on her wrists. "Do I look like I have money?"

"Store," Abbey said. "Screen us Closed for the day. But plug the Barbie special." She wandered over to the multilounger and sat down. The chair sighed as her weight forced stale air from its depths.

"You ever hear of Zachariah Smith?"

Renalda pursed her lips. "That guy with the fragged-out followers? Over at the old high school? Vitt wasn't involved with *him,* was she?" Her eyes widened in the ensuing silence.

Abbey picked up her tea and sipped it, allowing the cold brew to slide down her throat before it swelled into a blockade.

"Because Father O'Conner says they worship the devil."

"Yeah, Father O'Conner sees the devil everywhere."

Renalda opened her mouth to rebut, then reconsidered, retreating to the door. At the threshold she turned and said. "Maybe he is."

Abbey looked up quizzically. "Is what?"

"Everywhere." Her roommate hovered at the door while Abbey turned the diary over in her hands.

"You gonna be OK?"

"Ask me later." She grasped the small locket hanging around her neck, and even before she heard the front door close behind Renalda, she turned to the diary's first entry, *January 7, 2012,* and began to read.

An hour later, she found herself in the souped-up, double discount multilounger in the apartment, doing a Net probe on Zachariah Smith, downloading his spending patterns, 3D Web hits and every other public-access scrap available in the vast digital imprint that he, like everyone else, left in the communal Net.

~ 2 ~

By lunchtime, the sky was dark as pitch. Some storms are like that, with blue-black clouds reaching for the next horizon. At 1:00 the wind came up, and whoever wore hats in Medicine Falls saw them blown to hell and gone. Folks had been saying since the day before that the weather was changing, and when they heard the distant thunder, they reminded you they'd said so.

Gilda Tupper pulled her coat closer around her neck, turning every so often to see if she was followed. Lightning over the distant alfalfa fields soaked the sky with a green-white tea, reflecting in the office-building windows.

Passing by, Mrs. Prescott said, "Storm, by gad," nodding to Gilda briefly, and nearly slipping on a patch of ice. Her face was a ghastly white, tinged with lightning.

The bulge under Gilda's coat felt like a growth on her sixty-eight-year-old body, but it wasn't flesh, wasn't death, even if sometimes over the past few weeks it felt like it. Kevin called it a game. She called it a damn contraption.

Pausing in front of an alley, Gilda ducked in and headed for a large green Dumpster. Stealing the contraption had been a spur-of-the-moment impulse. Kevin took a bathroom break, and in an instant, Gilda had grabbed the tangle of wires, ejected the tab from the game appliance and rushed for the door, sweeping her coat off its hanger. She unbuttoned that coat now and carefully removed the game assembly, a surgeon excising the tumor. With an expert toss, she chucked the mass into the garbage.

And turned smack into the enraged face of a total stranger. Her son, Kevin.

His words stabbed out at her: "Just what the fucking

hell do you think you're doing?" His jowls shook with an angry tremor.

She drew herself up, but still fell far short of his towering height. "It's my apartment, Kevin."

"Yeah," he said, not pleasantly, his face the same lambent white as the lowering clouds.

He looked up at the Dumpster, and for an instant, Gilda had the shocking thought that he would dump her body there. Like in the vids, bodies were always ending up in Dumpsters. But he jumped to grip the high edge of the container and climbed up and over the top in a surprising show of agility.

"You crazy old bat," he muttered from the depths of the canister. Out of the Dumpster sailed rotten fruit and plastic bottles like cherry pits from a monster's mouth. Finally he emerged with the contraption in hand.

It was true she'd taken it. All right, stolen it. But what was she to do? Kevin hadn't paid his share of the rent in months, just sat on his fat ass most of the time, plugged into this retina game like some thirteen-year-old who just discovered virtual sex. True, times were hard, with lots of people unemployed. But he'd used that excuse for long enough, doing nothing but gaming with those damn sunglasses on, never even seeing friends. Not that anyone saw friends anymore, now that you could send instant duplicate letters to your whole Net mailing list.

And here he was telling her to get out of his face, to go play bingo. Bingo! As if she were some mindless oldster with nothing better to do than gamble her 401(k).

As Kevin jumped down from the Dumpster, the first drops of rain hit like overripe tomatoes, splatting against the alley pavement and driving into the remnants of blackened snow.

He thrust the mass of wires and visor in front of her nose. "You ever pull something like this again, I'll send you to the home."

She sniffed at this outrageous threat. He didn't mean it. "I don't know what you see in that game." She recalled the time she'd given it a try herself. Nothing happened. Static noise, was all. "It doesn't even work very well."

"Oh, it works. And keep your thieving mitts off it."
Then his face softened. Maybe he had just caught a
glimpse of himself. As he was becoming.

After a pause he said softly, "Let's go home, Mom."

Tears sprang to Gilda's eyes. At times he was still her
boy. Fewer and fewer times.

They trudged back in the slushy rain, his hand locked
on her elbow in what she took to be a caring gesture, but
which might also be a controlling vise.

The fleeing anger had taken her resolve with it. Nothing was going to change. She found herself wondering if,
like people said, spring was canceled this year.

~ 3 ~

Abbey pushed through the outer doors of the town's
most historic building, the three-story Grummel High
School, converted in the last decade to offices now that
physical schools had Netted out. The old landmark
smelled like one hundred years of varnish and wood soap
with an ancient patina of sweat clinging to the whole like
wax on an apple—familiar smells from her graduating
class of 2001, Grummel's last batch of real students. In
this new era of edutainment, teachers were reduced to
crunching spreadsheets and kids enjoyed the seamless
world of Net play and Net school. She took a seat on a
bench outside the doors of Zachariah Smith's Dimension
Institute, which was these days occupying most of the old
high school and, ironically, producing its own brand of
knowledge.

Institute. Fancy word for a crock of bull. Called himself a Server, this Zachariah Smith. His eerie Web zone
offered knowledge from "the other side," *and have your
credit card number handy,* no mistake.

"Zap psychology," she said under her breath, drawing
the attention of a young girl dressed in shimmering white
streamers that parted as she walked, showing painted
white skin beneath. The girl smiled at her. Abbey stared

her down before she could approach. No thank you, don't need your brand of salvation. Not that desperate. Yet.

The girl was one of many young devotees wandering the hallways. Each wore a different color, tied, they said, to their resonance color—which only Zachariah could bestow. It was a scam. And all perfectly legal.

As for the diary, nothing illegal in there either, according to the police. Nothing irregular, nothing to investigate, case closed.

The door opened and she heard, "Ms. McCrae?"

Abbey looked up into the eyes of a woman dressed all in red. Even her contact lenses were red, giving her the look of a cat that just looked into a flash.

Turning to follow, she heard her daughter's voice, as she had so often over the last few years, commenting, rankling, dwelling inside her.

Oh God, Mother. This is all so stuuupid.

Yes. Maybe it *was* stupid. So where did smart get you in this world? All the worthwhile things she'd ever managed to download were products of stubborn persistence, hanging on till her teeth hurt and the other side gave up.

Abbey entered the front office, which had once been Principal Malkovich's office. There was a long counter facing the door. Once full of sign-out sheets and PTSA announcements, now it was pulsing with miniscreen flash ads of the Institute's many services and satisfied seekers, whose faces she scanned for Vitt, always Vitt.

"This way."

Abbey followed the red blouse and skirt down a hallway, where she was ushered into Zachariah's office, which looked and smelled more like a gym. Instruments of supposedly healthy torture filled the room, like huge metal Tinkertoy constructions. Zachariah—if it was Zachariah—was hanging upside down from an exercise bar, facing away from her toward a sunlamp. Red woman didn't seem to notice this, announcing Abbey and then retreating, closing the door.

Monitors glowed from niches in the walls. Two ultra-tek chairs faced each other, a little too close.

"Those sunlamps can cause cancer, you know, Mr. Smith."

Slowly, his body curled up toward the bar, which he grasped with his hands and allowed his legs to unhook. His feet hit the floor soundlessly. He faced her. "Call me Zachariah."

His voice was melodious, like a singer's. He was her age, but with the muscled body of a younger man and the tan look of someone with too much money. Black workout pants and a yellow muscle shirt gave him a slightly carnival look. The aquiline nose, sensual mouth, and perfect blue eyes were right out of a facial-enhancement catalogue. But something in the roundness of the face and skull made him miss his mark, if handsome was what he aimed for.

"You ought to try it sometime, Ms. McCrae." He toweled off, draping the towel around his neck. "The warmth feels relaxing and the tan's flattering. We can allow ourselves to feel good about little things."

The little tidbit of advice darted in, pricking her. "Even dangerous things?" She glanced up at a row of blank monitors, glowing milky-blue, like blind eyes.

He shrugged affably. "Your message said you wanted to discuss your daughter, Vittoria." Seating himself, he gestured her to the number-two chair, propping his elbows on the chair arms and forming a steeple with his hands. His wrists sported a set of richly understated mobes.

"Vittoria was interested in the approach we take here. She was seeking. She was a lovely girl. She was a Blue." He nodded, a quick duck of his chin toward his chest. "Yes, a Blue. Blues are the deep ones, strong psychic powers. Did you notice how she always knew what people were feeling?"

"No. Never noticed." Keeping her voice calm, calmer than she felt, with the hunch overtaking her that she was in for more bull than she'd bargained for. . . .

"Parents seldom pay attention when their children grow up. They still see the child. A form of veiling. Seeing what they want to see."

"Are you saying I didn't know her?" Abbey kept her voice nice. Years in the store had taught her how to make nice to assholes.

"Did you?"

"She was my *daughter*."

"Did *your* mother know *you*? At seventeen?"

The comment stopped her. Abbey at seventeen. Her mother always off at church . . . the house of silences . . . And how the hell had the conversation gotten off on her *childhood*, for Godsakes? And her feeling all of a sudden like she'd taken off a few too many clothes.

"Strike a chord?"

Her smile coiled at the edge of her mouth, as she searched through her arsenal of comebacks, and paused—evidently just a second too long.

"They did the best they could, Abbey. The same as you. Sometimes it's not enough. No blame."

That did it. She hunched forward in the chair as though she might grab him and shake him. "Wait a minute. Get this straight, Mr. Smith. I don't blame myself. I'm trying to find out why a beautiful young girl would end her life at seventeen. How nobody had the slightest clue that she was in trouble. If you know something, tell me. If you don't, spare me your zap psychology." She sank back, feeling the chair moving under her, silently matching her moves.

Zachariah's expression remained the same, friendly, concerned, and infuriating.

"Just how far was she into your stuff, here?" she batted into his court.

"There's no law against philosophy," came the lob.

"How far? I know she came here." And back again.

"Far enough to know she was a Blue."

"How far is that?" She heard her voice, sparrow sharp, and thin—no match for his firm baritone.

"Abbey." He closed his eyes for a moment, as though mustering patience with a young child. Then he stood and walked around the desk to the treadmill in front of a huge mirror occupying the entire wall to her left. He switched on the machine and stepped up, starting to walk at a moderate pace. He looked her in the eyes, from the mirror.

"Vittoria studied with us for five or six months. Or thereabouts. Then she left. She was depressed when she arrived here and I'm afraid she was depressed when she left. She needed to stay on the path. But she felt you wouldn't understand, for one thing. In any case she left. Several months later we heard she was dead." He began a jog. "We were all very sad."

Abbey jumped up and strode over to the machine. With an angry flick of her wrist she switched the toggle, shutting the machine down. "What do you mean, 'afraid I wouldn't understand'? Just what the hell are you saying?"

His voice was warm frosting: "I can imagine how you hurt, Abbey. I wish I could help you. Maybe I could, if you'd let me."

She stared at him.

He stepped down from the machine. "I think you're a Yellow, Abbey. I'd have to spend more time with you to be sure, but there's a good chance you're a Yellow. Like me."

She just had to smile, a wolfish, baked-on smile it must have been, but he didn't flinch. Rather he smiled back, as though they understood each other. Maybe they did.

She nodded at him politely. "Fuck off."

"Aren't you the least curious? Initial sessions are three hundred and sixty-five dollars. But we have a scholarship fund that allows half-price packages."

"You're really something, you know? I'll bet you treat funerals as a marketing opportunity." She stalked to the door.

"Such a lot of anger, Abbey. I was like that once . . ."

She slammed the door on his voice, his soothing, droning voice.

Red lady hurried down the hall toward his office, bestowing a worried look at Abbey.

"He's OK, Red," Abbey threw at her. "Just a bad case of terminal jerk."

Abbey pushed past the startled woman and out of the

office door, nearly colliding with a Yellow who got in her
way.

"Be calm," the Yellow bleeped.

"Be madder than hell," Abbey spit back.

She made her way home, through the downtown neighborhood she'd lived in all her life, walking on automatic,
barely acknowledging friends and acquaintances. Like
Mrs. Kozlovsky with her shopping cart stuffed with
household treasures; Joe Mills, holding down his favorite
street corner; Buz Conrad, checkout boy at the corner
mart, hurrying by, VR visor shoved up on his head but
still plugged into his hip pack. Sometimes her heart was
that heavy, so that even the hellos were buried under
heavy snow, laid down storm after storm.

Lobo was working her side of the street today. No way
to avoid him. He saluted her. "I got megalinks today, Ab,
and a plasmic retina ride." He pointed to the eyepiece
dangling from his skull cap, fumbling to click it in place.
"Not as good as my personal own, but a great starter
piece. Two hundred greens, discount."

"Catch me when I'm in a better mood, Lobo. Today is
not a good day."

His voice followed her. "One seventy-five?"

Half the storefronts along Lowell Street were closed.
These were hard times, and no shame to be broke and
struggling. Medicine Falls wasn't the only place struggling
to keep up with FPEC taxes and the techno revolution,
and she wasn't the only one in town who couldn't afford
Lobo's toys. You wanted to farm or sell antiques, fine, but
if you wanted to really make it, you got into technology,
Net gaming, Net retailing, retina VR. Or pseudo, psycho
religion, like the Institute. For the rest, well, Medicine
Falls paid its taxes and sucked at the Net tit, wondering
what the future would bring, hoping it was something
different than the future had been lately. And Brazil's forest barons held the world by the toe, using the hated
agreement on Forest Preservation and Economic Compen-
sation—FPEC to the bureaucrats, the air tax to the poor
droid that had to pay it. It was only fair, Abbey supposed.

Brazil produced the oxygen, and the rest of us used it, breath by breath. You can't give things away.

When you did, you ended up like Abbey McCrae, with nothing.

She entered her shop. "Store," she said, thinking to open up. But then: "Back at three o'clock."

Climbing the stair to the apartment, she found Renalda sprawling easily in the multilounger, geared for VR, tiny shades flickering at the edges.

Abbey hung up her coat, greeting Harley's eager slurps with a quick rub on the head.

Her roommate put aside her shades. *"Hola,"* she said, dreamily. She stretched, pointing her toe to the ceiling in a sensual display.

"Hello yourself. What're you playing?" Abbey curled into the couch—which stayed *put,* thank God—pulling a blanket over her legs. Not needing a hug from a damned couch, but maybe hoping for one from her roommate.

"Nir."

"So what's it like?"

"It's like . . . it's like nothing you've ever seen. The color, the peripherals, the sensation . . ."

"But what's the *game?*"

Renalda frowned. "It's not so much a game. It's more an immersion."

"In?"

"Different things. It has lots of options. Mine is . . . fairly sexual."

"Sexual?"

"Nothing trashy! But like Lobo said, you *go* there."

"Lobo sold you? Isn't his stuff is mostly stolen?"

Renalda tossed her head, clattering her earrings. "Such a prude." She stretched the other leg. "I think it's love."

"Geez, Renalda, *that's* your new boyfriend? A retina game?"

Renalda's playfulness dimmed a few watts. "So? I'm enjoying him. It. The game. What's wrong with that?"

"Nothing's wrong with it. It's just that—it's not like you have a *boyfriend*. It's a *game*."

"More than that." Renalda swung the lounger to face

Abbey. "It's like nowhere I've ever virtually been. I can feel what DeVries is thinking, like I can be both him and me at the same time. It's just been getting more and more intense, like the story builds each time you play." Renalda looked at Abbey a long moment. "I guess you must think I'm desperate, huh?"

"Enjoy the story, Rena. But *love*? What happened to Evan?"

Renalda snorted. "Evan! God, he's a *shoe salesman.*"

"Nothing wrong with that, selling shoes."

This was met with an ironic stare.

As Harley brought a pork-chop bone into the living room to gnaw on, Renalda shoved herself out of the lounger. "I don't think you should criticize me for trying a little fantasy. Look at this dump." She gestured at the tiny living room littered with secondhand furniture and cast-offs from the shop. "Are *you* satisfied?"

"Sure, why not?"

"Bullshit. You want a little love and adventure in your life too. Maybe somebody like Evan isn't what any of us have in mind. Maybe Medicine Falls isn't what any of us have in mind."

"But Evan is real. He exists. He probably looks at the women in this town, and would rather have . . . a countess or a vid star. But all we get is each other. It should be enough."

"You're so full of *shoulds*, Abbey. Listen to yourself. Should, should, should. You're afraid to dream, afraid to fantasize, afraid of everything!" She got up and hauled her coat from the closet. "I'm going out. I don't need this shit."

Abbey sprang up. "Come on hon, don't leave mad. I'm sorry."

Renalda turned at the door. "You always think *sorry* fixes everything." She left, slamming the door.

The afternoon now felt bleaker than the drizzle that had started to pelt the living-room windows. Abbey moved to the lounger, sweeping aside the VR gear and staring at the screen. She was a modern woman, a woman of the Net, and no prude about virtual sex. So why trash out Renalda for a little retina ecstasy?

Settling into the lounger and toggling the seat backward to rest her back, she brought the screen arm into viewing position, switched on the back vibrator, and punched the chair arm control pad for her mail. As always, her bouncer had subfiled all the ads, offers, come-ons, incentives, and free-zone lures to find all the Vitt-related mail, answers to her standing query: any information about Vittoria McCrae's death . . . signed *Venus,* her Net name. A query sometimes could score you at least a few lost souls, but not today. In fact, not lately, not in months.

She quickly upgraded her Net probe to reach a wider base, debiting her account. Then, on impulse, she dropped into a directory of people who advertised fast, confidential results. She muted their promo voices and scanned their faces carefully, searching for evidence of someone who knew, really *knew,* how to listen.

And would stick around if the going got rough.

Chapter 2

~1~

No matter how much a town has lost, Simon Haskell reflected, it can usually depend on its name. No wonder then, when a movement began to try to change the name of Medicine Falls, many townspeople drew a line in the sand. They'd watched the jobs leave, their kids leave, the railway line, and the Marshall Fields. Enough already.

It was true that the "falls" were dry since the dam went in eleven years ago. But some folks were quick to point out that sometimes, after a summer downpour, water spilled over the falls. Besides, it would be confusing to have *Medicine Flats* right next to the *Medicine Falls* Indian Reservation. Those people being like they were, they would never change the reservation name for the sake of geographical consistency. Others held that since the town was flat as piss on a plate—situated as it was in a wide valley between rocky bluffs—that Medicine *Flats* would keep half the old name going while having the advantage of accuracy.

The two camps became known as the Falls and the Flats factions.

Simon Haskell was one of those folks who tried not to take sides. But since the Haskell and Ginestra agency was tucked into the heart of the business district, and a short walk from his favorite hamburger joint, it wasn't long before a Flats petitioner buttonholed him, and he signed the petition to change the town's name. The week before, he'd signed the Falls petition, so it was as though he'd signed neither, but without the annoyance of arguing with pushy canvassers.

As a petitioner argued with the man standing in back of Simon in the line at Dave's Deli, Simon ordered his hamburger, speaking loudly into the screen face of the mech attendant, which intoned, "The Surgeon General warns that animal fat is bad for your heart."

"Make it a cheeseburger," he said.

A server arm slapped a strip of processed cheese on the burger, and hot-wrapped it, shoving it over the counter in his direction.

Making his way past a long line of ragged outers queued up at the Salvation Army for lunch, Simon trudged the three blocks back to the Professional Arts building. Along the way, he was passed by runners half his age. No one walked anymore. Their lean, muscled bodies were reflected in the display windows of the retail frontages, and among them his own image: a fifty-four-year-old man with fifteen extra pounds crowding his belt; wrinkled brow creasing a tall forehead full of junk thoughts to match his junk food. Or, alternatively, a mature man, just this side of handsome, an interesting loner in a town of Net-heads and pasty vegetarians.

Simon took a bite of his cheeseburger. *Yeah, sure.*

It had been a bone-wearying day, and he hoped the late-afternoon cheeseburger would help. It was the kind of day where each step is a conscious effort, and the breakdown of the world is reflected in all things. The cleaner lost his favorite jacket. The cheese on his burger wasn't melted. The lift was dead at his office building—a building that over time he'd come to refer to as the war-ren.

The Directory Girl shimmered to life, a perfect Myrna Loy, including that classy, arch way of saying, "Unfortu-nately, the elevator is out of service. The stairs to your right . . ."

Simon stared balefully up at the lift cage, trying to guess which floor the damn thing was stuck on this time. He finished off the burger there in the lobby and turned to the stairs, climbing slowly and passing Roland Waler, who was headed down.

"Time to quit, Haskell," he said cheerily.

"Not everybody's got a rich wife, Waler. Some of us poor droids got to put in a full day." It was 4:00. Why didn't he just go home?

Afterward, he thought about that moment a lot. He could have turned around and followed Roland Waler down to the parking garage. Life tips its balance over the smallest decisions.

She was waiting for him outside 307. Shit. A client.

The woman leaned against the wall, one foot braced against the cracked plaster, the other dug into the reedy carpet. Her hair sparkled in the last spray of daylight. Her shirt magically twinkled. To Simon it looked like energy radiated from her body, as from an apparition, or—and here Simon was already chiding himself for his imagina-tion—a visitation of a goddess.

As he came closer, walking the walk of the four-o'clock-in-the-afternoon-and-still-working man, he saw that she was wearing a pink shirt, blue jeans, and cowboy boots.

The cowboy boot came down off the wall and she turned to face him. Early thirties, nice-looking, layered brown hair almost to her shoulders. Looking closer, he saw that the sparkles came from song chips on her T-shirt.

"Mr. Haskell?"

"Yeah," he heard himself say. "Simon Haskell. You need a detective?" He slipped his keycard in the door and she followed him in. "Because I got a full client list al-

ready. Be glad to give you a referral." He threw his coat
on the nearest chair and turned to her.

"All you need is love," her shirt sang, just loud enough
to be heard, chips pulsing to the beat of a song he vaguely
recognized as an oldie.

She cleared her throat, expertly killing the music, then
stood there looking like she had plenty to say, but letting
her eyes have the saying of it instead. Not an accusing
look exactly, but maybe one that said, You don't look so
damn busy to *me*.

This seemed to be a good moment to rummage through
the top desk drawer for his referral list. Maybe he could
just hand her off to his partner, Rocky. Rocky went home
at 2:00 every day for a meeting with his bottle of Glenfid-
dich. But he was a damn good detective.

When he looked up again she was still watching him.

Her silence would be a kind of permission to roll past
this one and hand her Rocky's card. But that quiet poise
or the sparkling vision from the hallway, or the quirky
urban-cowboy routine of jeans and fancy boots—one of
these, or all, propelled him to slide the drawer closed.

"But I suppose it depends on what you need. . . ."

She brightened. "Just research; that's all it is."

He opened the window blinds a narrow slot to lighten
up the room. Slumping into his chair, he mentally ticked
off the likely *research* she had in mind: husband skated on
child support, teenage runaway, a business deal gone bad.
From the expression on her face, it had to be deep files of
trouble. He arched an eyebrow at the client chair. She sat
down and hung her purse on the back of the chair. "OK,
what've you got? Ms. . . . ?"

"McCrae. Abbey McCrae." She stood, extending a
cool hand across his desk. He looked into her dusty, hazel
eyes, fringed with long lashes and little wisdom creases,
and shook the hand, somehow knowing it was the seal of
a bargain—simple, ordained, and fatal.

He sat back, feet up on his desk to get some distance.
Jesus, Haskell, he told himself. *Get a grip*. He poked at
the corner of his left eye with his knuckles, trying to dis-
lodge a speck of dust.

"It's my daughter . . ." Abbey began. She faltered. She looked up at the corner of the room as though the thread of her story might dangle there for the grasping. The window blinds threw stripes across her face and body, and across the wall behind her.

"Missing?" Simon prodded.

"Dead."

"I'm sorry." He allowed a respectful pause. "An accident?"

Abbey pulled on her thread. "Vittoria was seventeen. She was a lovely girl. Dark hair—long—and slim as a princess. She could've had the world at her door, Mr. Haskell. You should have seen her. Knew her own mind. Even Dean couldn't push her around."

Simon found the eyelash he'd been digging for, wiped his cheek dry of the tear that seemed to mock her story. "Dean?"

"The guy I was living with when she died. He took off right after it happened. Took my best vid tab with him, and left me his dog. The dog's OK, but he sheds. That long kind that the lint brush doesn't pick up?"

"Where's her father?"

"Lyle." She nodded, eyes hard as enamel. "Vitt used to have a picture of her sitting on her dad's lap. But that was all she had. Lyle put up with fatherhood as long as he could, then one day he was gone, leaving a hundred-dollar bill on the pillow." She was fingering a silver filigree locket the size of a nickel. "He meant well."

"Yeah."

"Vitt loved him, I think, though it was hard to tell just what she felt. She was a private girl. Self-contained, I guess." After a beat, she said: "They found her body at the bottom of Vogel Tower."

Simon nodded. If you wanted to jump off something in Medicine Falls, it would be Vogel Tower, the tallest construct around except for the grain elevators.

"The police called it suicide, and after a long while I guess I did, too."

"And this happened—when?"

"June 2, 2013. Almost two years ago."

She was looking at the ceiling again, giving him the chance to get up and plug the coffee in. Morning coffee, but what the hell. Woman was going to keep him here awhile. He waited by the coffeepot, which was slow to heat ever since Simon had yanked its connection to the office manager system, a monstrous assembly of networked appliances that Rocky referred to as Jeeves, and Simon as Big Brother.

"Do you have children, Mr. Haskell?"

"No."

"That's too bad. A man your age should have children. Never married?"

He wanted to remind her it was late in the day and he was looking forward to a brandy, a good book, and his favorite chair. But at the same time he found himself wanting to hear her talk, and most anything she had to say would do.

"No, never married," he said, and wanting to say, *And you?* He raised the pot at her, offering coffee.

"No thanks, I don't drink coffee."

He poured himself a deep cup. "Go on," he said. "I'm all ears."

"They want me to believe she killed herself, Mr. Haskell. A young girl with everything to live for." An ironic smile played at her lips. "I know what you must be thinking, that I'm grasping at straws. I am . . . I *was* . . . her mother. Maybe the last one to accept things like this. But if she took her life, I want you to find out why. So I can sleep."

Simon sucked in a deep breath of stale office air, full of electronics and dust. Christ almighty, what a thing to carry around. "Sometimes these are things we can never know."

Out of nowhere, she threw out: "Do you believe in justice, Mr. Haskell?"

Justice. When the bad guys lost. Which was seldom. "I've seen it a time or two," he said.

"You look like a man that believes in justice."

He thought that he looked like a man in need of a brandy, but found himself stupidly flattered by this sum-

mation. Still, he didn't want to play Superman to her Lois.
It was an easy game to play, and he always tried to avoid
it. "Have you talked to the police?"

"The police! I've talked to them until they don't answer my calls anymore. They know me, all right. They
ignore me." The room darkened as the day's stripes crept
up the wall to the ceiling. Abbey leaned forward. "Don't
turn away from me, Mr. Haskell." The voice soft, but the
damn hazel eyes stoked. "A woman loses her child, she
goes a little crazy. She paws at the body, tries to blow
second life into it. Then she paces and waits, paces and
waits. Finally, she carries that child's face in front of her
every moment of the day and far into the night. All she
asks for is somebody to say, Yes, she died because of *this*.
Without that, every day is the same, the day of her death.
You try living like that."

The coffee lay in Simon's stomach like an oil spill. He
gazed at her, wondering whether she was going to prove a
little nuts or just bulldog persistent. Wondering if it would
make the slightest difference to him. "OK, Abbey," he
said, "I'm not backing away."

She looked at him a couple beats and then she dug into
her handbag—some cloth monstrosity about a mile
deep—and pulled out a small black book.

"It's no proof," she said. "But you read this and tell me
if you can figure out what Vittoria McCrae was dealing
with."

Simon took the black book. "Diary?" he said. She nodded. A teenage girl's diary. What a dependable chronicle
that was likely to be. He tossed it on his desk. "OK, Abbey. I'll take a look." Then, scrambling for some distance,
he said, "No promises, you understand?"

She nodded, and produced the first real smile he'd seen
from her. Though it was small, it dazzled him. Damn fool
that he was, and knowing better, goddamn it *knowing*
better, than to let a female client affect him like this.

"You got a thousand dollars?" His voice was gruffer
than he meant it to be.

"I could borrow it. I've got friends."

"My retainer."

"I don't care what it costs." Her voice had grown calm, but her eyes . . . her *eyes* like LED lights in the gloom.

He smiled his *yeah, I'll bet* smile. Sometimes the cost is more than money. But you can't ever tell clients that at the beginning. Or the poor droid they put on retainer.

~ 2 ~

She was nothing, she couldn't touch him. Proprietor of a threadbare junk store, with a high-school education, living over her shop with a roommate. So she knew that Vittoria came to the Institute. Lots of people came to the Institute. She couldn't touch him.

Zachariah clicked in a probe for either her driver's license or fedmedcard, but routed it through a few remailers for cover, stripping his address in the process. While the probe burrowed in, he gazed up from the screen a moment, leaning back in his chair. Here in his attic, the wall in front of him sloped up to the peaked roofline, distorting the photo scans serving as changeable wall-paper. The center one showed Lonnie holding him as an infant, with her face—at the top of the picture—unnaturally large, and the baby disproportionately small, making the whole all the more tender when you considered how . . . big . . . mothers were, and their absolute power . . .

A chime interrupted his musings: the computer had completed its chore:

Profile complete: pers.search.zachariah

He ran the profile, a list of information research requests aimed at him. Scrolling down, nothing unusual. A credit search by SiliconBank; Institute eligibility update from fed.irs.nonprofit; attempts by marketing firms to perform keyword searches of his online transactions—rebuffed by his paid privacy feature. And, in the last three months, two probes by anti-cult groups digging for dirt on the Dimension Institute. Let them dig. And, oh yes, here we go, on 31 March, from Ms. Abbey McCrae, an artless grab at his Net activity . . . wait, she *did* manage to find a pointer into his global Web zone queries. Annoying, that. But outside the U.S. and Canada, the barbarous state of privacy features, virtually—in every sense of the word—useless, made him cautious when linking internationally. She got little out of that.

He scrolled down, shaking his head. She was an amateur. He'd set up looped phantom Net imprints to snag and stall exactly this type of nosy search. And, sure enough, she was snagged. He hoped it cost her plenty to download hours of worthless info.

Yes, minor league, this Abbey McCrae, except for the fact, the all-subsuming fact, that she was Vittoria McCrae's mother. This changed her profile considerably. It didn't take a database search to figure out that a woman in her situation would be highly motivated, morally certain of herself, and fueled by anger and guilt. A potent profile.

Vittoria . . . you could say that he remembered her, could say that he thought of her. Often. She made herself hard to forget, beyond that she was beautiful and eager to please. That much described many young girls. But, in truth, she was entirely in a league of her own. . . . He swiveled his chair around to the other large, slanting wall behind him. There were versions of Vittoria, stages of Vittoria—all beautiful, even the difficult ones. You don't shrink from that part, the deep and painful part, or you become like most people, skimming the surface, content with an inch of life where fathoms beckoned.

But, no question, Vittoria was dead and gone. And none like her, perhaps ever again.

The computer chimed.

Packet received: spend.pat.retail.12mos.amccrae

OK, Abbey, here's how it's really done. His earlier search packet was back, bearing info: a long list of the subject's online retail habits, which told you more than a hour's conversation with her could reveal. Case in point, as he scrolled down the page: Cybermart faux leopard coat, $45, discount. Her taste, atrocious. WearRite cro-

cheted ladies' white gloves, eight pairs. She collected silly
things, perhaps compulsively. And her book orders, beyond belief: *Secrets of the Ancient Mummies, Turn Your
Spare Time into Dollars, The Complete Guide to Guys,
Hawaii on a Shoestring, Motorcycle Mamas* (motorcy-
cles? oh well), *The King's Vixen* . . . And more, more
and more of the same.

Then, a swift browse through her recent credit applica-
tions, personal mail, standing queries (feckless pleas for
news on Vittoria), responses to queries, and user-group
postings . . . and then he keyed out to answer a new
chime:

Search complete.fedmedcard.amccrae
Please wait, downloading photo

And starting at the top of the screen and threading
down, the lovely mother of the lovely daughter, Abbey M.
McCrae, 536–17–8030, 774.12.016.95.410. And all the
other numbers that meant much to fedmed, but which
meant nothing to him, not now that her full face was
smiling at him from his personal screen—charming, to
actually smile for your medcard photo—and she was, un-
doubtedly *was*, so very much like Vittoria. This much had
generally escaped him during that ugly little interview at
the Institute.

This close-up view was . . . nerve-racking. The dia-
mond-shaped face, plunging to the delicate chin, the
eyes—their directness, their color, deep hazel like tropical
waters, the pencil-thin eyebrows that arched a little far to
the side, the narrow-bridged, slightly hawk nose, the
creamy white skin, still flawless. And well, the luxurious
soft brown hair in the unfortunate layered cut, so unlike
Vittoria's silky black tresses. But still, *remarkable*.

It was a quick matter to superimpose Vittoria's face
over Abbey's. An idle exercise, and one he fussed with a
long time, enhancing first one, then the other, until, back
and forth, forth and back, they looked like sisters, *versions* of each other, to his mind's eye. . . .

Like daughter like mother? But, no. Vittoria was utterly in a class alone.

~3~

Rose stood at the bottom of the staircase leading to the master's attic retreat. Through the window at her left, she glanced out at the wine-red barn, with its low shed of a milking parlor and the bunkhouse beyond, watching for movement. In the distance, a few Guernseys munched on the neighboring pasture with that maddening calmness of cows, who would, Rose thought, chew cud on doomsday, and still count it time well spent. Down the hallway, old Verna finally shut off the vacuum cleaner, and the house sank into perfect quiet again. Not a sound from the upstairs den where Mr. Zachariah was still surfing the Net, she dearly hoped.

Calculating that she had at least a couple minutes of privacy, Rose hurried down the stairs and through the foyer to the door leading to the basement, the only place she hadn't checked out yet. Quietly pulling the door shut behind her, she snapped on the light and descended the creaking stairs. Deep in the cool cellar, the furnace made a sighing noise, as though it lived and breathed. The only other sound was the soft thud of her shoes on cement as she paced through the dim expanse of this subterranean region, checking out the shadows with a small, high-intensity flashlight and paying particular attention to the floor itself.

But if the basement held secrets, it wasn't about to divulge them. Rose stowed the flashlight in her pocket and crept up the stairs, listening at the door. Nothing.

She opened the door to come face-to-face with Verna. Her companion carried a large bucket brimming with spray cleaners, rags, and red vines candy, which she considered her go-power for the housecleaning business.

"I finished with the bathroom," Verna announced. "Mr. Z is asking when we'll be done."

"I guess we're as done as we're going to get."

"Good thing, because Johnny's here."

Rose nodded. The sooner they were out of here the better she'd like it. "Did you leave the lights on upstairs?"

Verna waved her rag at Rose and lumbered off down the hallway. "Waste of electricity," she said.

Rose hurried upstairs to check on Verna's work in the bathroom, a room Mr. Z was finicky about. She gave the room a once-over with her cloth, and peered under the claw-foot tub. A spider the size of a dollar coin crouched within a few inches of her face.

"What you want to live in a place like this for?"

Spider stared, not flexing even one leg.

Verna's cleaning had only reached about a hand's distance under the tub. Spider stood on the line of demarcation, defying the encroachment of soap and water.

"Just don't let Mr. Z see you, then," Rose admonished him. She turned on the light and hurried down the stairs.

"We're leaving, Mr. Zachariah!" she called in the foyer. After waiting a short second, she hurried to follow Verna out onto the porch. Johnny's '95 Nissan minivan, now parked in the driveway, rumbled like a kettle boiling rocks. Johnny was at the wheel, smoking the stub of a cigar—the same stub, it seemed to Rose, that he'd been smoking for weeks. He reached over to haul Verna by her outstretched hand, and Rose squished herself in beside them.

Turning toward the house for a last look, she saw Mr. Zachariah standing on the front porch, a silhouette among the bright windows.

Verna leaned past Rose and waved at him, as though he would wave at a crazy old Indian cleaning woman!

"Put that cigar out, Johnny," Rose said. "Mr. Z don't like smoking on his property."

Johnny shrugged and threw the butt out the window onto the gravel driveway, gunning the engine as the old heap lurched away.

"The cigar!" Rose hissed. "On Mr. Z's driveway!"

"It's OK," Johnny said. "I got more."

"I could use one of them smokes myself, after today," Verna said.

•   •   •   •

Zachariah watched as they peeled out onto the highway. These people who never hurried at working were suddenly in a hurry to do whatever they did on the reservation. Which was little, judging from the condition of the place. He strode down the porch steps to the smoking cigar butt.

He stood in a large, circular driveway originally made for welcoming a stream of visitors but these days seldom used except for Zachariah himself and the occasional cleaning lady. Behind a dense stand of poplar trees along the highway, the sound of a speeding car would now and then break the country silence, along with the lowing of the Guernseys from the adjacent farm. Because of the cows' popularity—there was no better way to describe it—Zachariah sometimes wondered if they weren't a major reason for his being chosen, as unflattering as the thought might be.

To the east, beyond the driveway plantings, lay a barnyard large enough to load hay wagons, and behind and off to the left a low bunkhouse, newly whitewashed outside, but inside . . . another matter.

He didn't much care for Rose and her fat helper, except they kept things tidy, and the clunking of pails and the roar of the vacuum formed a background of social contact without his having to interface. Now the house silences took over, magnifying occasional small noises that his brain tended to supply meaning to. Highly unpleasant meaning, though so far—so far—his house was inviolate.

In the kitchen, Zachariah blended up a supper drink of kelp, pollen, and rice milk and sipped at the brew, thinking about Nir.

Nir was selling like hotcakes. It had been dicey at first, with the beta version coming on a little too . . . strong, but since then it had exponentially improved, and on the street the word was *Nir is hot*. It was a—cash cow, actually. But he needed to keep that spigot open, yes, to pay for the things he wanted—needed. The ranch, the Institute, Lonnie.

Lonnie. Finally he could afford high-class care. Unlike the old place, a bestial hive full of smelly old people, forgotten and forgetful. Feeling a surge of satisfaction, Zachariah flexed his forearm, bringing the wrist cuff to pulsing life, and punched in Harvest Home, shunting the visual to the kitchen wall screen.

In a moment Lonnie's face appeared, her lipstick leaking into the cracks around her trembling mouth and her puffy blond wig askew on her tiny head. Nurse Aziz straightened the wig, patting it in place.

"We're doing just lovely today, Mr. Smith," she said in a throaty voice that caused Zachariah to stir in his chair.

"Not!" croaked a voice like a bird gargling a worm.

Lonnie turned her wheelchair around to confront the viewing eye. "Tell her I don't have to take a bath, Zachy."

"Well," Zachariah began, "it might be . . ."

"Where have you been? Living high off the hog, I 'spose? Leaving me with these perverts!" She glared to the side. Her face filled the wall between the refrigerator and the microwave. "I want to go home."

"I'm sorry you're not happy, Lonnie." His voice rose in pitch, shedding years as his throat constricted. "There's no one here to care for you, even though . . ."

"Oh God, a dummy for a son! I don't mean home with *you*. I mean back where I *was*. My old room, where my things was and where the nurses"—here she looked over to the door—"where the nurses don't try to undress you all the damn time."

"Lonnie, they didn't even *have* nurses. They had dirty mechs, and . . ."

She started to cry. Tears rolled down the arroyos of her face, dripping off her chin onto her lace white blouse that was pocked here and there with a reddish sauce.

"We played checkers," she cawed, "me and those mechs."

"I'm sorry, Lonnie. I'm sorry you're not happy. I'll come visit as soon as I can."

I'm sorry, Lonnie. He was eight years old and kneeling by his mother, large welts rising on her face as the sound of Dad's car screamed out of the yard.

Lonnie snorted, forcing a trickle of liquid out of her nose.

"Did you try the Nir game yet?"

"You and your games!"

"But did you try it?"

"He just shuts me away," Lonnie whimpered to Nurse Aziz.

Shuts me away. The words cut like shrapnel. The best nursing home in the county!

"I'm sure he loves you very much," the nurse said.

"Ha!" Lonnie coughed at the nurse, her grey tongue trembling between her teeth. "What would he know about love?" Her face jerked back to stare at Zachariah. "Just like your father. I shoulda knowd you'd turn out like *him.*"

Zachariah's dinner festered in his gut. "Just try the game, Lonnie, please."

"And if I do, I can go back home?" Her face was so small and pleading, it was tough not to forgive her little outbursts.

"We'll see," Zachariah said.

"Well then, maybe *we'll see* about the game."

Lonnie jerked one side of her mouth, her version of a smile since the stroke. "Aren't you going to tell me you love me?"

"I love you, Lonnie." His eyes blurred, and he bit his cheeks to stay neutral.

Her smile slowly evaporated. "Dummy. What would you know about love?"

The nurse moved onscreen. "She's just tired, Mr. Smith, really. Call back in the morning." Her kindness made Zachariah want to slap her.

"I'm not taking my clothes off!" Lonnie screeched from offscreen.

He stabbed at the mobe, breaking the phone link. Lonnie never changed. There was familiar comfort in that. He drained the last of the vegetable brew, staring at the kitchen wall, still seeing his mother's face. *Just like your father. He just shuts me away. Dummy.*

He took his plate and glass to the sink, washing them carefully. But the glass broke in his hand, cutting the fleshy part of his palm. He washed the cut and bound it with gauze from the first-aid kit in the pantry. The hand felt nothing.

In the hallway, he took his winter parka from the closet and left the house, walking down the driveway to the side path toward the old barn and beyond, the bunkhouse.

After a call to Lonnie, facing *them* was easy.

He knew what he would say to them. He was a well-known man, a public figure. People in his company just couldn't turn up missing, not so often, surely that was simple to understand, even for them. They wanted what he had, and he wanted what they had. A simple business proposition.

They were the spigot of Nir. They could crank up the volume.

The barn doors were ajar, broken on their hinges, exposing a long black crack of an opening. No need to go in *there* . . . not this time. He walked down the snow-packed stretch on the north side of the barn, where the spring thaw was at least a month behind. He felt his socks grow wet through his loafers, and his throat tightened from the frigid air.

Outside the bunkhouse the usual fleshy, sharp stench lay soaking in the air, mingled, blessedly, with an infusion of rotting silage. Although blanketed, the windows allowed a wan glow to escape at the edges, confirming his guests' presence, confirming that what was about to happen was neither hallucination nor nightmare. No. They were real, more real than Zachariah seemed to himself at times, when Lonnie's voice dissolved him utterly, like a body in a vat of lye. He climbed the three sagging steps and opened the door, entering quickly and shutting the door behind him.

Their scent rushed at him, tugging at his stomach. Oftentimes, from the look on their faces, he felt his scent affected *them* the same way.

Two kinds of beings inhabited the bunkhouse. One was child-sized, and pearl-white. It hovered about six inches off the floor, with the demeanor of a slave. This creature was nowhere in sight today, but its master very much was.

An ancient pole lamp and a red plaid couch occupied

the center of the room. The creature weighed down the middle cushion of the couch so that its—feet—touched the floor. It sat as if it belonged there, and had been waiting for him. Maybe it heard him coming. Zachariah glanced down at his bandaged hand. *Smelled* him coming. A bright slash of blood colored the center of his palm, lying wet and heavy in the bandage. He thrust his hand in his pocket.

His guest's face parted in a huge slot from side to side. Zachariah had come to believe this was a smile.

Chapter 3

~1~

Simon got himself a cup of coffee and leaned back in his chair, propping his feet up on the desk. The diary's lock had a broken hasp, making the act of reading the damn thing feel even more intrusive than it already was. Hoping Vittoria's mother wasn't making him snoop for no cause, he opened the book and began to read.

January 7, 2012
Dear Diary,

I hope you know how to keep secrets. Well duh, I have a key, don't I? This is so stupid. Who does diaries? It's like all that junk Mom keeps and tries to sell so we have to live in this stupid apartment and never have anything nice. All I want is somebody to talk to. I won't call you Diary. I'll call you . . . Yes! Favorite band, Cereal Killer. Cereal for short . . . unless you like Killer?

Dear Cereal,

Just be a friend and listen. Because, like, boys don't listen. We know that. What they do and what they don't. But you, you'll be a friend. No choice, is there?

So this is what happened. I logged my Net time in schoolgroup and then hit the mall, where of course, I see Scott and Macky straggling around. The way Macky looked at me, I knew Scott gave him an earful, the way he promised he wouldn't, when he was pleading with me and being sweet. Him and his vid looks. So Scott moves in on me and tries to grab some, and I push his hand away and I say, Keep Away From Me You Frag. And they go laughing and bugging their eyes at each other, and Scott grabs me again, and when I push his hand off I hurt myself. That really set them off.

And then Scott was mad because I wouldn't perform in front of Macky. So he shoves a hot spot up my nose. It started to make the world go wobbly, and especially my stomach. And so I ran to the lav and used water but mostly it was too late. Scott always wanted me to hit spots with him and now he has his revenge.

I came home and felt sick and Mom was going, Are You OK Honey? And then I locked my door and closed the blinds and lay there thinking about how guys have all the power to look at your chest and make you feel like a whore or a freak and make sex your fault whether you give it to them or don't.

So if you ever wished you had big yoyos like mine, don't. My current craze song? "Flat Chested" by the Reamers!

Simon closed the diary with a sigh. He ruffled the pages, noting that about half of it was blank. Blank, like the rest of Vittoria McCrae's life.

He got up from his desk to refill his coffee cup. These kids, he thought. They live in war zones, with bombed-out minds, craters marking their passages of puberty. Young Vittoria, with the body of a woman, and the boys behaving like assholes. He shook his head.

At times like this, in the early morning, the office had a certain peace. The screens were blind, the comps silent, the Net passed him by. It became for Simon a sanctuary where he could perform his everyday work at the speed of Simon, instead of the speed of light. One of the pleasures of living in Medicine Falls was its backwater peace. Up-valley was nothing but the reservation and Chief George Dam. Nobody was ever just passing through. Down-valley was the rest of the world, in a hurry, stressed out, deluged by the outfall of the Net pipeline and other insults of modern life.

He glanced at Rocky's desk, scattered with Net manuals, computer tabs, and gadget add-ons, proof that even in the Falls you could plug in and fast-forward your life, if so inclined. From his desk, Rocky looked like a busy man. Rocky *was* a busy man. For somebody who worked eleven to two, he had to push hard to make a living. Unlike Simon, who found that *contemplating* his cases required a full day. Contemplation, Simon told himself, was a lost art. He leaned against his desk, cradling the coffee cup and listening to the shurring of tires through slush on Lowell Street, contemplating Vittoria McCrae. He had a pretty good sense of the girl. He would get to know her better, but he always learned ninety percent about people in the first five minutes of meeting them. The only time this wasn't true was for psychopaths and women he'd courted. These could keep you off-balance for a long time.

She was a seventeen-year-old girl. That told you much, right there. Witless, hormonal, and desperate for friend-ship. Trading occasional sex for male regard, and inno-cent enough to be surprised when betrayed. Conned by the vids into loving the handsome ones, the ones Most Likely to Be Bastards. But foremost, betraying herself big-time by giving herself away cheaply. Why did the comic universe give adolescents adult bodies? Mistake number 6,007. This was not the *cosmic* universe the New Age stalwarts prattled about. The *comic* universe.

Simon's higher power had a sense of humor. A down-right vicious sense of humor at times, but a damn sight more digestible than that soothing, lavender haze of mystic mooning.

Speaking of hazes, here was Rocky, couple of hours early, by God, and about to impinge on his morning peace.

His partner closed the door behind him, hanging his heavy corduroy jacket on the coat hanger along with his stocking cap.

"Why don't you throw that thing away," Simon remarked. "Makes you look like a bank robber."

Rocky Ginestra waved a newspaper at him, and lowered himself into his chair, all five-foot-eight, two hundred pounds of him. "I love that hat, Hassle. I'm going to be buried in that hat. Don't you forget it, either."

At fifty-one Rocky was just beginning to get a few grey hairs. His squarish face defied a good shave, ruining what might otherwise be a nice, Italian chiseled look. He had the neck and shoulders of a football player. In the navy they'd called him The Rock, partly from his build and partly from a steady, determined personality. With Rocky, you knew what you were getting. If you were navy, a client—or a friend—he was yours for life. The kind of man about whom it is said, "He'd do anything for you." Except take advice.

"You die with that hat on, Rocky, I've never seen you before."

"I am no slave to fashion," his partner responded in all seriousness, flipping on the comps and their appendages, sitting amid a pile of disorder wearing a slightly wrinkled Sears short-sleeved shirt with his undershirt peeking out the unbuttoned neck. He unrolled the newspaper, revealing two hamburgers wrapped in Dave's hotfoil. He handed one off to Simon and unwrapped the other for himself.

"Jesus, Rocky, it's nine o'clock in the morning. Even *I* don't eat hamburgers for breakfast."

"You're welcome."

The comps screamed into action, making the electro-whine of the species, filling their anemic glass faces with facts, choices, lists, icons, reminders, blinking dates, and scrolling titles. To Simon, any person sitting in front of a comp looked as though they were losing a battle with the Honduras flu. As to the bells, whistles, gongs, ditties, and voices that announced the silicon duties of Rocky's comps, these were banished from their shared office by way of a prenuptial agreement between the Sinbad of Cyberspace and the last of the living holdouts from Netopia.

"Hey, listen to this," Rocky said, reading the morning news. "Our man in Congress finally killed the manned Mars project. Deader than a doornail."

Simon laughed soundlessly. "Why explore outer space when cyberspace will do?"

Rocky stopped in the middle of chewing. "That's true," he said thoughtfully. "I hadn't thought of it that way."

"Well, *think* about it. We're squandering technology on the ultimate retina game, the perfect face-lift, the supreme easy chair."

Oblivious, Rocky went on to read his messages, getting absorbed in the work, the endless creditor harassments, missing persons, infidelities, and other pesky and profitable flies in the ointment of life.

Simon refilled his cup and circled back around his desk facing Rocky's. He picked up the black book.

"You finally got a client, Hassle?"

"Yeah. Only she's dead."

"Makes it hard to collect those high fees you don't earn."

Simon propped his legs up on the desk, leaned back in the wooden swivel chair, and resumed his reading.

January 22, 2012
Dear Cereal,

Two things happened today. I'll save the best for last. First, after school me and Drool went to the Social Security office at the old Grummel High School. She wanted to see if she could change the name on her card to Drool. Amy Lund is what the card says now, but even her parents call her Drool, because she won't answer to anything else.

So while she's in the office, I'm waiting in the hall. And this guy sits down next to me.

And he says, You Have Business At Social Stupidity? And I say, I Guess So (brilliant!). And he says You Think The Government Is Going To Take Care Of You? Or something like that. This guy is old—but he's got this real deep voice, like a vid announcer or singer. Anyway, we talked for a while and he never once looked at my bobbers, if that's what you're thinking.

So he runs this Institute or whatever, that's got all these offices there. He said to drop by down the hall to see him sometime. Then he said You Don't Have The Slightest Clue, Do You? And I go, About What, and he goes, About Why You Came Here Today. And I was thinking no, I don't know, I don't know anything. And he says, Come See Me Vitt, and gets up and walks away. So What's Your Name, I say. He turns. Zachariah, he says. Zachariah Who? Just Ask For Zachariah, Vitt. And I wondered how does he know my name? Then I saw I wrote my name on the math book lying next to me. Then Drool comes out and she's just flaming and no, she can't. Have to be twenty-one or parents' permission.

The second thing that happened is that I called Scott and when he got to the phone I told him it was the humane society and did he have a cocker spaniel with a white belly and a splotch on one ear. He says Yes, sounding worried. And I tell him I'm so sorry but that same dog was crushed by a gravel truck this morning and could he come and pick up the body? And I give him the address and tell him there'll be a twenty-dollar fee for processing. Just to make it sound real. And he's crying. And he goes, Is A Credit Card OK? And I go, No, Cash Only. So he cries even harder!

How's it feel now, Scott?

Rocky's comp was making that irritating quacking noise of a download.

"Five gigs for four hundred dollars. That's street price, Hassle," Rocky said without looking up from the keyboard. "You know what that costs at the Mall?"

Simon set the diary aside. "Your soul?"

"Five hundred and twenty-five dollars. Not including maintenance. It's a racket."

"That's a tad harsh." Simon walked to the front door to retrieve their paper mail, which had just hit the floor, cascading from the mail slot which had been installed a few years ago in a fit of retro-remodel mania. Simon pawed through it. All ad tabs, jackets dancing with sneak previews of the software. He dumped them in the trash on the way back to his desk, noting, as he passed Rocky's desk, the blip of game markers on his screen. His partner was knocking off early today.

"You know, you really oughta try this game, Credit Crunch, it's a real kick."

"I play that game every day of my frigging life."

Without looking up from his joystick, the words came: "You are, my man, what they call a class-by-yourself technophobe. But I love ya anyway, God help me."

"Not a technophobe at all. I drive a car don't I?"

An ironic eyebrow shot up. "Yeah? Well look at your desk. You could let a computer organize that paper mess. And think of the trees you're killing." He shot home a winning score, to the flash of pulsing lights.

"Trouble with you Rocky? You've got too much information, too little significance. There is, I do maintain, a difference between data and meaning."

"Sounds like some of that existential crapola."

"Rocky, you wouldn't know existentialism if it bit you in the ass. That's the trouble with people these days. Nobody *thinks* anymore. They're too damn busy coming to *conclusions*."

He heard Rocky's bottom desk drawer slide open, from whence appeared a bottle of scotch, and an unwashed tumbler, into which his partner poured a dainty half-glass. Leaning back and cradling his drink, he looked up at Simon. "Help yourself."

"Maybe later."

Instead, he refilled his coffee cup and stared out the window at downtown Medicine Falls, thinking of Abbey McCrae. Drowning her grief in a crusade to explain Vittoria's death. People had their ways of unloading grief and rage. Some ingenious, like pretending to off a pet dog; some ordinary, like the bottle or a doomed crusade. And he would help them. He would help *her*. Most definitely, and damned if he knew precisely why.

Rocky shut down his comps. He'd talk about the old days now. About Lydia. Simon turned away from the window and leaned on the sill, waiting.

"Sure you don't want a drink?"

"That's OK."

Rocky nodded, resigned, now, to drinking alone. After a moment he sighed. "Remember the time she knitted me a new hat?" He shook his head, smiling fondly.

"Yeah. I remember." Memory was not a problem. Simon Haskell had it to spare.

Rocky frowned. "Some funny color, what was it?"

"Blue."

"Right. Blue."

"That was a real funny color, all right."

Rocky looked up. "But it was funny-smelling, you got to admit."

"It was *clean*, Rocky."

Rocky laughed silently. He stared into his drink, where, apparently, Lydia could often be seen in the amber liquid.

February 16, 2012
Dear Cereal,

It's been awhile, don't be mad. A couple days ago, we're like, at the Mall, and Scott sneaks up behind me and hangs two enormous balloons connected by a string around my neck—balloons with nipples drawn on them. The kids were all standing around laughing. Wouldn't you know that was the day I wore a sweater where my bobbers really stuck out. But it didn't stop me. I flicked my lighter and popped the balloons. We all laughed like hell.

I couldn't eat lunch so I headed out of there and I ended up at the DI. (Dimension Institute, OK?) Everybody there says I'm too old acting to be just seventeen. Right!

Zachariah leads everything. We sit in a circle around Zachariah and people ask him questions and he just answers about, like, friends who are passed over (that's dead) and where you should go with your life, or anything. I never ask him anything, but I listen. Most everyone is older, but they all seem to be in trouble. Like me!

I'd say, def, Zachariah knows things. I don't know if he really hears voices from people passed over. But he might. What if he did hear—passed over people? (We're not supposed to say dead.) That would be plasmic. Last night after everybody else left, we sat and talked a long time. I don't even remember about what!

—Had to go to dinner. Tofu and peas. Mother says too much meat is bad for you, as though we could afford meat! This is what her mother always said to her. So now I get to hear it, and someday I'll say it to my daughter. Kill me first, OK?

Drool and I had a fight. Her parents won't let her frag around with me anymore. They said I'm cheap. I go, Why Don't You Tell Them To Give Themselves A Brain Job? But she doesn't have the nerve. So, bye, bye, Drool, I guess.

February 19, 2012
Dear Cereal,

Here's what happened: I was at the DI, and Zachariah was done with Serving a big round, so it was nearly midnight and everybody left but me. And he goes, Talk To Me, Vittoria. So I told him about zombo Scott and my zombo body. And he goes, Your Body Is Perfect. So I watch to see if he's going to palm the big Bs. But he doesn't even look at them, OK? And then he drags out this retina game, and do I want to play Nir? Do I know what that is? No! Do I want to play? Def! And I hook up—he's got these teeny little glasses—and *only one can play at a time, but a second person can watch. So I played. I became. You'll never know, will you, Cereal? Too bad!*

Nir just grabbed me by the face. It took me to this beauty salon, with weird machines, like to do your hair, your nails and bathtubs for soaking and like that. In a flash I knew what I could do, what would make it all just fine—beyond fine. And then I was operating one of the machines and Vitt was sitting in front of me. And, "Do me," she goes. So I pulled out all her eyelashes and inserted really long ones. It must have hurt! All the time we did these machines, Zachariah is sort of there with me, at least I could hear his voice in my ears, not that I cared. "Do me," she says again. And I go, "Can I?" We were both crying, but happy! I took a sharp blade and fixed her fat ankles by shaving them down so nice and thin. And I curled her hair and did her nails. The messiest part was working on the yoyos. At first I was just going to make them smaller, but then I just felt like going all the way. All the trouble they are, and that they have ruined my life. So I cut them off. So then she washed up and dressed and I got to see my perfect self. Like that transvest singer, Acrid. Then we put the game away and I go, Let's Do It Again.

And he goes, Tomorrow, OK? We'll play it tomorrow.

Dean and Mother are fighting about something. Dean is pretty nice. But he's not my father. When me and Dean play around with Harley, we really laugh. Harley is my favorite, except that he sheds. Later!

Rocky poured himself another drink. The sour smell laced the office as the analog wall clock lurched toward noon. "Time for lunch," Rocky announced.

Simon closed the diary, still thinking about Vittoria's little dungeon of beauty. The hamburger from Dave's still lay untouched in its bed of congealed grease.

"You go ahead," Simon said.

Rocky rose from his chair, measured and slow. "Believe that I will, Hassle. Man was not made for work alone."

"I'll drive you home."

"The TraveLink will do." Rocky held up his wrist, revealing the broad band of his glittering, man-sized mobe. "Already made my booking. What's in the little black book?"

"A descent into hell."

"Need a tour guide?" Rocky asked. He snorted through a smile. "Let me know." He moved toward the door, turned. "We're always gonna be pals. That right, Si?"

Simon nodded. "Always. Take care of yourself, pal."

He closed the door, on his way to the LinkStop.

Back at his desk, Simon thought about the little black diary. This Zachariah was a real piece of work: self-styled guru of a bunch of pathetic mystic types, and, not content with adults who should know better, he hits on Vittoria. Yet that wasn't what bothered him the most. It was the retina game. *Game,* indeed. The damn thing was as sick as anything he'd seen lately, and, in this business, he'd seen a lot.

Simon picked up the phone. He called Abbey's number and let it ring. Finally her messaging center switched through to e-mail. Simon scowled at having to talk Netish. *I'll take the case,* he planned to say. *Come see me. Don't worry about the money.*

Instead, peevish, he hung up the phone. He sat thinking a long while, staring at the little black book with the broken hasp.

~ 2 ~

All of a sudden, Abbey was in a hurry. When things have been glacier-slow for going on two years in your life, you can get a thirst for speed, can wish for things like maybe a car of your own, or a tricked-out motorcycle, or for folks to return your calls in something under a month of Sundays. But Simon hadn't called back and now, here on Lowell Street, she couldn't find Lobo, either. The local girls were starting to eyeball her, and not too friendly, mind you. She punched in her TraveLink booking and waited. Simon Haskell, she thought. Another gutter ball in the bowling game of life.

Out of all the linked transport options of buses, maxi-taxis, and minicars, here came her luck-of-the-draw, an ancient maxi-taxi, a low-riding, seen-better-days sedan, packed with five other riders, amid whose grocery bags, pet dogs, and knapsacks she managed to shoulder her way, passing forward her SmartCard, and receiving it back through a relay of hands. From the looks of her fellow-passengers, she was headed in the right general direction, into derelict land, where Lobo lived, Renalda said. Headed out to find a retina game you couldn't buy at the Mall, couldn't swipe from your roommate—who looked at you like you'd asked to share her toothbrush—all in pursuit of a vapor-thin hunch: Vitt and Nir, a bad pairing.

Out the windows she could see the block-by-block deterioration of this end of town, including metal bars over storefronts, broken windows, and refuse sprouting from gutters and the stoops of once-tidy brownstones. In the distance, anchoring the far end of Defoe Street, she could make out the strutted dome of the old Lowell Street Rail Station, once proud, and now, it was said, a palace for rats. As the taxi stopped at a traffic signal, a round-eyed freaker newly lit with a hit of Xstasy crossed in front, smiling at them with his freaker's smile.

The taxi deposited her in front of her destination, the St. Croix, a narrow and pockmarked apartment building. This was maybe not the smartest move she'd ever made, she thought, coming here alone . . . but she clomped up the stairs and peered at the roster of names by the doorbell. The names were faded, torn, and missing, like the current tenants, most likely. Just as she got ready to knock, the door jerked open. A boy of about eight confronted her. "Nobody's here!" he shouted.

Her hand met the door as he tried to slam it in her face. "Lobo," Abbey said, just as loudly, matching his tone. "I came to see Lobo." She pushed into the foyer, where, beyond the boy's greasy head, a tall stairway climbed into darkness. Not promising.

"Lobo's not here," the boy proclaimed. Something in his eyes made him seem remote, perhaps retarded.

"He's expecting me," Abbey lied. "I'm a friend." Which might be stretching it. But no pint-sized runaway was going to push her off this easy.

At his split-second pause, Abbey sidled by him. The noise of a slamming door several floors up proved *someone* was home. The boy banged the door shut and raced up the stairs ahead of her blurting out, "It's the Blooos, come for some scrooos!"

Doors creaked open and small faces peered out, sometimes stacked, short to tall, like totem poles. As she passed, the doors pinched shut.

"Where's Lobo?" she asked, shotgun style, hoping to hit something. From the closest door, a lisping, sweet voice said: "Up at the top."

She hesitated, looking at the murky stairway. Maybe this wasn't such a good idea. What if Lobo wasn't home? Come to think of it, what if he *was*? Lobo smiling on Lowell Street with his sales pitch on automatic might be a different Lobo than the one who retreated each night to the top floor of the St. Croix.

But she began the climb. On the second floor, a window at the hall's far end provided at least a dim view. She walked to the next flight of stairs, past doors she just hoped would stay closed.

At a noise in back of her, she turned to find a group of four youngsters standing at the head of the stairs as though blocking her retreat. "You got five dollars?" asked a girl of about eight with an off-center, long blond ponytail. She lifted her skirt and swayed her naked hips. The smallest boy knelt in front of her demonstrating what the five dollars would buy.

Abbey took a step toward the nasty creatures, edging them backward a notch. "You should be in school! Shame on you!" The girl lowered her skirt, looking doubtful.

"Hey Sooze," one of the boys said, "she ain't your

mother!" At this, Sooze turned and jumped on the bannister, sliding into the shadowy depths, laughing raucously,
followed by the others like monkeys on a vine. Resuming
her climb, Abbey found floor after floor of hollow-eyed
children, standing on the thresholds of their respective
holes, most scattering as she passed.

On the fifth floor she looked up and saw that the staircase ended at a single door. Like a penthouse. Like an
attic. She wasn't afraid of Lobo, or the wild children or
the dark. She could handle those things, she figured. But
not the attic. Attics were places you put all the things you
didn't want anymore, the things you wished you never
had, the dark things.

"Lobo's home," a piping voice said from one of the
baby dens, maybe impatient with her.

"Lobo!" Abbey yelled. It came out a high-pitched
mewl. She sucked in a breath and belted out again,
"Lobo!"

From nearby came a repeated "Lobo!" and then down
the hall, a chant of "LoBO, LoBO, LoBO," and this echo
floated deeper and deeper into the building as though the
house itself had mouths. Abbey turned to face the pande-
monium. These children were pitiful and tragic, and, just
now, annoying as hell, calling up the urge to pull a few
ears, put someone on a chair in the corner.

From behind her she heard, "Who the fuck wants
Lobo?"

Abbey swirled. Lobo had come halfway down the
stairs in the confusion. He peered at her in the gloom as
though *she* were the strange sight, and not him. He wore
his skullcap, with gadgets dangling like insects around his
cheeks. A torn, baggy sweat suit hung from his stick
frame.

"Shit," he said. "What you doing here?" Silence
reigned in babyland. Abbey too, felt tongue-tied.

"How'd you get by my guards?"

That snapped her voice back. "These children are living in filth, Lobo. And so are you."

He grinned easily. "Well, we could move in with you,
Ab. How'd that be?"

"Ab, Ab, Ab," came the chant.

Behind Lobo, up at the top, his door was open. Beyond it lay his grey den, where Abbey could just make out motes of dust highlighted by some distant window or flame.

"Wanna come up?" Lobo asked.

"Not right now." A trickle of sweat left the nape of her neck and traveled slowly down her spine.

"Somethin' I can do for you, Ab?" His voice took on a prodding, sarcastic tone. He glanced down at the fifth-floor doors, perhaps posturing for his audience.

Abbey straightened. This could get out of hand. "You listen to me, Lobo," she said. "I haven't got time for foolishness. I came to buy something. You don't want my business, just say so."

"SAY so, SAY so," the house repeated.

His hands went up, fending her off. Then a cough shook him and he dug in a pocket, finally pulling out a rag so repulsive that Abbey had to look away. He blew his nose, and looked at her over the wad of cloth.

"It's that game," she said. "What do you call it? Nir? Sounds like fun. I'd like to try it. I brought money." She plunged a hand into her bag and pulled forth a crumpled bunch of greens.

Lobo visibly started at the sight of the money. He lunged for her arm and yanked her partway up the stairs, pulling her close to his face. "You're fucking stupid." His breath might have come from a waste vent. He pivoted on the stairs and practically carried her with him down the steps to the hallway. It all happened so fast she didn't have time to react, except she *did* notice he pulled her down, not up, not up to that lair of his.

He was dragging her down the hallway. "Get out of my way!" he croaked at the youngsters who began streaming out from their warrens. "Get out of my way, all of you, or I'll cut you off!" he shouted.

"Money!" the kids shouted gleefully. "Money, money, money," sped through the corridors.

"Fucking stupid!" he whispered hoarsely in her ear. He plunged on, elbowing his way through the crowd of children, now sprinting from doors, up the staircase, down the bannister. There were so many of them, it was a stampede, a swarm. "Money, money, money!" came the refrain from all mouths.

Abbey let him pull her along as his left elbow angled through the bodies like an icebreaker forging a channel. Looking up at her from all sides were little faces contorted with demon energy, screaming, the girls screaming in high-pitched ululations, the boys chanting money, money, money. She slapped at the insistent hands goosing her from all sides. As they stumbled down the stairs leading to the third floor, a thunderous drumming of feet pursued from behind, threatening to surge over them and pitch them headlong down, down. And then, for a moment, Abbey saw something glitter, could have been those feral eyes . . . could have been a knife. Dear God, just two more floors. Her heart lurched against her ribcase in time with an accelerating storm of Money Money Money Money . . .

And then down the long run of stairs to the lobby, met by an upswelling tide of children from below, through which Lobo shoved and cursed his way until at last he strode across the foyer, reaching for the door handle of the front door.

Abbey jerked out of his grip and flattened her back against the door.

"Get out of here," Lobo cried, gadgets swinging wildly from his techno cap.

"Not before you sell me the game." Abbey glared back, as the children hung from all levels, screeching over the railings, crowding the stairs and pounding the walls.

"I don't have it! I'm all out, see?"

"I came all this way, Lobo!"

"Yeah, and you lucky to leave. Get out!"

"Please, Lobo." She grabbed his skinny arm beneath his armpit, looking into his eyes, trying to find their center. "I've got to have it."

"Shit, I'd *give* it to you if I had any! Just to get rid of you. You still gonna end up dead on my front steps, you know?"

A pause, and then Abbey believed him. On all counts. A fine mess, this time, for sure. A simple black-market purchase turns into the Attack of the Killer Babies. Disappointment turned to anger. She stepped forward and pointed at the stair full of children. "You!" she shouted. "I hear any more nonsense from you, and I'll *really* get mad!" Then swirling, she pointed down the long hall with its mob of youngsters. The girl called Sooze was standing in front, looking round-eyed at Abbey's pointed finger, her yellow ponytail flopped over her shoulder like a dirty stole. "And you! Next time I come here, you're going directly to school. No stops!" She yanked open the door, feeling the fresh air like a welcome, cold cloth on her face.

She turned back one more time. The foyer was eerily quiet, the children standing as though carved from stone. "Shame on you" was all she could think of to say, holding them in a fierce scowl. Then she turned back and went down the front stoop.

From behind her she heard Lobo's voice, softer now, and perhaps tinged with respect:

"Be seeing you, Abbey."

~ 3 ~

Abbey pressed her nose against the door to Simon's office, trying and failing to see through it. Neo glass. Even had the little bumps all over for effect, but definitely that tacky petro/recycle stuff. The whole office building was a mixture of true retro, lovely repro, and horrid fakes. She knocked again. But no one was in. After yesterday at the St. Croix, it seemed like more than a good idea to get some help—not that she hadn't handled most of her problems herself all these years. Not that she hadn't screwed up a lot of them, either. But finding a man to really count on, well, try finding a snowball in hell.

She had hoped to find Simon in his office, have her conversation, and if he didn't want the case, retrieve the diary, and be back to open the shop by ten. She turned and leaned against the door, closing her eyes. "Crap."

"You need help, lady?"

Abbey snapped her eyes open. A man in a shabby suit stood a little too close to her, peering closely at her. His breath smelled of old refrigerator air, stale and vaguely vegetable.

"You waiting for Simon or Rocky?"

"Simon Haskell."

"Simon Haskell," the man repeated. "Looks like he's not here yet."

"Who's Rocky?"

"Rocky's his partner, so to speak." The man's eyes, dark as ball bearings, flicked in the direction of the closed door. "Looks like *he's* not in, either."

"Well, I'll just wait, then."

"You'll just wait," he said, nodding. "Not a bad strategy." His eyes traveled the slightest bit over her chest. "The name's Roland Waler." He extended a hand bearing a large class ring sporting a cheap, bright blue stone.

Abbey shook the damp hand. "You a friend of Simon's?"

"A friend!" he exclaimed. "No, no, not a friend. A business associate," he said. His attempt at a smile came out as a smirk. "I'm in 315." When Abbey didn't respond, he added, "Down the hall."

She glanced toward the elevator, hoping Simon or his partner would appear and rescue her from this guy.

Waler plucked a card from his lapel pocket. "My card," he said.

Abbey scanned it:

ROLAND WALER

SECURITY. INVESTIGATIONS. CONFIDENTIAL.

"I'm in the security business. Same as Haskell."

Now Abbey got the picture. She handed the card back. "Mr. Waler, I've got my business with Simon Haskell. I don't guess I need more help." She hoped this was true, but if it wasn't, she wouldn't be picking a man like Roland Waler.

"No! Of course not. It's just that if you're in a hurry . . ." Here he waited in vain for her to react. "Some people are in a hurry."

"Well, I'm not." She held out her hand, wishing she hadn't. "But it's been nice to meet you, anyhow."

Waler looked at her hand a moment before shaking it. He started to turn away, fumbling in his pockets, perhaps for his keycard. He turned back again. "Sometimes Haskell is in the field all day. Been known to forget an appointment. And Rocky, well, he's never in until eleven. Sometimes twelve. But you don't want to get mixed up with Rocky, a nice gal like you."

"Why's that?" Abbey heard herself ask. Vitt's voice whispered: *Brilliant.*

Waler sidled back in her direction. "Why's that? Because he's a drinker, a lush." He said the last word with an offhand relish that made Abbey tighten up inside.

"Not that there's anything wrong with a good belt now and then. I've been known to indulge a time or two myself. But Rocky Ginestra never met a drink he didn't like."

Abbey's mobe went off in her purse, with the rattling, teletype sound effect she'd selected. She thrust her hand into the bag and groped for it, finding that it had slipped from its Velcro fastening on the rim of her purse, into the depths of the bag.

"After that business with his wife, I don't blame him, though."

"What business with his wife?"

Noting her dig through her purse, Waler said, "I always wear mine here," pulling up the elastic wristband of his dress shirt. An impressive mobe hugged his forearm, running practically from his wrist to his elbow, twinkling like a live tattoo. He smiled a second time, a quick, nervous show of yellow teeth. "Chinese," he said. "You want a really good mobile info unit, buy Chinese."

Abbey gave up on the main compartment and started

on the outside pockets where usually she tried not to keep it on account of having lost one too many that way.

"The deal with Rocky, well that was a hostage situation. His wife was killed."

Abbey stopped her fumbling. "Killed? That's awful."

"Awful, sure it was. Especially since they'd only been married a couple years. Like newlyweds they were, even though Rocky's this old bachelor that hadn't been with a woman for decades." The smile again. "Well maybe that's *why* he doted on her. She probably gave it to him every night, the lucky son of a bitch."

Abbey plunged back in her purse, ignoring Waler. Found the mobe. She punched in for her mail. It was hard to see in the dusky hallway, and she squinted to bring the screen in focus.

"Is it Haskell?" Waler asked.

She rotated the mobe to catch the light from the wall sconce. The message came up, finally:

To: Venus
See Rose on the rez. If you want to know about V and Z.
Medfallsrez.tribes.com

"On his way, is he?"

Abbey read the message again, heart beating in her throat.

"Haskell on his way?" Waler asked again.

Abbey looked up at him absently. "Hmmm?"

"Stood you up, didn't he. Simon Haskell hasn't come through on a tough case in years. Hasn't got the balls anymore, if you want to know."

Like a mosquito that wouldn't give up, this guy. "Look," she said, leveling her best killer stare at him, "I *don't* want to know. I think our conversation is over, Mr. Waler."

He backed up. "OK. You don't want to know."

Abbey's mind was racing. Who was Rose? V and Z, that had to be Vitt and Zachariah. Someone knew that Vitt was involved with him. Someone named Rose. Abbey glanced down the hallway again. If she had to go to the reservation, she'd like Simon along.

"Just don't blame me when he lets you down."

She booked the TraveLink system through her mobe. As she jammed down the hallway to catch an intercity taxi-bus with a nearby real-time ETA of under fifty seconds, she heard Waler call out behind her:

"Sometime ask Haskell what kind of shot he is."

Chapter 4

~1~

Zachariah followed the girl for several blocks, trying to figure out if she was a prostitute or a runaway, though down here one usually meant the other.

Inky rain slashed at the windshield, making it hard to keep the girl in view. Occasionally the girl would pass under a streetlight, and he watched as she inspected street garbage and the lumpen forms of outers huddled in doorsteps.

Disguised in a stocking hat and in a beater of a car, Zachariah felt he was safely anonymous, but still, it was no time for dawdling. He pulled up next to the darkhaired girl—he figured her for about ten—and lowered the window on the sidewalk side.

"Kid, you need a good meal?"

The girl looked up to the window near the stoop. Two faces—looked like children—were pressed up to the glass, watching. Damn. Zachariah had thought this row of apartments was abandoned. Then, looking up at the apartment building again he saw that in fact, every window had its tiny watching faces. A house of children.

Plunging his hand to his wallet and pulling out a thick sheaf of bills, he slid over on the seat and waved them at the girl. He had her attention now. Zachariah smiled and nodded. The girl strolled to the curbside and then lunged for the bills, just as Zachariah jerked them back. She staggered into the gutter.

"Get in," Zachariah said.

She pulled up on the door latch and drew the door partway open, but another child was behind her, suddenly, and slammed it shut again.

The second girl was younger and blond, her hair drawn into a ponytail reaching to her waist. "Cut out," she ordered. She yanked the dark girl's hair to make her point, causing a wailed "My maaaaaan."

"He's not your man, he's mine." She leaned on the window and looked into Zachariah's face. "Aren't you?" She smiled, a lopsided parody of a come-on smile. But the smile vanished as the first girl shoved her, sending her sprawling on the pavement. The darker child took time for a look of triumph, then pulled open the door and flopped her wet body down on the seat, slamming the door.

Zachariah gunned the engine and the car squealed down the street. He had her. She practically *chose* him. Now, this was easy pickings, much easier than outers and adult hookers. Why hadn't he thought of children before? He looked over at the girl, who was methodically stripping off layers of filthy clothing.

"Leave them on," he said.

She scowled and threw the clothes on the floor of the car where they hit with a sodden smack.

"Put them back on."

He didn't need a naked girl beside him, here on a public street. But he glanced sideways at her while she sat pouting, dressed only in a slip and leggings. He could have her, too. He could take her to his house, upstairs, first. He gripped the steer stick and tried to remember the way home.

She noticed his glances. "Let's see the money again. You can wave it at me, like this." She mimicked Zachariah smiling and leaning over with his hand stretched out, waving the bills.

This is a little brat who deserves what she's going to get, he thought.

"Even if I do it all dressed, I still get paid." Her voice was muffled as she pulled on a large turtleneck sweater. Up close she was younger than he thought. Possibly only eight or nine, though she acted fifteen or forty.

"You got to pay first," she said.

Pulling the crumpled bills from his pocket where he'd stuffed them, he gave her a twenty. She looked at the other bills disappear back into his pocket. "Two twenties, at least," she said. "This one guy, he gave me three." She wiggled into her soggy jeans. "But I did him twice."

He gave her another twenty. "That's all," he said, making it gruff.

This donation was going to get him another full load, worth fifteen thou on the street. And even better, he'd found a lair of children who'd fight to get in his car. He slapped the steering wheel. Yes. This could work, this house of children. Once past the unsavory aspect of donating *children*. Even though she and all her little cohorts were filthy little low-lifes, probably diseased and marked to die, anyway. Certainly his guests could get what they wanted, if not from him, then surely from someone else. Maybe *lots* of people worked for them, although he liked to think he was the only one. He might ask them next time, but they tended not to answer questions. Not in the way you meant them, in any case.

"Where are we going?" she asked, squirming. "It's too hot in here."

He flipped the heat off.

"What's your name?" she asked.

"Zachariah."

"Mine's Carma. Or Caramel. Which do you like better?"

He looked at her. "Karma," he answered.

He pulled into his driveway, watching carefully to see that no other cars were on this stretch of highway, then drove around to the back of the tool shed.

"This your house?" Carma wiggled around to gape out the rear window. "The one with all the lights?"

Opening her door and grasping her firmly by the hand, he opened his umbrella and slammed the car door shut. He led her to the barn, barely visible in the steady downpour. Carma stomped her feet in the mud, splattering him.

"Stop it!" he ordered.

"Stop what," she asked, stomping again.

He yanked her around to face him. "Stop splashing mud," he said in his nicest voice.

She minded then, as best she could, considering the swampy barnyard. He pulled her forward toward the barn door. It stood slightly ajar.

"Can't we go in the bright house?"

"No."

He had to close the umbrella and hook it on his arm to open the barn door and still keep hold of the girl. They stepped into the spiky fragrance of the barn interior, redolent of old silage and manure, where the needling of the rain on the roof echoed softly, muted by bales of hay and the blood thrumming in Zachariah's ears. Here was a much safer place for his guests' little doorway than the train station where any bum might stumble upon it.

As he had that day. That vividly remembered day: It had been raining as he drove around, hunting a warehouse to store Lonnie's few household items after her move to the home. As he searched for the address he wandered into the wrong part of town. He'd strayed a few blocks from his car, and by the time he noted a gang of freakers moving toward him, there was only time to duck into an alley then scramble between buildings, finally ending up at a dead end next to the old train depot where a fence blocked his escape. Clambering over it, he raced along the platform; one of the boys pounded after him. Then Zachariah spied a hole in the depot side door—

maybe used by outers to find a dry sleeping spot—and crawled through, losing a shoe to the freaker who now reached to pull him back. He ran for the nearest door and threw it open, thinking to barricade himself in, except the room was empty of furniture, and in a moment the freaker was through the door, knocking him flat.

A vortex of curdled light sliced into the room, and the creature came out of nowhere.

It seemed to regard Zachariah and the freaker with a long, appraising stare. The freaker panicked and made a fruitless run for the hall. He was instantly struck down. Expecting to die, Zachariah shrank into the corner in a crouch, saying, "Don't kill me. I can give you what you want. Name your price." Everything had a price.

Over the next few hours Zachariah learned what that price would be. . . .

"I don't like it in here," the girl was saying.

He took her to the side where he kept his lantern. He turned it on, checking the empty stalls to make sure they *were* empty. The horses were gone, of course. They didn't like horses. Actually, the horses didn't like *them* either. But it was different with cows. Sometimes he brought a cow to them, leading the dumb beast on a tether from his neighbor's field. They would pat it and gently put their faces on its flanks. Like it was a pet or something. The thought of them catering to a *pet* made him shake his head.

He led the girl to a burned circle about two meters in diameter. "Stand here." She stood there obediently, waif-like.

"What for?"

Zachariah hesitated. "I don't know," he said. "I really don't have the slightest idea."

They waited. The leak of rain into the barn kept them company for a few moments. But they would come for her. They always seemed to know when anything entered the circle. And then they came and got it. From the loft, coarse flaxen strands of hay extruded through the planks like the frazzled hair of desiccated women.

Then, around the girl a circle erupted on the floor, like

a trailing of gunpowder set alight. From this ring, filaments of light began branching and growing upward in a million hairline fractures, climbing to surround the girl in a cylindrical vase. The filaments burned incandescent, and then blacked out to reveal a murky interior, as though filled with gel. The child fell to her knees, in slow motion, it seemed, an afterimage, following her downward motion. She began crawling out of the circle. "I want to go home," she whined. Despite having seen all this before, Zachariah's heart beat wildly, like a beast trapped in his chest.

One of them appeared within the gel tube, ushering his scent into the barn. It looked at him, and Zachariah backed up. *Not me,* he thought. *Don't get this confused.*

It lumbered forward and took the girl by one ankle and pulled her into the cylinder.

"It stinks!" she hollered, as though this was the worst she could say about what was happening to her. Then the gel burned bright and the tube collapsed into a circular sheet about eight feet off the ground. This luminous plate spun and spun, creating a buzzing sound like insect wings. Then the shining plate flung its glowing matter to the circle's perimeter, creating a hoop. The hoop faded until nothing was left but a ring on Zachariah's retinas.

They were gone.

He felt peaceful this time, without that little twinge of guilt. He didn't know what happened to his donations. But it was their Karma.

~ 2 ~

Simon ducked into the covered entryway of Abbey's Anteeks, escaping the cold, staccato downpour that couldn't decide if it was rain or ice. Though the shop was dark, he tried the door. It was unlocked.

He stomped his feet, shaking off a cascade of water, and entered the shop. The windows facing the street admitted a dusky light, enough to get a sense of the place, with its maze of secondhand marvels like slide rules, a

Ouija board, a fur stole on a tailor's bust, a telephone stand, and a row of dolls, glassy eyes reflecting the last of the daylight. Damn it anyway, Haskell, can't this wait until morning? Why the hell was he out in this miserable weather about to bother Abbey McCrae at home when a phone call would do?

Well, but a phone call might not do if he couldn't catch her at home, and he was damned if he was going to play the e-mail game with her: my machine will call your machine, and when you get around to it you'll compose a message for my machine and vice versa, and we'll call it communication.

"Hello?" Simon called. "Anybody here?"

"Shop hours are nine-thirty to five," he heard from a ceiling speaker. "Come back soon!"

A flash of lightning lit up the shop, bringing him face-to-face with Elvis Presley in porcelain, sporting a lampshade. As thunder grumbled far away, Simon made his way toward a stairway leading up to the second floor.

"Anybody here?" he called out. A dog barked from behind the door at the landing.

It can wait. He knew that. But he found himself climbing up the stairs and knocking at the door. *I'll take the case, Abbey. No promises on what I'll find, that's all. And answer your damn phone sometimes, OK?* He knocked again. The dog whined behind the door, scratching at the doorjamb. Sounded like a big dog. Simon took out his business card and wrote on the back: "Call me. Simon."

He was halfway down the stairs when the door opened. He turned.

"Yeah?" A woman stood in the doorway. Not Abbey. Shorter than Abbey. Dark hair. Simon climbed back up to the landing.

"I'm looking for Abbey McCrae." The room behind her was dark as though she'd been sleeping. She wore stylish black slicks and garish earrings.

"Abbey?" the woman repeated.

A large black dog with a sparkling chain collar poked his nose out to investigate Simon. Another whine seemed to indicate that Simon passed inspection.

"Is she here? I'm sorry to call so late, but I need to talk to her on business."

"Business?" the woman asked. Her lipstick was smeared on one side of her mouth. Maybe she had a boyfriend in there.

"I'll come back some other time," Simon said.

Lightning charged the windows in the apartment, throwing wavering light into a small living room cluttered with knickknacks and tacky furnishings. No one in sight.

The dog shouldered his way past the woman to sniff at Simon's shoes, then raised its head, panting eagerly. Simon patted him. "Nice dog."

"Do you want him?" she asked.

The remark startled him, and he looked at her closely to see whether she was joking. Her face had been passive since she first opened the door, and it still was.

"Looks like a nice dog, but no thanks. Will you give Abbey this card?" He stooped down to pick up his business card that had fallen to the floor. Cruising on automatic, Simon thought. If this was Abbey's roommate, she'd chosen a strange one.

"Harley," she said, fingering the card.

"Beg pardon?"

"His name's Harley."

"The dog?"

She smiled, a false and ingratiating little smile. Maybe she was actually trying to unload the dog on him.

"I'll tell her," she said. "That you wanted her."

"If you wouldn't mind. Sorry for the interruption." Simon turned and descended the stairs, feeling her eyes on his back, not hearing the door close. At the bottom, he turned around and looked up at the shadowy figure on the landing. "Your shop door is open, by the way."

"I'll tell her," came the reply.

Yeah. You do that. Simon yanked his coat around him, preparing to get soaked again, for nothing. Who was this Abbey McCrae, anyhow? The woman presided over a damn junk mausoleum and other dead memories, sharing a dingy apartment with a nitwit and a hound the size of a Volkswagen.

And never answers her goddamn phone.

He made his way back through the shop and closed the door behind him, nearly stumbling across some poor bum huddled under the awning, out of the weather. He pulled his coat around him, and dashed for his car through a hard rain.

Renalda closed the door and tucked the business card into her side pocket, relieved to be rid of whoever that was. What did he say he wanted? Couldn't be a boyfriend, he was a little old for Abbey. And he was all *wet* for some reason.

She snuggled back into the multilounger and pulled on the Nir shades, gazing into their silky depths until a small dot of light appeared like a distant star, and then rushed toward her. . . .

A thick infusion of nectar crowded her nostrils, that achingly familiar scent of the overgrown honeysuckle that nearly blocked the secret garden entrance. The world was washed silver-grey in a heavy, drifting mist.

"Where have you been?" His voice startled her, and she swirled around to face a black coach with a driver snapping the reins of a team of horses. The coach door was ajar and DeVries' silken arm emerged, the lace at his wrist drooping in the pervasive mist.

"Hurry!" His voice was a harsh whisper. From far away, the sound of dogs approaching. The grounds-keeper.

The driver struggled to restrain the horses as they balked at the sound of the dogs, and amid their thrashing and the gathering downpour, she plunged across the road toward the carriage, lifting her taffeta skirts, but splattering her pantaloons and soaking her velvet shoes in the muck.

The barking grew louder and voices broke out, "Halt! Halt there!" Renalda looked over her shoulder as DeVries hauled her forcibly into the coach.

"My bags!" she wailed, thinking of her fine dresses. All the more tragic if lost, now that this one was ruined.

"No time!" he barked, and then to the driver: "Make haste, and spare not the horses!" The door crashed shut as Renalda was thrown back on the seat and the coach launched down the road. DeVries pulled her firmly to himself, helping to cushion her from the jostling, his spicy cologne sending a wave of pleasure over her, side by side with the terror of her father's determined pursuit.

He shuttered the window, plunging them into twilight. "We have the lead on them, they'll not pursue." His eyes captured her in their sharp gaze. He felt it too—he must— the thrill of the chase, the triumph of their daring escape, flaunting the suffocating conventions of her family. It was wicked, ruinous, and intoxicating. "My darling," he said, with the lightest touch on her earlobe, a touch she felt race along her entire skin.

The coach thrashed across a gauntlet of ruts, then swerved onto the main road, a somewhat smoother ride. Calmer now, she was about to say, "Tell me that you love me," wanting to know, to hear, that she was everything to him.

He drew out his linen handkerchief and dried her face. "You're everything to me," he said, looking at her as though his heart was as full as her own. Then he pulled at the ties securing her cloak and drew her wet taffeta cover away, bringing a sharp chill to her bare shoulders. Before she could accuse him of rushing their intimacy, he reached in back of her and pulled a frothy fur cloak entirely around her, pressing its sumptuous loft against her shivering body.

It was ecstasy already, and they had just begun.

She batted at the damn dog as he continued to scratch at the arm rest of the multilounger. Finally, he gave up on Renalda and returned to the kitchen and his food bowl. It was still empty.

~3~

"Kevin, would you like a ham sandwich?" Gilda stood in the doorway to her son's darkened bedroom. He was sitting in front of his computer screen, his back to her, as he had been for what seemed like weeks. "Kevin?"

He swiveled in his chair as outside, lightning flashed, flooding the room with a milky light. She blinked, trying to see his face. "I was just going to make myself a sandwich. Would you like one?" She was intruding, she could tell. "I didn't bother to make dinner. It's too much effort, cooking for just one." Even to herself, she sounded peevish. Well, she had a *right* to be peeved.

"People are just fucking irresponsible," Kevin said.

Gilda was so startled to have him actually talk to her that she hardly noticed his cross tone of voice. "Irresponsible, dear?"

"Human doings." He snorted. "Just human *doings.*"

Gilda searched for a grip on this conversation. But it was smooth and self-contained as a pool ball.

"Not human *beings,* human *doings.* Doing this, doing that. And what for? What's the purpose?"

Ah. Now she got his drift. "Happiness, maybe?"

He was silent a few beats. Maybe she could cheer him up a little.

The screensaver displayed a lawn mower, eating up a field of grass, line by line. "Politics, football games, aerobics"—the words came out like hurled rocks—"movies, road trips, all the little diversions to fill up our little lives."

"Well," Gilda began, "it's not . . ."

"And those little *contests* you enter. Rhyming jingles to sell cornflakes and whatnot."

That particular rock struck a nerve. "I *enjoy* contests. And I'm *good* at it." She was just marshaling a nice surge of anger when he veered off again:

"See, there's a difference between liberty and *liberties.* People always think they want freedom. But deep down, it's really liberties they're after. Fucking irresponsible."

"You think it's *responsible* to sit here and play VR games and live off me?" It was more than she planned to say, but she was damn good and angry. That he could lecture *her* about responsibility—his own mother—it was insufferable.

An eruption of thunder garbled his next words. ". . . teaching us respect for *authority*. Obedience to a higher authority. The ultimate authority." His voice cracked as he put his hand to his forehead.

"Headache, dear?"

When he spoke again his voice was drained of malice: "When I wear the visor . . . it all seems so clear. So obvious. But do you get what I'm trying to say?"

She bit her lip. "I'm trying to. . . ." Though at a depth just below the surface, she didn't truly want to get it.

"It gives things a purpose, Mom. See?"

She found herself kneeling at his side, patting his arm. "Oh, Kevin." Tears formed, heavy and warm against her eyes. "It'll be all right, honey, don't you worry."

He nodded. His own voice, thick with emotion, came out in a whisper. "I know it will. Soon."

Chapter 5

~1~

The morning haze burned off as Abbey stood on the outskirts of the reservation village of Sun Rock. She walked down a narrow mud street passing a succession of small cinder-block houses and tar-paper shacks and, in the street, children playing, surrounded by barking, mongrel dogs. Her hair fluttered around her face as a few warmer currents chased away the cold morning breeze. Her spirits climbed. Maybe this would be a break. And if so, wasn't it about damn time?

Getting directions at Ducky's, the town tavern, she managed to find Rose's house. In front of the tidy, aluminum-sided mobile home, bits of colored cloth fluttered on the lower branches of a lone aspen.

Answering her knock, a young Native American woman opened the door. She wore a red plaid shirt, jeans, and canvas tennies.

"Rose?"

"Maybe. Who are you? If you're Jehovah's Witness, we got our own religion."

"Abbey McCrae," she said, hoping it would mean something.

The woman's face brightened. "Oh. I didn't think you looked like Jehovah's Witness. I never saw one in cowboy boots. Not like those."

Abbey looked down at her red boots with the black cut-away flower designs.

"Come on," the woman said. "There's somebody I got to take you to see." She grabbed a sweater from a peg near the door and shepherded Abbey down the driveway to the road.

"Was it you that sent me the message?" Abbey asked, walking fast to keep up.

"Yeah. But we don't have much time. How come you're so late?"

"I got here on the first intercity," Abbey said.

"I thought all you people had cars."

Rose strode on, with Abbey rushing to keep up. As Abbey walked, she cracked the ice on the puddles with her boots, and as she did so a surge of memory hit out of nowhere, a memory of Myra stomping through ice puddles, daring Abbey to do the same. And she did dare, because Myra did, because they copied everything the other one did. Until Abbey learned never to copy again. Learned it good . . .

They stood before an old house-trailer nearly engulfed in a leathery, leafless vine. A wood shack extended the trailer on one end. Rose opened the front door without knocking. There, in a small kitchen, stood a large-boned, portly woman, her short, dark hair threaded with grey. She was cooking furiously, with pans on four gas burners.

"Verna, this is Abbey," Rose said.

Verna looked her up and down. "I figured." She scrounged in the refrigerator, retrieving an armload of vegetables, saying, "If you're hungry, there's plenty."

"No thanks."

The two women began chopping onions and potatoes

as Abbey stood there in confusion. Finally she blurted out, "Did you want to see me?"

"Nope. Jaguar does. Did you bring a giveaway?" Her eyes narrowed when Abbey hesitated. Then, wiping off her hands on the sides of her dress, she gave Abbey an unopened pack of Take Fives. She walked to the back of the kitchen and opened a door, turning around to beckon Abbey.

She followed the woman through a dark room built onto the side of the trailer. At the back of this room Verna opened a door leading outside, where the midmorning sun exactly shone through the rectangle of the door, blinding Abbey for a moment.

"You coming?" Verna asked.

She made her way outside onto a sagging porch, rubbing her eyes, trying to bring them in focus. In a blurry outline off to one side she saw someone sitting in an overstuffed chair.

When her eyes cleared, Verna was gone and she could see an old man with a pronounced hawk nose gazing out to the vast marsh that formed the backyard. His white hair was cut at ear length, and he wore moccasins, jeans, and a denim jacket with an American flag skillfully embroidered on one arm. By his side an upright ashtray stand, vintage thirties, held a bowl of white sand.

Again Abbey found herself at a loss for what to do. Then, remembering the pack of cigarettes Verna had given her, she placed them on the railing in front of him.

Ignoring this, he turned to look at her. His dark face framed eyes of deepest black, with lines forming a network across his face and a large lower lip protruding in a hint of cruelty.

"Sit down," he said in a heavy accent, and from far down in his throat.

There were no other chairs. She sat on the edge of the steps, turning sideways to face him. From inside the trailer Verna's and Rose's voices could be heard, muffled—and far in the distance, children laughing. Unsure of what to say, she waited for him to speak. As she watched this man they called Jaguar, she tried to figure his age, and guessed seventy or thereabouts. He sat in his chair as though commanding the porch, although the only person to command so far was her.

Finally she said, "Do you want . . ."

His hand flashed up, stopping her. "Quiet," he snapped. "Listen to the fields."

Abbey took a moment to listen past Verna and Rose and the village children. "I don't hear anything," she said finally.

"No," he said. "You don't." As he turned toward her, Abbey saw that one of his front teeth had a square black stone embedded in it.

"What am I supposed to hear?" she asked.

He didn't answer, but gazed back over the marsh, turning his remarkable profile to Abbey. It was different in a way she couldn't place. Larger, more defined features. He had the attitude of someone waiting for something, his eyes scanning slowly, with a deep frown of concentration cutting into his forehead.

After a moment of quiet, he said, gazing past her, "My people aren't around anymore. All gone to the high gods. Still, I have my ministry, so I come here. No one can stop me. Not yet." He looked directly at her, a look that felt like a slap. "Who are *your* people, Abbey?"

She hesitated, groping for an answer. "My people—my family—is dead. My mother and father. My daughter."

He turned away, scowling.

"Can you tell me about my daughter?"

"Your daughter is dead."

She waited, summoning breath. "How did she die?"

His eyes narrowed. "You think I can tell you this thing. You make demands. That is not the way it is done."

Abbey took a deep breath. She wanted to hear how it was done. Maybe if she waited long enough *someone* here would tell her something.

"The round-faced man holds your power," he said.

The round-faced man. Instantly, Zachariah's face came to her mind.

"Was he involved in Vitt's death?"

Jaguar reached into his pocket and brought out a tiny

packet. He unwrapped the paper and placed a bit of incense in the sand of the ashtray. Taking a book of matches from his inside jacket pocket, he lit the mass and a sweet odor arose in a haze. "You waste time," he said, shaking the match out. "There is not much time."

Abbey breathed deeply, resolving to be patient.

"Listen to the fields," he said. "The birds flew away, you can't hear them anymore. The rustle of snake, can you hear him? Or the scratching of mole? No, you can't hear him."

Abbey listened, and then she *did* hear it, the silence, the empty calm of the marsh, like a vid screen on mute.

"They are gone, or burrowing deep. They know a darkness is coming," he said, face in profile again. "The high gods will abandon you. When the gods leave, your power will slip away with the birds."

A wisp of incense threaded by, rather like an image of power slipping away. "What darkness is coming?" she asked.

"The same that destroyed your daughter. It will take your people." He fanned the incense toward his face with the broad paddles of his hands. "You will prevent this. If you fail, your name will be cursed and your death will be a misery."

Great, Abbey thought. The mummy's curse. Out loud she said, "I don't know what you're talking about. I'm sorry. And I don't know what this has to do with me."

"There is nothing you have to know. I will tell you what must be done." With short yet graceful fingers, he took the pack of cigarettes from the railing and slipped them into his jacket pocket.

"Please," she said. "I do have to know. And I think . . ." Here she raised her chin to fix him with a candid stare. "I think if you know something of my daughter's death, you have no right to keep it from me."

A beat. "No right?" It was a throaty phrase, a growl.

It took all her resolve to return his level, black glare. "No. No right."

Jaguar stood up suddenly. "You are unworthy," he

said. He stalked over her outstretched leg and down the stairs, striding toward the marsh.

She sprang up and pursued him. "Hey wait." Then it happened. She had followed him down the steps and across the short clearing toward the tall grasses of the marsh. At the edge of the tall grass, as she stared into the morning sun, squinting against its brilliance, he shimmered for a moment, then vanished.

She stood staring, then ran into the edge of the marsh, finding nothing but a small, burned section of grass.

After several minutes of searching, she went back through the house to the kitchen.

Rose looked up from a plate of food she was eating, and Verna turned from the stove, spatula in hand. They both stared at her.

"Have you seen Jaguar?" she asked, feeling especially stupid.

"I hope you didn't make him mad," Verna said. "You won't get far with Jaguar once you make him mad."

They returned to what they'd been doing, as though that were the end of it. In frustration, she blurted out, "Look. I need to find out about Vittoria, can't you understand that? Can't you help me?"

Verna held her spatula, looking at Abbey as though she were a crazy white woman talking gibberish. "You shouldn't speak the names of the dead," she said.

Abbey cast about for something to say, some way to *be*, to engage these women.

Finally, Rose put down her fork. "I'll take her," she said. "Come on."

Abbey looked from Rose to Verna, who shrugged. Then she followed Rose out the door.

"You lost your daughter, huh?" Rose asked as she led her down the road from Verna's.

"Yes. A couple years ago."

"You should let her go, then."

"Yeah. That's what everybody says."

"Hope those boots are comfortable, we got to get up to the ridge."

She could have asked *why*. Why, for starters, she

should trust Rose. Why Jaguar—if that was his real
name—should know anything about Vitt. Why she should
believe he did, and why she was about to hike into the
backwoods to find an arrogant old man intent on pulling
vanishing acts. But the answer was easy: because she'd
damn well tried everything else.

She followed her guide off the road, down a narrow
path into a patch of woods. After about twenty minutes
they began a steep climb over a talus slope and finally
reached the foot of a ridge with a path the width of Abbey's shoulders. It edged sharply up to the top.

Rose nimbly tackled the path, and Abbey followed,
hugging the hillside and picking her way upward, boots
sliding on pebbles and her right side brushing the crum-
bling hillside.

At the top of the climb they looked out on the entire
valley of Medicine Falls. Turning, Abbey looked past
scrub trees and patches of sage into the dry riverbed leading to Medicine Falls dam.

Abbey followed Rose's gaze to a figure about two hundred meters away, seated on the edge of the ridge. "Will
he help me, do you think?" She searched the woman's
face for some hint of what her part in all this was.

"He'll help you. But he won't make it easy." She
turned and began walking down the trail. "Just watch out
coming back down. If you come back down."

If I come back down. What else would she do?

Abbey approached Jaguar, gathering her wits. She
crouched next to him and looked out over the patches of
forest below, as far as the curve of the highway in the
distance. She waited for him to acknowledge her presence.

"That's a tough climb in boots," he said eventually.
"Sneakers or moccasins are best."

Did you climb it? she wanted to ask. But, instead, she
looked out over the vista, avoiding his eyes, as he seemed
to avoid hers, and asked, "What do you know about my
daughter?"

As she waited for him to speak she heard the wind
whistle softly as it blew over the lip of the cliff, through a
deep groove in the stone.

"She was the first to die," he said. "If you wish to avenge her, you must be truly worthy. About that, I have my doubts." He glanced at her skeptically. "*Are* you worthy?"

Abbey's mouth was dry and she looked at the soil near her boots. How does somebody answer a question like that?

"You are like this river, Abbey. Dry. Your power held back by a giant dam." He turned to look up the canyon. "Medicine River used to thunder over this ridge. Right here, where we sit. It was a good thing to see. Now . . ." He snorted, and looked at her. "You must snatch your power, before it is gone. Find the round-faced man and steal back your power. Then you'll have strength to meet the Others."

Abbey watched him carefully.

"That's all," he said.

In the bright sunlight Abbey could see that the stone in his teeth was green, not black. "I don't understand," she said softly, trying not to offend. "Any of it."

"Do you want to lay your daughter's spirit to rest?"

Abbey bit her lip, suddenly unable to speak.

"Do you want to lay her spirit to rest?" he asked, louder and more sharply.

"Yes." Her voice, threadbare.

"Then listen. You will never do this until you undertake a great thing. Do you see that you must earn your peace, your glory?"

"I'd settle for peace. I'm not sure about glory. . . ."

He stood up in a burst of energy, slapping the dust from his jeans. "Do you see that you are, like your daughter, dead! A spirit cannot bury a spirit!"

Abbey felt her throat swell nearly shut. "Yes," she whispered. Yes. Dead. That was the word for her. Simple and ugly.

"Then find the round-faced man. Force him to play the game. It is very dangerous, this game. Do you comprehend? But he must play it, and you must see that he does. No tears and woman-excuses. Then you must find the point where the Others enter, and tell me. If you don't find it, I can't help you." He turned away from her and looked out over the valley, saying matter-of-factly, "If you fail, your people will sleep forever. Unburied, like your daughter."

Abbey's tears filled her face, just under her skin. "Who are the Others?" she asked. White people, the federal government, progress, all these might be Others to Jaguar.

"If I told you the name, you would still be ignorant."

"Tell me."

"The Hhso." He pronounced the name like a garbled breath, like a rush of wind.

"Sooo," she repeated, attempting his pronunciation and failing.

He squinted at her, lip curling. "You should be a man."

"Why single me out then? And how did you find me?"

He shrugged. "From the Net. In the Net, you are only one fish. But you did not give up; you have passion—unlike the rest of your people. Afterward, I discovered we share a common enemy. The round-faced man. Therefore I chose you."

As usual his answers were partial and unsatisfying. It was almost useless to ask him questions, but she asked: "Who are the Hhso? What do they want?"

His eyes narrowed. "Your fields."

"Fields?"

He nodded, once.

"What is going to happen to Medicine Falls? Is the town in danger?" A dread built up in her, *had* been building, ever since she'd first laid eyes on this man.

"They will create wealth—for themselves."

"In real estate?"

"Real estate!" he snorted. Taking a step closer to her, he faced her squarely, saying, "They will kill you all. All."

"How?"

"The Leap Point is opening."

"The Leap Point?"

He nodded, slowly. "Yes."

He was always on the verge of incoherence. Who were the Hhso? What was their scheme? What was a Leap

Point? "Why can't you tell me?" she blurted. "Just tell me!"

Continuing on as though she hadn't spoken, he said, "The gods have abandoned your world."

"There are no gods," Abbey said, speaking her heart. For if there were gods, wouldn't they have had some pity on her or Vitt?

"When they are gone," Jaguar continued, "then you will believe. Like the hills and grasses. When they are silent, then you remember their songs." He took off his jacket. "We will come for you in the morning." He thrust the jacket into her hands and walked away. She watched him walk through the grass and go down the path in the cliff side. The hard way.

"Wait a minute!" she yelled, running after him to the head of the path. "I'm not staying up here all night!"

He turned at the head of the path. "This is the least of what you will do." His eyes were locked on hers as she struggled to frame her response. He went on: "Prove to me you are not soft and weak. Then we will have a *real* talk."

As he ambled down the path she shouted after him, "Is this some kind of *test*?"

He mumbled something, continuing down.

"Well *is* it?"

She thought she heard him say, "It is the first test." She watched him descend, easily striding down the scratch in the side of the cliff. She stood a long time there, until he disappeared into the trees below.

~ 2 ~

Except for the wind whirring through the cleft in the rock, it was quiet on the ridge. Abbey tugged at the locket around her neck, pulling it out, and fingering its molten warmth, its textured, filigree surface, as she scanned the late-afternoon sky. The good news was, it would be dry tonight; the bad news, colder than hell.

The easy way was to just scramble down that path and

book the first public vehicle heading in the direction of
Medicine Falls. Forget this Jaguar, forget his story of bad-
things-coming. She could have told him bad things were
coming, God, they'd *been* coming. Anyone in Medicine
Falls could tell you that. The town was slipping into
oblivion, and her own life, just part of the landslide.

But Jaguar wasn't one to slip into oblivion. She felt he
could, all by himself, hold back the landslide with those
broad hands, that he could teach her how to ward off the
flood of dark things into her life. But first, in Jaguar's way
of doing things, came a test. Perhaps he knew that tests
were something she could relate to. Give her a test, a race,
a contest, and she would beat her way to the finish line;
do or die. She squinted at the fleeing sun, and found herself turning and walking slowly through the gully, hunting
for firewood.

Under the scrub pine trees of the riverbank, amid
patches of snow, she managed to scavenge several loads of
sticks and boughs. These she carried to a spot in the
riverbed where the embankment formed a slight overhang
of about three meters' height, her best bet for shelter. She
had one book of matches that Jaguar had left in his jacket,
one book that had to last her through the night, though
her firewood was far from dry. She looked up to see the
sun dipping toward the horizon and hurried her pace,
scavenging for dried weeds and grasses to serve as both
tinder and mattress, working swiftly, methodically, while
trying not to get spooked by the awful quiet, without cars,
without people—without birds. As the daylight leaked
away, she began framing a lean-to, using her largest
branches, and then shoved the weedy stalks and grasses
inside to sit on. Standing back to assess her nest-building,
she saw a great pile of sticks and pine boughs, more akin
to a haystack than a shelter. Dusk came on with a brutal
chill. By God, it would have to do.

Pulling Jaguar's jacket on over her own, she crawled
just inside the hut opening and drew out the precious
matches.

Fifteen minutes later she was down to two matches and
the most she'd accomplished was a blackening pile of

grass, producing much smoke and little warmth. A scythe
of a moon rose in the east and Abbey was, she admitted at
last, getting cold. To generate some heat, she got up and
started to walk back and forth in the riverbed, squinting
in the moonlight to see her path, but stumbling over rocks
just the same, feet starting to feel as cold as stones themselves. The sound of her boots clobbering over rocks was
the only sound, though she listened—intently—for the
sound of Jaguar arriving to say it was enough, two hours
was enough wilderness experience for a city girl. . . .

Twenty paces away from the nest, twenty paces back,
then out again (away from the edge of the precipice, make
no mistake about that) then back to the nest, and Vitt's
voice in her ear, saying, *You're going to freeze your ass
off, you know.* . . . She stomped her aching feet as she
walked, pumping her arms, scuffing her boots for sure,
beginning to wonder if she could possibly make it down
that damn goat path in the side of the cliff in pitch-black
night.

But no, damned if she would. What was comfort, her
warm little life at the store with Renalda and Harley? She
had taken her comfort from her tea and her antiques for
years, and no, *damned* if she would go back to *that*. It had
felt like warmth, had felt like life. *Felt* like . . . As she
mused, she marched, and the cold immersed her in its
rising waters. Her feet were turning painfully brittle, and
a steady breeze pushed icicles up her nostrils. Deep in her
pockets were the only remnants of warmth, there in her
own clenched fists. But damn, it was life, wasn't it? The
real thing: dangerous and in-your-face.

Then a snapping sound, a branch cracking. She
stopped, listening. Quiet reigned. A flat, disconcerting
quiet as though her ears were stuffed with cotton.

Then again, a crack. A shadow moved, and she saw a
dog or a wolf about fifteen meters away on the bank.
Well, certainly a dog. Nothing to get jumpy about. Then,
nearby, she heard a long, throaty howl.

Back down the riverbed she ran, crashing into the dark
pocket of her haven. They couldn't be wolves, she
thought, heart banging against her rib cage. Who'd seen

wolves near Medicine Falls in twenty-five years? Dogs sometimes howled like that, like Harley, when the fire trucks screamed by . . . She grabbed a large deadfall limb off the lean-to, and pivoted as the howl came again, this time closer. Across the gully, where the line between deepest dark and moonlit field defined the bank, scrubby trees poked up into the star-spangled sky. Then a streak of movement there, and she saw two dogs—no, not dogs, wolves—trotting along the bank, their breaths a smoky plume in front of them. She backed up, stepping on a branch and snapping it, drawing their attention. Two pairs of yellow eyes flashed for a moment, turning toward her. They were in the riverbed, approaching. She stood, trembling, until instinctively she took an aggressive stance, fending them off, waving a pine bough at them, shouting, "Get out of here! Get the hell away!"

She could see nothing, but she sensed their presence. Near. Whirling, she checked behind her, then raced back to the shelter. The embankment was behind her, a protecting flank. But they might use that perch to jump down on her. This sent her racing out to the middle of the draw again, panting for breath, swiveling to watch all sides.

Just at that moment she saw one of them scramble up the opposite bank, a black wolflike form, and as it reached the top, a flash of a white tennis shoe appeared for a moment before melding into the night.

Her mind sank into quiet. From deep in the well of her body, something stirred, and began to move. She felt it gather momentum, plunging upward toward the surface, gathering force as it climbed. Bending down, she laid her hand on the nearest and largest rock she could hold, and rose to her full height, lunging toward the bank.

"Damn you, Rose! I saw you, I saw you, you, you . . . fake!" She shook the rock over her head, screaming, "And you, Verna! I saw you both! Come then and fight if that's what you want!"

Abbey scrambled up the bank, falling and clawing her way to the top, still holding the rock, and yelling, "Come out! Come on you cowards!"

No answer, no yellow eyes, no white tennies, nothing.

Her whole body was on fire with a strange fury. "I'm ready for you! You wanna be a wolf? I'll be a wolf too! So come on!"

Abbey pivoted to one side and the next. Then, down in the draw she spotted movement. Like wolves, if you were gullible. Like a couple of Sun Rock women, if you weren't. Abbey slid down the riverbank into the gully and hurried after them, shouting, "You think it's *funny* to scare me up here? *Funny* to leave me here to freeze?" She raced after the shapes, raced too far, too fast, skidding to a halt . . . Oh God, where was the lip of the ridge?

She was standing on it. Beneath the toes of her rose-colored boots lay a ten-story drop to the valley.

Her stomach lurched, her skin zinged with shock. Pebbles rolled beneath her soles. She perched there, looking down into a hole of darkness. Resting on small, round stones, her boots became roller skates. She was afraid of making the slightest movement. Her stomach hovered somewhere in her body, quivering at the thought that she was an instant short of safety, had stopped an instant too late, and now—in a split second—would pitch over the edge. A pebble stirred beneath her left heel. The stars watched, their icy eyes calmly pointed at her. Heartless, those stars. They had borne witness to all the deaths of the world, of which hers was only one, her daughter's only another.

So she would die like Vittoria, by falling.

One of her boots shifted. Where was the ground, the edge? Safety was so close—just a step away. It was a risk to move at all, but it was that or let the pebbles decide. "No . . ." she whispered. "No."

She stepped back from the edge. The stars blinked.

On her knees. She found herself on her knees, hands tingling against the immense earth, as it shifted under her, still tilting in the direction of the valley. Her stomach clenched and clenched, sending currents of nausea through her. There was a rock in her hand. Gripping it like a lifeline, Abbey shuddered, feeling in her stomach the long, slow plunge down the chasm. She crawled from the edge, far back from the edge.

After a long time she got to her feet. Her eyes felt icy, like the stars. Everything was clear, she could see miles away, across the treetops below, across the years of her life. Walking slowly back to her camp, she sensed the wolves were gone. She was alone, and alive. Not her time to die, or to be dead.

But time to build a fire. And get it right this time. She gathered small sticks by touch, feeling for them underneath the boughs where she'd been sitting. Two matches remained. She lit one and coaxed it into a small, lasting flame, and twig by twig, built it into a fine roaring blaze, oddly exulting in the fact that she still had one match left.

~ 3 ~

In the morning she made her way down the narrow path and through the woods to the road. The sun toasted her face and sparkled off the icy puddles crusted over during the night. Smells of rotting winter grasses combined with the first green thrusts of crocus and new weeds to create a fine spring stew. Her mind and body were empty, scoured clean.

Up until the moment she caught the smells of bacon frying, just outside Verna's front door. Then her thoughts turned powerfully to food.

At her knock, Verna opened the door and blinked. "You're back," she said.

"Surprised?"

"She's back," Verna announced to Jaguar and Rose, who paused at their breakfast. Abbey noticed that a fourth place had been set at the table. The smells of eggs and beans enveloped her in a fragrant embrace.

Verna pulled a pan from the stove and filled a plate with heaps of bacon, fried eggs, and what looked like mashed yellow beans. "Have yourself some breakfast," she said, smiling for the first time since Abbey had met her. Jaguar and Rose stopped eating and watched her.

She washed her hands in the sink, took off Jaguar's jacket and her own, hanging them on the back of her chair, and started on her breakfast with intense concentration.

Verna poured her coffee from a huge blue ceramic pot. Abbey judged that the likelihood of camomile tea was low, and began sipping at the black stuff. Verna also brought her a beer mug full of milk and a glass of orange juice.

Slowly, Jaguar and Rose went back to their breakfasts, with Rose checking out Jaguar from time to time, out of the corners of her eyes. His face, impressive as it was, looked a little more ordinary, less imposing, chewing food.

Again, Rose looked surreptitiously to the side, this time to Verna, who finally sat down to her own meal, ignoring Rose.

At last Jaguar said, "Well," pushing his plate away and wiping his mouth with his napkin. Behind him on the wall stretched a large wolf pelt, one paw dangling from the top with a loose nail in its clutch. Abbey finished off the last of the bacon and held the coffee cup between her hands, savoring the warmth.

"Well," Jaguar said again, his voice softly booming like a drum in the distance, "tell me everything you saw last night."

Abbey considered a moment. "I saw wolf-people." She kept her face carefully blank.

"Wolf-people," he repeated. "Yes." He pursed his lips, perhaps wondering what she knew of his little ruse with the wolf skin.

The three of them watched her with what might have been a tinge of respect.

"And," she continued, "I saw my own death."

"Ah." Jaguar's eyebrows raised with new interest. "Was it a good death?"

Abbey thought for a moment. "It was clean and fast. By falling from a great height."

Jaguar watched his cup as Verna refilled it. "That is the death of a great personage, a king." He paused. "Or a sacrifice person. Which was yours?"

Abbey looked at him, eye to eye. "I chose not to fall,"

she said. It wasn't a matter of luck or fate. She had decided. She placed the cup slowly down on the checkered oilcloth of the kitchen table. As her hands trembled, she held them locked between her knees.

They sat for a time, drinking coffee. The morning sun streamed in the window over the sink, casting an oblong of light on Verna's tablecloth, a great red and white chessboard, stretching impossibly far in all directions.

Jaguar broke the silence once again. "Good thing you built a fire," he said. "It got a little chilly last night."

Abbey shrugged. "A little."

Then, without preamble, Jaguar rose from the table, saying, "Come," and walked to the back of the kitchen, leaving through the rear door.

Abbey picked up her plate and turned to the sink. Rose came around the table to meet her. "I'll do that," Rose said, motioning with her glance to the rear door.

"Thanks."

Rose smiled.

Abbey smiled back and glanced up at the wall hanging. "Nice pelt," she said, and turned to follow Jaguar through the back door of the kitchen.

The room adjacent to the kitchen was in darkness as before, except for the wan light of a computer screen, where Jaguar was sitting, intent on the keyboard. Without looking up, he said, "You may sit."

She sat on a nearby cot. Now, with food in her belly, a heavy weariness settled on her, beckoning her to sleep.

"From now on it will be necessary for you to hide yourself," Jaguar said. "Do not go back to your home." He watched her carefully. "You understand this."

"Am I in danger? From who? The Hhso?"

"Now that you have been here, anyone may be your enemy. Mark me: even the police."

"Why would I have an enemy? Who are the Hhso? And why is Zachariah your enemy? You don't tell me a thing. Why?"

"I cannot. It is not time. There will come a day for telling. Until then you will wait."

"I could just walk away from all this."

Jaguar nodded slowly. "Yes."

Abbey was the first to break eye contact.

"Bring me information," he said. "The Leap Point. Then I will tell you more." He snorted. "You are lucky that I stoop to bargaining."

"Lucky! You're lucky I don't take a walk and let you find somebody else to play mind games with!"

"Mind games," he said, seeming to savor the phrase. "Apt. Apt."

She put her hands to her face, sighing in exhaustion and frustration. After a time, she looked up again.

"When do I find out about Vitt?"

His mouth fought off a sneer. "I have told you this. The round-faced man has this knowledge, and much else. Discover what you can, but above all, see that he plays the game."

"What happens when he plays the game?"

Jaguar stalked to the window. With his back to her, he was a mere shadow. "He will lose . . . all his power."

"And when *I* play it? Do I lose power too?"

"No." Said with finality.

She took a deep breath. "And you can't just do this thing—find the Leap Point?"

"No," he said.

"Why not?" She could do worse, to have Jaguar at her side.

"There are many reasons, not the least being he would suspect me if I approached him. I do not know your ways." He turned back to face her. "But you, if you must, you may bring a helper."

"Who?"

Jaguar shrugged.

She held his gaze for a long while.

"Do not hesitate," he commanded. "Run swiftly! Your time vanishes, do you comprehend?"

"Yes," Abbey said, looking into the shadow of his face. "But I have to sleep," she said. "I have to."

His lip curled in disgust. "A few hours, then."

He left her, and she sagged back onto the cot, grabbing a folded blanket to cover herself, tired as the ancient rocks that had been her bed last night. A part of her suspected this would be the last good sleep she'd have in a very long while.

Chapter 6

~1~

It had been a good night, Lobo decided. He'd unloaded twenty-four games—just like that! Poor zombos would pay anything for the glory game, falling like flies. When Lobo gave them the pitch, they just had to swing. Three thousand dollars, he exulted, a good kick for one night, even if a bunch went to the Big Z. Still a great kick for one night. And he could've got more, a lot more. Zombos would pay more, like he'd told the Z-man, they'd pay lots more!

No, get 'em out on the street, Lobo, he says. *It's our advertising. Then, when we're ready to spike, we'll be in mega greens.*

In the wind, the icy branches of the trees made a clattering sound as he passed, each twig an icicle, after a light snowfall had melted and then quickly frozen in the night. Click, click, went the trees. Lobo looked up at the branches, imagining frozen hands reaching for the tote, his three thousand greens, his mega games. Click, click, like bones cracking, like his own thin bones, clanking and cold even in his new wool jacket. Not too new. No target for crashers, this Lobo. Too smart to spend his kick on zombo clothes. And too smart to go against the Z-man.

"Stay off the Nir," he says. *"That's my hard rule, my only rule. The rest, I'm gonna trust you, Lobo,"* he says. *"But don't plug in, is all, and you'll be a fraggin' cake eater before long."*

"Why," Lobo says. *"Why not give her a run, this Nir?"*

"We're still working out the bugs, Lobo. It's not always safe. Sometimes bad things happen."

"But not like the beta version."

The Z-man's smile crashes. He don't like to remember, no better than Lobo. *"No, not like that. It won't fry you. But wait until I tell you, then you can crank up Nir. Later, Lobo, later."*

Lobo hugged his jacket around his chest and hurried on, watching for patches of ice. Almost spring and still this zipping snow and ice! Maybe winter coming up for another play. Maybe the Old Man leaned on the Repeat button. Yeah, that was it! Lobo chuckled, a startling, bubbling sound, not like laughter at all, but more like pipes squeaking, many floors down, in the St. Croix.

Later, Lobo, later. Yeah, it was always later, later we'll be in mega bucks, later we'll make a killing. Meanwhile, he was a fraggin', flea-bitten fence, with a houseful of half-size whores to babysit.

But *later, Lobo,* he says.

Reaching home at last, he trudged up the stairs, forming his intention: Fuck this *later* stuff. He'd done tabs and hot spots and even slime. The Z-man's sunshades were just the next step up. He was improving himself, like his sister and Dad always used to say. What're you gonna do to improve yourself, son?

The mega-game, Dad. A step up. You'll see.

At the second-floor landing, Sooze was waiting for him.

"Carma never came back," she said, hands on skinny hips.

Lobo paused, then pushed past her. "Yeah, she'll be back later, then." He walked down the hall, annoyed to be dealing with one of the little shits.

"It's been four days. She left with a john and never came back."

"Well then, she's making a load."

"She isn't," Sooze insisted, following him up to third.

"Yeah she is, she's making a load."

"Carma isn't. She's hurt or dead because she's never gone three days!" Sooze's voice grew into a high screech. Doors opened along the hall and faces peered out.

"Lobo!" a few of them murmured.

"OK, she's not coming back, let's say." Lobo rounded the bend to fifth.

"So what're you gonna DO?" Sooze asked.

Lobo whirled around. "Do? DO? I'm not gonna DO anything! Carma chose her john. I ain't her dad. Now frag off!" Lobo stomped up the final flight of stairs to his apartment door, with "Lobo, Lobo, Lobo," chanted behind him from the kiddie warrens, like the bratlings liked to do.

From below him on the fifth-floor landing he heard, "You beat up that crasher that time he tried to do me."

Lobo turned his head around a bit as he turned the key in his lock. "That was on *my* block. Nobody rips us on my block." He shut the door behind him, fumbling for his matches. As he lit a few candles, a soft glow bounced back at him from the festooned spiderwebs, legacy of the long arachnid ancestry of the St. Croix attic. Stealthily, he opened his tote and extracted a gauzy pouch, tendrils waving, sucking at his finger tips, and pulled it apart, removing the goggles. He sat down on his tattered multilounger, tucking his jacket over his knees and lap.

He fondled the glasses, blue-black and lean, hesitating a moment. Just once, he told himself, as he slid them up the bridge of his nose. Just once, and the Z-man will never know.

•　　•　　•

Sooze watched Lobo disappear into his hangout. "You're supposed to be the dad," she whispered. When Sooze and her pals gave him some of their money, he said it was because he was the dad, and he was taking care of them, except like now, when he didn't.

She walked down the hall toward 502, stomping on a skittering cockroach along the way. "You're a goner," she said to the roach.

From one of the open doors came the remark, "Carma's a goner!"

And then the refrain began, "Carma's a goner, Carma's a . . ."

"Stop it!" Sooze shouted. "You bunch of freakers, just stop it!" She slammed her door, plugging up the voices, and stood wiping her nose with her forearm.

From the window facing South Defoe, a street light cast its fluorescent moonlight onto her tea table. She sat at the mother's place and pulled a Wownow candy bar from her pocket, cutting it into three pieces, and serving dinner. Dad and baby loved Wownows.

"Chew your food," Sooze told them. "If you're good, tomorrow I'll make you a turkey dinner with pineapple slices."

"Where's Carma gone to?" baby asked, her one good plastic eye dangling from a thread.

"Oh," Sooze replied, "she went off and got married."

Dad leaned forward, his bear paw sticky with chocolate. "Her hubby'll take care of her," he said, winking.

"Maybe he already has," she replied, her appetite gone.

As Sooze listened for Carma's return, the streetlight just outside the window sputtered, strobing the faces of the diners, giving them a fleeting and comforting vitality.

~ 2 ~

"Oh, for Christ's sake, Gwen." Lieutenant Joshua Dern was looking forward to the basketball playoffs on TV and here comes the wife with another *togetherness* idea.

Gwen gripped a snarl of wires, from which hung a thin pair of VR glasses. "It's really fun, Josh. Give it a try."

He sighed noisily, scratching his Saturday-afternoon stubble of beard. He just wanted to be left alone. They'd tried marriage encounter; honeymoon cruises; group counseling. Now a VR game was supposed to bring marital bliss?

"It's not just VR," she was saying. "It's a retina game. The latest thing. Maybe you'll get a . . . sexual fantasy. Dottie Phillips did."

"What, it's potluck? Some get sex, some get Pac Man?"

"Sort of. And I'll plug in and watch." She held up a second set of goggles, with a blue-black iridescent sheen to the lenses.

He snapped the TV off. She was determined to talk, to interrupt his well-deserved rest from the three criminal cases and one missing-person investigation that'd been driving him nuts all week . . . now she wanted to explore their sexual problems.

She held up the visors.

If he didn't give it a try there'd be hell to pay.

The first thing he saw was a glowing marble of light.

He watched it with mild curiosity for a moment before it swelled to fill his vision with a drenched light. He felt a bounce of impact, a soft but pervasive press of light against his eyes. If he were an imaginative man—and Lieutenant Dern was not—he would have said the light flooded into his braincase like a breath into a collapsed lung. Gradually, a sensation began, like being suspended in a tank of water. He relaxed in the warm fluid, both intensely aware and oddly peaceful.

Voices murmured, just out of deciphering range; blurs of color welled up, receded; and now and again, a spike of vivid memory: roller-skating down a hot sidewalk, with the cracks making his skates go ka-thunk, ka-thunk; that time in Scouts when he got to carry the flag at the PTA meeting; football practice and tackling a muscular red-headed boy . . . and then, tackling him again, in an embrace of consuming passion . . .

He ripped the visor off. Stunned for a moment, he sat utterly still, then looked up at his wife, who was removing her own goggles. "What kind of garbage *is* this?" He fought off the intense arousal of the fantasy and turned it into something safer. Anger. "Well? This your idea of a good time? This pornography?" Dern wetted his lips, trying to get his bearings.

His wife stammered. "I didn't think it was going to be . . ." A flush of embarrassment brought her freckles out in full force, making her look girlish and vulnerable.

Even after twenty years of marriage those freckles always disarmed him. Softly he said, "Where'd you get this anyway?"

"Dottie had an extra. I'm sorry . . ."

"Look," he said. "It doesn't matter. It's only a game. Just not my sort, OK?"

"I thought it would be harmless."

"Of course you did." He conjured up a reassuring smile. He wanted her to feel better. He also wanted her out of the room so he could put on the visor again.

"You're not mad?" Gwen looked hopefully at him, gathering up the game paraphernalia.

He put out his hand, patting hers. "Just leave it. I'll clean it up."

Later he revisited the red-haired boy with a mixture of terrible shame and joy.

In the next few days he went back to Nir again and again. And while thus engaged, another part of his mind was otherwise occupied, learning: that there are more things in heaven and earth than he'd quite realized before . . . for example, certain massive and hulking—individuals—of undeniable presence; and their requirements of a rather strict obedience. He also learned that for the time being what they required was that he play the new VR game.

Lieutenant Dern gladly complied.

~ 3 ~

Megan waited until everyone left the Institute. The Clearing session was over. Before seekers were granted a session with Zachariah, the true followers sat in a circle and cleared newcomers of wrong ideas. If the seeker resisted . . . well, Zachariah had enough to do without wasting time on them. But sometimes the followers could be overzealous, with Clearings lasting well into the night, like tonight.

A group of talkative Violets went home at last, their chatter still grating on her as she locked the Institute doors behind them, ostensibly staying behind to clean up. When their voices finally died away, Megan smoothed out the creases in her long red skirt and walked down the hallway to the storage room next to Zachariah's office. The walls twinkled with ad plaques for his Resonance video series: *Gray Grace, Red Reverberations, Violet Visions*. A path for each color, a prescription for happiness unless, like Megan, you had a little more in mind.

She used a flashlight to locate the sacks underneath the rear table. It had been weeks since Megan first figured out that Zachariah was distributing the Nir game. At first it perplexed her why he was secret about it. But from what she was hearing lately it was the latest rage, and apparently the mystery of where it came from only added to its market appeal. Whoever figured that part out was smart. They could've downloaded a popular game like that from the Net and sold millions, but instead they parceled it out on the street a little at a time until people were desperate for copies.

She was desperate. Her hands trembled a little as she pushed aside the sacks to find the small packet hidden behind. She removed the shades and cords, plugged in her compact, and hooked herself up to paradise.

A sound outside in the hallway brought a sharp stab of fear to her stomach, and she removed the glasses. Then she recognized the air-filter system clicking on. She regarded the glasses again, feeling both guilt and resentment. He trusted her. But she was only borrowing a copy of the game for a few minutes each evening. What harm could it do? Besides, wasn't she practically running the Institute now that Zachariah was seldom around? Didn't she handle every damn piece of paper this enterprise ever generated, keying, filing, calling, and remembering every detail? Didn't she cover for Zachariah's frequent absences by saying he needed privacy to meditate and connect with the Beyond? She wasn't sure what the man was doing these days, but she was pretty sure he wasn't meditating.

Didn't she deserve a little happiness? She caressed the visor, resting it over one knee.

Then Megan fixed the glasses in place once again. A small, molten dab of light pulsed to life and threaded from the eyepiece into her right eye and points beyond.

It was like looking into the heart of the sun, forbidden and blinding. She faced the stage spotlight that created this island of light in the vast, dark theater. She could feel their eyes, in a thousand faces, enraptured faces, all turned to her, seeing only her, waiting to breathe in unison with her. The silken costume was an emanation of softest gold, an aura produced, it seemed, by the ecstasy of her skin. The conductor raised his baton. As the exquisite strains of the symphony seized her body, she pirouetted, gliding into the dance she knew so well, soaring into the music while the audience watched, enthralled.

Megan, the flawless prima ballerina, at one with the light and the adulation of the thousand faces.

~ 4 ~

Annie checked in on her sister every couple of days to make sure she was all right. What *all right* meant under the circumstances was hard to know, but she figured she'd recognize it when she saw it. A little less moping around playing VR games would be a good start.

Though it was past midnight, after her late shift at

Dave's Deli, she wasn't afraid of waking Cherilyn. Cherilyn stayed up late these days.

She let herself in the front door and walked toward the living room, the only room with a light on. The living-room vid screen was playing on mute, and blankets and pillows littered the couch where her sister must have tried sleeping. Magazines and newspapers, formerly residing in orderly stacks on the coffee table, were strewn across the floor, among them her stacks of petitions to keep the name of Medicine Falls . . . her untiring crusade of the past few months—until Nir. Annie shook her head. Here, in a house where you used to be able to see your face in the polished tabletops, Cherilyn and Jeffrey's thirtieth-anniversary picture lay facedown in a layer of dust on the credenza. She began to set the framed picture back upright, then replaced it facedown. Maybe Cherilyn couldn't bear to look at it right now, this remembrance of happier times, before that day Jeffrey passed out on the bedroom floor in the middle of a VR game and ended up in a coma in the hospital.

Looking up at the ceiling, she wondered if Cherilyn was still up. No footsteps stirring, though. Chances were that she was getting some sleep at last, but, on impulse, Annie turned from the living room and climbed the stairs to the second floor. In the dark upstairs hallway, the House Manager must have had a program glitch, producing a suffocating heat that Annie could hear rushing from the vents.

She turned on the hall light and opened the master bedroom door, peering in to see if Cherilyn was in bed. She wasn't. The light streaming from the hallway showed that the bed hadn't been slept in. Annie was about to close the door, when she was startled to notice someone sitting in the multilounger.

"Lights," she told House. As the room brightened, she saw her sister sitting there in her nightgown. "Cherilyn?" she asked softly.

Moving closer, she noticed that her sister wore sunglasses . . . no, VR shades. As Annie nudged her gently on the shoulder, Cherilyn fell heavily to the side, mouth gaping. Shaking her by both shoulders, Annie called her name, once, twice, again. Then, tentatively, she placed her fingers against Cherilyn's neck, feeling a sporadic pulse. After a few moments she saw that the side table was littered with pill bottles.

Using the part of her brain that always kicked in for an emergency, she called an ambulance, but the rest of her was numb, too numb to notice the note at first. Just as the ambulance drove up, she found it where it had fallen onto the floor. It read:

> *I've given my soul to the devil. And oh, it is sweet. If these are the tortures of the damned, then I guess I hope to be damned. God forgive me, if He can.—Cherilyn Hoyle*

~ 5 ~

Renalda squinted into the blasting light of the refrigerator. Her eyes hurt and she had a headache. Probably from hunger. Maybe she'd forgotten to eat dinner. And maybe lunch too. She noticed that three of her fingernails were broken. She'd have to fix those.

Scanning the refrigerator shelves for a long while, Renalda rummaged through the fridge contents, the jars of pickles and barbecue sauce, the tub of margarine and moldy ham slices. Something slimy occupied the vegetable drawer. Time to hit up the grocery store, maybe, but what time was it? Two A.M. And nothing open. Pushing Harley out of the way, she slammed the door. Goddamn, but the place stank.

Harley whined for the ham.

"Tomorrow," Renalda said. "Tomorrow I'll get a bunch of groceries, OK?" For now, DeVries was waiting.

Chapter 7

~1~

It wasn't as though Simon Haskell didn't have work to do. Sitting in his office in the early morning amid stacks of papers and documents, he had plenty of work. But there he was, leaning back in his chair, feet up on his desk, hugging a cold cup of coffee and thinking about Abbey McCrae.

Simon wasn't one to believe in love at first sight. He wasn't sure he believed in love at all. Or that it was love, specifically, that he felt for Abbey McCrae. But that he felt *drawn* to her, there was no doubt at all. A woman he'd seen once, dressed like a cowboy queen, out for revenge or justice or a little of both. And she was threading in and out of his thoughts like a pop tune. Get a grip, Haskell, he told himself. Get to work.

He was staring at the doorway, unseeing, when she walked in, smiling tentatively, closing the door, and then backing against it as though needing something to lean

on. He thought at first she was conjured from his imagination, since he'd been thinking of her at that very moment. Had been, in fact, searching for her and calling her
for days. And now here she was, saying:

"Mr. Haskell? Sorry to interrupt. Am I interrupting?"
As he fumbled his legs down from the desk, covering his
consternation, she said, "I can come back if . . ."

"No," he interrupted, louder than he meant to, "no,
this is fine, Abbey." He stood up as she approached the
desk, hugging her big purse to her chest and looking a
little ragged around the edges. "Coffee?" he asked; then,
remembering she didn't drink coffee, he pulled a stack of
files off a chair for her.

She sank into it and locked on to him with those eyes.

Simon found his chair and sat on the edge of it, where
he pulled together his detective persona, impersonal, help-
ful. Phony. "I've been trying to find you." All my life, he
wanted to say, feeling utterly ridiculous that he'd even
had such a thought.

"To find me?" she asked, clearly surprised. She un-
zipped her jacket, under which she was wearing a brilliant
blue crushed-velvet shirt tucked into blue jeans. The blue
made her hair glisten with red highlights. Then Simon
noticed that it wasn't a crushed-velvet shirt, but a very
wrinkled velvet shirt.

"I wanted to talk to you about the case," he said.

Abbey looked back to the door. "Can we lock the
door?" she asked.

Simon hesitated, then said, "Sure." Smart office or not,
he walked to the door and swiped at the lock plate, returning to his desk under her close gaze. She had something to say, clearly, and she'd come to say it. For some
reason, he had the unpleasant feeling that it wasn't what
he wanted to hear.

"I came to see you," she said. "You weren't here, so I
went to the reservation. Because of Rose."

Simon narrowed his eyes, concentrating. She was fid-
gety, grasping at the locket around her neck, looking back
at the door, where now and then through the opaque

glass the shadows of tenants passed by for the start of the workday.

"Who is Rose?" Simon asked.

"A friend of mine on the reservation. Only I just met her yesterday." She paused. "Do you believe in medicine men, Mr. Haskell? Native American wise men?"

Simon paused. Only the truth would do. "No," he said. With a sinking feeling in his stomach, Simon waited for her to go on.

"Well," Abbey said, "even if you don't. He's helping me."

"Who is?"

"Jaguar. He's an elder. Rose and Verna say he's a man of honor, of respect."

"A medicine man . . ."

"Yes. He says Zachariah's the key, that Zachariah knows about Vitt."

"That's a good possibility," Simon admitted. "But how does this—Jaguar—claim to know?"

"I didn't ask him. But he knows."

"But he wouldn't say how?"

"I think he has access to another . . . realm."

"Oh for Christ sakes, Abbey."

"I know how this sounds. I think it would help if you'd been there."

"Yeah." Simon leaned forward from his chair, hands clasped in front of him on the desk. "Sorry I missed it."

She smiled, a small, ironic smile, a casual net cast over his heart. "At first I was like you. I didn't trust him, or Rose and Verna either. Why should I trust them? But then I spent the night up on Medicine Ridge, Mr. Haskell."

"Simon, please."

"I learned some things about myself, Simon." She studied her hands. "That I've been living in Vitt's life, in the past. That I've tossed away my life like she did. That I've been dead." Her look snapped up to him suddenly. "But I'm back."

Despite his skepticism, Simon couldn't doubt that something had happened to her, maybe something that wasn't all bad. Still, he profoundly wished that this particular conversation were not happening.

"I've got to reclaim my life if I want to move forward," she said. "I need to confront my enemy. That's what Jaguar said. I need to act. You know? I think I believe him."

Simon struggled to conceal his disappointment. Medicine man. Zap psychology. Why, oh why was she involved with this stuff? Well, that was the Comic Universe for you. He didn't trust himself to speak.

"I'd like you to help me."

She waited long enough that he felt forced to reply. "I'm not sure you need my kind of help, Abbey."

"Oh, I do," she said.

He raised an eyebrow.

"There's more."

Oh shit, he thought. He got up and rinsed his coffee cup in the small corner sink, futilely scraping at the brown sludge in the bottom of the cup. "Let's hear it," he said, circling around to get a refill at the coffee maker.

She began to recount the events of the last few days, her call to the reservation, and, in detail, Jaguar's story of the vanishing animals, the enemy he called the *Others,* and a place where they would enter. Wrapped into this tale was the game of Nir, and, through the game, her *act of power,* as she put it—or Jaguar put it—in which she would pit herself against Zachariah Smith. And with every sentence, Simon's mood grew darker. Medicine man and acts of power, indeed. He saw by the passion in her eyes that her voodoo man held some sway over her, saw that his own warnings would be about as welcome as a preacher at a bachelor party. She'd found her advisor. And it wasn't him.

"How much did he charge?" Simon asked.

"Nothing."

Well, that'll come later, he thought. "I'll tell you frankly that I don't believe in medicine men—or clairvoyants or channelers or astral projection or anything of the sort. And I don't think this guy can help you. He may even be harmful. At best, he's a waste of your time." A crease appeared between Abbey's eyes, but Simon plunged on, steeling himself for truth telling, the damned, inevitable truth. "I want to help you, Abbey. I've read the diary and I want to look into Zachariah Smith and this Institute of his. But I can't help you with the other stuff." He watched her carefully. "I'm sorry."

Sorry wasn't the half of it.

"But I need a helper," she said softly.

"For what, exactly?"

"Something bad is going on, Simon." She looked at him with great, luminous eyes. If she'd been selling tickets to the Firefighters Ball, he'd have bought a bunch.

"I'm not sure what it is," she went on. "It's a threat to Medicine Falls, somehow related to the game—the Nir game that my daughter played. Vittoria was the first to die. She won't be the last."

"Abbey. We're talking about a computer game, here. Listen to yourself."

"*You* read Vitt's diary." Her voice rose in pitch. "Was it harmless?"

"Compared to what kids call entertainment today? It was sleazy and disgusting. I don't think it killed her."

"I think maybe it did." She said this so quietly, it was almost out of hearing range.

"Let's get a copy and look at it, then."

"I've tried. I think they have a supply problem." Abbey had turned very quiet, maybe giving up on her argument. Giving up on *him*.

"And the locked door?" Simon glanced over toward the hallway door.

"I'm in danger. The nearer I get to Zachariah, the more danger I draw from the . . . Others."

He wasn't going to touch the *Others* bit with a ten-foot pole. But mystic mooning aside, he worried about her crusade taking a bad turn.

"What do you plan to do?"

"I'm going to play Zachariah's game."

"Which one? He's running a bunch."

"All of them. Just like Vitt did."

"Just like Vitt?"

"She was . . . naive. I'll face him prepared."

He let out his breath slowly. "I wish you wouldn't do this, Abbey. The man's a charlatan. Granted, he might know what happened to your daughter. But it doesn't have to get supernatural. Keep it grounded in what's real, would you please? Then I'll help you." His heart sank slowly as he heard himself talk. How often had he sat in this chair and advised clients not to do what they were bound and determined—against all logic—to do?

She smiled a rueful smile. "I don't blame you for not believing me. I sound like I've gone off the deep end, don't I?"

"Abbey, it's not . . ."

"Please." She rose, slinging her bag over her shoulder. "I'm sorry we couldn't do business, Simon." Her eyes hardened, and in them he imagined her view of him was chiseled in stone. A man incapable of the refined perceptions of the spiritual plane. Well, and wasn't it so?

He heard himself say, "I'm sorry. Maybe my colleague, Rocky Ginestra, can help you." He fumbled in the desk for Rocky's cards, failing to find any, and then walked over to Rocky's desk. Abbey followed, gathering up her jacket.

She glanced at the small framed photo on Rocky's desk, an old picture of Rocky and Simon, in navy uniforms, side by side, smiling, palm trees in the background. She bent down for a closer look. "Is that Rocky?" she asked.

"Yeah. Me and Rocky. A long time ago." He found a card, handed it to her.

Abbey took it, turning it over in her fingers. Finally she said, "I'd like the diary back."

Simon went to his desk, dragging his stomach behind him. Of course she wanted it back. But handing it over would be like giving up his last connection to her. Stupidly, he hesitated.

"Oh, I guess I owe you your fee." She began digging through her purse.

"No. No fee. I haven't done anything." Except shoot myself in the foot. Except give this woman a hard, cold shoulder.

"Oh." She looked at him doubtfully, then slowly removed her hand from her bag. For a moment he allowed himself to believe that she was reluctant to leave.

He handed her the diary. It disappeared into her purse, and they mumbled their brief goodbyes.

When the door closed behind her, Simon's mood was as black as the coffee he was drinking. Well, he thought, get over it. What would Abbey McCrae have seen in an old fart like you anyway? And can you imagine how a woman like that would disrupt your quiet, orderly routine? Your leisurely evenings reading books and eating junk food? God, you're lucky to have escaped.

He got up and refilled his cup, then opened the window, letting in some desperately needed fresh air, cold as knives. He stood there, looking out, hearing the downtown traffic in the street below, and in the distance the brief wail of a police siren, and finally, he realized, listening in vain for Abbey's vanished birds.

~ 2 ~

"Mr. Ginestra, this is Abbey McCrae. Simon Haskell gave me your name." An unfinished chicken sandwich lay in front of Abbey as she clutched the phone close to her mouth, trying to speak quietly. The smell of mold and disinfectant in her tiny YWCA room drove away her appetite. For a moment she glimpsed Vitt standing there, hugging herself as if she didn't want to touch anything. *Can we leave now?* Vitt, eternally seventeen, never changing . . . never leaving . . .

"Yeah, I heard of you," came the voice, hearty, and a little too loud. "My partner said you might call."

"What did he tell you?" The vision of Vitt faded, leaving behind a long water stain on the wallpaper where a slow leak peeled the wallpaper along one seam.

"Not much. Can you speak up a little?"

Abbey glanced at her locked door. The hallway outside was filled with creaks and coughs of roomers walking past, sometimes talking in low voices. In the next room over, more voices. The Y had thin walls.

"Yes," she said, turning her back to the door. "There are some things I have to do. I need a little backup. It could be dangerous. Are you interested?"

"Interested? Sure. Come on up and fill me in. You know where the office is."

"I'd rather you came here. I may be followed."

"Okaaay. Where are you?"

"You know the Purple Haze tavern on Loyola?"

They arranged to meet there in an hour. Abbey had scoped out the tavern and figured it would provide some privacy in the way of crowded places. When she arrived, however, the place was almost empty. In the depths of the murky bar, Abbey could see the bartender polishing a set of VR goggles. He looked up at her, nodded, and replaced the visor, moving on to wipe down the next set, one to a stool, where customers could plug in to the perpetual gaming tables of the virtual casino.

The only other person in the Purple Haze at one o'clock in the afternoon was a man with black hair and a stocky build, sitting at a corner table. She threaded her way among the tables as a spitting lavender neon sign in the front windows ignited the smoky air into a violet gauze.

"Mr. Ginestra?" she asked.

"Rocky." He put out a great paw of a hand and shook hers.

The bartender approached, peering at them over the minivisor perched far down the bridge of his nose. The visor glowed faintly with his personal entertainment, which he had the good taste to opaque from the front. He took her order for an iced tea and Rocky's for another beer with whiskey chaser. When the bartender left, Abbey took a long look at Simon Haskell's partner, and liked what she saw. A good face. But still, it was Simon Haskell she wanted to see. Simon Haskell had something she liked—a quality of caring a little more than money strictly could buy. There was about him an air of . . . was it steadfastness? An old-fashioned word, but one that seemed to fit in the way he had of listening hard and thinking hard about what you were saying. Steadfastness? But hadn't he boogied on her already?

The bartender came back with their drinks and pressed the charges into their tabletop running tab.

"Would you rather have a beer?" Rocky asked, looking doubtfully at her iced tea.

"No. It's OK." She looked up at Rocky and realized that if Simon was put off by her story, odds were that Rocky would be skeptical too. She decided to take a different approach.

When the bartender left, she began: "I'm going to see a man who may have been involved in my daughter's death. He's a dangerous man, and a powerful one. But he's not a criminal, so he'll look respectable. I may need some help. I can't give you the details, so you'll just have to trust me.

"There's nothing I'm going to do that's illegal. And if you don't want to do something that I ask you to, then just don't. But I need someone to stick by me in case I get in trouble. Maybe it'll be no more than knowing where I am and checking to be sure I come back. Can you do that?"

Rocky took a long drink of beer and followed it with a slug of whiskey in a shot glass. "Sure. Sounds easy." He wiped his lips with the back of his hand. "So who's following you?" He raised his eyebrows a bit, a sweet but patronizing look on his face.

Abbey winced inwardly. He couldn't help her if he didn't know anything, and the more he knew the less he would believe her.

"You don't have to tell me," Rocky said. "If you say you're followed, you're followed."

She knew in that moment that Rocky wasn't her man. It was all wrong. The bar, the man, the whole damn business. But here he was waiting expectantly to hear her story. So, against her better judgment, and while he went through a few whiskeys, she told him some details of her quest—leaving out Jaguar, leaving out the hard part. A few customers finally dragged in, and as the tavern noise grew, Abbey felt a little more comfortable. She ordered a sandwich, and took that opportunity to shift the conversation away from her, to him.

"How long have you and Simon been partners?" she asked, suddenly ravenous, and recalling now that she'd been running on little but raw nerves for the last couple of days.

"Oh, we go way back," Rocky answered. "Far and deep. Far and deep."

A man walked into the tavern, looking directly at Abbey a moment before sitting at the bar and casually visoring into the casino. He swiveled his chair, elbows braced on the bar. Abbey focused on her conversation, trying to stay calm. She didn't even know what her enemies might look like.

"Met in the navy," Rocky said. "Best friends ever since."

"I had a friend like that once. Myra. We were like sisters."

"There you go. Me and Simon are like that. Blood brothers, I guess you could say."

"Where did you see action?" Abbey asked.

Rocky sipped his beer. "The home front." He watched his drink, then looked up at Abbey. "We've seen a battle or two right here. Don't have to go far to find hell, Abbey. It's right around the corner."

She shivered to hear him say that. As the neon sputtered outside, it raked the smoky tavern atmosphere with a sporadic, sleepy lightning. "Hell?" she asked.

He looked into her eyes. "You might know a little about hell, eh, Abbey?"

"Maybe I do."

He nodded slowly, eyes squinting in apparent concentration.

"What do *you* know about it?" she asked. The sandwich arrived, and was better than she'd figured it would be.

"Oh . . . what it looks like. What it feels like. Things like that." He smiled then, tossing off the somber mood. He was a little drunk, for sure, but not succumbing to self-pity. She liked him for that.

He finished off his beer, ordered another.

"How about some coffee?" Abbey suggested. "Too much booze is bad for the liver."

"Nah," Rocky said. "The day is young." The bartender brought him another set, punching in the charges and swimming back through the growing tide of customers and smoke.

"You were married once, weren't you?"

"Hard to believe, isn't it?"

"No. It's not hard to believe." She paused before saying, "You can tell me, Rocky. I'm a good listener."

"Not a very pretty story, the Rocky Ginestra story."

She wanted to hear. Hoped it wasn't just morbid curiosity, hoped it was compassion, in fact.

As the silence between them stretched on, Rocky took a deep breath, inflating his barrel chest, and letting it out through his nose. "Well"—he glanced up with a self-deprecating smile—"her name was Lydia. The love of my life, et cetera, et cetera." He made a backhanded wave, dismissing the phrase, *love of my life,* rushing past it. "Let's just say we were happy. You ever been happy?" He cocked his head when Abbey didn't answer, surprised, maybe, that she couldn't say she had. "Not many people been happy, I guess, not like Lydia and me. Anyway. One time we—Simon and me—had this case, a psycho kind of guy."

He spoke in a soft, matter-of-fact manner, tracing a pattern of beer in the dark surface of the table. "Somehow this psycho gets ahold of Lydia. To get to me, see? Revenge, or something, I dunno. And he calls to say he has her, and what he's gonna do to her. And Simon and I rush to my house, but Simon gets there first." He took a drink of beer and looked just over Abbey's shoulder, as though at a vid screen behind her. A vid he doubtless had seen countless times before. "So Simon is first on the scene. And then he sees the psycho standing in my living room, and Simon has a clear shot. Simon fires, except that Lydia comes running toward him and the bullet hits her instead. And it killed her. One shot. Right in the head."

He paused. "I got there a few minutes later. She was

already dead." Rocky took a revitalizing draught of beer.
"We put down the psycho. Not that it mattered."

Abbey put her hand over his. "Rocky . . . I'm so
sorry."

"I told you it wasn't a nice story."

They sat in silence for a few minutes. The man at the
bar got up and left without looking toward their table.

"Simon always was a lousy shot with a pistol."

"Do you blame him?"

"Simon? Nah. He did his best. And he loved her too.
For my sake, he loved her. Nah, I don't blame him."

For a few minutes then, Abbey forgot her own problems and thought about Rocky and the love of his life.
And his brother for life, and how love is both the reason
for it all and the price for it all. She found herself warming
to this man, wanting to comfort him. So she stayed a little
longer, as the afternoon deepened. Finally Rocky ordered
coffee, and when that was gone he asked her if she was
sure she didn't want help, and she found herself saying,
No, no thank you.

After Rocky left, Abbey stared into her tea, wondering
if in fact he could have helped her. If anyone could. A
woman at the far end of the bar lit up a cigarette and, in
that way of smokers, blew out a long, thin stream of
smoke, seeming to savor getting rid of the smoke as much
as inhaling it. A woman like that, who smoked, and
dressed in plasmic tights and tube top, a woman like that
could be a spy, an enemy. Abbey felt in desperate need of
a friend.

She fished in her purse for her mobe and punched in
her home number, waiting for Renalda to answer.

"Hello?"

"Renalda. It's Abbey."

"Abbey."

It was such a relief to hear Renalda's voice, and be
talking to someone from her old life, her real life.
"Renalda, God, I'm glad to hear your voice." Abbey's
throat constricted. She realized how tired she was after
the last two days. "Hon, I'm in trouble, sort of."

"Harley's here."

"Harley? How's he doing?"

"Harley's fine. Where are you?"

"That's a long story. Renalda, I'm not going to be home for a few days. I'm sorry I can't tell you why, but I can't." She paused, waiting for Renalda's assault of curiosity. When it didn't come, she went on, "I just want you to take care of yourself and not worry about me."

"Where are you?"

"I can't tell you, OK? Please just trust me. There's something very big happening, and I can't come home for a while. One thing I can tell you is, that lots of people are playing that game you have. Nir. And it could hurt you, you know?"

"Lots of people are playing Nir," Renalda said.

"I *know* that." This conversation was not going as she'd hoped. There was no comfort in Renalda right now. "Look. Just take care of yourself. And give Harley a hug for me."

"Harley's here."

Abbey watched as the woman at the end of the bar stubbed out her cigarette and lit another. The room was unbearably smoky. The world seemed unbearably bleak. "I just feel so afraid and lonely, that's all." She said it more to herself than her roommate.

"When are you going to come home?"

"Soon."

"Somebody needs to go grocery shopping."

"Goodbye, hon. Say a prayer for me." Now she was getting sloppy. "Renalda, are you still playing the Nir game?"

A pause. "I'm not playing a game anymore."

"Good. Take care of yourself, OK?"

"OK."

"Bye then. I'll call in a couple days." Her heart was plummeting. There was no comfort.

"Bye then," Renalda said.

Abbey clicked off.

No comfort at all.

~ 3 ~

Zachariah arrived with Lonnie's gift at suppertime. A cloud front bearing the smells of cooked carrots met him at the door, along with the murmur of voices from the dining hall.

The first thing that he would change was the menu, the disgusting hamburger casseroles and other animal-fat concoctions, along with the habit of cooking everything to death. The next thing was the name. It would be Smith Manor, a name with class. Class was generally what was lacking in people, content as they were with their common denominator lives. Now that he owned the place, there'd be some changes, all right.

Starting with this little gift. At his side, it rode a short cushion of air, its domed top purring under his hand, responding to the merest directional pressure. Its face screen was lit with a pleasant digital face, and the thin tubular arms were crossed amiably in front. Lonnie's beloved mech nurse. The comfort they had denied her, citing their *policies*, what they called the *human touch* of Harvest Home. Well, some people didn't want the human touch. The home needed to learn to give the customer what she wanted. The first rule of marketing: Don't try to make people want what you have; just be sure you have what they want.

"Mr. Smith?" The manager was smiling anxiously.

"Zachariah."

"Yes, sorry." He stumbled on *sorry* as though swallowing something unpleasant, his new deference as ill-fitting as a cheap suit. "Your mother is expecting you."

"You didn't tell her about . . . ?"

"The gift? No. She'll be surprised, she thinks it's only you."

Zachariah cocked his head.

"That you're alone, I meant!"

Zachariah and the mech pushed past him.

An old man in a red plaid robe had been laboriously making his way toward the front desk with the help of a hover cage. He stopped in front of the mech and leaned over to pat it on its rounded top. "I've seen these before. It's one of those janitor things, isn't it?"

"This is not Lonnie," the mech enunciated in male tones.

The old man's hand jumped away from the mech.

"No," the manager said. "It's a . . . nurse."

"I am the Welby Three," it intoned. They still couldn't quite get human cadence into the speech patterns, but each word by itself was lovely.

"Nurse! That's against the rules, isn't it?" the old man asked in indignation.

"Was. Yes, it *was*," Zachariah replied. He turned down the hall toward Lonnie's room, the mech following. The oldsters were displaying grandchild vids on their door-screens, and cranked up the volume as he passed. "My sixth granddaughter," one of the tenants barked out at him, hovering next to the perpetual vid on her door. He hurried to keep pace with Welby Three as it picked up speed and aimed for Lonnie's room.

Nurse Aziz stood watching him approach. She looked worried, the closer he got. Worried about being replaced, no doubt, by legions of cheap machines. Her uniform was spotless white, her black hair pulled into a tidy roll in back, and her name tag perched on the sharp curve of her breast like a toboggan ready for the ride of its life. There would be things about Nurse Aziz that he would miss now that Welby made her redundant.

Lonnie was in her wheelchair, facing the door. She looked alert and unhappy, not a good combination.

"Hello, Lonnie." Neutral was best with her; don't give her a handhold.

"Hello Zachariah." Mock pleasant.

"How've they been treating you?" The mech was still hidden outside in the corridor.

"Just hunky-dory." She licked her lips. The room was overpoweringly hot, and Zachariah removed his overcoat.

"Planning to stay awhile this time?" She jerked to face Nurse Aziz. "Nurse, take Zachariah's coat." Nurse hurried to do so.

Now that he was facing his mother, words left him, as

always. Every sentence was a trap, every word a potential offense, a ladder to his throat. "Lonnie, I've . . . there's something . . . someone here to see you."

"Hell's bells, I can see that!" she exploded. *"You're* here, ain't ya? Think I've gone nutty?"

Zachariah turned to the door. "Welby Three."

As the mech appeared in the doorway, Lonnie's jaw trembled. "Booger!" she squeaked. She looked at it, then at Zachariah, with a flash of what might have been surprise or joy. Zachariah took it for joy. Yes. This was all she needed, and stupidly he had withheld it. He hated himself, then forced it down. No. *Feel good, Zachariah. She smiled at you.*

Her hands fumbled at the wheelchair arm, slapping the Forward button, forward, forward. And rolled to the mech, placing her twiggy hand on its side.

"This is Lonnie," it said.

"Damn right, lovie. It's me. None like me, is there?" She laughed, a dry cough.

"No one is like Lonnie."

At that, her eyes filled with tears. She patted the mech, turning back to Zachariah. "Booger's come to take me home?"

The overheated room pressed in on him like a pillow over his face. "Not exactly . . ."

"Not exactly! Is he or isn't he?" Lonnie's wig began to pitch over her forehead.

"He isn't."

She squinted, waiting.

"He'll stay here with you."

Her lips shook as the words pushed out: "You worthless piece of beetle dung." Her eyes accused him. Of the wrong gift, the wrong life. Zachariah felt his chest constricting smaller and smaller, into a dense, pulsing fist.

"Booger, tell that female over there to leave."

Booger turned to the nurse. *"Now you will leave the room. You upset Lonnie."*

Nurse Aziz fled.

Lonnie nodded, over and over. "Booger, take my food away, it's garbage."

Booger glided to the food tray on Lonnie's nightstand.
It extended its arms and, picking up the tray, held it far in
front of it as if it had a foul smell. The mech deposited it
outside the door, its arms descending to floor level along
two grooves in its sides.

The manager arrived at the doorway in time to protest.
"You should eat your meal, Mrs. Smith. You haven't been
eating, have you?" He looked uncertainly down at Booger
as the mech's faceplate began tilting up at him with a soft
whirr. He appealed to Zachariah. "The mech is programmed like a house attendant, no nursing skills, it just
follows her orders. It could be harmful."

"You're fired," Zachariah said.

Lonnie guffawed. The manager paused, then said,
"Please, Mr. Smith . . ." He looked into Zachariah's
eyes as though trying to find a hold on an icy wall.

Zachariah shrugged. "You're fired," he said again,
even more pleasantly than before.

Lonnie gave Zachariah a long, appraising look. "You
got a little of me in you, after all." She turned to Booger.
"Not such a little tit-sucking weakling as I thought. Let's
play checkers, OK, Booger?"

A checkerboard appeared on its screen. *"Red or
black?"*

"Red!" A tendril of a smile burst forth on the live half
of her face. "He lets me win, Zacky," she said happily as
she made the first move on the board, keying the move
from the chair arm pad.

"I own the home now, Lonnie."

Her hand jabbed at the arm pad, and the checkerboard
blipped.

"We can do what we want. I bought it for you." Mistake. That was a hook. She'd pounce on that one. *I
bought it for you,* too much like fishing for a thank-you,
too close to showing his underbelly. He waited for the
claws to extrude.

And they came, gleaming: "For me, was it? You bought
this shithole for *me?*"

He waited for the rest of it, stomach sinking as though
into a sucking mud.

"I could tell you where to shove this whole damn place. Up the arses of all these high-and-mighty rich bitches that live here!" She laughed soundlessly. "You think somebody like me'd ever fit in here? Think they don't talk behind my back and roll their eyes when I use the wrong fork? Think they don't know I come from the wrong side of town and still got a likin' for cheap whiskey?"

"Lonnie, it's not . . . they're not . . ." He was skidding on the muddy bank, flailing for words. . . .

"Not what? Not different from me? Not lookin' down on me?" She was rising up, pushing on the armrest, her elbows trembling, looking as though she might catapult herself at him. Instead she spun her chair around and skidded to the dresser, where she grabbed a small vial. "Take your damn perfume back, it don't help!" She hurled the bottle at Zachariah, and it sailed, end over end, shattering against the wall behind him.

The smell of lilac forced its way into Zachariah's nose.

"It don't cover a thing, see? Take all your damn presents. I don't want 'em."

Zachariah's hands fluttered in front of him, trying to calm her, fence himself off from her.

"I want to go . . . HOME," she whispered at him, her eyes like small blue creatures trapped in her face. "Home . . ." Her wig plopped into her lap. A few strands of white hair lay matted against her head like a bleached spiderweb.

He took a step forward, wanting to comfort her, wanting to squeeze her to stop her from being unhappy, wanting to stop her from saying, over and over, *I want to go home.*

The mech followed him. *"You will leave now. You upset Lonnie."* It whirred as though winding up to physically eject Zachariah from the room.

When his back hit the doorframe, he turned and staggered into the hallway. A few patients were clustered around the doorway, in their chairs and hover cages, gaping at him.

"Get out of here!" he barked, slashing his arm at them

to scatter the group. For a moment they stood frozen, then slowly dispersed.

Nurse Aziz was at his elbow. "Mr. Smith, can I help you?" Her face was a knot of concern.

Here in the corridor he could breathe again. Even the stench of the dining room was refreshing compared with the poisonous lilac atmosphere of the room in back of him. He leaned against the wall for a moment, hands shaking, wanting to smash the wall with his fist, but conscious of eyes upon him, Nurse Aziz and the now wary tenants of Lonnie's corridor.

"You could get my coat from the room."

She disappeared, doing his bidding.

When she came back, Zachariah was much improved. He asked for a tour of the facility, riding a slow wave of heat generated by Nurse Aziz, with her dark hair, so much like Vittoria's. The crest of arousal, gathering mass as it traveled, scattered his worries like so much debris.

In the laundry room, Nurse Aziz seemed to understand what was expected. She looked up at him for confirmation, starting on the first button of the starched white front of her dress.

"Yes," Zachariah said, in his true voice. He nodded once.

"My job . . ." she said, pausing.

"You're the new manager."

Her eyes widened.

He walked over to the door and locked it. "A little gratitude is in order."

Her clothes dropped to the floor next to the front-loading dryer. He could see her backside reflected in the glass door. His hands closed around her, grabbing fistfuls of her, as she stood in front of him, eyes closed, docile, and as he rode the wave a little higher, flowing over the top of her as she moved down to the cement floor. Then Nurse Aziz showed her gratitude for a very long time.

Before he left the laundry room, Zachariah gave Nurse Aziz her second set of orders as the new manager.

"Next time I visit Lonnie, I want her in a good mood." It was time to take control. Past time. Years and decades

past time of asking Lonnie to be happy. Now she was
going to be happy whether she wanted to or not.

Nurse Aziz looked uncertain as she struggled back into
her clothes. "A good mood?"

"You have pills. Use them."

~ 4 ~

As Abbey drove into Zachariah's ranch, a harsh moon
vied for prominence with the flood of light from every
window of the great house. Here was a self-centered person. Don't spare the electricity. Let it roar. The waste of
electricity gave her a surge of annoyance, just enough to
overcome her lingering doubts, enough to propel her out
of the rented car. *OK, Zachariah. You got a special introductory rate for Abbey McCrae? Swell. Here I am.*

She got out and slammed the car door, announcing her
presence.

To her right, beyond the semicircular gravel driveway
and a span of grass and plantings, a red barn stood, its
color sapped by a bleaching moon. Beyond the barn, low-
lying outbuildings crouched, completing the picture of a
working ranch, except for the absence of any sign of life
or noise of animals—not even a dog.

Another light broke out. It was the front door opening.

Abbey turned toward the porch, seeing Zachariah
standing there, dressed in jeans and a yellow T-shirt and
wearing a glittering mobe on one wrist.

He remained silent as she mounted the wide front
steps, into *his* territory, *his* lair, but armed with wariness
at least, if nothing else. She would run a number on him,
and the thought provided a certain satisfaction and
grounding. She would outfake the great faker.

He was frowning at her, not welcoming, no.

"I guess this is kind of late to be coming by . . . ?"

"What are you doing here, Abbey?"

"I should have called." Behind Zachariah was a great
hallway with white-carpeted stairs leading up to a second
floor. It flashed into her mind that those white stairs

would show every trace of mud, every footprint, and this thought conjured an image of Vitt climbing those stairs, slowly, reluctantly, disappearing into the upper recesses of light, fading as she went. . . .

"What do you need, Abbey?" His voice sonorous as a struck gong.

"I was hoping we could talk." She stood face-to-face with him, with only the doormat between them. His hair was backlit, standing out from his head slightly as though electrified, his face pale in the glare of the porch light.

"I've been fighting coming here, Zachariah. But I've been thinking about what you said—that Vitt was in trouble and that I didn't know. I *do* want to know. Maybe there's something I can learn from you. I'd like to try." He made no move to invite her in, but kept her standing there, his eyebrow now arching, waiting for her to go on. "And yes, you're right, I'm angry. It's eating me up inside, all of it. And I don't know whether it's Vitt or me or both. But you offered a session. And I'm willing to pay."

He looked past her, toward the car, toward the road, and might've been looking for this to be a setup, might be looking for the likes of Simon Haskell, but she was innocent on that count, if nothing else.

For a moment his eyes took on an unmistakable leer. "We can take care of this at the Institute, Abbey. I don't work at night. You must learn to relax, you're agitated." He appeared to be searching her face, waiting for her to deny or confirm, to *reveal* something. Here was a guy, she figured, who thrived on prying out little intimacies.

"Yes," she said. "I'm nervous, coming here like this."

"I'll see you at the office, Abbey. Call for an appointment."

"Zachariah."

He was about to close the door, and stopped.

"Zachariah, I don't want to be in a group. I need something personal. Please."

He threw a darting glance out past the car again. "We'll do a private session, then. But you don't make demands. You don't come here at night."

"No, I'm sorry. It's just that I'm ready now. I have the courage now. I don't know about tomorrow."

He looked past her again, toward the road. "Go home, Abbey, and get some sleep. You're overwrought. Call me tomorrow."

She mumbled a good-night and turned dejectedly away. It wasn't hard to play dejected. Getting next to him was going to be tough—and getting him to play Nir, maybe impossible.

She got in the car and drove off the property onto the highway.

As soon as the road curved and her headlights were masked from Zachariah's house, she turned around and headed back to a deep pull-out where a stand of trees bent low to provide some camouflage for her car.

Leaning on the steering wheel, she stared at the distant blaring lights of his house, trying to think of her next move. Call me tomorrow, he said. But a session at the Institute wasn't what she had in mind. Somewhere in the bright darkness of that silent ranch was the ghost of her daughter, and possibly, the *Others* that Jaguar said threatened Medicine Falls. And the Leap Point, the place where they entered, whatever that might mean. And the knowledge of one led to knowledge of the other, whether you wanted it or not.

Turning off the interior car lights, Abbey quietly opened the car door and stepped out. Curdled, moonlit clouds floated in a vast sky, brightening the road, which she now crossed, feeling as if her every move were exposed on a photographic plate.

A cold wisp of air threaded down her neck, and Abbey zipped her jacket tight to her throat and fished in her pockets for her gloves. Stepping across the ditch by the side of the road, she heard the frozen grass crinkle underfoot.

The field belonged to a ranch abutting Zachariah's property. It was inhabited, she thought at first, only by the shadows of the skidding clouds. But after a few moments she saw something move, and peering closer, saw the shapes of two cows in the center of the meadow.

A car sped by on the highway. She froze, hoping she looked like a fence post, hoping that the passengers saw only what they expected to see: dark highway, sleepy fields. The headlights receded, leaving behind a silence so keen it seemed the world was holding its breath. It was one of those moments when the sense of time suspends, stretching the present to a thin, cutting filament. Then snaps back with an event in tow.

A smell crept into her senses. A disgusting stench as thick as paste that knocked her back a step. Looking down, she expected to see a rotting carcass gutted open beside her boots, but saw only frosty, glittering weeds. The odor came on even stronger, a complex mulch of flesh and rust. A smell that *might* have been barnyard smells, for all her experience was worth. And then the clouds tore off the moon and she saw it. A figure a little taller than the cows, a grossly fat man, swaying from side to side behind the cows. As she stared, he moved to the other side of the cow, and just his head could be seen, a great, swollen head sloping to shoulders. And then he turned, a massive rotating movement, and he looked at her—no, she couldn't see his face—but he *seemed* to be looking at her . . . and then the clouds closed ranks and the field darkened, dissolving the image.

The glassy spikes of grass crunched as she stepped backward, a sound she could feel in her teeth, on her skin, as her nerves hummed and she strained to see the fat man again. Revolted by the smell, she slowly backed up, heart thudding. She turned and stepped into the ditch, breaking through a plate of ice, then staggered up to the road and edged toward the car. The car sat in deep shadow where she'd parked it close to the trees. *Get in the car. Get in the car and lock it.* She crossed the road in four strides and got in, punching in security.

A part of her—a primal, limbic part of her—knew what she'd seen and smelled, even if her civilized mind pretended otherwise. It knew danger, and issued the command to flee. Before she had consciously decided, the car was in gear and she was putting mile after mile of highway between her and the field.

As she drove, her mind raced. Who would be in the pasture late at night? Or what? For the first time she started to think that Jaguar's *Others* might not be just a catch-all term. What was the matter with her, anyway? Maybe she was becoming hysterical in a slow, day-by-day progression. Seeing wolves, seeing a medicine man disappearing like a bubble popping and a creature too broad to be a man, lurking among cattle. Maybe Renalda was right, she should have left the diary in the bread box, left that knife-edged discovery back on the store shelves. Now its sharp edges lanced deep, releasing half-human animals and half-animal humans. . . .

Not a chance, came the response. Not your imagination. That profoundly organic smell, *not* a barnyard smell, not from any barnyard she could imagine. Her scalp tingled in exquisite awareness. That thing out there, that thing was what Jaguar tried to tell her about; it was real. And no wonder he couldn't tell her. Who would believe him?

~ 5 ~

Gilda Tupper sat in the Commons, her favorite refuge lately from the cramped condo—and her erstwhile roommate, the boy-man with the black visors and the black thoughts. The Commons was a rather puffed-up name for one square block of lawn and a few park benches, Gilda thought, absently chewing popcorn. It tasted like cardboard. In front of the bench where she sat a rusted fountain lay clogged with last fall's leaves, a remnant of the days when the town could afford to spray water in a park just for aesthetics.

She was startled by a car blasting its horn at someone in the street. Gilda sighed. That was another sign. Nobody honked their horn in Medicine Falls. It was rude, like spitting in public. Yet lately, people honked at you. Didn't they? It was very hard to know what was so, and what was not. One could draw the most sinister conclusions from seemingly harmless trifles. This was possibly a

symptom of creeping senility. Pray God she would be
dead before she would start forgetting her name and spitting in public. But still . . .

She pulled the little blue notebook out of her purse and
recorded the incident of the car honking. Then she read
over what she'd written that day:

*It's been three weeks since Kevin's had a civil word for
me, sitting as he does with that damn contraption. I don't
think he's showered this whole last week. One of the Lost
Ones.*

*Oh, they're everywhere now, the Lost Ones—the ones
with the vacant faces, the guarded eyes, the little black
visors—more of them this week than last, people who
don't bother to say hello on the street anymore, don't
bother to call.*

She looked over the list of Lost Ones. *Fred Marshall,
Glenn Englestadd, Jenny Allen, Kim Hoppe, Patrick
Dyer, Eileen Cziske, Bernard Koops, Lorrie Weddle . . .*

*I was sorry to see Lorrie Weddle go lost. Each time, it's
such a shock. Last week Lorrie showed me the bag the
game is sold in—a fuzzy sack without any printing on it.
(They don't advertise who's responsible for this deviltry!)
"Look, Mrs. Tupper, Steve bought this for me, one of
those retina games," she said as though I'd be impressed.
"Oh dear," I told her. "I understand they're going to
recall that game. Causes cataracts, they think." I don't
know why I said that. Or maybe I do.*

*This morning I saw her at Peavy's Drugstore. She was
subdued, like the Lost Ones get at first. "It's not bad for
the eyes," she said, staring at me. For a moment I was
almost afraid of her. But I held my ground. "A bad case
of cataracts makes your eyes cloud over like cottage
cheese," I told her. But, "I don't think so," was all she
said, low and throaty.*

*Bill Flynn's another one. Real far gone. Got his game
about the same time as Kevin, so I believe the more you
play the more lost you become. There he sits at Flynn's
Books, plugged in so you have to tap him on the shoulder
to buy a book. And then remind him for your change. Not
that people buy books anymore. The only people in that*

store were me and old Kate Milhaus. Which is another matter. From what I can tell, nobody over sixty-five can even make the contraptions work. I asked Noah Penrod, who's my age, if he'd tried it and he said it was a dud. So it doesn't waste time on oldsters. It likes younger folks.

And yes, I know how I sound.

Then there's the matter of the people it's killed. I don't have proof, and maybe no one's actually died yet. But they will, mark my words. Cherilyn Hoyle tried to kill herself. She's been lost for weeks, and finally went off the deep end. She'd taken the cure for pills and alcohol, and now this, poor thing. Maybe if you tend to be the addictive sort, the deeper your dependence on the game. It makes you wonder: didn't they test this thing before they put it on the market?

Andrew Chin walked by just then clutching a furry packet, a little hurry in his step. She sighed, and dutifully logged his name in the list. Then she finished off the last of the popcorn, fighting within herself whether she was losing her marbles or whether there really was something ugly going on. And wondering which was worse.

As she tucked the little blue notebook away in her handbag, she heard the screeching of tires and a car horn. It took her a moment to see that a few people were gathering in the street out in front of Peavy's.

Oh dear lord, someone was hurt. As she drew nearer, she saw that a man lay in the street, blood pooling around his head . . . there was actually a great deal of blood . . . her heart was drumming hard against her rib cage as she hurried forward. She didn't really want to see, but suppose it was someone she knew? Three others including the driver were staring at the injured man. No one moved.

"Call an ambulance!" Gilda blurted out. The man lay awfully still . . . perhaps the others were as horrified as she was. But the damn fools could get help, couldn't they? "You," she said pointing at a fit-looking young man, "run to the drug store and call nine-one-one." He looked doubtful, but she fixed him with a powerful glare. "Run, you hear me?"

He moved off, but no one else so much as lifted a

finger. "Does somebody know first aid?" she cried. She looked from one person to the next, then finding them useless, she knelt by the injured man and listened for breathing. Yes. Breathing. She took off her coat and draped it over him, her hands shaking and her mind rummaging back into its depths for how to treat a bleeding wound. Don't move someone with a head injury. Or was it with a back injury? In consternation she looked up to find that the young man she'd sent to call 911 was hanging about on the fringe of the now swelling crowd of onlookers. The injured man still made no sound or movement. She turned to the gawkers, swiveling her head to encompass them all. "Somebody, *somebody* run and call an ambulance." Leaning closer to the man, she saw that blood was still streaming from his head. She removed the coat from him and gently tucked it against the bleeding wound, applying a little pressure. He couldn't be much more than twenty years old, dear lord. "Just lie still, we're getting help," she whispered to him." Then she looked up again.

No one moved. Not to run for help, not to aid her. "Give me a coat to cover this man."

A portly woman who looked more stricken than the others struggled out of her coat. Then she stood there, holding on to it as though confused about what came next. Gilda looked at her pointedly. "Call . . . nine . . . one . . . one." She said it slowly, with venom. The woman nodded once and walked away. Slowly. Dear God, who knew how far she would get?

The minutes scrolled by while the lookers looked and the young man bled. Gilda's knees hurt from the pavement. As she knelt there, her skirt sopping wet from the street slush—and perhaps the blood—a breeze sucked the warmth from her body. The onlookers stood silently. She was alone in a figurine world, the only flesh-and-blood moving creature among a collection of porcelain people.

She checked the injured man's pulse again and again, weeping with frustration. At last she realized that he was dead.

After a time she struggled to her feet. Unaccountably, a man who'd been watching at her side helped her up, bracing her elbow with his hand. She turned to him in anger. "Why didn't you *do* something?"

The skin between his eyes furrowed. After a moment he said, wonderingly, "I really don't know."

Gilda slowly pulled her arm out of his grasp. No, he didn't know. But she did. She took one more look at the pathetic circle of Lost Ones. Of murderers. She took a deep breath to speak her mind, looking from one to the other, trembling. Then the breath leaked back out, wordlessly. She picked up her purse off the street and staggered away. The wind fluttered bitterly through her thin clothing as she cut a swath through the Commons.

On her way out of the park she threw the blue notebook in the waste can. She was beyond the note-taking stage—way beyond. It was time to set things straight.

Chapter 8

~ 1 ~

It was an eerie feeling, watching your own home from a hiding place. Things that you took for granted, hardly saw in the day-to-day flow of things, took on new appearances, much like words you say over and over until they don't sound like themselves. The tacky storefronts looked shabbier than Abbey had convinced herself they were, her neighbors less familiar and innocuous. Even down to the resident bag lady—who, like everyone else on this street, could easily watch her come and go, from kitchen to bedroom and back again.

If she were up there, that is, and not watching from her parked car.

She took another swipe at the condensation on the car window and watched, hoping her roommate would at least come out if she wasn't going to open the store. It was eleven o'clock, and Renalda should have opened the shop by now, but she was mucking about in the apartment, taking her sweet time. Come on, Renalda, don't make me come in after you. She squinted again through the window aperture, her eyes feeling like jellyfish in a sand pail after a sleepless night at the Y, replaying in her head the scene at Zachariah's.

No reply yet from him. She'd e-mailed him asking whether he could find an opening for her, today or tomorrow . . . and he was making her wait, no doubt part of the scam.

A figure at the shop door.

Abbey leaned forward. Renalda was leaving the shop, slouching more than walking down the sidewalk on the other side of the street. She wore nothing more for a coat than a baggy sweater, her hair pulled back into a low ponytail with—was that a piece of yarn? Devoid of her signature heavy makeup, this hardly looked like the woman she knew—Renalda with her flash, and her stiletto strut.

Abbey sat back, shaken. Then, determined to follow through, she pulled her muffler around her face and got out of the car to follow her, to intercept her somewhere that might not be watched.

With a winter cap pulled down over her head, and the muffler, Abbey hoped she was disguised enough. The boots couldn't be helped, but who looked at feet? She crossed the street at the intersection and kept Renalda in view at a safe distance.

"Hi Abbey."

She jerked around to see Joe Mills hawking his dailies there on the corner. Damn anyway. She wiggled her gloved fingers at him, hoping to brush him off, but he persisted: "Where you been, Abbey?"

"Busy," she answered.

"Yeah, a lot of people been busy lately." He gestured with the *Medicine Falls Daily*. "Business is lousy."

She nodded at him and quickened her pace to keep up with Renalda. She needed some different clothes. She could pull some stuff out of the shop, vintage stuff, or grab something old and nondescript from her closet. . . .

Renalda was retching into the gutter. God, she was

sick. She wiped her face on the hem of her sweater and stood up, tottering a bit on her heeled boots.

Something in that careless swipe of sweater over her mouth; an ugly, sloppy gesture, so un-Renalda. And then she turned and walked across the parking lot into the Food Galore.

Abbey stopped. The woman was sick, but here she was staggering onward to grocery shop. Yesterday she'd said nothing about being ill. Yet even sick as a dog, Renalda would never step outside looking like that.

As Renalda disappeared into the grocery store, Abbey began to rethink the situation. She started to doubt the wisdom of talking to her old roommate at all, though she desperately wanted to talk to someone who wouldn't think she'd gone crazy. But something held her back. Maybe doubt instilled by Jaguar, maybe a leftover unease from last night. But she passed on her little chat with Renalda.

Noon traffic filled the streets, tires churning through snowmelt as the sun tried to assert itself against the stranglehold of five months of winter. As the patches of snow melted, the rivulets carried soot and litter away, damming the storm sewers with debris, and pushing lakes of water onto the sidewalks. Picking her way around these, Abbey retraced her steps as far as the alley behind the store. Here the two-story brick buildings plunged the narrow corridor into a frigid shadow. A flagpole jutting from an upper apartment sported a frozen bandanna and bra. Thinking to avoid the paperboy by cutting through and approaching the car from the other direction, she walked past the back door of the shop, where she noticed the garbage can lid had toppled off. In the intermittent breeze, sodden papers lurched down the alley like crippled birds. A long rope hung out of the can.

No, not a rope. Harley's leash.

At that moment, Abbey didn't ask herself what to do, she just did it. Reaching into her purse for her keycard, she strode to the back door, where she let herself into the shop storeroom. She was blind in the sudden blackness, but blackness was also her cover. She felt her way for-

ward, hand sliding along the shelves. Aiming for the door
at the foot of the apartment stairs, ears straining for the
slightest noise.

As she slid her hand along the shelves, her fingers
rested on the random contents of the storeroom: a cast-
iron pan handle, a set of binoculars, the leg of a doll,
bizarre handholds leading her across the room.

The door now should be just to her left. If she hurried,
she could check on Harley, grab some clothes and be
gone, no one the wiser. She rested her hand on the doorknob, then opened the door a crack and then slowly
wider.

Through the front shopwindows, the daylight burst
through to the twilight depths of the shop. Abbey started
up the stairs, suddenly in a desperate hurry. It was all
wrong, everything felt wrong—the shop, the neighborhood, Renalda. She'd get in and out fast. A spike of noise
as the stairs creaked. If someone waited for her in the
apartment, then they for sure knew she was coming.

The apartment door was ajar. When she pushed it
open, the first thing Abbey saw was the multilounger's
comp screen glowing dully like a block of ice housing a
flame. The room stank of moldy food and perspiration.
Clutter lay everywhere, shoes and underwear and paper
cartons of take-out food with forks abandoned in them.

"Harley, here boy," she whispered. But no Harley.

She hurried to the bedroom, almost stepping in a dried
pile of dog shit. Fury pulsed through her. What the hell
was going on? Damn it, Renalda . . . savagely, she rummaged through her drawers, grabbing this and that, and
stuffing the items into a turtleneck sweater, for lack of
something better. Then, after pushing the dresser drawers
shut, she fled the bedroom, fled the reeking apartment.

Traversing the storeroom again, she threw open the
alley door and staggered out, arms wrapped around her
improvised bag of clothes. Abbey hurried down the alley
and out onto the main street.

Lobo appeared in front of her, startling her.

"I got Nir today, Ab," he said.

He smiled a grimy smile and cocked his head. "Ninety-five, bargain basement, even though I know you dyin' to buy."

"I thought you were all sold out," she said, trying to sound conversational, frantic as she looked, clutching her armload of clothes. She looked around, wondering how he'd found her, wondering if he'd been following her.

"I *was*. Now I'm flush. But if you don't want it, I got plenty that do." He was buoyant and cocky, and looking prosperous, with gold ear studs and a clean jacket. Followed or not, she *did* want a copy of that game, and cash terms were no problem, now that she carried a good bit of cash to avoid an electronic trail. She pulled out the money as the breeze fluttered the bills in her hands.

Lobo groped in his knapsack, producing an odd-looking, oval sack, covered with a coat of gossamer fur, rippling in the wind. "The packet's all you need besides your comp," he said. "You don't need your old goggles and glove. Just tab in the game and hitch on the Nir shades. And if you want to do partners, connect the leads, is all. One plays, one watches." The money disappeared into his jacket pocket.

He made her a little salute, jarring the tech appliances that swung from his skullcap. "Have fun," he said, "and thank you for shopping with Lobo."

~ 2 ~

Sooze peered out of her door at the noises of clattering and swearing. Lobo stumbled down the stairs from the attic, a little higher, a little earlier in the afternoon than usual. He swirled around and growled at the hallway, the prying eyes. Lobo was getting meaner these days. You never knew when he might swing on you. A dozen doors slammed shut.

All but Sooze's. She slipped out the door and watched him stagger down the six flights. She listened for the front door to slam.

Then noticed he'd left his door open.

Just a crack. From the long, thin slit a soft glow sprayed onto the upper landing.

She took the stairs two at a time, avoiding the worst creaks, with Hipe close on her heels, followed by his fragging pals. She swung to face them. "Look. I saw it first. One of you can come. One."

Hipe and his two sidekicks hesitated at her commanding tone. First Come was a pretty big rule; but so was Up Yours. "Who says?"

She assessed her competition, standing there like hyenas trying to steal her kill, and one of them with the neon-looking eyes of a slime-user. A freaker. "I'll share," she said, raising her chin. "But I ain't gonna make a mess with four of us pounding around up there. You want Lobo to find out?"

"Get lost," Hipe said to the others. He elbowed by her and they scrambled up to the door of the many locks, none of which—none—were locked right now. Usually, he'd be gone a couple hours at least. Even so, she looked down the stairwell, checking for a hand on the bannister somewhere. The sidekicks were moving off, afraid to challenge Hipe.

"Hurry," she urged.

As Hipe leaned in, peering into the room, Sooze brushed by him.

Lobo's den smelled like mice droppings and mold, the way Lobo himself smelled sometimes. He'd left a stubby candle burning next to his big chair. That could set the whole place afire. Sooze considered whether to blow it out. Would he remember he'd left it burning? Was he coming right back?

"Guard the door," she whispered to Hipe. She rifled quickly through piles of clothes and a few boxes of wares, probing by touch, hoping not to find something slimy. What to rip? There was so much. Food was her first thought, and games. Lobo was zipping stingy, never handed out nothing lately, but knew how to take, he did. Sometimes Sooze even wondered if he'd taken Carma, killed her and stuffed her in a chest up here, like he said he'd do if anybody ripped him. Sooze's hands got tingly, her nerves peeled back, waiting for Lobo's footsteps up the stairs.

"Whadidya find?" Hipe was getting restless.

She stuffed some tins of gourmet sausages in her pockets, and little packets of ketchup. "Not much, shut up!"

When she found the mounds of fuzzy balls, her hand shot back so fast she fell on her butt. The floor thunked resoundingly. She scuttled backward. Then, when the pile didn't move, she crawled closer.

"What izzit?"

"You freaker, shut UP! You want him to hear us?"

"You're the one making the noise!" Hipe hurried to her side. "What izzit?"

They staggered back again when something black and shiny jumped out of the sack Hipe was holding. "Jesus-god!"

Sooze snatched the open package from him. "Totally meg!" She thrust the visor on. "It's that game. It's meg, I'm telling you." She pranced around in the candlelight, holding the too-large glasses on her face. "Am I plasmic, or what?"

"What's in that visor?"

"Stupid! It's a ret game." She flounced over to Lobo's chair where he'd taped a game appliance to the over-stuffed arm. "Plug me in, honey!"

She slipped the tab into the port and hooked up the wires to the shades. "These don't work." She tossed the visor to Hipe. "Give me that other one."

He hucked her the smaller shades, then tried jacking in the other for himself. "No glove," he said. "What kind of eyeball game got no glove?"

"I TOLD you that one don't work. Go watch the stairs, then you can try."

She was in a sparkling chamber. Golden light flooded around her as though the air were a lake of butter. The walls themselves were the source, all crinkly and glowy. It was, Sooze thought, like being inside a pineapple on fire.

And that's just what it smelled like all of a sudden, sweet, tangy pineapple, so good it made you dizzy.

On the floor was a stick. She picked it up, releasing music from all the walls at once. As she pointed the stick toward a section of wall, the wall got lighter and then thinner until she could almost see through it. There were shapes moving out there to the beat of the music. Moving the stick sideways made the walls get thick again, and moving it up and down made it see-through. It was a magic stick. The kind you used in a retina world, like rich folks plugged into.

Something was out there. She jumped back and swished the stick, disappearing the thing. Pointing the stick again, the figure put its hands on its hips and looked at her. It was an action figure with no real face, just a tube was all it was, an icky white tube that moved. The fun music said this was a funny toy, but Sooze wasn't so sure.

She thinned all the walls, turning them to yellow glass.

She was in a big field with big, clunky cartoon animals everywhere, chewing grass beneath a sky like a tent of honey from one end of the world to the next. Sooze wanted to fly into that sky, where everything was light and the world tasted like pure joy.

One wall fizzled away with the sound of popcorn exploding.

She stood next to the action figure whose name was I-haar. It was maybe not so fun after all. It had too many arms and it floated off the ground instead of having legs. She made it disappear, but the music got sad, so she brought it back.

I-haar pointed above his head where a thread of light snapped into the air like a crack through ice. Sooze reached up to touch it, and then it swept her up and, with I-haar next to her on another thread, she swept over the animals, the pineapple wind rushing past her face, and the flowers zooming below. Then, whoosh! She pointed the stick and they turned the other way, and she laughed so hard she almost had to pee, but then she didn't have to anymore, because she was magic. For a moment she thought she heard I-haar laugh too.

The I-haar would be her friend. There was nothing to be afraid of.

Someone was shaking her arms. The visor fell off her face, and she found herself looking into Hipe's scrunched-up face. "Lobo!" he hissed.

She sprang from the chair, ejecting the tab and grabbing up the visor. A can of pork sausages rolled across the floor as she bolted toward the bag of ret games. Hipe fled, leaving the door wide open. From down below, the sound of doors slamming followed the progress of Lobo up to his pad. On her way out, Sooze slapped the Off button on the game appliance, and then knocked into the candle, sending it splattering onto the floor. She picked it up, spilling hot wax on her hand, slapped it back onto the side table, and jammed for the door.

Just as she closed the door behind her, she heard Lobo's footsteps below, rounding the corner to the sixth floor.

She hopped onto the bannister and skidded to the bottom, coming face-to-face with Lobo as he stalked toward her. Her pockets were heavy with cans, her heart fluttering like it would take wing. "Hey, Lobo whadidya bring me?"

He looked up to the landing where his door stood closed. Fishing in his pockets, he at last drew out a hard candy wrapped in thin paper, and tossed it up in the air, so she could catch it.

"Shitalmighty," he said. "Thought I left my candle burning, you know?"

"Maybe it just gutted itself out," she said, her mouth full of watering cherry candy.

Lobo trudged to the top of the stairs. When he got to the landing he examined the door locks, frowning. By the time he turned around, Sooze was leaning against the inside of her door, eyes squeezed shut, listening for Lobo's steps. Instead, she heard his door slam shut, and quiet descend on the house like a net.

Ah, the unimaginable, sweet world of grown-ups. The

world of food, of mommies and daddies. And the glory world of Nir.

~ 3 ~

A creme-de-menthe-colored carpet that had seen better days lapped up to Simon's apartment. Abbey's hand hesitated above the brass knocker, as she listened for sounds within. Nothing. Then she let the knocker fall.

After a few moments the door opened and Simon stood there, wearing a shirt with rolled-up sleeves, casual slacks, and bedroom slippers. A pipe was in his hand, and a pungent haze dimmed the room beyond.

"Pipe smoking is even more lethal than cigarettes," she heard herself saying.

"Abbey," he said, looking startled.

"Your address is in the phone directory. I hope you don't mind." He was silent a couple beats. "I have something you should see, Simon."

His voice was softer than she remembered it. He looked tired. "Not my case, remember?"

"I don't have anyone else, Simon." And obviously, she didn't have Simon, either. But despite his skepticism she was determined to win him over, this man with the steadfast core, whom she barely knew. *Another loser, Mom,* Vitt said in high disgust. *You always pick losers.*

"You can trust Rocky," Simon was saying. "I'd bet my life on it."

She plunged her hand into her purse, retrieving the packet. She thrust it at Simon. "Just take it. It's the Nir game. A virgin copy. You try it if it's so harmless."

He made no move, but sighed a deep, infinitely weary breath. "I don't think so, Abbey."

After another moment Abbey broke off looking at him and turned to leave, taking a few steps before turning back. "I know this woman? She can cure a smoking habit with an herb tea that she concocts by looking at your irises. It worked for a friend of mine's brother." That last wasn't something she'd planned to say. Truth was, she hadn't planned at all, beyond getting that game into Simon Haskell's hands. After that, she figured curiosity would win him over.

She wound up for one more try.

But he had already opened the door wider. "Abbey." He moved his head a little sideways, toward his apartment. "Come on. Let's play Nir."

She hitched her purse up higher on her shoulder and hurried toward him before he changed his mind.

Simon's flat was not what she expected. This wasn't bachelor-mess, it was museum-curator-neat. His small parlor held a loveseat, overstuffed chair, and coffee table with a stack of books, one of them splayed flat, as though he had just now been reading. Wood bookcases covered every available wall. Lamps spread a honey glow in two circles near the loveseat and chair.

No decaying socks or piles of clothes draped over chairs. Simon was a tidy man. Abbey thought about proposing marriage.

"My humble abode. Have a seat."

Abbey sank down on the loveseat, gazing up at the row upon row of hardbound books that surrounded the room like a coat of armor.

"You've read all these? Must've taken a long time."

"I've *had* a long time."

She nodded, scanning for what was obviously missing here: the electronics. But not a piece in sight: not a comp, not a vid screen, phone, stereo, fax, or remote control. "The retro look," she said, trying to sum up his decor in a positive way.

"The contemplative look," he responded. "I like to muse, let's say." She must have been staring like a dolt at his bookcases, because he said: "Reading. You ought to try it sometime. Keeps the brain in shape. Stems the tide of techno-trivia."

"Someday the trivia will be collector's items," she said. "Tomorrow's antiques."

"You ever seen a two-eighty-six PC in an antique store?"

Abbey paused, then smiled. "Don't tell me you never

indulge in a chat over the Net?" She paused as it dawned on her he likely never had.

"Remember when people used to drink coffee in cafés and talk—in person?" He sighed. "No, probably you don't. I rest my case." Still standing, he turned the packet in his hand. "So this is the nasty Nir, eh?"

To her surprise he began pulling books out of one of the bookcases, piling them on the floor in regular stacks. He turned to look at her. "Guess we've got to plug it in, don't we?"

"You have a comp?"

Simon continued pulling books off the shelf. "I'm not entirely behind the times. I do have a computer, it's just a little tucked away." He dragged the empty bookcase into the center of the parlor. There, set into the wall in the style of the old built-ins, was a comp screen and key patch. "Came with the flat."

She knelt beside him among the books, as he opened the side panel and pulled out the shades and joystick. "You won't need those. Nir has a personal display system upgrade." She examined the seamless Nir packet, watching as the fine hairs of the bag adhered to her fingers for an instant, then snapped back. Tearing the bag apart, she withdrew a crumpled black item that sprang to shape: a pair of tiny goggles, black and wet-feeling. Peering inside the pouch, she saw more hardware, dark and glistening. She pulled out a second visor set and a mini-looped cord with a prong on either end.

"You know how to use this stuff?" Simon asked.

Abbey extracted a comp tab and held it up between them. "Nir," she said. It looked like an ordinary game tab to fit any machine.

Simon had turned on the old machine. It whined and thrummed, emitting a smell of burning dust.

"How old *is* that thing?" she asked.

"It may be old, but it's wired to the same carrier that the rest of the town sucks in, so never worry." The screen pulsed into life.

Abbey held the game tab, hesitating.

"Your medicine man give you a little ceremony to purge devils?"

Her eyes snapped up to meet his, gauging if he was sarcastic or playful, and decided it was fifty-fifty. As Simon reached for the larger of the visors, Abbey touched his wrist, stopping him. He looked at her in a funny way, narrowing his eyes.

"The primary player uses the small pair." She handed him the smaller shades, barely as wide as a man's thumb, with a small appendage jutting out to provide a minuscule earpiece.

"So I'm to be the main player?" Simon said.

"You're the main skeptic, right?"

He smiled as though to say, *touché,* and reached up for the old VR joystick.

"We don't need a stick, either."

"Just sit back and enjoy the ride?"

"Simon. This is dangerous. Are you sure?"

"Nobody's ever died from virtual interface yet. Let's get going."

She uncoiled the cords, examined the two visors for plugs, and used the patch cords to connect their visors together. "We're wired," she announced.

"Pretty soon you people are going to look like cyborgs." He paused, looking at her as though waiting for her to say something, or waiting to say something himself. Then he smiled. "OK, my dear. Let's party." He slid on the goggles, adjusting them on the bridge of his nose.

She reached over and pressed in a small button on the rim of his glasses. "Start button," she said.

Goggled herself, at first Abbey saw only the black of the shades, and at her side, a pulsing light. After waiting a few moments, she pulled the visor onto her nose and looked at Simon. A gentle halo of light escaped from the edges of his visor. When Abbey pushed the shades back into place, her sight fell into a vast, inky pit. Then, with breathtaking suddenness, she was enveloped.

. . . they were sitting in Simon's office. At least Simon was sitting there, behind his desk. Abbey was watching from somewhere off to the side, at a distance farther than the office walls. The images wavered now and then, shimmering as though seen through a layer of water.

She heard Simon say, close, next to her ear, "The ultimate fun game. I'm at work. Terrific."

The room was a startling re-creation. How had they done this? The smell of coffee, reduced to its blackest essence, along with a faint overlay of Rocky's cheap cologne. His partner's stacks of computers, looming like high-rise buildings over Simon's own humble stacks of files labeled: Jakowski, Lemmert, Rowe and Rowe, Billable Hours. . . .

How the hell?

Simon began reading some papers at his desk, testing the words. And he could actually read them, as though straight out of a familiar file . . . A hot sun beat in through the windows, infusing the air with a heavy lethargy. He settled deeper into his chair, a movement that produced an eerie, dead-on simulation of his office chair's rocking motion. He was half-aware of sitting in his apartment, on the floor with Abbey, but that awareness seemed to be trickling away by the moment.

Except that the cologne was wrong. Rocky didn't wear cologne. Not since Lydia. He felt a bead of sweat trace a path from his hairline past his ear. The clock read 1:25. A feeling swept over him, that he'd done this before. A pronounced certainty that he'd sat here just like this on a hot summer day, reading this very file . . .

Lydia, he thought. And then he knew what would happen next.

The phone rang, and he knew who it would be, what news he would hear.

Hell no, Nir. Not going to play this little horror story. No.

But he picked up the phone.

"Simon," *the voice said,* "it's Rocky. He's got her. He's got Lydia." *The last word came out like a moan.* "He's at the house. I'm on my way, but it'll take me, God, twenty minutes. Si, he's got her."

Simon rose from his chair. "Rocky, how . . ."

"He called me . . ." His voice was breaking. "He said
he'd . . ." and the words strangled in his throat.

"Jesus. I'm on my way, I'm on my way. . . ."

"Hurry," his partner said in a hoarse whisper, "just
hurry."

Simon pulled a gun from his drawer. Small, black,
smart-wired. It went in his belt on his way out the door.
The part of him that sat next to Abbey on the floor of his
living room had faded to a small kernel, embedded far
beneath the radical presence of Nir. Within that tight
knot, his resistance shriveled. He abandoned himself to
the sensory assault, and plunged onward, down the hall.

When he reached the lift, it wasn't operating. His fist
crashed into the lift door. Damn, damn! He raced for the
stairs. Could call the blues, but they'd botch it for sure,
try to negotiate. Horse shit.

He tore out of the stairwell into the parking garage,
cold as a mine shaft, yanked open the door of his beat-up
Mitsubishi and squealed out of there onto Lowell Street
on two wheels. He raced through downtown as fast as he
dared, sweat peeling off his face in sheets, not bothering
with the AC, weaving through lunch traffic, just passing
on the right and miraculously making every green light,
and still going slower than molasses in January, slower
than he by-God had to go. And all the while thinking of
gentle Lydia with that psycho, and feeling the hot metal at
his waist urging him to kill this bastard, if he laid one
hand on her—he'd kill him in a New York second—if he
didn't kill himself first, barreling down the street like a
pinball in a berserk machine. Hurry, just hurry. That
voice, looping through what remained of his thoughts,
Rocky, his best friend for thirty years, and Lydia the
woman who saved Rocky from the fate of lonely, desperate middle age. A life like Simon's, maybe. He fairly stood
on the accelerator and flew past the outskirts of Medicine
Falls, all in a blur.

Outside the house all was quiet. The summer afternoon
framed the small clapboard house like a doily around a
nightmare. Climbing roses twined along the porch railing

and over the door, and the vegetable garden slumbered in a profusion of corn, tomatoes, and beans. Simon crouched behind the bushes to get to a view of the side windows. Not a movement inside. He ran, crouching low, and flattened himself against the house, listening past his own gasping breath.

Then he heard it, a muffled scream. Lydia's buried cries, and he used her cries for sound cover as he leapt up to the back porch and pushed through it to the kitchen where the cries clattered off the white ceramic counter tiles, shards of her voice, piercing him . . . and now, Simon knew, he—the monster—would appear in the living room just beyond the doorframe.

He did. And Simon had a clear shot, a clear shot, and he watched, horrified, as the gun swung up on the end of his own outstretched arm. A terror filled him; there was something he was supposed to remember to do—or not do—but all he could think of was steadying his arm as his hands gripped the gun, two-fisted, his finger dimpling the trigger.

Lydia! . . . the thought sliced in. But Lydia was no-where to be seen, as the psycho turned and saw Simon, and brought up his shotgun.

Simon fired. The psycho took the slug in the stomach, and the shotgun fell slowly from his hand and he turned his head to watch it hit the carpet and discharge into Lydia's porcelain table lamp, while he fell onto his rump, now holding his reddening middle, looking at his hands fill up with gore.

Simon paced forward, calmly shooting the writhing figure in the crotch and each leg. Yes, kill him, once isn't enough, kill him so he never rises again, never breaks into your life, your dreams: grinning, casual, and demented. As Lydia's captor lay in shock, spread-eagled on the floor, Simon removed the knife from the man's belt and turned it before his animal eyes, so that the light from the dangling bulb of the shattered lamp flashed and flashed from the blade. Yes. Watch it coming. Then Simon slit his throat, ear to ear, in a slow, neat slice, as methodically, calmly, as the Sunday roast.

Rocky burst through the front door with three officers behind him, as Lydia rushed to meet him, hands tied behind. Rocky yanked at her bonds, tearing them away, and they collapsed to their knees together, clasping each other, and Lydia's voice called Rocky's name, over and over. The blues stood back, watching the reunion. Their eyes raked over the now unmoving body, and they nodded at Simon, at his well-earned revenge.

Rocky looked up at Simon, past Lydia's dark, sweat-drenched hair. "Simon . . ." His voice faltered. "Simon . . ."

Lydia turned to Simon, her face deathly pale and wet. "I knew you'd come."

As she turned back to Rocky's arms, Simon thought he heard her say, "Practice makes perfect."

He threw the knife on the floor. "I need to clean up," he said.

Abbey pulled the shades from Simon's face.

"I need to clean up," he said, his voice a scrape deep in his throat.

"Stay right where you are." She rummaged in the kitchen for a tissue, found a clean dish towel, and brought it to Simon, cold and wet. He buried his hands in the towel, covering his face.

Abbey stroked his hair and they sat for a long time in silence. The old built-in began a series of wheezing blips. She crawled over and shut it off. When she turned back to him, Simon was staring at the cooling screen.

"Can I make you some tea?"

"Brandy."

"Alcohol is . . ."

He flashed her a certain glance. One that discouraged advice.

She found the brandy in the kitchen. Simon was behind her, reaching past her toward the cabinet. He brought out two snifters.

He poured a stiff one and a small one, leaving hers on the counter as he took his glass and the bottle into the living room. She took her glass and followed him, sitting on the loveseat, as he sat in his chair.

"Quite a gadget you got there." He nodded at the comp. "Wish fulfillment of the highest order." He took a long drink. "Or the lowest."

"How do you feel?" Abbey asked. Her own hands were shaking. She'd never seen a person die. Never seen a gunshot wound. Never seen . . . what Simon did. Nothing even close. She found herself staring at the brandy in the glass.

"I feel terrific. Just nearly cut a man's head off. Feel terrific."

Simon's gaze was off across the room, toward the comp screen.

"She was the one to die, wasn't she, Simon."

He looked up at her for a brief moment, then away.

"Rocky told me," she said.

"Well then you know this—version—amounts to a fairly bizarre fantasy."

"But *whose* fantasy?"

"Mine, I guess." After a moment he placed his glass down on the side table and got up, walking through the bedroom to the bathroom.

Simon's fantasy. Getting it right this time, and executing the villain. And Vitt's fantasy of the new body that would free her of male attention and derision . . . and how, *how* did this program come into being?

Simon came back, looking pale. "Used to like that brandy," he said ruefully. He stood there looking so vulnerable, it made her want to protect him, heal him, forgive him, if that's what he needed. She got up and walked over to him, taking his hand and leading him to the loveseat, pressing him firmly into the small couch, and sitting beside him.

Simon reached for the brandy bottle. Abbey beat him to it, pouring him a half glass.

"Jesus, woman. If I drink that I might make a pass. Or pass out."

Abbey flushed. The comment, and his nearness, seemed acutely personal, his gaze almost tender. "Well then . . ." she floundered a moment. ". . . then I'll help you drink it." She took a drink of the harsh and aromatic liquor. Coughed.

"Just sip," he said. "The slower, the better."

Looking at him at that moment, Abbey thought she could stand to love this man. She could take care of him and maybe end up with a little from him in return. She allowed herself to think about living with him . . . cooking him a nice meal . . . sitting next to him watching TV late at night, with Harley snuggled down between them. . . .

"Do you like dogs?" she asked.

"You see any dogs here?"

The fantasy evaporated. Get real, Abbey. You'd end up with the guy's pain and no guy.

After a long silence he asked: "Where did you get the copy of Nir, Abbey?"

"A street contact." She told him about Lobo, what little she knew of him.

"I wonder where he gets his supply. I'd give good money to know just where. And how the damn thing works."

"Do you think it's dangerous?"

"It could be."

"But then, Renalda—my roommate—used it and just fell in love."

Simon smiled humorlessly. "Maybe that's her nemesis. Falling in love."

"What was Vittoria's?"

"Nemesis? I don't know, Abbey. There's a lot I don't get about this thing. Like, how does it know this deep background stuff on us? Is it accessing our brains somehow? If that was the case, this would be very big news. We'd be hearing about it everywhere. Why the mystery?"

"Because they don't want the light of publicity."

"They?"

"The Others," Abbey said.

The edge of Simon's mouth twitched in the beginning of a smile. "I don't think you need to get supernatural to find evil in the world, Abbey. Dig deep enough, you find it in everyone. Scratch the surface of a rich infotainment company with a technology breakthrough, and you'll find it, big time." He refilled the glass, offering it to her.

The liquid plowed a fiery trail down her throat. "*Is* it a breakthrough?"

Simon held her gaze. "A quantum leap."

"I still don't understand how they expect to sell very many if it turns people off," Abbey said.

Simon frowned. "Is that what it does?" His eyes narrowed, watching her closely. "Something you should understand, Abbey."

She waited as he took a long drink. Then he said: "I enjoyed it. Nir. I enjoyed it." He looked at her, waiting.

It wasn't what she wanted to hear. But it was hard to fault him for lusting after revenge . . . she'd dreamed of revenge herself, and knew its power.

"Not pretty, is it?" He smiled sardonically. "I think I'd like to run that program again."

"Don't."

He snorted. "No. But I think whoever owns this little game is going to make a billion dollars."

She was full of confusion and brandy. She put her head back on the couch, closing her eyes a moment. "Can't hold my liquor."

"Goddamn, woman. You almost drank me under the coffee table. Don't sell yourself short."

"That's been my problem all along. Selling myself short."

"Well you have no earthly reason to ever do that."

The room started to slant to one side.

"I think I need to lie down."

"You can sleep here, if you want. Couch is damn comfortable, actually."

"I shouldn't." But she lay down, and soon felt a blanket surround her. The couch had a problem sitting still, and had begun a slow, clockwise rotation.

"Simon?"

"Yes." His voice was very near.

"Will you help me? Even if you don't believe, will you help me?"

"Anything," he said.

"What?" She was starting to tumble away to sleep.

"I said, I'll take the case."

She dreamed she was floating down a rain-flooded street on a hot summer day. She was standing on a round snow-saucer, the kind that children use to sled down hills, turning as they go. She turned and turned, trying to keep from falling in the river that was now commanding the entire street. The river carried her past tall apartments, with steps leading up to them. Watching for the right one, she sprang at last from the saucer onto the front stairs of a large brownstone building.

A doorman in a red uniform with epaulets and brass buttons said: "We're ready to start."

She was climbing the stairs inside, her feet leaving muddy footprints on the white carpet. At the top stood the St. Croix girl, she of the long ponytail, the one they called Sooze. The girl stood with lustrous blond hair, wearing a white dress and leggings.

"Hurry!" Sooze said, laughing, running up floor after floor.

Hurry, hurry, came the chant of the hidden children. . . .

The air smelled like late summer, just on the turn to unbearably hot, with a tantalizing fragrance of baking fruit pie, like Mother made.

Mother looked at her watch. "I was afraid something happened to you," she said. Sooze reached for Abbey's hand and pulled her forward to the open door where everyone waited. Dad and Mother and Uncle Richard and Cousin Helen, all happy to see her.

Down the aisle, an aisle that stretched out a block long, stood the waiting minister, holding a tall lighted candle. From the mosaic glass windows, a rose-colored light stained the air, people's faces, Sooze's dress.

The girl was about to start the procession, but turned and ran to Abbey. "My shoes!" She was barefoot. Abbey gave Sooze her own boots, relieved that they fit, and then

Uncle Richard said, "Parents have to watch from the balcony." Abbey kissed Sooze on the top of her head and hurried for the balcony stairs as Mother and Dad waved at her from the pews.

At the bottom of the stairs, she noticed that she was in an older part of the church. The window was boarded up. Pieces of stained glass lay on the floor, shattered.

Cobwebs hit her bare shoulders. Why was she naked?

She opened the door and entered a cavernous, black room. This wasn't the balcony. She'd gotten it wrong. Those weren't the balcony stairs. The floorboards creaked like attics do.

Turning to find the door, Abbey found herself surrounded by a huge, vacant blackness. She was lost. She felt her despair rise in her throat and come out as thrumming music, softly pulsing against her temples, then filling the space around her, reverberating as though in a great drum. The sound grew and grew. And something hid in that sound, behind her. She spun around, blind.

Somewhere in the middle of the room was the light, with a long string to pull, and the drums would go away if she could turn the light on, and the thing that waited would go away, but it meant she had to wave her hand out in front of her, hitting cobwebs, touching the creature that waited for her, the slime and the insects.

But the ceremony below, the drums, she had to hurry. Where was the string? She knew it would be dripping with slime. She had to touch it. Frantically, she waved her hands, turning, turning. The light. The light. The drums boomed. The dark, the slime. She didn't care, she reached for the cord.

Pulled on it, flooding the attic with light . . .

"No," she heard herself say, the sound of her voice booming in her head.

"No, Myra, no."

Chapter 9

~1~

If you were over ten years old, you shouldn't wear loud colors, Simon decided. That was another thing he didn't like about Zachariah Smith's "Dimension Institute," besides being in the place on one of the few spring days lately when the sun actually bothered to show up. These idiots should try looking in a mirror sometime. Here was a young man dressed all in blue-green, giving his complexion the pallor of glue. And lounging over there next to the coffee stand was a plump woman doing a bright orange theme. Looked like a damn tomato. He supposed he looked a bit out of place, with his brown corduroy jacket, jeans, white shirt, and maroon tie. These clothes fit right in anywhere he'd ever been, except in this hive of crayon-colored kooks.

Simon waited until the coffee stand was clear of loud colors, and then bought himself a triple. He shook his head, thinking: Abbey McCrae asleep on my couch. Most

of the night he'd thought about that, lying awake, intensely aware of her. If he slept, damn if he noticed.
Maybe she'd had a restless night as well—she was sleeping when he left that morning.

What the hell ailed him, anyway? Fifty-four years and
he'd known exactly who he was: no one especially complicated; a straightforward guy with a penchant for good
books, hard truths, and ironic humor . . . especially at
the world taking itself too seriously. Willing to let the
ultimate question of life get settled in the Net chat rooms
while he wrestled with whether to take his burger with or
without cheese. And in the space of a few days he felt
alternately like a sadist and a love-struck teenager.

He walked past the Institute office again. A woman
dressed in red still sat at the desk. He checked his watch.
Maybe she'd leave for lunch. He hoped it'd be an early
one.

Simon wondered if they'd throw a fit if he lit up his
pipe out on the front steps. The health Nazis might blow a
circuit, but damn, Haskell, live on the edge. He pushed
through the double set of doors onto the ice-crusted front
stairs and stuffed his pipe, lighting the sweet, aromatic
tobacco and cupping the familiar bowl in his hand. Tobacco was a blessing, a misunderstood physical pleasure
in a world of mental meandering. He sucked on the pipe-
stem and felt his body relax. Probably killing himself with
this stuff, Abbey said. Well, since the woman had already
deprived him of every pleasure, could tobacco be far behind? When he wasn't worrying about what she thought
of *him*, he worried about what he thought of *her*, and
why she'd sunk a hook in his heart as big as an anchor,
and how he would exactly go on if she didn't reel him in.
Now, that was a bit of melodrama. How he would go on.

Get a grip, Haskell.

And this morning, when he wasn't—all right—mooning over Abbey, he was savoring last night's naughty pleasure, hooked up to the infernal game of Nir. After six
years of reliving that hour at Rocky's house, now comes a
new and improved—oh, vastly improved—edition. With
Rocky breaking down the door, and Lydia alive in

Rocky's arms and "I knew you'd come . . ." and then the act of perfect and immediate justice. Butchery, he would have called it on a better day. Not that he hadn't thought of killing the bastard. He'd thought it. But not . . . like that.

And then there was the question of the technology. What exactly was the virtual interface with the computer? He suspected—hell, he *knew*—the thrills and chills of this particular game were in his own sweet head. Maybe that weird, white light at the beginning was hypnotic. Then, combined with some kind of subliminal messaging from the program, the hapless gamester ends up paying a bunch of cash for his own damn daydream.

Except that it was an impossibly heightened daydream.

My God, the world was becoming an opium den of technological fantasy submersion. Was he right? Was he one of the few humanists left in a world of infantile pleasure-seekers? Or was he just an old man fighting against change?

The pipe was cold in his hand. He tapped out the bowl and slid the pipe into his jacket pocket. Screw it. He had work to do.

He pushed through the doors back into the musty halls just in time to see the woman in red leaving the building by a side door. He tried the Institute door. Locked. Picking this old lock was no problem except for drawing people's attention, especially the coffee-stand operator.

Simon climbed the stairs to the second floor, where only a few businesses anchored a mostly empty corridor. Finding an old-fashioned glass fire alarm, he pulled the handle and waited a few beats. As the alarm jumped into action, bellowing around him, he hurried down to the first floor, where people were swiftly leaving the building. Jimmying the lock, he slipped into the office, closing the door behind him.

As he quickly learned, the office was not a paper office. Most weren't, but he could always hope. He slammed another drawer shut and eyed the computer, where, perhaps, something of Vittoria McCrae lived electronically.

Something of Vittoria that a technophile like Rocky might retrieve, but not Simon.

Time to get out of view of the hallway, where the last stragglers hurried to obey the alarm. Down then to the far end of the office hall, where he spent a few minutes on a fancier lock on the door of Zachariah Smith. He opened the door a crack, to feel along the side of the doorjamb for sensing wires. Found them: the crumpled ridge of a wire so thin you had to close your eyes to feel it.

He closed the door slowly. Zachariah liked his privacy, and he could have it for now. This was just a reconnoiter.

Simon checked another office—empty—and then a storage room. Outside in the main corridor, he heard noises and shouts. Probably a fire crew arriving. He rifled through boxes, finding pamphlets and office supplies, but nothing to the point. Then, under a table in the back of the room, he spied sacks, duffel sacks, bulging full. When he opened one and reached inside, his hand grabbed a fuzzy package, recognizable even before he pulled it out and stared at the grey, oval mass. As he pulled it apart, the contents sprang into his hand like a jumping insect released from an egg. The visor lay wet and glistening amid the coils of electrical wire. It was Nir all right. Hundreds of them. Zachariah was selling this shit, but not outright. He was funneling it to some street outlet. If Nir had been hard to come by—and Abbey said so—the shortage was about to end. He shoved the duffel back into place and turned his attention to slipping away before the red lady—or Zachariah—came back.

He waited by the office door until people began coming in the building, then made a hasty exit, putting on his best blank expression. In this business you learned how to look ordinary and innocent, no matter what villainy you were up to. It was easy to look innocent. He *was* innocent—in the larger sense of things. He'd done worse in this business. And never for profit, not directly. Always the highest motives, Haskell, highest motives, now get the hell out of here before they throw your ass in jail.

Across the street at a pay phone, he punched in his credit password and then Rocky's mobile number.

"Rocky, it's me."

"How's tricks at the Institute?" Rocky asked.

"Terrific. How about you, you got anything?" Simon watched as the fire trucks rumbled away.

"You should see what I got. Seems our brothers in blue are squirreling away a thick file on people who just up and disappeared lately. Now, I haven't seen this file, but we're talkin' lots of homeless—you can bet *they're* not a high priority—but also some regular folks."

Simon considered. "How come nobody ever heard of this?"

"Dunno. I had to take a cop to breakfast just to find out all this. Cost me twenty-five bucks, pal. You covering expenses?"

The line clicked and an automated voice came on. "This account is overdue and your call is being terminated." Shit.

"Jesus, Haskell, you late paying again?"

"Look Rocky, give Abbey a call will you? She's at my place. . . ."

"*Your* place?"

"Yeah, she had a bad night."

"I'm not surprised."

"Just see if she's OK. . . ."

The line went dead. Simon glared at the receiver. Goddamn phone. "Check's in the mail, you great, slow-witted pile of electronic crap." He hung up a little too hard. Didn't anyone know how to open an envelope anymore? If it wasn't electronic, they got confused. Didn't fit in the system. That was the problem with systems. They rejected everything that didn't fit in, no matter how relevant.

Like Simon himself, he admitted.

Rocky knocked on Simon's apartment door. Abbey hadn't answered the phone, so he figured to drop by in person. He wasn't sure it was a good idea, Simon getting personally involved with his clients. Hell, he *knew* it wasn't a good idea.

A woman's voice came through the door. "Who is it?"

"Rocky Ginestra."

A pause. "What do you want?"

"Simon asked me to check on you."

In a few beats the door opened. "Why did he want you to check on me?"

He took a new, appraising look at her. Nice-looking, Rocky had to admit. Pretty damn good-looking, in fact, but that was no excuse.

She opened the door wider and stepped back for him to enter. "Rocky," she said as soon as he was inside and she'd shut the door, "something's come up. I've got to go. Tell Simon I've gone to Zachariah's ranch." She began folding a blanket heaped on the couch. Maybe that was where she'd spent the night.

"Zachariah's ranch, huh? That a good idea?"

"Maybe not. But he just e-mailed me, so I'm going. Before he changes his mind." She gathered her purse and jacket and turned to him.

He was standing there, barring the door. Simon wasn't going to like her traipsing off to this bad-ass without some cover. "I'll come with you," he said.

Abbey's forehead wrinkled for a moment.

Rocky went on: "This Zachariah sounds like he could cause trouble. Didn't you say you needed a helper?"

"Where's Simon?"

"He's checking some stuff out. You wanna wait for him?"

She pursed her lips, then checked her watch. "Zachariah said twelve noon." She pulled on her jacket. "You can come if you want." Then she brushed past him, out the door.

He took out a piece of paper and jotted Simon a note: "Off to Z's ranch. I'll watch out for her. Get a mobe, will ya?" He left the note on the coffee table and hurried after Abbey.

~ 2 ~

Just down the road from Zachariah's ranch, Rocky hesitated before getting out of the car. "Are you sure you want to do this?"

Want might be the wrong word, but, "Yes. I'm sure," Abbey said.

"I don't know if you're gutsy or stupid."

"Me either."

After a pause, he said, "Give me a few minutes. Then go ahead. If he tries anything, just tone me out on your mobe. I'll be on him like a cheap suit." He patted her knee. "If he even looks at you cross-eyed, you punch in my button, you listening?"

"What if he has a security system or something? Or guards patrolling."

Rocky smiled. "I've crawled through backyards laced with land mines and faced off with Pakistani suicide squads. Don't worry." He gave her a thumbs-up and got out of the car, heading for the deep woods adjacent to Zachariah's property.

Abbey locked the doors and waited. This felt like overdoing things. Two detectives helping her. Planning to signal Rocky if Zachariah got out of hand. *No kidding,* she heard Vitt say. *Go ahead, totally dumb yourself.*

Abbey answered the voice: Looking cool isn't everything, my dear. The palms of her hands tingled, as though her body knew more than her head, knew to keep the hell away from Zachariah, knew to stay out of Jaguar's strange conspiracy. Knew she wasn't going to.

The windows were fogging up, making it hard to keep watch. Rocky had melted into the woods. As a car or two sped past her, she rolled down her window and let in the cold, bright day. Then, after checking her watch for the umpteenth time, she started the engine, pulling out onto the highway. Just beyond the next curve, where a stand of skeletal poplars marked Zachariah's property, she pulled into the driveway.

He was standing on the front porch. That threw her for a moment. Abbey clasped her locket a moment, caressing its lacy-rough surface, and, taking another deep breath, got out of the car, walking to the foot of the stairs. In his yellow tunic with black tights and boots, Zachariah looked curiously mismatched against the formal white porch.

"I'm glad you found time for me," she said, forcing her voice into its deepest tones.

He nodded. "Come in, Abbey."

She followed him into the great house, between two white pillars that gave the impression of established grandeur, not simple sleaze—but it was all a practiced image, as everything about this man was creation, his own creation. While she kept up a steady steam of conversation, he hung her coat up in the hallway closet. "You live here alone? A big place like this?" Her voice had a disconnected, amplified quality in this tiled hallway, sounding for a moment eerily like Vitt.

"Do you find that unusual?"

"No. Well . . . yes, I suppose."

He led her into the parlor where he took a seat in a chair opposite her. A fire crackled in the fireplace. "Nice," she said, smiling at the fire.

"I wanted you to feel comfortable."

On the wall behind him hung a painting of a woman leaning against one of the white pillars; her blond hair swept over one eye, but with the other she fixed Abbey with a cold, appraising stare. They sat in silence for a long moment. Finally Abbey said, "I don't know how these things are supposed to go."

"No." He raised his chin, frankly staring at her.

"I'm sorry about the first time we met, Mr. Smith. I was . . ."

"Zachariah, please." He picked idly at the brocaded arm of his wingback chair, as though mildly bored.

"Yes. Zachariah. I was upset. Upset to think Vittoria was involved with the Dimension Institute. She never told me. It hurt."

"How did you know she studied with us?" His voice was calm and deep, like his posture as he sat there, settled into the chair, seemingly relaxed and reflective. She realized she was sitting on the edge of her own chair. She put her purse on the floor and sat back.

The lie was ready: "I found a letter she wrote to her dad. She never sent it. It mentioned that she was happy at the Institute. It seemed harmless. But, from what I've heard of you . . ." She paused, in feigned embarrassment. "I'm sorry."

"What have you heard about me, Abbey?"

"Folks in Medicine Falls aren't very tolerant, Zachariah."

He cocked his head. "And you?"

"Me?"

"Yes, you."

A pop from the fireplace made her jump.

He smiled.

"I'm not used to being around a psychologist." She thought she'd flatter him. To her surprise, she thought maybe he *was* flattered.

"You're a lot like Vittoria." He looked at her a few beats. From the bank of windows behind her, the sun flooded the room, gilding his tunic in a fiery display. "Did you know that?"

It was designed to be an intimate statement. She *felt* that, deflected it: "Thank you. She was a wonderful girl."

"But I won't appreciate it if you make trouble for me and my work."

"Trouble?" Her stomach contracted, forcing the word out a little too high. He had veered off from pleasantries and lobbed this to test her return shot.

"My work is to serve, Abbey. To help people expand in ways that transform their lives. I can't do that very well if townspeople make up stories about me and undermine my credibility."

Abbey leaned into her game. "I'm not undermining you, Zachariah. I've come to learn from you. Believe me."

He sprang up from his chair and strode to the fireplace, picking up a poker and jabbing at the burning logs. "But you've mentioned me to the police?"

"No!"

He turned to face her. "Others?"

"Others? Look, I'm really starting to feel like I'm on the witness stand. Was this why you decided to see me?"

He stood there with the poker, eyeing her with that same sardonic coolness as the woman in the painting. "No. But your behavior has been a little strange. And I need to be sure you're sincere."

Abbey thought of Rocky and the reassuring mobe in her purse. She eyed the poker, sure that despite the smiles and the velvety voice, he could erupt, could lose the control he so carefully cultivated. Yet she wasn't ready to call for help, not by a long shot. Zachariah was only probing her motives, all to be expected.

"I've been a little strange," she admitted. "This is what people tell me. Maybe I'd like to move past it, and maybe being here is a start."

"I'd like to hope so." He replaced the poker in its nest and remained standing, back to the fire, hands clasped behind him. "But I can't know for certain, can I?"

He wasn't moving away from the topic of trust. Not good. "Do you ever," Abbey ventured, "know anyone for certain?"

"But you, Abbey, have many secrets."

"Secrets?"

"Oh, I think so." Abruptly, he said: "Do you think it's cold in here? Come sit by the fire." He sat down on the floor next to the hearth and gestured for her to join him.

He was good, this one. Come sit by me, Abbey, show some trust. Hoping the smile she pasted on wasn't as phony as it felt, she rose and joined him on the floor, sitting cross-legged.

Zachariah watched the fire for a few moments, then looked over at her, an arm's distance away. "We all have secrets, you see. We hold on to them, thinking they're treasures. But they're trash. Give them away and you're cleared up for your real work. Your deep work."

"My problems aren't secret. I've given them to everyone who'll listen."

He looked into her eyes with an intimate, unswerving gaze until she looked away. "You're being secretive," he said.

Damn, but he could manipulate. She thrust against the current of his intention—toward her own. "I think you're being secretive, too." And looked into his pale, blue eyes. In those depths, she felt sure, swam a pathetic creature, a bottom-dweller, with no tolerance of sunlight. But she looked at him steadily.

He blinked. "This isn't about me."

"But I need to trust too, don't I?" In the ensuing silence, she pushed on: "There's something I'd like to do. But I'm not sure if you'd be interested."

"Why don't you try me?"

"Nir. I'd like to play the game that Vittoria was into. With you."

A twitch in his cheek was the only indication that he might be surprised. Might be intrigued. "That's very tempting. It could speed up our work." He watched her closely. "But I'm afraid I don't have a game set here at home."

She was certain that was a lie. But she was ready: "I do."

A chime rang out, a repeating bell tone, issuing from the foyer. Zachariah looked at her sharply, then rose in one, athletic motion. "Wait here."

When he'd left the room, Abbey scrambled to her feet. An alarm. She rushed to the window, drawing aside the curtain. Outside, the porch and the gravel driveway were empty, but she knew that the alarms had reason to scream. Knew that it must be Rocky who'd set them off. Knew it was time to leave.

The alarm bell subsided, but her own alarm still raged. Over, it was over before it had begun, her match with Zachariah. She headed for the door, stopping to peek into the foyer. No one. She judged the distance to the front door, then charged back to the tall parlor windows, looking for an inside release to crawl out a window. But the windows were fixed panes, every one. She ran back toward the foyer. She bolted across the entryway and turned the doorknob.

"Abbey."

His voice stopped her. As she turned, she saw him standing there, with a gun.

"Maybe I'll just shoot you now and get it over with."

"Zachariah. What are you doing?" Her voice warbled, escaping from her throat like a trapped bird.

"What are *you* doing?"

He was pointing a gun at her, a *gun*, with a spiral of sensing wires flaring, searching for their target. "I want to go home. You scare me." Her hand was still gripping the doorknob. In a split second she could be outside. Could be dead.

"Come here, Abbey."

When she didn't move, he said: "The rules are extremely simple now. We're not playing cat and mouse any longer." He lifted the gun a fraction. "The cat won. Come here."

Her mouth was dry and sour. She couldn't speak, even if she could think of something to say. She walked slowly across the tile floor toward him, waiting for Rocky to burst in upon them, waiting for something to happen to turn the tide of events. Things would not end this way, not murdered by the same man who murdered Vitt. Not this way.

Not, as the last hellish piece, to die in ignorance.

He latched on to her arm and thrust her in front of him. Opening the hall closet, he grabbed two coats and handed hers to her. "Down there," he said, pointing to a door leading back, deeper into the house. They walked into a narrow corridor, lights flicking on as they approached, the House leading them into its depths, a smiling, witless tour guide.

"Who's your friend out there, Abbey?"

"Friend?"

"The one trapped in my net. That's why you were leaving, wasn't it? Because you knew your friend tripped my alarms?"

He poked her in the back when she didn't answer. "Well?"

"I came alone. I don't know who it is."

"Let's go ask *him,* then."

Her thoughts were scattering like oil on water, she couldn't grab them. Nothing cohered, and meanwhile he pushed her along faster, through a kitchen, all stainless steel and uncluttered, on toward a back door and then a sunny mud room. "Please Zachariah, if you have an intruder, I understand why you'd use a gun. But don't turn it on me."

He swung her around to face him. They were outside, with a bright sun overhead. "Shut up. No more lies. You're nothing but lies." His face crumpled at the edges. "I knew you were lying." His voice compacted, words now coming fast: "That's why I brought you here. I knew you were snooping in my fields. I know all about you, oh yes. And if you tell me another miserable lie, I'll kill you on the spot."

"Okay, no lies. But if you kill me, the police will come looking, Zachariah."

"No. The police don't listen to you. You're a crank, a loser. Or so they tell me."

He gestured her to move on, down a brick walkway. Then led her off the path and through the shrubbery toward the woods until the sky was cloaked by a dense pack of trees.

He prodded her in the back and she hurried on, while under her feet the ground crunched like small, brittle bones. In her path, a squirrel lay frozen, its wide-open eyes capturing a last moment of panic. Then she saw a crow covered with a mottled rime of ice and twitching feebly. A coldness began to replace the first surge of hot fear, as though her body had shed every nonessential thing except muscle and cunning.

Rocky lay next to a creek, one leg in the water, the side of his face in the mud. His eyes were open and he blinked, but the rest of him didn't move.

Zachariah nudged him with his foot. "Who are you?"

But no sound from him. He lay as though paralyzed.

Zachariah swung the gun around, pointing it at Abbey's head. "Tell me your name or I'll shoot her face off."

Rocky's eyes squinted with an effort to speak. He grunted his name, unintelligible.

Abbey said, "It's Rocky Ginestra. A friend of mine."

"Get his wallet and if he has a weapon, take it out and throw it over here. Don't touch the frost."

She kneeled down next to Rocky. "God, I'm sorry," she whispered. He was covered with an uneven cocoon of a shiny, transparent film, like the animals.

Abbey found Rocky's billfold in his jacket pocket, and his gun in a holster under his arm. She threw the wallet to Zachariah. Going back into the jacket for the gun, her wrist scraped on a bit of the rime, tingling her skin like acupuncture needles. She withdrew the gun, being more careful. As she threw the gun to Zachariah, the needles marched down into the back of her hand.

Zachariah picked up Rocky's gun and stuffed it in his pocket. Then he pawed through the billfold. "Rocky Ginestra, Private Investigations." He looked sharply up at her. "Lies. That's all you are. Lies."

"I was afraid to come here alone. But the reason I came here, that's not a lie, Zachariah."

"You think I'm that dumb?" His eyes, nodes of blue ice, stripped her of every remaining defense. From his jacket pocket he extracted a bag, the size of his thumb. Yanking it apart, he set it on Rocky's stomach, where what looked like sand poured out onto Rocky's jacket, dissolving the cocoon in an ever-widening circle. He noticed her watching him. "The frost," he said, nodding. "A little present from my guests."

"Guests?"

He gestured at Rocky. "Get him up."

Abbey stepped forward to steady Rocky as he rose to his feet, staggering. While he leaned on her, together they lumbered back through the woods, across Zachariah's backyard and around to the opposite side of the house. His weight was like a huge sandbag loaded on her shoulder, slowing their progress to a crawl, but giving her time to think, to hope, despite her desperate situation. He could have killed them both by the stream. He wanted them alive. . . .

He urged them toward the barn. As they stumbled into the barnyard, a rancid smell hit Abbey's nostrils, the instantly recognizable odor from the cow pasture, the odor that wasn't cows, that even in this extremity made her stomach rebel.

Zachariah was pushing her forward into the twilight of the barn interior, where the smell subsided amid the pungent, decent smell of hay and manure. He threw her a coil of rope and had her tie Rocky's hands and feet. When she finished she looked up at Zachariah, taking another stab at engaging his common sense, his humanity, or any handhold at all on this sheer cliff. "Why are you doing this?"

"You always want to know why, don't you?"

"Zachariah. You're not a murderer." She rose and faced him. "You're a psychologist. A healer. Killing isn't your way. You have your Institute. Are you going to throw all that away?" Abbey's hand was growing cold and tingly.

"You think the Dimension Institute matters?" As his voice rose in pitch, it broke like an adolescent's. "You people, none of you know what I can do. Medicine Falls doesn't know. You don't know my true power."

"All I see is a man with a gun. That's easy, Zachariah. That's not true power."

"A woman like you hates to admit a man's power. You don't give respect. And you're too stupid to know when to be afraid."

"You *wish* I was afraid. I'm not."

"You will be." He motioned with the gun toward the barn door.

Back out in the barnyard the estate was quiet. No police to the rescue, no Simon, not even a bird sound, only the intermittent sound of cars on the road.

"It might be fun to pay a call on my guests," he said.

"Guests?" The stench now saturated the air, making her loath to bring it into her lungs.

"The creators of the glory game. I'm going to be a very rich man, Abbey. A very powerful man." He pushed her along a walk where packed snow was turning to slush in the noon sun. "And all they ask in return is a few . . . playthings."

"Playthings?"

"I call them donations."

They stood in front of a low outbuilding, weathered and radiating that sharp, hot odor. Here was the source of the miasmic stench, there could be no doubt.

He nodded at the three sagging stairs leading to the main doorway. "Open the door. And stay absolutely quiet. Any kind of fuss, and they could kill you. Do you understand?"

He was bluffing, trying to terrorize her. Bluffing. But: "I don't want to go in," she heard herself saying.

"I know!" he whispered. His face loomed close, his eyes trying to glean something from her. . . . "Open it."

The gun was against her back. She stepped up to the door. White paint was peeling off the door panels like the sloughing of dried skin. From the field behind the bunkhouse, the lowing of a cow seemed to warn her, don't enter, but he was pushing her in the back, and she opened the door, Zachariah stepping in behind her.

A dim light seeped in through the heavily curtained windows. She stood in a small room with a coffee table and plaid couch, and the almost palpable presence of the smell. Off to the left was a closed door toward which Zachariah urged her.

"Be very quiet. They sleep during the day. Acclimatizing. Sensitive skin, actually. They're not from here, believe me." He put the muzzle of the gun up to her temple, then reached past her and opened the door wide.

At first all Abbey could see was a row of beds. Square borders of light defined eight boarded-up windows, four on one side, and four on the other side over the beds.

The bunks were occupied.

Nearest to her, she could see one of Zachariah's guests. Not . . . human, no. A short yet massive creature with an ovoid head. She scanned down its torso to its impossibly thick legs, like long stumps, and flat circular feet pointing toward her, with toenails like short, grey beaks. Abbey stepped backward, bumping against Zachariah, who put his arm around her waist, holding her tightly against him, gun still against her temple. She began to shiver. The darkened room, the smell, the . . . toes, it was monstrous, she had to get out, leave now.

Zachariah held her firmly and whispered, "Meet my guests. Oh yes. Want a closer look?"

Abbey shook her head, saying No, but No wouldn't quite come out, and meanwhile she was pushing her body back against Zachariah as he pressed forward to meet her.

"Shhh," he said. "We don't want to wake them, believe me." He walked forward, pushing her along, closer to the bunk. She turned, trying to push Zachariah backward, backward toward the door. He shook his head, one slow, back-and-forth movement, and savoring her reaction. He turned her firmly around, and she looked down on the creature.

Its face had two heavily lidded eyes—closed—and a mouth, very wide and thin. The head melded into a broad, short torso clothed in what might be leather. Like the shape in the cow pasture that night, the head sloped to the shoulders in a huge, neckless mass. Muddy-red skin, the color of old brick, with a short nap, like horsehide and scarred in places, or tattooed. Two arms lay at rest at its side—beefy upper arms tapering somewhat to muscular lower arms and blocky, four-digit hands. From the wrists, a thick flap of hide extruded halfway over the hands, in a half glove.

To the left, in the next bunk, an identical . . . Hhso. It stirred, eyelids twitching.

All was silent except for the squeak of the floorboards under Abbey and Zachariah's feet, and the occasional ping of the electric baseboards, which filled the room with a hot and reeking soup.

Abbey's thoughts were only to flee that room, except for a thread of logic that kept superimposing explanations over the eight sleeping forms: constructs, automatons, mutants, animals, disguised humans, creatures from another world—the attempts at matches failed, could not stick, and she felt her body backing away . . . felt Zachariah relenting, pulling her slowly backward several steps.

"We could wake them," he whispered to her. "They

wake instantly. And they . . . react instantly. Let's see
what they'll do."

"No. Zachariah. Let's not . . ."

"Oh?" He sounded mock-disappointed. "No curiosity?" Then, turning her around, he guided her toward the
door to the outer room. He prodded her through the
door, and all the while the back of her head bristled lest
the creatures get up from their bunks and follow her. The
stench cut a path down her throat, an invading taste that
turned her stomach into a cauldron. . . . She began to
retch, while Zachariah hurried her out the door, shoving
her down the steps, onto her knees in the muddy snow.
Her stomach spasmed and spasmed. When she was done,
she bathed her face in snow. Then she turned to
Zachariah, standing above her, contemptuous. "For
God's sake, what *are* they?"

"Hhso." He cocked his head. "You don't like them?"

Hhso . . . my god, these were the Hhso . . .
"They're disgusting."

"Ah yes. The famous open mind of Medicine Falls."

"Open mind!" Abbey got to her feet. "What *are* they?
What kind of—animals . . ."

"I told you. They're not from here. Now get moving."
He motioned her back down the path.

Abbey looked back at him as she walked. "What hold
do they have over you?" When he didn't answer, she continued: "They'll kill us all. You know that?"

"You're scared shitless, aren't you, you helpless bitch?"
He pushed her along, toward the barn. "You're scared of
everything. Scared of me too."

"I'm not scared of you, don't flatter yourself." No, not
once she'd seen the Hhso.

Zachariah grabbed her arm and yanked her toward the
barn door. "We'll see who's not afraid." He jammed her
in the back, pushing her into the barn, where she stumbled to her knees. Bright squares of light from missing
roof shingles and dust-occluded windows poked through
the darkness to create a hazy atmosphere, redolent of
straw and rotting wood.

A voice came from the recessed shadows. "Drop the gun, Zachariah, or you're a dead man."

Simon. Simon Haskell's voice. The sound of what might be a gun cocking.

Zachariah pivoted to one side, then the other, waving his gun in several directions. Abbey began inching away. But Zachariah zeroed in on her. "I'll kill her," he said.

Abbey lay almost touching a scorched circle in the center of the barn.

"And then you'll die. I have a bead on your head."

A moan. Rocky stirred. The ropes around his feet were loosened, as much of the job as Simon must have had time to do.

"Throw the gun out, Zachariah."

A long moment passed. Finally Zachariah pitched his gun onto the wooden slats of the barn floor.

Simon walked out of the nearest stall, holding a pistol. "Put your hands behind your head."

Slowly, Zachariah did so. "I have friends nearby," he said in a quavery voice. "Dangerous friends. She can tell you." He turned toward her, trying to net her with his eyes.

"Yeah, good for you." Simon stooped to help Abbey to her feet. Her head swam from Zachariah's blow. She staggered against Simon, and with one foot he stepped a few centimeters into the blackened circle.

"All of you are trespassing on my property," Zachariah said. "I had a right to protect myself." His voice, turning deep and commanding, assumed its disguise of civility.

"I think you used a bit of unnecessary force with Ms. McCrae and my partner here."

"Ah. So you are a detective also, yes?"

Simon shifted his weight. His foot was now firmly planted in the circle.

"Rocky," Simon asked, turning to him, "do you have your mobe?"

Rocky struggled to rise, failed. He fumbled to pull it from his wrist. "You finally admit," his voice came harsh and breathless, "that you need one?" He slid it along the floor toward Simon, who picked it up.

Then a humming sound, and a molten loop suddenly formed on the floor around Simon. Startled, he jerked away from the circle as though stung. In the same moment, Zachariah's hand plunged into his jacket pocket and he stepped forward, his hand balled into a fist as though squeezing something. Out from his hand spewed a thin stream that hit Simon in the leg, and another that spurted over his head. His gun dropped from his hand as he sank to one knee.

Rushing forward, Zachariah grabbed up the gun and stood gasping for breath. Finally he said, "I'm getting real tired of you, Abbey. You and your hired guns."

He shoved one gun into his pocket and strode over to Rocky, grabbing the back of his jacket collar. Pushing the barrel of his gun in Rocky's face, he snarled, "Get over here." Rocky crawled in the direction Zachariah was pulling, until he lay crumpled in the now quiescent circle.

Zachariah backed away several meters. "Now let's see who's not afraid."

He kept the gun pointed at them until at last a hoop of fire crackled to life on the barn floorboards. It traced a circle around Rocky except for where his arms and one leg sprawled outside of its confines. The bright crack widened as pressure appeared to build from underneath the floorboards, and filaments leapt up, traveling like mycelium in fast-forward, reaching, shooting upward to form a cone up to the rafters of the barn. Through the million hairlike roots, the cone interior appeared bleary, as though turned to gel.

Now, as he struggled to rise, Rocky created trails of motion, as though he were in more than one position, in fact many positions, all at the same time. He turned to Simon and Abbey, and his eyes might have seen them through the tracery around him, for he stretched out one arm in their direction. In a matching movement, Simon did the same, while struggling to his feet. Then a great Hhso flickered into existence, its massive form straddling Rocky's body. It lifted him by the head, so that amid a growing crackling sound a pronounced snap could be heard. In the next instant this scene contracted to a spinning disk as the fizzing noise rose out of hearing range. A hole appeared in the center of the disk, growing larger and larger until nothing was left but a ring of molten light. Rocky and the Hhso disappeared.

All of this took only a few seconds. Simon's charge forward came too late, leaving him staggering around where Rocky had vanished.

The next thing Abbey heard was a great roar that filled the barn, an animal bellow that might have come from a slaughterhouse. It was Simon. She saw him lunge forward at Zachariah though Zachariah fired the pistol directly at him. Turning and running, Zachariah made it to the barn door before Simon collided with him, bursting the barn door wide open.

Abbey ran out into the barnyard, transfixed for a split second by the ferocity of Simon's attack on Zachariah, who now lay beneath Simon trying to shield his face from blows. Then, in the corner of her eye, she caught a movement. Turning, she saw a short, massive form moving down the pathway at the side of the barn. It moved slowly, in a plodding, syncopated lope, but the path was short. "Simon! Behind you!" Abbey hollered, her voice subsumed amid Simon's continued bellow and Zachariah's screams.

And then she was running toward the ranch house. In her jacket pocket somewhere were her car keys. Fumbling for them as she ran, and still screaming at Simon, she strained her legs to carry her faster, calculating her chances, the timing of it all, which seemed a few seconds short of possible. Reaching the car, she managed to get her hand on the keys, and yanked the car door open and jumped in, stabbing the key at the ignition, missing, thrusting again and then hitting the slot, as a second later, the car throbbed to life.

In the next instant she was thundering over the lawn and onto the muddy barnyard.

Simon looked up at the approaching car, still straddling Zachariah, apparently unaware of the creature just rounding the corner of the barn and a second Hhso close behind the first.

She leaned across the front seat to throw the passenger seat door open. "Behind you!" she yelled.

And then still holding Zachariah down, Simon turned around. The first Hhso lumbered forward, a broad mass of compact muscle, a foot shorter than Simon, advancing in jackhammer steps, now close enough that Abbey could see the color of its eyes, a deep, creamy brown. Simon crawled off Zachariah and started backing up slowly.

"Get in!" All she could see of Simon was his back. "Get in the damn car!"

The brick-colored form was stomping forward, as Simon backed up another step, and another. "What in the name of God . . ." she heard him say.

"Get in!"

The Hhso raised its forearm, extending a finger, and pointed at Simon. Abbey hauled herself across the seat toward the passenger-side door, leaned partway out of the car, and yanked on Simon's arm with her full strength. He staggered slightly, muttering, "Jesus H. . . ." In the next moment Simon threw himself into the front seat of the car, slamming the door shut with great force. For a moment Simon's window was eclipsed by the creature, just before a thousand cracks slithered across the pane, and just as Abbey slammed her foot on the accelerator, jolting them both back against the seat. They sped across the barnyard, where they hit a patch of lawn, and sank a few inches into a shady patch of snow. The car wheels sped uselessly.

"Let me drive!" Simon ordered.

"Shut up!" The wheels spun and spun. She threw it in reverse. The same. Finally Simon yanked on her arm and she relented, sliding under as Simon climbed over her, cursing.

"Can't drive a goddamn car!" he was shouting as bullets began thudding into the vehicle.

"And you don't have the brains God gave a turnip!" she screamed back.

"Get down on the floor!"

But there was no time as the car lurched out of its rut and the tires connected with gravel, and she was thrown sharply to one side as they rounded the corner of the driveway. They swung onto the wrong side of the road, then wildly corrected to miss a truck, and, finding solid traction at last, sped away.

Chapter 10

~1~

In the bunkhouse, Zachariah stood before the Hhso, his face hotly swelling and his rib cage aching. *Simon was a dead man.* Yes, and soon. Zachariah clung to this thought, a healing salve against the humiliation of the blows, the loss of Abbey. . . . They were the next donations, the next to embrace the Hhso.

"I need a chair," Zachariah said.

The chief Hhso, the one he called Big Dog, gestured toward a chair by the door.

Zachariah dragged it forward and fell heavily into it. He found himself thinking that with his nose bleeding, at least he didn't have to smell the bastards.

Big Dog's heavy-lidded eyes glanced at the coffee table. Zachariah had forgotten to get the slate they used to talk to him. *His* speech was no problem for the Hhso; but *their* speech, that conglomeration of glottal smacks and susurrations, might as well have been modem static for all the sense it made. He dragged himself up again. As he reached for the tablet, a drop of blood fell from his nose on the coffee table. He hurriedly brushed at it with his hand, smearing it. Big Dog smiled, with a horizontal crack in his face beyond which could be seen a few flat teeth. It smells with its mouth, he thought, hurriedly reshuffling his idea of the Hhso smile.

There was another Hhso in the room, the smaller one with a few long hairs bristling from a patch on its . . . neck. He called this one Little Dog. Occasionally it made noises and gestures, sitting there in the overstuffed armchair, filling it from side to side with four hundred pounds of alien muscle and bone.

When Zachariah settled back in his chair, Big Dog began speaking. From a deep recess inside its mouth issued the Hhso-speech. Its mouth barely moved, and when it did, it wasn't clear that it was connected to the speaking. Perhaps it was a twitch, or a gesture.

On the tablet appeared block lettering:

Identify the members who prepared you.

Sometimes they got words wrong. *Prepared* had to be wrong. But Zachariah knew what they were asking. "Abbey and Simon. Abbey follows me to find out about her dead child. Simon works for her. They will notify the police."

More guttural clicks.

Where are the herds of these ones?

They'd used that term, *herds,* before. Zachariah assigned it the best meaning he could. "They don't really have followers. Abbey has no family. Simon Haskell, I don't know. But they'll call the police. A big herd." She was a nuisance, his police sources told him. But the police would surely investigate, nuisance or not. He had to run, throw his things together, grab Lonnie from the . . .

The slate was forming a new message:

We know this herd. This herd will help you prepare these ones.

"The police are your enemy. They will hurt you." And me. When the police get an eyeful of you fat bastards, he thought, all hell will break loose, especially if you start that squirting business. "You should hide. Before the police arrive."

The police do not arrive.

Zachariah stared at these words, hope surging for a moment. *The police do not arrive.* Clearly, the Hhso were not alarmed, were perhaps in control in some way. . . . He looked again at these repulsive creatures wondering just how far their abilities went. . . .

"Abbey will call the police. They will bring guns."

The police member Dern will call Zachariah. This herd will help you.

"Why would the police help us?" He was mightily confused. Who else did the Hhso deal with? He liked to think they relied on him alone. And then a hairline crack threaded across his concept of the Hhso. Unbidden, the idea flitted into his mind of the game, and the visors, being part of a communication system . . . which could be useful, yes, but which meant that . . . that he was perhaps only one of several, or one of many, business partners. . . .

The slate formed the words:

This herd are calm.

Calm. That was a familiar Hhso word. Sometimes it seemed to mean loyal. Or happy. And if the police were *happy*, maybe they weren't a problem just now. Maybe all was not lost. He smiled. Maybe there was hope.

You are damaged?

Zachariah puzzled once more, then realized that the Hhso were responding to his facial expression. "No. I was smiling. I'm happy—calm."

Big Dog leaned forward, his hands braced on the sofa cushion.

Zachariah separates from the Hhso?

This question startled Zachariah. Big Dog's lids retracted to produce a dark stare from the egg-sized eyes. "No! Not separated."

You play the herd game?

A gargling sound from Little Dog snagged his attention. What were they talking about? He'd been told not to play Nir. So that was easy. Were they asking about disobedience? "I never played Nir. Only observed. Second player."

Big Dog remained canted forward, staring unblinking at him, the couch creaking under the stress of the creature's weight.

Never play Nir. In primary position.

"No."

No?

Zachariah grew hot underneath the jacket. He dared not move. "I will not play Nir. I stay with Hhso." He had the sudden alarming sense that the creature was going to strike him.

But after a moment Big Dog sat back up, his movement matched by a protesting squeak of the sofa frame. Another noise to one side of the room brought Zachariah's attention to the door to the sleeping quarters. The door slowly opened, revealing a Hhso wearing something Zachariah had never seen before, a close-fitting head cap, crusted over with shiny humps and ridges. Behind him, several others with bare heads. They watched him, quietly. Beneath the short, creamy-yellow leather of their tunics jutted the columnar legs upon which they swayed unsteadily, as though gravity could not quite hold them.

From between the foremost two Hhso, the tube-creature sidled to the front. It had two thin, almost normal arms, one on each side, and another, shorter pair protruding from its chest. The top body unit of the creature's three-part, segmented body bore a round orifice that Zachariah thought of as a mouth. Otherwise faceless, the creature nevertheless appeared to be watching him along with its Hhso companions or masters. Zachariah had seen it bring bags of food to Big Dog, bags with feeding siphons attached, from which the leader drew an occasional sip. So it was likely a servant, or perhaps a robot, the way it rested on a cushion of air.

Big Dog took no notice of the assembled watchers. Instead, the message came:

There is no price now for the herd game.

Zachariah grew faint from the tension and stuffiness of the room, his face so hot it felt like it would blister off, and the odor beginning to filter past his blood-caked nostrils. . . . "I don't understand," he finally managed to say.

There is no price now for the herd game.

Zachariah waited, a vein throbbing in his temple. The lesser Hhso creatures watched from the bunk room, passive, looking for all the world like curious children spying on parents.

You give away to all.

"Give away?"

You give away to all herd members.

This couldn't be right. They had never told him what he could and couldn't charge. Nir was his reward for providing donations. "The price is important to me," he said, starting to smile in a conciliatory manner, then wiping it.

Now Little Dog also canted forward. The stench in the room was making him sick. It seemed to hang in the air in layers, drifting, so that the smell hit his nostrils in nauseous waves.

You refuse?

"No, I don't refuse. But . . . I feel bad." He was wary of the Hhso leaning forward like that, but he just had to press on: "Don't you need the donations I bring?"

Find these ones Abbey and Simon. Kill these ones. The police herd now help you. This one Renalda now helps you.

They didn't answer questions. It was maddening. But they didn't understand how things worked. "She won't help me. She's Abbey's . . . friend."

This one helps the Hhso.

"She'll make trouble. Renalda is . . . in Abbey's herd."

Renalda lives the life of Nir.

Zachariah's thoughts floated in a suspended, expectant state. Any moment they would coalesce into meaning . . . and then, like dots connecting in a child's puzzle, the outline emerged, of hundreds of visored people plugged into one great, pulsing machine. It was hideous. But audacious, and in its absolute control, also thrilling.

Except now they didn't need him. If they weren't trading Nir for his donations, then they didn't *need* him.

The two Hhso had been in conversation, and now projected onto the slate:

Provide Nir to all. Go away.

It was so confusing. The police would help him. But: *Give Nir to all? Give?* Why would they think he would serve them now?

Go away.

Little Dog smiled. It was not attractive, that spreading crack on its face. Zachariah hesitated, thinking to protest once more. They were the cash cows, he needed the . . .

In an instant, Big Dog lurched to his feet. Tilting to the side with his entire body, and raising his arm, he struck the coffee table with a mallet-sized fist. The movement seemed no more than a bow, but the heavy wood table shattered into two pieces with an explosive, sundering crack. Zachariah staggered to his feet, chest hammering, brain urging him to flee, feet locked in place.

In a slow, graceful rise, the Hhso straightened to his full height, and looked at Zachariah.

Zachariah began backing up, his chest still registering the crushing sound of splintering wood. . . . The Hhso was going to kill him. It looked directly at him, eyelids fully retracted, its smashing arm just returning to its side. Zachariah edged to the door. Little Dog sat transfixed in his chair, while Big Dog swayed in place.

An undulation of putrid air crested over him. He opened the door and fled.

Staggering down the path, he slid now and then on the hard-packed snow. He chanced a backward glance, saw and heard the door slamming shut. Big Dog almost killed him, could have broken him in two with a swipe of his steely arm. . . . He made his way back to the porch and slumped against a pillar. Big Dog had *erupted*. Over nothing, over nothing. When he failed to leave, when he hesitated to obey.

After a long while Zachariah went into the kitchen and ran cold water, drenching his face over and over again. Then he sat down to wait for the calls the Hhso had said would come, his mind a blank, except for seeing Big Dog snap the thick wood table in two like a pane of glass.

Joshua Dern thought he'd take a fifteen-minute break and hook into the game. Hell, maybe he'd take an hour break. Take all the coffee breaks he'd skipped in his life, they equaled all the hours he was planning to use up now. He slipped in the game tab—and as usual, the comp screen just went to blank white—then jacked in the goggles and watched for the little ball of light. Which came, barreling out of black nowhere, straight for his eyeballs.

Instantly he was transported elsewhere. Where, he didn't know, but it had to be somewhere else. No game was this vivid, with touch, taste, sound and visuals . . . he entered that world. He embraced it.

And at another level, he grew anxious. Something was wrong, terribly wrong. This woman, Abbey McCrae. Terribly wrong. She opened the herd to danger. She and Si-

mon Haskell—rogues, disruptors—and the herd needing his protection . . .

Zachariah jumped when the phone rang. His throat was dry. "Hello?"

"This is Lieutenant Dern," the voice said. "You are Zachariah?"

After a moment, he answered: "Yes." He was nervous talking to the police. But they would help him.

The lieutenant said: "Where are these ones Abbey Mc-Crae and Simon Haskell?"

It was as strange a call as Zachariah could remember having. But after a few minutes it was clear: Lieutenant Dern was on the case.

An hour later, the woman named Renalda called.

~ 2 ~

Drivers in passing cars stared at Abbey and Simon in their near-wreck of a car, with two of the side windows shattered and the rear window a ragged hole.

"My leg is going numb," Simon said. "You'd better drive." He found a side road and parked. They were at least five miles from the ranch, probably farther, but it was no comfort. Abbey checked out the main road, but no pursuit so far.

"Jesus Christ, Abbey," he said, "what were those things?" Simon slumped back against the seat, closing his eyes.

"Are you all right?" Shattered glass littered the seat, the floor, crunching under them with their slightest movements. An indentation in the dashboard revealed the puckered socket where a bullet had lodged.

"My leg. Pulled a muscle or something." His voice fell into a husky tone, as though he were straining to speak. "You drive."

Abbey squinted, looking closely at him. Simon was rubbing his leg where a small patch of frost was soaking

through his jeans. "Don't touch your leg, Simon." She
pulled his hand gently away from his thigh where it had
been resting. "That frost on your leg—it's a kind of poison." As she took Simon's hand, she saw the rime forming
on his right-hand fingers. Using his wool scarf, she bound
his hand. He let her do this, growing quiet in an unsettling
way.

She got out of the car and walked around to the
driver's side. God. The car looked like a bomb hit it. No
wonder people were staring. She staggered a moment,
feeling dizzy. Slapping her hand against the car for support, she leaned for a moment against the remains of the
windowpane, cutting her finger. She pulled out a delicate
sliver of glass, wiping the blood on her jeans. Her leg was
trembling. Actually, it was her whole body, which, now
that there was a moment's peace, took the opportunity to
be scared as hell. She remembered the image of the Hhso
. . . behind Simon . . . in the barn . . . Rocky, oh,
Rocky . . . and in the barracks . . . all asleep, row
upon row . . . each under a window, as though stamped
from the same discreet nightmare image.

She took a deep breath and got in the car. Simon was
looking out the broken windshield at the long dirt road in
front of them. He appeared stunned.

"Rocky," he said. "Where did they take Rocky?"

She started the car. "I . . . don't know" was all she
could bring herself to say for now. After about a mile she
found a deep pullout where she drove into a thicket of
bushes.

"What are you doing?"

Abbey shut off the engine and turned to face him.
"We're going to hide this car."

"We're going to call the police." He reached for the car
phone.

Abbey grabbed it first. "No, Simon. We can't." In her
mind she heard Jaguar's throaty voice: *Anyone may be
your enemy. Even the police.*

He raised his eyebrow, was all. Staring at her.

She took a deep breath to respond, but nothing came
out. This wasn't going to be easy. "Simon," she said fi-

nally. "You think the police are any match for those things? There's lots more where that one came from."

She told him about the barracks. About what Zachariah told her about the Hhso acclimatizing.

He just looked at her. "So what are they? Some kind of genetic-engineering thing?" He closed his eyes, leaning back again, saying faintly, "And Rocky . . . got to get Rocky."

She opened her mouth to say something, not sure what would come out. Nothing did. She looked closely at Simon, his head inclined back against the seat, eyes flitting open, then shut. She felt tears building, but it was no time to cry. Not her right to cry for Rocky, not in front of this man, Rocky's best friend.

"I'm . . . going back . . . to find him," he said, face set in a stubborn scowl.

"We'll go back. But not right now. Wait here." She got out and began hunting for grasses and weeds to drape over the car. Fortunately the car was a dark blue color, and blended in underneath the growing thatch of deadfall and winter grasses. Meanwhile, her thoughts turned to the reservation and to Jaguar—the man who seemed, more than ever, the key to everything.

Back in the car, Simon was huddling against the passenger door. "Let me drive," he said, his voice now a mere whisper.

"Simon," she said gently. "Do you understand we have to hide?"

"The smell." He tucked his chin down next to his chest. "The way they smelled."

Searching the trunk, Abbey hunted for a first-aid kit with a hot cover, but the damn rental car skimped on the extras, apparently. Back in the car, she moved close to him, putting her hand on his forehead, which was cool to her touch. They sat quietly, Simon breathing deeply, eyes closed, Abbey's hand on his face, trying to comfort him, as she would a child, stroking his face. Simon had a nice face. When you really looked close, Simon was a handsome man, especially when he wasn't scowling. "You'll be OK," she said, hoping it was true. "I'll take care of you."

"I love you, Abbey," he said.

"Shhh. You rest. I'm going to call for help."

"Don't go away." His voice was slow, very slow.

"No. I'm here."

His eyes were closed. She thought he might be falling asleep, but he said: "If I die . . . it was worth it. Do you see?"

Abbey looked at his face a long time. What was this talk of love and death? He was delirious, and perhaps deathly ill. A seed of fear began to sprout. If something should happen to him . . .

She called her apartment number. Simon moaned when she removed her hand from his forehead, so she kept it there. "Renalda? Is that you?"

Renalda was taking a very long time. Every now and then Abbey would leave her post by the road and check on Simon. He was sleeping, his face ashen and slack.

As cars sped by on the main road, Abbey paced. The fields were still, and no bird sang. Renalda was always late, and would be for her own funeral. Maybe she was still sick. But no matter what was going on with her, she would be a welcome sight.

The trouble was, would Renalda believe her? The situation stretched friendship to the limit. Well, if believing was going to be a problem, then she would have to lie to her roommate, at least for now. Thinking again about the barracks with its sleeping Hhso, she realized she would lie to Renalda, was planning on partial truths if not outright lies, and all because no sane person would believe even half of what had just happened, not even a best friend.

The long spine of Medicine Ridge eclipsed the late afternoon sun, lending a new chill to the day, and turning the wide trough of the sky a waxy blue, as though rimed-over with poison frost. For a moment Abbey had the feeling that she could see the entire world. That horizon to horizon, everything began and ended here, and beyond the hills all else was only potential, awaiting release from a foregone conclusion of death.

At last, her dark mood was dispelled by the sight of Renalda's minicar as it turned off the main road and slowly approached. Abbey waved as Renalda pulled in to the turnout and shut off the engine. When she got out, Abbey knew at once that she was sick. Her complexion looked waxy, and her unwashed hair was pulled back as before into that uncharacteristic ponytail.

They looked at each other a moment. Then in a great flood of relief, Abbey stepped forward and hugged her. "Thanks for coming." She held Renalda at arms' length. "God, I'm glad to see you. But you look terrible, hon."

"Do I?" A frown appeared between Renalda's eyes, and she touched her face with what seemed a sudden and genuine dismay.

"Are you sick?"

"Sort of. I haven't been eating."

"The flu?" The closer Abbey looked, the worse she looked.

"Let's go home."

"Can you drive me somewhere first?"

A pause. "OK." Her eyes, like glassy marbles.

"Do you have anything to eat in the car? I'm starving."

"I haven't been eating," Renalda responded.

"Not even a piece of fruit or a pop?"

Renalda's frown returned. "You were supposed to get groceries," she said in a petulant tone.

"Hey. I've been in a lot of trouble, Renalda. I told you I wouldn't be home. Now I'm supposed to do your grocery shopping?" Abbey was getting tired of this distant Renalda. No concern, no warmth.

"Let's go home."

Silence stretched between them. She must be really sick, Abbey thought. She decided to humor her. "It'll be nice to be home."

"It's a little messy," Renalda said apologetically.

"That's OK, we'll clean it up. Can we bring a friend of mine?"

"Yes, bring Simon."

That stopped her. How did Renalda know she was with Simon? Abbey fought an unwelcome feeling. Suspicion. She searched Renalda's face, trying to shake the ugly feeling that she was hiding something. Reluctantly, and because she couldn't think of what else to do, she plunged ahead: "Let's go get him. He's in my car. He's not feeling well." She led Renalda into the bushes where the car was hidden. Oddly, Renalda made no comments either on the heavy damage to the car or the camouflage. While Abbey opened the passenger-side door and tried to rouse Simon, she found herself sincerely wishing that she didn't have her *back* to Renalda.

What *the hell* was going on here?

When Abbey couldn't urge Simon to his feet, they half carried, half dragged him to the minicar. Abbey saw that Renalda was struggling with his weight, perspiring heavily. God, Abbey. You call her when she's been sick for days, pressure her to help you with what she thinks is merely a flat tire, ask her to move Simon—and then you wonder why she's acting cold. What's happening to you? You're becoming paranoid.

They slid Simon into the backseat of Renalda's car, where he lay, silently. Abbey turned to face Renalda. "I'm sorry about all this. You should be home in bed. I'm really sorry."

"I didn't want to come," Renalda admitted.

"Well, I don't blame you." She felt the tug of a smile, but hadn't the heart to let it come.

"Let's go home," Renalda said.

On impulse Abbey said, "I'll drive," putting her hand out for the keys.

Renalda hesitated. The moment stretched on in a long, awkward pause that Abbey decided to wait out. Finally: "That's OK. I'll drive," her roommate said.

She went with her hunch. *Get the keys.* "OK. But let me have the keys a sec to check the trunk for our first-aid kit."

"First aid?"

"For Simon." Abbey smiled at her, holding out her hand again.

In slow motion, Renalda handed over the keys.

Now that she had the keys, she followed through with

the excuse of the first-aid kit, inserting the key in the trunk and opening it.

Inside lay Harley, unmoving. His body was stiff and thin, his chrome collar sparkling with more life than Harley would ever have again.

Abbey's stomach clenched up, as though Renalda had struck her. "Harley." The words formed in the back of her throat, barely audible. Tears blurred her accusing look at Renalda, who drew near, looking into the trunk.

Not looking at Abbey, but wrinkling her nose at the animal's body, Renalda said, "I had to bury Harley anyway, so I came."

At this incredible statement, Abbey shouted at Renalda, "You said Harley was fine! What happened?"

Renalda looked startled by Abbey's verbal attack. "We didn't have any food," she said defensively. Then, with a sullen tone, "You were supposed to get groceries."

"You killed him!" She restrained herself from rushing at Renalda.

Her roommate looked up at her, blankly, a mask of childish resentment fending off Abbey's accusation.

"And . . . you don't care," Abbey said in a calmer tone. Shoving away her sadness for later, Abbey concentrated instead on the fact that Renalda was scaring the heck out of her. She was changed. This wasn't Renalda. This Renalda was her enemy, and Harley's death proved that in a way nothing else quite could.

Poking out from under Harley's body was a tire iron. Abbey grabbed it, jerking it back and forth until she could pull it out. When she turned around, Renalda stood there with a very long kitchen knife. As the knife came down toward Abbey, she slashed out with the tire iron, connecting with the knife blade and little else. It was enough to force Renalda back a step, leaving a space between Renalda and the car. Abbey backed through this space toward the driver's-side door as Renalda stood there, swaying in place.

Renalda lunged for her again, knife held high, then plunging down, but no match for the heft of the tire iron, which Abbey swung in a two-fisted swipe across

Renalda's balled-up fist. As Renalda winced from the blow, Abbey brought up her boot to kick her as far away from the door as she could. The boot made contact with Renalda's side, causing her to stagger backward.

Using that split second to open the car door, Abbey put one foot in the car and threw the tire iron at Renalda's head. She missed as Renalda crouched to avoid it, but it provided enough time to fling herself in the car and slam the door, locking it. She started the car and pulled it around in a tight circle to face the road.

Renalda stood ten meters away, looking small and helpless, their biggest kitchen knife, the one from the set they'd bought together last Christmas, drooping from her hand.

Abbey had to make a sharp turn onto the dirt road to get out of there. She decided to take it slow. She inched the car toward Renalda, who remained motionless. As Abbey passed her, she looked up at her roommate and friend.

Renalda moved slowly toward Abbey's window and slid the point of the knife in little probing circles on the glass, lightly, her face lost in thought.

Abbey's foot hit the accelerator, and she flew around the turn onto the road. Rocks and dirt sprayed out from the wheels as the car lurched down the road and out onto the highway, trunk flopping open, and the steering wheel shaking hard beneath her clenched hands.

~ 3 ~

By the time Abbey got to Verna's, Simon was unconscious. Verna took charge, directing Abbey and Rose to cut off Simon's clothes and stuff them into grocery bags. Then, with Abbey helping, Rose burned the clothes in a pit in the backyard. The fire flared now and then with green static, perhaps the Hhso frost giving up its poisons. As they watched the flames consume Simon's clothes, Abbey asked where Jaguar was and learned only that he wasn't there, but was expected back soon.

As Verna bathed Simon and dressed him in spare clothes, Rose persuaded Abbey to eat a bowl of venison stew, though she could hardly bare to think of food, much less swallow it, her thoughts lurching from Simon, to Renalda, to Harley . . . to the Hhso.

Then Verna inspected Abbey's hand and wrist and, after a thorough scrubbing of the area, she brought her into the bedroom and gave her a pile of fresh clothes. "I'll trade you," she said. "New clothes for old. Then you can sleep in here."

"First I've got to bury Harley," Abbey said.

"We'll bury the dog."

"No, I'll do it."

"Huh!" came Verna's response. "You're sick. You need to sleep."

"I don't feel sick."

"You can't tell the difference, can you?" Verna's tone grew softer. "You sleep. I know how to bury a good dog. Don't worry."

When Verna left, carrying her old clothes, Abbey put on the pair of cords and a wool sweater she'd been given and lay down on the spare cot in the corner, pulling over herself a heavy quilt smelling of pine needles and tobacco. Sleep was swift in coming.

The next morning Simon was stirring: delirious, and murmuring. Occasionally they could hear him call out Rocky's name, and then Lydia's, and Abbey knew whereof he dreamed. She would have wakened him if she could, would have substituted the Nir version even, if she knew how—any version but the one true nightmare of Simon Haskell's life.

For the next four days Verna and Rose fed Abbey huge meals of bacon and eggs, venison stew and a seemingly endless supply of cheese biscuit swirls—Verna's personal favorite—along with many cups of an oily, bitter tea. At night she slept on the cot in Verna's room with a heavy smudge hanging in the air from dried cedar that Verna burned in a large dishlike shell. At times, in the curtain of smoke, Abbey could see Vitt's face, bearing a flickering range of emotions: mischievous, pleading, ironic, fearful, and lonely, somehow the worst expression of all . . . except for a brief glimpse of Vitt in the bunkhouse, tiptoeing among the Hhso. . . .

On the fifth day, late in the afternoon, Simon opened his eyes and asked for Abbey.

She was there, had been for the last hour, watching him rouse from the deep, bobbing to the surface and sinking again. "I'm here, Simon."

"Where's here?"

She explained about Verna nursing him all week. Then reminded him of the ranch and their escape.

"Rocky . . ." he said, looking up at her, his eyes flat and dark.

"They killed him. The Hhso." As Simon closed his eyes, she said softly, "I don't know where they took his body, but it's beyond where we can go."

He took in a long, shaky breath. "Jesus Godalmighty."

"Do you believe in God, Simon?" Abbey hoped he did. It might help.

"Figure of speech," he whispered.

"I'm sorry, Simon." She hoped he would say something. Anything.

But he lay still for a long time, eyes looking toward the square of light from the room's lone window. Outside, the afternoon grew dark as a storm came on.

After a while Verna entered the room. "This is Verna . . ." Abbey stopped, waiting for Verna to say her last name.

"Lester," Verna finished for her. She came forward and felt Simon's face. "We have last names," she said.

Stung, Abbey turned in confusion to Rose, who'd entered the room behind Verna.

"Rose Labideau," Verna explained.

Simon looked up at both of them. "I apologize for the trouble I've been," he said.

"Give him some tea," Verna told Rose, and left for what seemed to be her permanent occupation; that of cooking to feed an army.

When she came back with the tea, Rose watched to

make sure that Simon drank it. Meanwhile, Abbey told him about Renalda . . . Harley . . . the kitchen knife.

He listened incredulously. "What the hell is going on here?" he asked. "Has everyone gone crazy?" He scooped up the contents of his pockets from the nightstand and put them in his pockets. When the two women remained silent, he placed his head in his hands, waving off the fresh cup of tea that Rose urged on him.

"I'll see that he drinks it," Abbey said.

When they were alone, Simon asked, "Have you called the police yet?"

"No."

"Abbey, why the hell *not*?"

She paused, remembering their conversation not so many days ago when her ideas drove him away. But in the end she had a kind of faith that the truth would win this man over, and so she stayed with that, the simple from-her-heart truth: "I'm afraid they might be hooked on Nir. Like Renalda."

"Hooked?"

"I think it controls people. If you use it long enough. And she's not the only one who's hooked. So I just don't trust anyone right now. Including the police."

He closed his eyes for a moment. Then, speaking slowly, as though she needed extra help on this one, he said: "Zachariah was holding you against your will. Rocky's dead. There's some kind of—animal—out there nobody's ever seen before. *We need to call the police, Abbey.*"

"You believe the police are always on the right side of things, Simon?"

He looked up at her, frowning. "Of course not."

"Believe me, they're not this time."

"And you know this because . . . ?"

"Zachariah told me."

Simon's hands flew up. "Well, *that* wins me over."

Abbey urged the tea into his hands. "You think those creatures are animals? Simon, *they sleep in beds;* they're getting used to our atmosphere. One of them was going to kill you."

"So what are they, then?"

"I don't know what they are. But they're evil."

"Not evil." A husky voice came from the back door. Jaguar.

"They're no worse than humans," he said.

He'd come in the back door, wearing, as before, the jeans jacket, and now, a heavy pair of leather gloves and a wool scarf. He threw the scarf and gloves on the table next to the door and walked to the bed. "Humans have enslaved other humans," he said. "Have taken their land, their language, their religion. They've killed the four-leggeds, and the tree people. The Hhso are no worse than that." He looked her up and down, nodding his head. "You did well."

"I found the Leap Point," Abbey said. "It's there, in Zachariah's barn. But they killed our friend."

"Who is this?" Jaguar glanced at Simon, then back at her.

"Simon Haskell. He saved my life."

At this, Jaguar looked over at him, one eyebrow raised. "True?" he asked Simon.

"And who the hell are you?" Simon responded.

Abbey was fairly certain that Simon had guessed who this was. And was unhappy with his conclusion.

As the two men faced off, Abbey blurted out, "We want to know where they took our friend. What happened to him."

Still eyeing Simon, Jaguar responded, "He disappeared in the circle?"

Simon's words were venomous. "Goddamn right he disappeared."

"Then he is dead, or soon will be. They watch for opportunities to pull in subjects through the Leap Point. If he stood in the circle, then he is lost. Forget him."

Abbey put her hand on Simon's arm, feeling it tremble.

"What *are* those things?" Simon said fiercely, looking like he would wring the information out of the old man.

They were interrupted by Verna announcing supper.

"First we eat," Jaguar growled. "Then we talk."

Abbey pulled on Simon's arm, hard enough to get his attention. He scowled at her, but held his protest.

They ate a long, silent meal. Simon started slow, and eased into the meal with growing enthusiasm, prompting Verna to pile his plate higher and eliciting a few smiles from her. In annoyance, Abbey watched Simon charm her just by eating. After supper, Verna insisted that he smoke his pipe at the table after supper, which he did with evident pleasure.

Rose and Abbey cleared the table, leaving the dishes piled in the sink, and setting cups of herb tea in front of Simon and Abbey. Then Verna and Rose donned their coats and headed out into the growing dusk. Simon was brooding over his pipe as a light rain plummeted against the windows like hurled sand.

Abbey broke the silence: "Jaguar," she began, "the Hhso—they're not human. What are they?"

The old man answered, "Creatures like you or me." The green stone in his front tooth was just visible for a moment.

"Yeah, right." Simon leaned back in his chair, cradling his pipe. "I had an aunt like that once. Four feet high and three feet wide. But her hugs didn't kill you."

Jaguar raised his chin so that he appeared to be looking down on Simon. After a moment he asked Abbey, "You trust this person?" She opened her mouth to respond, but Jaguar continued, "He is your servant?"

She winced inwardly at Jaguar's choice of words. "He's helping me. It almost cost him his life."

"Yes. And may yet," Jaguar said. "Do you have courage to go on?" he asked Simon.

"Yeah. After you answer some questions. Starting with those things that live on Zachariah Smith's ranch." Simon rubbed his thigh, grimacing in what Abbey took for an expression of pain.

Jaguar nodded. "Yes. The Hhso. They are from a different world."

Abbey interrupted. "Are you saying they're from some other place, not Earth at all?"

"Yes. Some other place. Are you prepared to know

these things? Or did you think your people were the center of creation? Were *all* of creation?" His expression indicated what he thought of that idea.

In truth, it was no more than she'd already thought. "I'm prepared," she said.

"Then yes, worlds apart, worlds away from this small kingdom. The Hhso are a mighty kingdom. You are right to fear them. They are not evil, understand. They are desperate, and that is worse. We have beaten them back, and now they come here. Easy pickings, you would say."

"So we're talking about other planets, here?" Simon interrupted. *"Please."*

In annoyance, Abbey snapped, "Try keeping an open mind for a split second, will you?"

Simon pressed on: "Who are you?"

Locking gazes with him, Jaguar said, "Some things I cannot tell you." As Simon began to speak, Jaguar continued, "Some things I *will* not tell you."

"OK, let's try a different question," Simon said, with elaborate patience. "If you know so much, how come you didn't know where the Leap Point was?"

Jaguar's words came out slowly, reluctantly. "I sent Rose and Verna to the round-faced man's realm. They found the Hhso. They did not find the hoop." He shrugged. "It was dark in the barn."

Through the kitchen window, staccato bursts of lightning flashed in the distance. Then Jaguar dug in his jean-jacket pocket and took out something wrapped in a red cord. As he placed it on the kitchen table and unwound the cord, Abbey saw that it was a small, cloudy square about the size of a baby's fist. Inside the square lay an embedded spiral, which, beginning at the outer edges, plunged deeper into the glass with every turn, until in the center, it disappeared. The red cord was attached through an aperture at the top.

He nodded at her, and she picked it up. Its surface was smooth, except for the indentation of the spiral, and had, overall, a lightly sticky surface. She squeezed it, and it gave under the pressure, bringing the spiral more fully into view.

Jaguar put his hand over hers. "Do not squeeze it until you're ready."

"Ready?"

"You will carry this when you enter the Leap Point," he said. "Grip it hard and it will guide you to a personage who will help you."

Simon leaned forward, eyes narrowing. "You're not suggesting she go back to Zachariah's ranch, are you?"

"I thought all I had to do was *find* the Leap Point," Abbey said in dismay.

"It was a first step."

Abbey looked at him, her voice faltering. "You want me to confront the Hhso?"

"That is not required. But you will go to the Regent, enemy of the Hhso. This will guide you to the right place." He scooped up the medallion, and hung it around her neck.

The square device was heavy against her breast. Looking down at it, she thought the spiral plunged like a corkscrew, diving straight at her heart.

"There is not much time remaining," Jaguar said. "The Regent is leaving. He is eager to go home. Who can blame him? The Earth is a lost world, far from important centers. Only you who live here could love it. Even I no longer care."

She paused in confusion. "If you don't care, why are you helping us?"

"What I care about is not your concern. Your concern is to make your journey. Then you must plead for your world. He may listen to you and decide to help. If not . . ." He shrugged.

From behind her at the other end of the kitchen table, Abbey could hear Simon's rather loud sigh.

Abbey's stomach was having second thoughts about sharing space with her breakfast. Enter the Leap Point . . . go through that ring of fire . . . to who knew where . . .

In the silence, Simon said: "OK, I give up, who is the Regent?"

"He is one in a long line of—tenders, you might call

them. Earth has been growing toward a great civilization for a long time. Thousands of years. Do you know how many other worlds are great kingdoms, already great kingdoms? While you grow and stop, grow and stop?"

Simon's eyes narrowed. "Tenders?"

He took a sip of his tea, made a face, and set the mug aside.

"Drink, Simon," Abbey urged.

"So I can get as nutty as the rest of you? What's in that tea, anyway?"

Abbey faced him squarely. "It's just tea, herb tea, OK? Are you going to pitch in and help, or just sit on the sidelines and complain?"

Simon drew in a long breath, looking from her to Jaguar. He looked ill, whether from the poison or Jaguar's story, Abbey didn't know. "I'm going to the john." He stood up slowly, steadying himself against the back of the chair for a moment, then left them alone, disappearing into the back room.

"So the . . . Regent has been watching us," Abbey continued. "What for?"

"Try to understand. The war has weakened us all. We have to be careful who we ally with. In Earth's case . . ." A sneer hovered at the corner of his mouth.

"Where is the Regent? And why do I have to . . . plead with him?"

"Understand this. Your world is of no significance. You have no culture, no Leap Points, no weaponry, no knowledge. I have told you. You are growing toward civilization. But some are tired of waiting while you dabble with your science. Games and luxuries and nonsense. This is your science. You grow soft and content." Thunder growled far in the distance, as though the Earth itself grew impatient.

"Who says? What gives the Regent the right to judge us?"

"The right?" Jaguar looked at her pityingly. "Because he is a personage of rank, representing a great realm. One that was traveling to the stars when your ancestors were still swinging from trees."

"Well, we're not exactly stupid. We've been to the moon."

Jaguar set his jaw and stared at her. Then in a slow, measured pace he said: "He looks for the unique, not the tired, the common. He has a standard."

"Who says we're so common?"

He shook his head. "You think like a child. Hear me: there are thousands of worlds, *thousands*. The distances are vast, the Leap Points are dear. Many worlds are not worth the trouble; they exercise great care in deciding who to ally with. You think to be an exception because you stamp your foot?"

Simon returned and sat down at the table. "Did I miss anything important?"

"You miss it all," Jaguar said. He paused, looking out the window, which was now occluded by a heavy rain.

Abbey pursued her thought. "In all of this . . . how can what I do possibly matter?"

"I chose you. I took sympathy on this minor kingdom. I intervened. If you fail," he said, looking sternly at her, "we will both be cast down." He leaned forward and grasped the medallion. "But you will not fail. You have the life within you."

"What life?"

"Is there any damn coffee around here?" Simon blurted. He scraped his chair back and pulled himself to his feet with evident difficulty. He sniffed at a pot on the burner, threw out the tea, and poured himself a thick cup of coffee. Then he leaned against the sink, frowning mightily.

Jaguar regarded Simon for a moment. "You must protect her, understand. The Hhso will prevent her, if they can."

"I'll protect her all right. Starting by getting her as far away from here as I can." He slammed his mug down on the stove and crossed the short distance to the kitchen table, leaning across it toward Jaguar. "Who the hell do you think you're fooling with this cock-and-bull story of kingdoms and outer space?" He looked at Abbey. "Her maybe. Not me."

Jaguar slowly rose. "You'll do," he said quietly. Turning to Abbey, he said, "This helper is strong and will not abandon you. Now you must hurry. You may waste a few hours only. He must heal—one day, no longer. Then you must return to the Leap Point and do as I have said. If the Regent abandons your world, the Hhso will have it to themselves. They are on the move, migrating."

"Migrating?" Abbey's mood sank at the word.

"Yes," Jaguar said simply. "Why else would they come here? To prevent them, you will need powerful allies. By yourselves you are helpless. Therefore you will persuade the Regent."

"How?"

"Tell him that your people are worthy. Tell him all that you love about your people. Tell him about Vittoria, all that you care for about her."

"Why should that matter to him?"

"Maybe it will not. As I have said, he is tired. He is leaving."

"Couldn't you find someone better than me? A leader? The president? A scientist, somebody who's somebody?"

"Such people are . . . predictable. They protect their power and imitate the ideas of others. At best they are dull, at worst, destructive. But you have no . . . knife to grind. Only a child you loved. And you would die for her." Here he looked at her pointedly. "And for your *people.*" He nodded to himself. "The Regent will listen to you."

"But not to you?"

"No! Not to me."

"And what if the Regent's gone when I get there?"

Jaguar looked sideways at Simon, then looked away.

"Well?" Simon asked. "If this Regent fellow is gone?"

"Then you won't get there. The medallion is set to take you to his Leap Point. If he leaves, you cannot land, so to speak. You will be lost in fire."

Abbey stared at him. *"It explodes?"*

"Still, it will accomplish much," Jaguar said. "It will produce a quake of great power in the realm of space. It will be a symbol, a monument to Earth's resourcefulness.

Possibly it will even damage the Hhso Leap Point here. The Regent will take note, perhaps reconsider."

Simon interrupted. "And *your* Leap Point won't do, huh?"

"No. You must undertake a bold move. You must snatch power from the very stronghold of the Hhso. Then the Regent may listen." More softly, he said, "And I cannot be seen to . . . interfere."

"Ohhh boy," Simon muttered. "My bullshit meter just hit overload." He charged around to Abbey's side of the table. Taking her by the arm, he said: "Come on, we're getting out of here."

"You must not keep her from her task," Jaguar growled. "That is my one fear."

"Watch me," Simon threw back.

Rose came in from the storm, stomping the water off her shoes. She had a backpack slung over one shoulder.

Abbey slowly pulled her arm from Simon's grasp. Looking at Jaguar, she said, "Wait. I haven't finished." There was more, there were volumes more. But it all started with the same question, the first question: "Did Nir kill my daughter?"

Jaguar held her gaze a long while. "I do not know."

"But it could have. Is that how they conquer?"

"People go back to Nir over and over, hoping for pleasure. Then also it teaches you the Hhso desires: to work for them and trust them."

"How far . . . has Nir gotten?"

Jaguar paused. Then: "It is trickling out. Trickling out."

Simon rolled his eyes. "*I* played your magic game, and had my pleasure, as you call it. You don't see *me* in a chain gang, do you?"

"That's right," Abbey said. "*I* played too."

Jaguar snapped back at her: "No. You did not play Nir. You watched. It was a copy, a reflection of Simon's experience." He turned to Simon. "But you, if you used the small visor, then you played the game indeed. And playing once—even twice—that many times is free. First they set the hook. Then they reel in."

"How do you end up *knowing* any of this?"

Abbey put her hand on Simon's. "Don't bother asking. He won't answer that."

Simon smirked at the old man. "You're good, you know that? Ever think of used-car sales? Snake oil?" Ignoring Abbey's glare, he pressed on: "Do you have even the slightest idea how that game taps into our thoughts? Is it drug-induced? Hallucinogenic? Or are you just as confused as we are? And don't like to admit it." Simon's own brand of a sneer tugged at his upper lip.

When Jaguar didn't answer, Abbey asked, "Why did you tell me to get Zachariah to play?"

"The round-faced man is unbalanced. He cannot endure the Nir game."

"Endure?"

"He cannot survive it."

A pause. "You wanted me to *kill* him?"

"Yes, and anyone else who stands in your way: the police, the one called Lobo, anyone."

"Lobo?"

Here Jaguar looked at Rose, who was leaning against the counter next to Simon.

"A guy named Lobo comes to Zachariah's house," Rose said. "Once I saw him there with your daughter."

Abbey looked at her, astonished. Lobo with Vitt?

Jaguar nodded. "This helper sells many games now." Rain pelted against the tin roof and the light from the kitchen windows barely lit his face.

Softly, Abbey said: "You promised me I'd learn how Vitt died." In the midst of this great disaster, she still felt her own life, her own hopes, surge. They might mean nothing if the world was to end. But her thoughts clung to these hopes like flotsam in a flood.

"I promised nothing. But you have already proven yourself to me by confronting the round-faced man. He should have played. He should have died. But now you have found the Leap Point despite him. Now you must enter it."

She spit out her words, one at a time: "You don't get it.

I'm in this for my daughter. I've always been in this for her."

Jaguar advanced on her, his eyes hard as fists. "And your people? One daughter for your whole people?"

Standing her ground, Abbey threw back, "She is my people! The last of my people!"

His sneer deepened. "Listen well: when the migration is complete, your people will serve the Hhso. The heat of your world oppresses them, therefore they will sleep much and work little. Your people's fate will be the opposite. Opposite."

They all turned as the front door opened and Verna rushed in, water shedding off her yellow slicker. "The police are here, looking for them," she said. "They're questioning everyone."

Abbey sprang up. "The police! How did they find us?"

"How indeed," Jaguar said, rising. He was looking at Simon, his lower lip curling back on itself.

Quietly, Simon said, "I called them."

Rose was thrusting a jacket at Abbey. "Put this on!" Rose had her own jacket on, and was swinging the backpack onto her shoulders.

"Where can we run?" Abbey asked.

"If I were you, I'd go *now*," Verna said, her back to them as she peered out the window.

"You betrayed us," Jaguar said, glaring at Simon.

"Hurry," Rose said. She took Abbey's arm and pushed her through the kitchen into the back room.

Simon followed them, saying, "I did it for you, Abbey. To protect you."

"Don't you understand?" Abbey cried. "We have to run. Now, Simon!"

The sound of a car in the front of the house, and a car door slamming.

"Go," she heard Jaguar shout from inside the back room. "Go!"

She pulled desperately on Simon's arm, and he moved down the first step of the porch and stopped.

"Hurry!" Rose called, dashing across the backyard. "The Leap Point!"

Abbey paused for another moment, then bolted after her. Just as she broke into a run, a policeman emerged from around the corner of the house. In one swift action, he halted, raised his gun, and shot directly at Abbey.

"No!" Simon bellowed. "Not her!"

The policeman, a young man with a likable, friendly face, swung the gun around in Simon's direction and shot again. A pane of glass shattered behind Simon.

Then a police car roared around the building—driven by Jaguar—and swiped at the policeman, sending him sprawling, just as Simon began running toward Abbey. She was holding out her arms, and when he reached her she grabbed on to him, pulling him close. Rose reached out and clasped the medallion dangling at Abbey's throat and in the next moment the world turned to brilliant phosphorescent blue, shot through with fractures of light. Then Abbey's skin seemed to forget its boundaries and began to release its tender hold on her being.

Chapter 11

~1~

Simon, Abbey, and Rose stood in a driving rain on a high bluff with clouds roiling in the valley below them. Simon felt as though he'd been thrashed in those turbulent clouds and spit out like a chicken bone.

Where in the name of hell were they? Rose handed him a heavy jacket, which he gratefully struggled into as she guided him away from the cliff edge. He remembered the police shooting, shooting to kill, and then he was running and Abbey held on to him while the air caught fire all around them. . . .

"He's weak! Take his other arm!" Abbey was shouting at Rose through the rising wind.

Simon allowed himself to be led by the women as thunder roared above them, loud enough to crack the stones he walked on. His legs were a little slow on the uptake, like they had to do committee work before obeying the brain. He stumbled.

"Just a little further!" Abbey's face was in front of him, rain sheeting over it, glistening, like the first time he'd seen her. Glitter. A goddess in the dingy hall of the warren, come to rescue him, or damn him.

"Over there. The hut!"

He felt himself pulled along, disoriented from the sudden physical exertion, the vortex of light, and the damn, numbing poison. . . .

"In here!" Abbey pushed him into a mass of branches piled against the bank. He found himself in a dark cocoon, smelling of mud and pine needles. Blessedly, it was dry. Rose thrust the backpack in next to him and Abbey crawled in after it.

"Rose! Where are you going?" Abbey shouted. Rose was gone.

"Where are we?" Simon asked.

"My shelter. I built this. We're safe up here. The police will never figure we got this far."

"But where . . . *are* we?" A gust of wind sprayed them with rain from the opening.

"Medicine Ridge."

Simon considered this a moment. He wasn't sure he wanted the answer to the next question. "How did we get here?"

"The Leap Point. Jaguar's Leap Point."

Outside, a pile of boughs was thrown against the opening of their hideaway. A dark shape moved there—presumably Rose—building up the outside of the hut.

Simon felt he should be out there helping her, but his bad leg felt like a piece of driftwood, unresponsive except for tendrils of pain. Lightning erupted outside, sending shards of light through the brush walls. It was followed closely by a bone-crunching peal of thunder. Maybe they'd been struck by lightning back there, he thought, and he'd passed out, and they'd carried him here. . . .

Rose appeared in the hut opening. "Take these to lie on." She passed in evergreen branches, and Abbey bustled around with them as Simon leaned against the bank and as the woods got colder and darker. Night was coming on, hurried along by the storm.

It had been forty years since he'd been in a tent. Some damn Boy Scout campout replete with lukewarm pork and beans and a tent that collapsed in the middle of the night. Simon was well aware that some people waxed rhapsodic about the great outdoors, convincing themselves it was transcendent—or at least pleasant. But he would settle for warm, dry, and within a few paces of a well-stocked refrigerator, thank you. Simon loved nature as much as the next person. He even wished it well. But, as with a raging grizzly bear, you could damn well appreciate something in a picture as easily as up close and personal.

A sluice of water hit his neck. From the outside came a whacking sound as more branches piled up, stopping the leak at least for the moment.

Then Rose appeared again in the doorway. "Is there room in here for me?" They sidled farther back as she crawled in.

Rose dug into the rather formidable backpack, pulling out a flashlight and using it to find other items. Next out was a hot cover. "Tuck this around him," she said, pulling on a tab.

Abbey plumped up the boughs in back of Simon. "Looks like we're gonna sleep sitting up, OK?"

"Sleep? Here?"

"You'd rather be out in the rain?" Abbey paused, eyebrow raised.

She could be a hard woman. He'd known that. Meekly, he settled back against the slope as best he could. She obviously was one of those outdoor types. Even had a standing shelter for godsakes, here on the godforsaken edge of nowhere. Abbey fussed over him, tucking the blanket around him, drying his face with her scarf, her hand rubbing his brow and cheek, and traveling down to his neck . . . all of which was as near to a sexual experience as Simon had had with a woman for years.

After a time, Rose passed him a cup of soup she'd fixed over a small camp stove. He held the cup of soup between his hands, savoring the warmth.

"Thank you, Rose."

"Are you getting warm?" she asked.

"Yes, this really helps." Outside, the rain kept up a tat-a-tat on the roof branches.

"Looks like you were packed and ready to run," Abbey said to Rose.

"On the reservation, we're always ready to run."

A pause, then he heard Abbey say: "The police were . . . trying to kill us, weren't they?"

"Yes. They were."

"What will they do to Verna and Jaguar?"

"I don't know." She sounded worried.

"Rose, who is Jaguar?" Abbey asked.

"A shaman."

"Why does he use a Leap Point? I thought shamans had their own mysterious ways to travel? You know, quieter, less flashy."

Rose turned on her side, snuggling under her hot cover. "He says this way is easier."

Simon groaned low, trying—and failing—to be respectful. Rose wasn't your typical mystic mooner at all, but still, she was letting Jaguar bamboozle her, the same as Abbey. He hated this. Hated taking this business of a Leap Point seriously. Where was his common sense? Only days ago he'd taken a pass on Jaguar's mystical conspiracy. No thanks, Abbey, he'd said. Said no to Abbey McCrae, with all the implications of that no. Now here he was, starting to wonder if the Medicine Falls police were under the mind control of aliens. Simon put down the cup and rested his head in his hands.

"Are you OK?" Abbey asked.

"Yeah."

"A headache?" She snuggled up next to him, her own blanket cocooned around her.

The touch of her body, even through layers of wool coat and chemical blankets, was electric.

"I guess we're going to sleep together and we hardly know each other," she said playfully.

"Well, I was never one to hang out with loose women." He put his arm around her. "But I could get used to it."

"Do you have a girlfriend, Simon?"

"A girlfriend?"

"You know, someone special?"

"No," he said. "Not for a long time."

"A man like you, I thought you would."

"Why's that?"

"Oh, I don't know. A sexy detective. Smart. Distinguished."

"*Sexy* detective?"

"Most women think detectives are attractive."

Simon was genuinely surprised. "They do? Why?"

"OK, knowing what to do. Take a tough situation: your detective will know what to do. Will a tax accountant?"

"There've been years accountants have saved my ass, Abbey."

"Well. But you know what I mean."

Maybe he wasn't quite tracking this conversation. Maybe he was a little wobbly around the edges; not surprising since he was so tired he could sleep standing up if he had to. But the fact was, he was delirious with happiness. He pulled her a millimeter closer, wondering if Rose was asleep yet. But even if she *was,* nothing personal was going to happen. Though hope springs eternal. . . . "What about you?" he asked. "Seeing someone?"

"Me? Usually I do. In the winter. But the last few winters, no." Answering his unspoken question, she added, "Since Vittoria."

"Ah." The quest for Vittoria. Vittoria's honor. Her doom. To which, at present, they all seemed headed in a straight shot.

As though thinking of doom herself, Abbey said, "I'm sorry about Rocky. It's my fault, and I'm just . . . so sorry."

"No. No, Abbey, don't think that way. It's a hazard of the trade. We faced death lots of times. We never thought of blame. Certainly Rocky never did." Tears formed somewhere in a secret cave behind his eyes, where the underground rivers flowed. No, Rocky never blamed. Maybe if he *had* it would have made it easier. "He wouldn't have blamed you, Abbey."

"Do *you* blame me?"

Simon shifted sideways to look at her, blindly, in that hut. "Never, Abbey." He struggled with what to say, not wanting to say too much. Then he brought her into his arms and she came to him.

Her hair smelled like a woman: shampoo, and a soft, musky smell which he took for her own, there under the wet strands of hair, near her scalp. He inhaled it like a tonic. At last he released her, not sure what that embrace meant to her, but figuring it for a sympathy hug.

"He died fast, Simon," she said in a whisper.

No, he died slowly. Years ago.

She went on: "I heard his neck break. I wouldn't want him to be with the Hhso."

In the cave of his mind the river flowed, cold and deep. It cut its bony passageways, leaving its salty deposits in fantastic shapes along the way: the image of Lydia, lost love of his friend; the image of Rocky, lost friend. You'd think tears would come. He wished they would.

He shifted position. Needed to shift topics. "Your roommate—Renalda—is she . . ."

"Is she what?"

"Well, unstable, easily influenced?"

"I never thought so. Maybe Nir is just that powerful."

"Nirvana," he said.

"Hmm?"

"Nir is Nirvana, heaven."

"I never thought of that."

He felt an uncomfortable smile tug at his lips. "That's because you never tried it."

Abbey stretched out her legs and leaned against the slope of the riverbank. "We'd better get some sleep. Are you tired?"

"No."

They were quiet for a while then. Rose lay breathing slowly, deeply.

"You're still trying to find logical explanations, aren't you, Simon?"

He sighed. "Abbey. All my life I've hated supernatural hoopla. People come to me with the damnedest stories.

Hauntings, clairvoyant dogs, and channelers investigating past lives. No end to the nonsense. I used to tell Rocky about the real zippos and we'd have a good laugh."

"You think Jaguar's lying about the Hhso, about what they are?"

"Come on, Abbey. Alien beings may be Jaguar's take on things, but I think he's been eating too much peyote."

"But, why couldn't there be aliens? We can't be the only life in the universe."

"Because, if there were advanced civilizations, they'd have been here by now. Hell, they'd probably have colonized us by now."

"Well, that's what the Hhso are *doing,* right?"

"No, I mean alien societies would have been here *long* ago. There'd be evidence they'd been here."

"Why?"

"Because the galaxy is very old, something like ten billion years. But our sun is young, so we're latecomers in the game of civilization. By now, even if the older civilizations traveled merely by colonizing one planet after the next, I think they say that the whole galaxy could have been visited in less than a million years." He wished he could remember the details of the recent article in *The Skeptical Mind.*

"Well, Jaguar said they've been watching us a long time. . . ."

"Abbey, think about it. Why would they watch? Why, for godsakes, *bother* to watch? If they were interested in us, if there was anybody out there, they'd *be* here. And they would have been mucking about in our affairs big-time for thousands, for millions of years, whether well-intentioned or garden-variety greedy. We'd have seen them by now, or their equivalents of old freeze-dried food packages and empty beer bottles."

"But if you want evidence, what about the Leap Point?"

"Well . . ." Well, what *could* he say about it? "I don't know. It doesn't prove anything, it just adds to the questions. We moved a couple miles in what seemed like an instant. If we're at the top of Medicine Ridge, as you say—well, we really can't be here, scientifically."

"Why not?"

"In la la land there may not be mass and distance and energy requirements, but in the real world, I'm afraid, you can't go 'poof' and be somewhere else."

"But we did."

After a moment he said: "Yeah. That's what's making me nuts."

"That you can't explain it." In the silence that followed, she pressed on. "Or the thought that you've been wrong all these years?"

Jeeesus. Woman could sock you between the eyes with a two-ton velvet fist. He didn't suppose he was the sort of man who couldn't stand to be wrong. Was he? And, he had to admit, being right was often a matter of perspective, as husband/wife clients had made abundantly clear to him over the years. But to be fundamentally wrong about the physical world and the general possibilities of the cosmos . . . this, indeed, bothered him.

"Did you ever think," Abbey said, "that maybe there is a normal explanation for all this? But it's just too advanced for what we know right now?"

"Oh Abbey, that's what the kooks *always* say."

"It is?"

"Yes." She was trying to fix this for him. It was sweet. But maybe for tonight, hopeless. "That's all right, Abbey. I'll survive." He contemplated his situation quietly for a time. In the long silence he thought that Abbey might be asleep.

But she asked: "What shall we do in the morning?"

This was the real question. What comes next? Jumping into another Leap Point was not high on Simon's list of options. "Get out of Medicine Falls, I'd say."

"Why?"

Simon pursed his lips together, hard, hating to say the words: "Because I don't trust the police."

"Yeah. The Hhso have them."

He winced. "Anyway, I don't trust them."

"They tried to kill us," Abbey said effortlessly. As though she'd said, *They don't return phone calls.*

Simon closed his eyes, letting his thoughts settle out. As the night deepened, the rain stopped and the temperature in the shelter drifted toward absolute zero. Simon shifted his position and considered sleep once again . . . but nope, he was goddamned wide awake.

"Have you ever been in love, Abbey?" Hell it was late. Just be blunt, Haskell.

"Sure."

Well, of course she'd been in love. "That him in the locket?" Damn stupid thing to say. It was Vittoria, of course.

"A lover?"

"No."

He waited a few beats for her to go on.

At last she did. "My best friend."

"Renalda," he said.

"A childhood friend. Her name was Myra."

He closed his eyes and pulled her a millimeter closer. "Tell me about her." A long silence, then. He'd pushed too far.

"If you *want* to tell me." He heard a slow exhalation.

Then she said: "I grew up here—in the Falls. My parents were religious. Hyper-religious, you could say. You're not religious?"

"No."

"They were. They loved me, I suppose. They wished for me to love God, they said. All I ever wanted was their love, not God's. Maybe I had it, but then lost it later, because of what happened." There was a silence. Then: "My uncle Richard moved in when I was ten."

Simon's jaw hardened, knowing in an instant what was coming. Yes. It was a common story.

"He was a construction worker and hurt his back in a fall. When he recovered he was on a small disability and my parents took him in. His daughter, Myra, a year younger than me, became my best friend. We shared everything. Except her big secret. One day, when my parents took me to church, I got to feeling sick, and they let me walk home. And when I . . . walked in on them . . . and what they were doing . . . my uncle got real angry and told me he'd hurt me if I told. After that, Myra acted mad at me. It was only later that I realized it was shame— shame for what I'd seen."

Simon took her hand and held it while she summoned the rest of her story. It took a while. Finally, she continued: "It was then that Richard started coming to my bedroom. He made me tell my parents I was too sick to go to church. So Sunday morning was Uncle Richard's morning. Then Myra and I were friends again. We never talked about it, but we were so close, like girlfriends can be. I miss her."

"What happened then?" He spoke whisper-soft.

"One day I went up to the attic where Myra and I kept our trunk of dress-up clothes. She was hanging from the rafter by a clothesline rope. Her head was way over to the side like it was fallen off a pedestal. . . . She took her own life. But I knew it was murder."

He held her close, caressing her hair. Sweet Jesus, what a load to carry around.

"After we buried Myra I told my parents about Uncle Richard. I wanted him to be punished, but instead they punished *me*. Richard moved out and then a couple years later he froze to death in the railroad yard. My parents blamed me, and really, I did feel responsible, especially for Myra because I was older, and should have protected her. Well . . . we were both children, and it wasn't my fault. But for a long time it wasn't so clear to me."

Simon whispered: "How long, Abbey?"

She paused. "About thirty years."

"Yeah," he said. "When did you finally let it go?"

"When Vittoria died, I guess."

When you had something else to feel guilty about, he thought but didn't say. As the thunder rolled in the distance, it seemed to him that it forged cracks in the world, releasing the world's latent evil.

After a long silence she asked: "Simon?"

"Yes?"

"Where shall we go in the morning?"

As Simon considered this question, Rose stirred next to them. "The dam," she said. "We got to get to the dam."

~ 2 ~

Verna looked down on the unmoving policeman, lying facedown in the muddy torrent. She hoped he wasn't dead. Jaguar sat at the wheel of the police car looking slightly dazed. She hurried to the back door of the house, grabbed an umbrella, and ran back to the vehicle. "Get out," she said. She opened the door for him and urged him into a run across the backyard to a small path that cut across the field to Mae Two Hawks' house.

The wind fought her for control of the umbrella.

"Simon betrayed us," Jaguar bellowed to her and to the marsh.

Betrayal, Verna thought. Well, let him worry about betrayal. She was worried about important matters, like the police finding this trail and coming after them. The path had become a water-filled ditch, soaking her new Casual Strides she'd found in the discount pile at Costless. It almost broke her heart.

As they neared her neighbor's house, she hoped Mae would be waiting as she'd asked her to when she'd called her just before the police crashed into the house. And then through a curtain of rain she saw Mae's car, engine running. Mae threw open the passenger door from the inside, and Verna guided Jaguar into the front seat. She collapsed the umbrella and climbed in the back.

"We got to get to Ducky'!"

"The blues are all over the place," Mae said, still not moving. Mae was a good friend, but she was cautious as a cat in a room full of rocking chairs.

"Yeah, and they'll be here in another minute. Let's go."

Slowly Mae backed the car out of the driveway.

"Step on it!"

"You want me to speed with cops around?"

"Gun it for once in your life."

Another pause. Jaguar leaned over to Mae. "Drive!" he thundered.

The wheels spun and they flew out onto the road. In the distance, flashing blue and white lights flickered. Mae got the car out of reverse and jolted them all back with a sudden pounce on the accelerator. As she drove, the windows fogged horribly, and Mae grabbed a cloth from the dashboard, swiping at the condensation while driving one-handed. The windshield wipers fluttered uselessly on the outside as the storm raged on.

"This piece of junk," Verna said. "My nephew had that nice Ford wagon for two hundred dollars. But nooo."

"The last time I saw two hundred dollars?" Mae responded. "It was when Gil won at cards and before he pissed it away. And that was fifteen years ago!"

"You're cheap, Mae. Everybody says so."

"Cheap!" Mae turned in anger, hands still on the wheel, driving by instinct.

Jaguar put his hand on Mae's head, grabbing a hunk of hair, turning her to face the road.

At that, she began to sob. Verna shook her head. With Mae, being direct was not the best, but Jaguar suffered fools badly, and Mae might be lucky he just pulled her hair.

When they actually made it to Ducky's Tavern, Verna counted it a miracle. Or maybe not, considering all those years Mae fetched Gil home from this watering hole. She led Jaguar up to the plywood door. "If the blues ask you something, act dumb. Say, 'I didn't do nothing.' and 'It's a conspiracy, man.' "

Jaguar brushed her aside and strode into the tavern.

Ducky's had a good crowd this afternoon. It was exactly the kind of scene she'd hoped for: a confusing, milling hodgepodge where Jaguar might not stick out like a sore thumb.

The stereo wailed out a country tune as the owner, Billy Joe, presided over a crowded bar, card tables, and two pool tables. Those at the closest tables turned to stare at them. Not everybody had met Jaguar yet, and some of those that had didn't trust him. Mae was a familiar face, but Verna hadn't been seen in Ducky's for years.

Billy Joe tipped his hat to Verna. He owed her twenty bucks, and that bought her a little respect. Verna nodded to him, then took Jaguar by the arm and walked him way into the back to the pool tables. These tables were in almost constant use ever since their own Dirk Kiefer won himself a national championship four years ago and went on to do acting parts in movies, when an Indian was called for, which turned out not to be often. This, Verna could have told him. People didn't want the Indian point of view: disillusionment, despair. Who wanted to hear? Even Verna didn't. Like the next person, she wanted a little good news now and then. Likely it wouldn't show up this afternoon.

She grabbed a pool cue off the rack and gave it to Jaguar, getting him to lean on the stick like the man next to him. "The blues are coming," she told the guys. She caught Billy Joe's attention and signaled for two beers.

He brought them over in paper cups, and she handed one off to Jaguar. Billy paused. He had nerve if he expected her to pay, but you couldn't put any venality past Billy Joe. He was proud to be a full-blood, but acted like a white man, cheating and lying. A real apple; red just on the outside. As Billy left, a renewed torrent of rain hit the tavern roof, like a tall cow pissing on a flat rock. She strained her ears to listen for any cars pulling up outside.

The guys had stopped at their pool game, smoking and staring at her and Jaguar.

"Wanted for murder," she said archly. "So if you don't want to end up dead, just play pool."

Will Lonecob started wheezing and laughing. He put down his cigarette at a precarious balance on the pool table edge. "Anything you say, Verna." Mumbling his call, Will jammed the cue ball, smashing it unintentionally into the six ball, which popped over a pucker in the felt and against a cup of beer on the edge of the pool table, toppling the contents onto Jaguar's legs, before sinking in the side pocket.

Even through the thick smoke, Jaguar's glare was terrible to see. Will, however, took no notice; as he bent to his next shot, the others watched him with new respect.

Verna sidled next to Jaguar. "Don't worry about it. You need to smell like beer anyhow."

The front door slammed open. Three figures appeared silhouetted against the grey light of the storm. The strobing of lights from several of the cars left no doubt who this was.

One man stepped forward, dressed in a suit and a long, transparent raincoat and hat with dripping brim. The bar got real quiet then. In the pause between jukebox songs, the moment stretched long. Verna's heart beat so furiously she wondered if it showed through her shirt. She took a sip of beer, with Jaguar following suit.

"Tastes like lizard piss," he said, his voice carrying to the ends of the earth.

The lieutenant looked in Jaguar's direction. As he removed his hat, thunder quaked the sky above Ducky's. This was a man known on the reservation. Lieutenant Dern. Never showed up but some Indian came to grief. The jukebox found its voice and sang out Lilly Valley's hit, "Virtual Lovin'."

Dern sat at the bar, where an empty stool had suddenly appeared in front of him. As he leaned in to talk to Billy, the tavern resumed its beery pursuits, and the click of pool balls punctuated Verna's thoughts. That Billy sure would suck up to the lieutenant, twenty-dollar debt or not. Or maybe *because* of the twenty dollars. All Billy knew about Jaguar was not much, but he still could do damage. Plus, if Jaguar opened his mouth again, he was jailmeat. Only thing Dern hated worse than Sun Rock Indians was Indians *not* from Sun Rock, especially if they came drifting through—a sure sign they were jumping bail or otherwise up to no good. Verna began to see she'd made a bad mistake, coming here. But no way was she jumping into that fiery door of Jaguar's, though now she thought of it, she should have pushed him through by himself. So much for presence of mind in an emergency. She held her breath and waited for the worst.

• • •

Lieutenant Dern turned from the bar and scanned the crowd. The regulars and a couple of newcomers. He'd question those. His hand strayed to the bowl of beer nuts that Billy Joe put in front of him. The McCrae woman and Haskell looked to have got away. These people had to be found. Their crimes, terrible. A pulse in his right temple signaled that the damn headache was back. Brain cancer, he thought again. I'm dying. Or losing my mind.

He pushed off the chair and wound his way through the tables to stand in front of the two new ones. The woman was dumpy, a little drunk. The old man was stocky, with a hook nose and thick lips.

"Names?"

"Ginny Two Hawks," the woman responded. "This here's Cougar."

"Cougar what?"

"Far Seeker," she answered. And didn't seem as drunk as before. Cougar glared at the old woman.

"He don't like his name given to strangers," she added.

"Yeah? Why's that?" Dern looked this Cougar guy in the eye. Cougar had not learned how to look at a white man. His eyes fairly growled.

"There a reason you like to hide your name?"

"I did not do anything. Man."

The pounding in Dern's head made him a little nauseated. Abbey McCrae. Dangerous. Threatening the herd: it was ugly, monstrous.

"Either of you know Abbey McCrae or Simon Haskell?"

They gave him the Indian stone face.

"She's five foot six, about thirty-five, brown hair. Haskell is early fifties, short sandy hair, a little grey. About a hundred seventy pounds."

Ginny looked at Cougar, shrugging.

Dern took out a pack of cigs, offered one to Cougar.

He shook his head. That about clinched it. Every Indian on the reservation smoked, especially if it was somebody else's smokes. Dern took one for himself and lit it, the inhale sweet and awful. He needed a smoke, but with this headache it made him sick. The cancer might be in his lungs. Abbey McCrae. Find her and kill her. His police career was over, you murder a suspect. But it had to be done. . . . Why, again?

His hand trembled as he took another drag. He saw that Cougar noticed this. For a moment he wondered if there might be a gleam of understanding, of sympathy, in the man's eye.

"Nobody like that around here," the woman was saying. "White folks, right?"

"Yeah, white folks." He turned to the man. "How about you?" Cougar, still looking at him real funny. Something arrogant, knowing and—unafraid. Slowly, the Indian shook his head.

"Don't say much, do you?" Dern stomped out the cigarette on the floor.

"I did not do anything."

This guy was as phony as a tourist shop curio. And hiding things. He motioned to Lou, his backup by the door.

"Where do you live?"

"He's staying with me," Ginny said.

"OK, so where do *you* live?"

"Mae Two Hawks'," she told him. "We're cousins."

"Search it," he told one of the men. "Meanwhile your friend here can come with me. You won't go anywhere, will you Ginny?"

"I'm an old woman. Where would I go?"

He nodded to Lou, who took Cougar firmly by the arm. "Let's go."

The stabbing pain in his head. He followed Lou and the suspect to the tavern door, a fury building in him. Then, he was pulling on Cougar's arm and swinging him around, using a flood of strength that got the son of a bitch against the wall.

"Where is she, you lying bastard?" Dern considered killing him on the spot, but no, get information first. He punched him hard in the stomach, once, twice. Lou held the Indian upright against the wall. "Where is she?" the sound coming out of his mouth was a gravelly raking of words over stones.

Slowly, the Indian stood up straight, looking right in his face.

Dern punched him once more, causing him to bend double. But the rage fell away, replaced by a sickening knowledge that his mind was going. Who were the Hhso, really? Sometimes he thought he knew, felt their power, their sweeping vision of law and order and belonging . . .

He nodded at Lou, who dragged Cougar out the door. Dern took one more look at the now-silent tableau of redskins, all watching him. They probably figured he was acting normal. But *normal*, Dern hadn't seen for weeks.

As they forced Cougar out the door and into the rain, the Indian bellowed, "It is a conspiracy!"

Dern held his gun in his hand. As they slammed the car doors on their prisoner, he looked down at the standard police-issue pistol. For a moment, he considered using it on himself. Right here, right now. Before he lost his manhood. His humanity. His mind. And then he remembered Abbey McCrae. Get her first. Find her, then maybe the headaches would stop.

~ 3 ~

With his eyes still closed, Simon heard Rose and Abbey rustling around and talking in low voices. It was dark and warm in his huddled space, and he sank back into his dream as into quicksand.

Abbey was shaking his arm. "Wake up, Simon. We have to leave."

He sat up slowly, trying to see her. "It's the middle of the night," he said.

"It'll be dawn in an hour. Rose says we have to hurry."

It had stopped raining, except for a persistent drip onto the back of Simon's head. Abbey thrust a cup of something warm into his hands.

"Drink this. It's breakfast."

It smelled like tomato soup. Never a soup drinker even in the best of times, Simon tried to stave off a wave of extreme irritability. If he had to get up at goddamn four o'clock in the morning, at least let him have bacon, three or four eggs, and buttered toast. A side of hash browns would go down well, and above all, good, black coffee and lots of it.

He drank the soup. "I don't suppose there's any coffee?" he inquired, feeling like an ass.

Abbey was just crawling out of the shelter. "No, there's not. Later we'll make tea." She crawled through the opening after Rose.

"Real men don't drink tea," he said, crabby and mocking himself at the same time. He tried to move into a crouching position, and found his left leg wasn't obeying. Using one hand to drag his thigh into a bent position, he painfully crawled to the shelter opening and out into the icy, clear air. After Rose and Abbey helped him to his feet, he began to feel the blood back in his leg, and tried walking a few paces. Painful, but operative.

"How far is the dam?" He looked up to the night sky, where the stars burned behind wisps of clouds.

"Only about three miles. But some of it's climbing," Rose said in the flat, matter-of-fact tone she had.

Three miles. Wonderful. He started to walk down the riverbed to find some privacy to relieve himself.

"Not that way!" Abbey said. "Over there's the cliff."

Simon stopped dead in his tracks. What a delightful place the outdoors was. No coffee, but cliffs, you betcha. After that, Abbey and Rose left him alone for a few minutes. The land around him was silent, sleeping heavily. There was something profoundly satisfying about taking a pee in the wilderness, Simon thought, allowing himself to contemplate how many aeons man had been doing just that, as opposed to availing himself of the odd technologies of indoor plumbing. Feeling better, he zipped up his pants and snapped his heavy parka as far as it would go, grateful for Rose's presence of mind in bringing it. Or had the plan been to flee up here anyway, and the police raid just pushed up the timetable?

He joined the women and they set out. From the shadowy banks on either side, Simon gathered they were in a riverbed—probably the old Medicine River bed. It was slow going over the rock-strewn gully. As the sunrise neared, the night took on some depth, with tones of black on black, including the shapes of Abbey and, in the lead, Rose with the backpack.

He badly needed to get his thoughts in order. The thready poison in his leg seemed to be taking root in his brain as well, setting him to wonder just how seriously he'd been injured. One thing was clear, if nothing else. He needed to get Abbey out of Medicine Falls. Whatever they were involved in was several orders of magnitude over their heads. Leaving aside the alien theory for a moment, even alternative explanations were astonishing. Even if they were some monstrous genetic-engineering mistake, even a disfiguring—all right, transformative—product of a hideous disease . . . Whatever they were, the county sheriff should be in on this, and the police down at Colson. Maybe the army base or the National Guard. Hell, call all of them and see who shows up. The *Colson Herald* had a couple good people, or why not go straight to the *Capital Tribune*? He stumbled on a slippery patch of rotten wood.

"Are you OK?" Abbey steadied him, holding on to his arm.

"Abbey, where are we going? We need to talk."

"The dam, Rose said."

"Yeah. I know what Rose said." A purplish-red dawn began at the edge of the world, like a bruise spreading. "I want to know why the dam's so—damn—important. Then I want us to make some decisions about what comes next."

Up ahead Rose had turned, listening to them. He included both of them when he said, "We need to call in outside help. And somehow, get out of the area right away. We'll need a car once we reach the dam."

"I've got a car up at the dam," Rose said.

"Good."

"Simon," Abbey said. "I'm not leaving . . . or hiding."

He swallowed, not wanting to have the argument that was looming. "For Christsakes, why not?"

"There's things I have to do. You go, if you want."

He didn't want. Not without her. "This Leap Point. It's dangerous, Abbey. Who knows where you'd end up?"

"I have the necklace, Simon."

"Terrific. Rub on the magic stone and we all fly to Oz? Only the Wicked Witch weighs about three hundred pounds and breaks necks like twigs!"

"You heard what Jaguar said. I have to get to the Regent."

"And maybe blow yourself to kingdom come instead!"

Abbey looked away, avoiding his eyes. "Not if I'm in time."

Simon took a deep breath to argue, but ended up in a long, frustrated sigh. Dawn bloomed slowly over their heads, bleaching the shadows. "At least let's agree on calling the authorities."

"Like who? Who's going to believe us? Who's going to believe that we've seen monsters on Zachariah Smith's ranch? Who's going to take our word against the Medicine Falls police?"

"I'm going to call someone. I have Rocky's mobe and I know a reporter or two."

"We should hide," Rose said. She was looking up into the eastern sky. "There's a plane coming."

Then Simon heard it too. A droning of an old-fashioned twin-engine plane.

"Into the brush," Rose said.

They scrambled up the riverbank and plunged through the scrub trees toward a thicket of bushes. Simon crawled among the scratchy branches as the plane passed directly overhead. After a few moments he poked through their hiding place to look at the receding plane.

"It's a crop duster," he said.

"That's good," Rose said.

"Good?"

She hoisted the backpack. "Maybe the police don't have any friends with better planes yet."

After that they kept to the riverbank, within a few steps of cover. The plane came over three more times as the day brightened. Simon was glad for their dark clothes among the green-black pines. Planned by Jaguar, no doubt.

"You always intended to take us to the dam, didn't you?" he said to Rose.

"Yes. There's something we've got to do."

"What?"

She looked at him as she hauled herself over a deadfall log. "We've got to get there for one thing." Rose didn't often look at him. When she did, it lent a subtle force to her statements.

"Your Jaguar doesn't divulge much, does he, Rose?"

Her eyes were on the path ahead. "He's afraid to interfere too much. That's how his problems started, from interfering with fate."

"What do you mean?"

A pause. Then: "I guess I don't tell too much either."

"Do you know about these Leap Points?"

"Not really."

"How did we get up to Medicine Ridge?"

After a while Rose managed to say, "The pendant was set to guide us there."

"To a . . . Leap Point?"

"I guess so."

From the tone of her voice, he figured the conversation was at an end. They walked on, with shooting pains crimping his leg. He worried that he wasn't going to make it to the next tree, much less all the way to the dam. If he lay down he would sleep. God. Even with the police after him, he could lie down and sleep. Not good, Haskell.

The sun rose in back of them, throwing their shadows before them. Simon doggedly followed his, like the murky image of his future. Black and distorted, maybe, but after all, *his* future. It beckoned him in a way his life had not before. For the first time he really had not the slightest idea what awaited him. Not the bland, dusty office, not the silent apartment full of books and familiar comforts.

And he would risk it all in an instant, to be where he was right now, even as miserable and uncertain as he was. Go figure.

As the air warmed, the sweet scent of pine needles infused the air—an air so pure it hurt his lungs, making him long for his pipe, left on Verna's kitchen table. Ahead of him, Abbey had taken a turn at carrying the backpack. Her hair fluttered in the breeze, its natural curl catching the morning light in stabbing red highlights.

She dropped back after a while to walk beside him. "I never thanked you for saving my life back at the ranch. If you hadn't come after us, I would have been dead by now."

"Well, likewise." He thought of Abbey barreling across the barnyard in the car and practically tearing him from the embrace of the Hhso. . . .

She was quiet for a few steps, then said, "I just wanted to thank you."

"And I'd do it again, Abbey." Things he wanted to say to her. Tenderness welled in his throat. Stuck.

"Simon. I've got an idea. Maybe you won't like it, but just hear me out." She eased the pack off and set it against the tree.

"Shoot."

"I want to meet with Lobo. I've been talking with Rose. She saw him with Vitt a few times at the ranch. I know him a little, and he might tell me something about Vitt. We can use the mobe to call him, have him meet us somewhere. I'll tell him I want to make a big purchase of the games. Lobo's greedy. He'll come."

Simon was stupefied. "Abbey! This has gone a little beyond Vitt, don't you think?"

"But you need to rest before we go back to the ranch. You need to get your strength. Meanwhile, I can talk to Lobo."

"That's crazy. He's linked to Zachariah."

"If he's loyal to Zachariah. I'll bet Lobo watches out for himself first."

"Abbey. Your roommate came after you with a kitchen

knife. A deformed set of monsters murdered Rocky. And you're planning to head right back into the thick of it!"

"And *your* plan is to run away?" Her face hardened. The eyes, loaded for bear.

"Abbey . . . I care about you. I . . ." He stopped, on the verge of spilling everything.

"Care? Why should you care? You hardly know me."

"I . . . just do."

"Simon," she began, shaking her head.

"Why can't you just accept it?"

"Because! Because it doesn't have anything to do with here and now. This is my life, Simon. Finding Vittoria."

"Abbey, that was *then*. She's gone, like Rocky's gone." We could have *each other*, he wanted to say. "You, all by yourself, are worth it."

"Worth what?"

He paused. "Life, for one thing. Going to Zachariah's—it's suicide, maybe. Please, don't be foolish."

"I'm being foolish?" Her voice veered sharply upward. Rose had come back down the trail to watch them volley.

"Yes."

"Have you thought about where we can hide while you recover?" she asked. "Have you thought what you're gonna do when you walk into the army base and find they're just a little preoccupied with a new retina game?"

"Keep your voices down, hey?" Rose said.

Ignoring her, Simon tried a new tack: "Let's just call in a few allies—from a safe distance. Don't go jumping into a goddamn hole in space and blow yourself to hell and gone."

"Look. If you don't want to work on this anymore, just say so."

"Oh no you don't. This isn't your case anymore, Abbey. I'm in it up to my ears. My best friend is dead, and he didn't hang himself, either. And I'm going to get those sons of bitches."

She bit on her lip, looking at him from narrow eyes.

"I'm sorry," he said. The comment about hanging. Pretty fucking thoughtless.

"Go to hell." She furiously grabbed the pack, trying to load it onto her shoulders. Simon put out a hand to help her. Abbey jerked away, struggling to fasten the hip belt.

They all heard it then. Rose had returned and stood turning her head to locate the sound.

In the distance, barking dogs.

"On the ridge," Rose said. "They've got dogs on the ridge."

Suddenly the fight with Abbey seemed pointless indeed. If only they had the luxury to fight, to have a friendship. But the dogs would find them. Sooner rather than later if they tried to help a cripple along. "I'll draw them off," he said. "If you two stay in the gully, maybe they won't pick up your smell."

"No," Rose said, "we stick together. Hurry." She urged them onward and they started down the bank into the riverbed. It was now a steep climb down, as the gully deepened into a ravine.

"Rose. I can't make it. My leg's going to buckle."

"Lean on me," she said. She took his arm over her shoulder.

"Abbey, tell her. You're better off without me." He wanted her to decide. His heart felt like a bubble about to pop.

Her voice came like a needle. "Maybe if all three of us separate, we'll have a chance for one of us to get to that car up at the dam."

"Look. We're staying together." Rose spat out the words. "The two of you are useless in the woods. And Simon, you're supposed to help Abbey."

"Like I'm some weakling or something?" Abbey snapped.

"You people always have to be independent. You have to be important. Why don't you try working together? There's no shame in that, you know. Besides, they probably think we're going up to the Pine Wood caves. Indians always hide up there."

Abbey walked on ahead, saying, "Well let's go, then."

As the sun rose over the cottonwood trees along the

banks, Simon pushed back the pain in his leg and with Rose's help he walked faster, metering out his energy.

"Chew on these," she told him. "It'll keep you awake."

Simon looked doubtfully at Rose's offering. "What is it?"

"No-Doz."

After a time, the yapping of the dogs receded. Simon mustered his strength and plodded on, no longer leaning on Rose, but rather on a sturdy walking stick that served as a cane.

Toward noon Rose called a break and handed around some beef jerky. They sat on a sun-dried slab of river rock and ate. A grouse erupted from the bushes and ran for a safer haven, proving that not all the animals had fled. Abbey sat facing away from him, despising him, no doubt.

Bowing to the inevitable, Simon reached into his pocket and handed Rocky's mobe over to Abbey.

She looked at it a moment, then slowly took it from his hand, slipping it into her pocket. "Thank you." She met his eyes for the first time in several hours.

"Rose is right. I don't know why it is, but I'm supposed to help you. Not control you." He could wish she were making other choices. He could wait until hell froze over for people to see things his way. He could be right as rain and still lose this woman.

"I'm sorry about back there."

She smiled, a stunning, broad smile. "I love a man that can say I'm sorry."

"Well, if that's all it takes."

"You'd be surprised how little women settle for," Rose said.

Simon hurried to help her with reloading the backpack, his heart soaring. Goddamn, but he hated to fight. "How far now to the dam?"

"Around the bend up there," Rose said. The walls of the ravine had slowly steepened until they found themselves in a small canyon.

Later, the barking of dogs could be heard again, muffled by ponderosa pines and, Simon hoped, several miles' distance. But as they hurried on, the barking grew nearer, and now and then, the shout of men's voices.

"Why didn't the Leap Point take us somewhere useful?" Simon asked. "Like the dam. Or Miami Beach?"

Rose climbed over a fallen log. "So we show up on the dam causeway in a flash of light? Out of nowhere?"

"Better than death by dog bite."

"Anyways, Jaguar . . ."

". . . decided. I know." Rose's usual explanation for every damn thing they did. Well, Jaguar wasn't taking an excruciating five-mile hike on a crippled leg. Jaguar wasn't facing a pack of bloodhounds and the entire Medicine Falls police force. Jaguar wasn't having a little tête-à-tête with caffeine withdrawal. Simon's leg felt like it was considering seceding from his body, and the pills were wearing off. Fact was, he could have draped himself over the nearest thorny nest of blackberry vines and fallen dead asleep.

Up ahead Rose stopped. "Here we are."

"The dam?" Abbey asked, quickening her pace to catch up.

"Yes."

When Simon rounded the bend in the riverbed to stand next to them, he could see the great Chief George Dam just a hundred meters away, its smooth, sculpted face rising some three hundred concrete meters in the air from the valley floor. The looming sides of the gorge at this point were dotted with scrubby pine trees holding on to a few more minutes of life before jumping off in despair.

"Is this the little climb you mentioned?"

"Yes," Rose answered.

~ 4 ~

Once the dogs got onto the fresh tracks they surged forward with eager, earsplitting, barking enthusiasm. Dern stopped a moment, partly to let the dogs get up-canyon a ways, so his headache didn't spike with each yap, and partly to sort out his thoughts. Lou and Kirk passed the canteen among the three of them.

If McCrae and Haskell were headed up the old riverbed, it wouldn't be long before they'd be trapped within a box canyon. Nothing up there but the dam, and cliffs like nonstop cell walls. So why would they flee in that direction?

"Lieutenant?" Kirk was eager to join the others, and looked at him, urging him to make a decision.

"Now, why do you suppose they'd go running up to the dam?" Dern asked Kirk.

Kirk chewed on his cheek a bit, glancing at Lou for help, which didn't come. "Well, they're scared?"

"Yeah." They were scared all right. But stupid? Maybe it was Haskell's doing. He'd called. He was leading McCrae to a dead end. But then, why didn't he just put her down? Why run? But if they had a way out of the canyon, the quicker the dogs found them the better. "Let's go then. Watch the gully sides to make sure they don't climb out."

They began to jog along the creek bottom. Up ahead, the canyon walls collected every dog bark and sent it round again, circling in and out of his ears like a swarm of gnats. The sounds fueled his feet, and he pounded ahead, scanning the gorge and placing his feet to avoid the bigger rocks. He and his companions fell into a heavy, thudding rhythm of boots on stone.

It felt good to run with Kirk and Lou. He'd known them for years, and had shared barbecues, kids' graduations, Nir . . . The three of them operated like appendages of the same body; Lou on the right, Kirk on the left, scanning the cliffs, all of one mind: to find the rogues, protect the herd, cull out the diseased ones, work together, protect the herd. . . .

The jolting of his feet on the rocks sent stabbing pains into his head. His heart was hammering like a machine gun. Why were they running like madmen? They were middle-aged, flat-footed, deskbound cops, not triathalon athletes.

Still, the adrenaline flowed, and he ran like a man half

his age, with a wild joy. Kirk and Lou ran beside him, connected, sharing, equal—as the visor showed—all equal, no one more important than any other, no one smarter, faster, better. Despite the pain in his legs and his head, joy flowed through him at what the Hhso offered, true life at last, true knowledge, true liberty. No mollycoddling the criminals with trials and appeals while they preyed on the innocent, getting by with murder because their father beat them when they were little or some teacher looked cross-eyed at them in the third grade.

The afternoon sun rested for a moment on the rim of the canyon, pouring a last benediction of warmth on his face, while, beside him, his herd ran, whose thoughts and hopes were his to share with the touch of a visor to the bridge of his nose. . . .

Kirk fell, crying out.

Dern waved Lou on, and walked back to where Kirk lay crumpled, rocking in pain. It was a blessed relief to slow down, but as soon as he did his legs turned to rubber and he staggered over to Kirk, where he saw a nasty bone protruding from Kirk's sock. The individual was screaming. Such pain. Oh God, the sound of his pain, and Dern felt it as his own. The ankle bone glistened wetly as the sun fell behind the ridge, throwing the canyon into cool shadow.

He drew out his pistol and stepped closer to the injured one. Tears flowed down the person's cheeks, and he smiled up at Dern through a terrible grimace. Dern nodded, and held out the pistol at arm's length, aiming for just the right spot, and pulled the trigger. The sobbing stopped.

He put the gun back in his side holster and stared at his companion's sprawled body. Untying the kerchief Dern wore around his neck, he crouched over the lifeless form and draped the scarf over his face. With a lump in his throat, he stood up and backed away, then resumed his run.

Damn, but he hated when that happened.

~ 5 ~

Despite the throbbing pain in his leg, Simon was stunned by the view here, halfway up the side of the canyon wall. On his left, as he looked out over the canyon, the layered pinks and greys of the gorge cut a rosy swath through clumps of spiky green pine until, far in the distance, deep violet plains flattened themselves in obeisance under towering thunderclouds. On his right, the slopes of Chief George Dam wedged into the canyon with the blinding whiteness of high sun on concrete, holding back the eight-mile reservoir of Medicine Lake. The spillway was dry, water being too precious to feed this mere riverbed, when the true needs of rye, flax, and durum wheat called incessantly from the twenty-five-mile radius of the irrigation demand catchment.

Rose led them up a narrow path that in places disappeared entirely, forcing them to follow her across bare faces of rock where a series of indentations afforded a precarious toehold. Beneath them, a low throb of turbines thrummed against their feet. Thirty meters deep within the canyon wall the great engine of the dam dispatched water in rhythmic pulses like a monster's heart.

"Hurry," Rose said. She had stopped and turned back to urge him on.

The path at this point was a shelf of rock at least nine inches wide. Across *this* he was expected to hurry as though it were an athletic running track. In the best of times, Simon was not a man to be hurried. He took a twisted pride in slowing down and being passed up, as his fellow humans jogged their way to the finish line. And women were the worst, always with more that needed doing—including this *little climb* of Rose's. He grumbled his way across the narrow shelf, foot dragging like Igor, trying not to look down. Then he saw in dismay that Rose was scaling a long, threadbare rope ladder.

"Oh God," Abbey was the first to say.

Her face was sweat-drenched and grimy and her hair lay matted in ropy masses around her cheeks. God, but she looked good. She ascended the creaking ladder. As

Simon waited for her to get to the top, he heard the distant report of a gun. One shot. Simon turned to look down the canyon, but heard nothing more. He followed Abbey up the rope ladder.

With the lag between brain command and leg follow-through ominously long, Simon strained to hoist his body from rung to rung. Ye gods, Haskell. Was he really scrambling up a ladder three-quarters of the way up the side of Chief George canyon? The gentle boredom of his previous existence could now be seen for the exquisite happiness that it was.

"Hurry," Abbey echoed, in what was becoming a highly annoying refrain.

"Goddamn it to puking hell, this *is* hurrying!" Simon muttered.

"The dogs!" she whispered harshly. "They're almost in the gully. I can hear them just beyond the bend!"

And they'll pick us off with rifles. Yes, he understood that well. He'd been dwelling on this obvious tidbit of doom ever since they started scaling the canyon wall. There was no increment of fear left. Well. Maybe of still being alive after the shot hit, and falling, falling the ten minutes or so to the valley floor.

Great cumulus clouds stacked up over the dam, like cartoon bubble diagrams waiting for dialogue. RIP, Simon offered. Or, Where's one of those damn mystery doors when you need one?

They hauled him up the last two rungs and dragged him into a fissure where a tilted slab of rock afforded safety and shade.

"Are you going to make it?" Abbey asked tenderly.

"Of course he is," Rose said.

"But he's weak."

Simon listened to them talk about him. No need to join in. Women didn't really need men for conversation. If you were quiet for a split second, they filled in the blanks. As he tried to catch his breath, he lay in a blessed prone position, considering whether they might let him sleep a few minutes. This furtive hope was soon routed when he felt himself summarily pulled to his feet. Far below, the dogs were yapping furiously, their nonstop yammering amplified by the canyon acoustics.

Their pursuers were here.

Rose was digging in the backpack. While they passed the canteen around, she pulled out a small, shiny bag and fastened it around her waist with a quick press of fabric on fabric. Drawing out a coil of nylon rope, she tucked this over her shoulder and under her armpit, then handed Abbey a set of keys. "The car is a brown Honda with a missing rear bumper. It's in the lower parking lot."

"Aren't you coming?"

"No. I'm going to lay the charges on the dam."

Simon jerked to attention. "Charges?"

"Jaguar gave me the explosives." She fished into the sack. It opened at her touch to form a slit that parted like sand falling into a crack. She pulled out a clip about as long as a finger. "Where's your necklace?" she asked.

Abbey pulled it out from under her shirt, and watched as Rose opened the clip to fasten it around the cord.

"The detonator," Rose said.

"Now, wait a minute," Simon blurted.

"No time to wait. You two go. Find a place to rest. Give your leg another day. And when it's time," Rose nodded at the dam, "blow it."

Simon closed his eyes. "Holy mother of Jesus."

Abbey's voice was an octave too high: "Blow up the dam? Rose, I'm not a terrorist!"

A pause you could have weighed on a truck scale. "OK, you're not."

"Why are we blowing up the dam?"

Rose looked at her as though she had just failed to name the first president of the United States. "Can you think of a better way to get the attention of the outside world?"

"What happens to Sun Rock? What about Medicine Falls? The lake will come down this valley like a freight train."

"Time to set the river free."

"Oh Jesus," Simon whispered.

"Just pinch the clip ends until they touch. It'll send out

an activating signal. But save it for the right moment,
when it'll do you some good as a diversion." She turned
up the path. "Let's go."

"What about the backpack?"

"Leave it, the next part is steep."

"Oh Jesus," Simon repeated.

For the next forty minutes they inched their way upward, using footholds that had been gouged out of the
rock, and pulling on scruff pine to steady themselves. The
cord around Simon's waist was the only thing that kept
him from falling. Rose and Abbey went ahead, and igno-
miniously he followed, practically swinging free on the
rope. The cliff face at this point was set back from the
lower canyon wall, protected from view by a sharp ridge
of stone.

Simon's mind went numb. The minutes passed as he
abandoned himself to his fate. If the rope broke, he would
be shattered on the rock ledge below. He knew now what
it felt like to be utterly dependent on someone else, to wait
for resolution with passive hope. It stank.

At last he belly-flopped onto the safety of the next
ledge . . . face-to-face with a plastic Coke bottle.

"We're here," Rose announced.

Simon looked up to find that, a short scramble away,
was a chain-link fence protecting an observation walkway.

"I'll watch," Rose said. "When it's clear, climb over
the fence."

Time was when the prospect of climbing over a four-
meter fence at the edge of a cliff would have given him
pause. Now Simon hardly gave it a thought. When Rose
gestured, he scaled the fence with the strength that comes
with last gasps.

And he was over the top, and then Abbey and Rose,
and they were running along a paved, flat path for the
cover of a squat building at one end of the dam causeway.
The place looked deserted. To their right the parking lot
held a half-dozen yellow Power Administration vehicles,
but visitors were nowhere to be seen.

Deep in the ravine, six or seven dark-uniformed people

with a batch of dogs were milling like ants over a table-cloth.

"They'll never figure we climbed," Rose said. She pulled Abbey back as she leaned too far over. "Unless they see us up here."

"Rose," Simon said, "think about this a second. You suppose you can lay charges along the causeway and not draw the employees' attention?"

"I'll walk across real casual. I press a small glob in a few spots, that's all."

He shivered. "Come with us. The most you can do is put a crack in this thing. . . ."

He stopped at the small, ironic smile on her face. "Don't worry, it'll blow."

Simon put his hand on his brow, suddenly over-whelmed. "Rose . . . people will *die*."

She looked at him with what seemed a hundred years of sadness. "It's a good way to die. Compared to what's coming. Let the river decide who dies."

"Don't do this, Rose," he said. Not that he believed Rose could blow up this adamantine fist of concrete. . . .

Abbey was pulling his arm. "Let's get out of here."

"Where will you go, Rose?"

"Back to Sun Rock."

Simon shook his head. Right in the path of the flood, if it came, but it was no good to argue.

Abbey moved to embrace Rose and slowly, Rose hugged back.

"Good luck, Rose," she said.

"Take care of each other," Rose said, looking point-edly at Simon.

He nodded. "And take care of *yourself*," he said.

Then she turned, and walked out onto the Chief George Dam causeway.

Abbey put her arm around Simon's waist and they half-walked, half-ran to the lower level of parking, where a brown car missing a back bumper and most of its hub-caps waited for them.

He made no argument about resting in the backseat while she drove. In truth, he was long past macho protests and questions of image. He wasn't sure what image Abbey held of him at this point, and perhaps it would be no worse if he let her call the shots—at least for now—as she seemed intent on doing, anyway. He lay in the back as she drove down the winding road from the dam, and he let the swaying of the car, back and forth from switchback to switchback, lull him into a deep stupor. At one point he heard Abbey talking to someone, but he couldn't rouse himself. It would have taken an excavation of major proportions to wake him, buried as he was beneath what seemed many miles of river rock piled one stone upon another.

~ 6 ~

Ever since the police searched Mae Two Hawks' house the day before, she was a nervous wreck. Which didn't help her driving any. She swerved to avoid a kid on a tricycle.

"At your age, you shouldn't be driving, Mae," Verna said, clucking her tongue.

"*My* age. I'm three years younger than you."

"So do you see me driving?" She pointed off to the left. "Stop here."

Mae pulled in front of a tidy white trailer, where Verna's daughter lived. Dawn's trailer was the nicest house on the reservation. But after yesterday's deluging rainstorm, her garden was nothing but mud, a small brown lake with stalks extruding like the arms of drowning men. To Verna, it looked like a sign of things to come. Except she was going to take a few precautions. Jaguar might be in the slammer, but he wasn't the only one who knew how to interfere. Verna figured she and Mae'd start at Dawn's trailer, and visit each house, recruiting a few friends along the way.

They had to evacuate. Nobody could stay in Sun Rock. The river was coming.

"Wait here." Verna got out of the car and hurried up the front steps, throwing open the door. The main room

was dusky, lit in the corner from a small screen, where
Dawn lay back in her multilounger. She turned toward
Verna. The little visor erased her eyes in one swipe of
shiny black. Dawn removed the glasses.

Verna snapped on the overhead light, leaving Dawn
blinking and annoyed-looking. "Do you have any trash
bags—the big, plastic kind?" Verna asked.

"Mom, I'm busy."

"I know." She planted her feet and fixed her hands on
her hips.

"In the kitchen under the sink," her daughter relented.

Verna started toward the kitchen, then turned. "Do
you have any idea what's been going on around here?"

"You mean the big rainstorm?"

Verna pursed her lips. "Rainstorm. That's a good one."
She pulled a couple bags from the dispenser under the
sink and walked back into the living room, where Dawn
was still sprawled in the multilounger.

She yanked the leads from the computer and threw the
whole visor assembly into the trash bag.

"Mom! That's expensive!"

"Who else has these?"

Dawn pulled herself to her feet, warily looking at the
expression on Verna's face. "Lots of us have it. It's just a
game."

"Get your coat."

"Why?"

Verna gathered the ends of the plastic bag into her fist
and swung the bag onto her shoulder. "Because we're
going to collect the garbage."

Chapter 12

~1~

Booger met Zachariah at Lonnie's door. *"Lonnie plays Nir. You will leave now."*

"Get out of my way or I'll have you melted down for hubcaps," Zachariah said.

The mech whirred for a moment, hesitating.

He strode past the mech to the hoverchair where Lonnie slumped, head thrown back in apparent sleep, the visor hugging her tiny face. Pressing his hand over Lonnie's, he felt her skin, thin as paper, her bony hand, frail as porcelain. She smiled in her sleep.

Lonnie was happy. She deserved to be happy, for all that she could be a cruel, maniacal old witch. Old people went nuts, and that was the truth.

Booger rolled to the other side of her chair. A checkerboard appeared on its screen.

"I've got better things to do than play checkers, you heap of slag."

"Red or black?" it said.

But the mech wasn't talking to him. An opening move appeared on its screen, as black moved one square toward red.

Zachariah stared at the checkerboard. He was black. The Hhso were red. And the game had begun. A new game. The old game had been tit for tat. Donations for Nir. Donations for power and all the perks that went with hosting the Hhso, like the custom version of Nir for Lonnie. Nir didn't "take" on old people, they'd said, but he'd bargained and they'd relented. And all to keep him happy.

He wasn't happy anymore.

So here's the opening move, you fat dogs: The institute sheep would all sell their quota of Nir on the street. Trusty Megan would be in charge. Hell, she'd *been* in charge for weeks. In a couple of days he'd skim the easy profits, buy a van, grab Lonnie—and her damn mech if she wanted—and head off to sunnier climes. When the hell-dogs found out, he'd blame the mistake on Megan— or better yet, he'd already be halfway to Atlanta before they smelled a rat.

For an instant he recalled their acrid, pulpy smell, and Big Dog slamming his fist in the center of a solid mass of lumber and cracking it like a twig. His stomach rippled with a slow inundation of acid. The dogs were getting stronger; he might not even yet know their true strength. But he'd seen a glimpse. If he was going to challenge them at their game, let it be at a distance.

Booger still displayed the checkerboard. Son of a bitch actually looked like it was lonely.

"Make sure Lonnie eats something," he said as he walked to the door.

"No one is like Lonnie."

Zachariah turned. "Actually, Booger, that used to be true. Now, she's just like everybody else. An improvement, don't you think?"

Booger whirred and whirred.

Out in the hallway, an old man was waiting for him. A big-boned man in blue jeans and a faded denim shirt with peace symbols from a bygone era.

"Mrs. Anderson's door is locked, and no one said any-thing about her leaving!" He pointed his finger at Zachariah's chest for emphasis.

"I'm sure Ms. Aziz can answer any questions."

"Ms. Aziz!" He snorted. "Who sees *her* anymore!"

"Excuse me." Zachariah walked away from this ha-rassment to find Aziz for his own purposes.

He felt his sleeve pulled at, and swung in a temper, now face-to-face with the old man, who was fairly sputtering with anger.

"We pay good money here! And people are dying, and oatmeal three times a day! No wonder she died!"

"Who died?"

"Mrs. Anderson, you damn fool!"

Residents were coming out of their rooms, drawn by the fracas.

"You don't need to shout. I'm sure nobody's dead, Mr. . . . ?"

"No? No? Well, you just come with me!" He yanked on Zachariah's sleeve, and succeeded in pulling him down the corridor. "She can't eat oatmeal. Allergic to oats, don't you know, and usually she ate fruit, even if lately it was just canned. The place has gone downhill since you bought it, Mr. Smith. You know what that's called?"

The old idiot eyed him, nodding, while Zachariah found himself temporarily speechless against this on-slaught.

"Absent landlord! That's what it's called. Oh yes, you think we don't notice because we're *old*!" He pulled Zachariah relentlessly onward, gathering cronies in an en-tourage, all headed to Mrs. Anderson's room.

"I used to be just like you when I was young. Oh sure, I was a big shot all right!" He gestured broadly with his free arm. "Yeah, a big shot!" he said, emphasizing *big shot* with great bitterness. "Too big for my britches. Thought everybody over thirty was old. *Old!*" Here, the nearest of the followers laughed at the notion. Obviously enjoying the platform, the old man was now declaiming in a loud, barking voice. "But let me tell you something: we don't have to stand for this treatment! *Hey, hey, whadda ya say?"* he intoned. *"How many oldsters did you kill today!"* Hey, *hey,* the chant repeated, as the hallway filled with the rhythm.

They apparently had reached their destination. A large group of curious and astounded residents formed a semi-circle around Zachariah in front of the door in question.

"Look," Zachariah began. "I don't have the keycard. Ms. Aziz . . ."

The old man waved this excuse away. He drew close, closing one eye in a gluey wink: "You can't fool some of us wily old foxes," he said.

"Hey, hey, whadda ya say? How many oldsters did you kill . . ." The chant died down as a ripple in the crowd drew attention. The crowd parted to reveal Ms. Aziz.

"Deal with this, Aziz. *Now."* Zachariah fixed her with a glare, methodically removing his sleeve from the clutch of the old nutcase.

She licked her lips and faced the crowd. Wisps of hair escaped her usually exquisite coiffure, and she paused, squinting. "She's dead. Now go to your rooms."

Zachariah grabbed her arm, whispering in her ear, "You dummy. I said *handle* this!"

She turned to him and stared impudently, removing her arm from his grasp. "People die. Old people die. She had a heart attack."

"But there was nothing wrong with her heart!" bellowed the man in denim.

She turned to him. "Are you a doctor, Mr. Cobb?"

"Well no, but . . ."

"Well, *the doctor* said it was her heart."

He turned to his supporters, raising his hands to orchestrate the chant: "Hey, hey . . ." he began, and stopped. Doubt and confusion lay on the faces of the onlookers. Irritably, he waved a hand at them, muttering, "Bummer."

"Go back to your rooms now, everybody," Aziz repeated.

As people started to trickle away, Mr. Cobb stood his ground, turning a scathing frown on Aziz. "You and your fancy computer game." He turned to Zachariah, raising an eyebrow: "That she plays *constantly* when she's supposed to be on duty." He backed up a few steps, noticing that his supporters were deserting him. "Well," he concluded, "if there's oatmeal for dinner tonight, there'll be hell to pay!"

Zachariah took a closer look at Nurse Aziz. She gazed at him without cringing. "Are these people being fed oatmeal three times a day?"

"The cook left," she said, as though that were the end of it.

This was not the Nurse Aziz that he knew. "These people expect decent food, and you'll see that they get it."

"These ones are old. Their time is past."

"Of course they're *old*. Why else would they be in an old folks' home?"

"They hold us back, these ones." Her eyes locked him out. He held no power over her. His mood plummeted. If this was Nir, she was definitely taking it too far. Couldn't she have held on just a few more days, until the last of the warehouse supply was sold, and he got Lonnie out of this insane asylum? She was incompetent. A hopeless dummy.

"You're fired."

No reaction. She just stared at him. This couldn't be Nir, it had to be tranks.

Zachariah stormed down the corridor and into the office, where he called the previous manager and offered him twice his old salary to come back if he arrived in twenty minutes or less. When he turned back he found Aziz plugged into Nir at the desk console, and settling into the chair.

It was outrageous. "Get out!" He ripped the visor off of her. "Get out of here before I throw you out!" God. People whose lives were so worthless they played ret games until their brains turned to custard. It was one thing if Lonnie cocooned with her little game. What else did she have to do? But Aziz had a responsible job. Used to have.

Aziz was slowly removing items from her desk.

"Get out of here. Take your purse and coat, and your

damn game, and get out." She moved to obey, but begrudgingly, as though there might be some *question* about his authority. He looked at her closely, entertaining a momentary curiosity about her Nir fantasy. Was there a sexual component? Did it include him?

As the nurse turned toward the door, suddenly Zachariah felt an impulse to detain her, to bring her to the laundry room. But at that moment Aziz was nearly bowled over by someone rushing into the office. Zachariah looked up in high irritation, expecting Mr. Cobb.

It was Lobo. Lobo glared at Aziz, who slipped quietly away, into the hallway, and out of Zachariah's hands.

"What are you doing here?" Zachariah hissed. Lobo had strict orders about being discreet.

"You ass fragger," Lobo sneered. "You cheatin' ass fragger." Lobo's face was punctuated here and there with patches of beard, like a rash. Light cascaded off the metal gadgets of his beanie, as he threw his head back and barked: "You're cheatin' me, Mr. Z. You're cheatin'!"

"Keep your voice down!" Zachariah closed the door, turning a stern look on him.

"I'll be quiet when I get my money! My share!" Lobo threw his arm out, pointing in the general direction of downtown. "They're selling cheap, way cheap, those zombos of yours. Selling our game, that was gonna make me rich, if I just followed along!" A string of saliva whipped out from his mouth, and swung back again to hit his stubbled chin.

"There's plenty of it, Lobo. Plenty to sell cheap, for a little promotional gimmick. Then we're back regular price. It's a marketing ploy. You'd best leave the marketing to me."

"Oh, marketing. Like I don't know when I'm getting fried? I ain't no zombo, and let me tell you somethin', you give me my kick off this thing, or I go to the police! I'll tell everyone what you're up to!"

"All right, Lobo, you go to the police." This guy was a loser, a liability. A sheep. Big mistake to challenge the wolf.

The sheep nodded, up and down, up and down, groping perhaps, for his outrage. "Well—where's my money?"

"All in good time, Lobo. But you have to wait for my promotion strategy. I'm not ready to share that strategy."

Lobo backed up and swung around, slamming his fist into the door frame. A crack erupted down the middle of the glass pane in the upper half of the door. "Frag off! This is the big frag off, man! You can't just dump me. I'm a partner!"

Zachariah paused. It had gone too far. "You're fired, Lobo."

The look on Lobo's face mixed amusement with horror.

"I've got a hundred more like you now. Better behaved. Better dressed. Better everything."

Lobo threw open the door. "You . . ." His face contorted, squeezing out his words. "You gonna pay, you ass fragger!" He paused another moment, then dashed out and down the hallway, crying, "You gonna pay!"

Doors along the hallway filled with curious, animated faces. This was more action than the home had seen altogether in the last year and sure beat sleeping in the multilounger or dozing over the meal tray.

Lobo barged through the front doors, taking little notice of an old man with a satchel who stepped aside to let him pass.

Max Cobb watched as the harried youngster stormed down the front sidewalk looking to be as mad as Max himself felt. Mrs. Anderson didn't die of a heart attack. Her heart was fine. But Nurse Aziz—her heart was a black stone. He had an awfully funny feeling about her, and now she *knew* he did. Calling the police didn't help. They treated him like he had Old Timer's disease, yessir. Heart a little wobbly, grant you, but his brain hadn't turned to macaroni yet. He could see something was wrong at Harvest Home, terribly wrong, and maybe it wasn't only Harvest Home, either, judging from all the phone calls he'd made.

He gripped his satchel firmly and walked right out the door and down the sidewalk with a little hurry in his step. Well, he might be old. But he wasn't ready to give it up just yet.

~ 2 ~

From the butte, a landscape of carved rock and twisted hills surrounded Abbey, combed by chill wind that whipped her hair around her face. The late-afternoon sun, a ball of pale ice, slid down the sky, barely illuminating the tower before her, with its dark stones and darker, gaping windows.

Vogel Tower had been built fifty or sixty years ago as a memorial to one who had loved this view; to Abbey's mind, it must have been someone who loved desolation. She cinched the collar of her jacket more snugly around her neck for warmth.

Marking the spot where Vitt died, a patch of snow hugged the base of the tower. Today would be a good day for ghosts, she thought. She quieted her mind, listening. The voice in her head, Vitt's sweet, heartbreaking voice, had nestled on her shoulder for years. Now all was silent, except for the consumptive breath of the wind in the tower windows. But lately Vitt's voice had been slipping from her life: the caustic remarks, the teenage posturing, the wry advice. . . . Replaced by another voice—Simon's. A flesh-and-blood voice, a flesh-and-blood person. But still she listened, prayed, for Vitt to speak. *Tell me, Vitt.* What did you have to do with this remote tower, with the likes of Lobo and Zachariah? *Tell me.*

A car door slammed in the parking lot, just out of view. One slam. That would be Lobo, unless Simon had wakened—which seemed unlikely.

She turned toward the head of the path, waiting. She found herself wishing Simon were beside her, wishing it with an intensity that surprised her. People had cut long slits in her life and stepped out: Vitt, Myra, Mother, Dad, Vitt's father, Lyle, all the other boyfriends, Renalda. Even

Harley was gone. But Simon had stepped *in*. She thought maybe he really liked her; after all, he was still *here*. Maybe it wasn't too late to start over. Maybe Simon didn't like dogs, and maybe he did smoke a pipe and read those thick books . . . but after everything they'd both been through, couldn't they be a comfort to each other, and stand by each other? And put the past behind?

Lobo appeared at the head of the path. He wore a thin jacket with a knit scarf wrapped around his neck, fluttering in the wind as though struggling to get away. On his head, his beanie bristled with tiny electronic attachments. A hip pack bulged with his wares, she guessed, or perhaps his portable computer and personalized game of Nir. He drew closer, a little sneer twitching at the side of his mouth.

"Well, look at you," he said. "Hunting up old Lobo again." His eyes shifted from her to the tower, as though he expected someone to be hiding there.

"Hello Lobo." She swallowed, alert to his provocative stare, his challenging persona, the one from the St. Croix apartments.

He paced around to the other side of the tower and back again. Then, standing in front of her once more, he sucked on his teeth for a moment before saying: "So what's this *big purchase* you wanna make, Abbey?"

"What's your price these days?"

"My price! I gotta price, don't worry. You get what you pay for. Lots of people out there claim they got the mega-game, but you know old Lobo's got the real thing, don't you?"

"I hope you do."

"Hope? Well, how'd you like the *last one* you bought?"

"It was just fine."

"That all? *Just fine?*"

Seemed he took everything a little wrong. While she was choosing her next words, he drew closer, voice growing raspy as he lowered his tone. "No roller-coaster joys? No hyperspace hits, no satanic dreams?" He walked back and forth in front of her, declaiming: "You lead such a zombie life! You got no dark little thoughts, no bright, hopeless urges? Where'd your high-school dreams go off to, huh?" He stopped for a moment looking at her with derision. "Or were you one of those homecoming-queen types? Yeah, you were Miss Cheerleader with the curly hair, weren't ya? You had all those tidy little dates. Sitting with your purse on your lap, covering up the place of dreams, didn't you? Looking at guys like me and looking right through our ugly faces. You were one of those."

"Lobo . . ." She had to get him calmed down, had to get him off this track. "I don't know what you're so ticked off about. I never went out with the football captain, that type of thing."

"Football captain!" he sneered.

"I'm ordinary, just like you. Got a little money for once. Thought I'd buy some games." Maybe he was high on drugs; Nir wasn't the only mind-bending ride in town.

"So why we gotta meet way out here? You think you can rip me? You got friends in there?" He eyed the tower.

"I'm leaving town, Lobo. I'm on my way out. I don't know if I can get that game from anybody else—you know, for gifts."

Lobo smirked. "Gifts. I can just see you passing out the forbidden fruit to all your little nieces and nephews at Christmas. Give me a zipping break! You think you can buy 'em cheap from Lobo and sell 'em high down in Colson, maybe!"

"Look, if you don't trust me, just name a price. I don't care."

That seemed to settle him down a bit. He looked over toward the door in the tower. "Nobody spying on us, huh?"

"No."

He wandered over to the rectangular cut in the stone that served for a door, and peered inside. Then he slipped into the black recess.

She waited for him to reappear. "Lobo," she said, finally.

Vogel Tower had engulfed him and now seemed reluctant to spit him out.

She urged her feet in the direction of the tower, calling his name again, *willing* him to come out, not wanting—definitely not wanting—to go inside. But as the minutes stretched on, and it was clear he wasn't coming out, she at last stepped through the deep lintel of the tower door.

The temperature dropped twenty degrees and sight slipped away. She listened for Lobo up on the curved stone steps, where a rectangle of light from the first window pierced the tube of darkness. When he appeared in this light stream, she jumped.

"Come out of there," she said. The stones radiated a cold, sharp as flint, and a decades' old odor of frozen moss and stale air.

"Afraid of the dark?"

"I guess so."

He turned from the light and disappeared up the stairs.

"Lobo! I'm not going up there!" She paused. "Please."

"Yeah," his voice floated down. "Vittoria. I know."

She paused, her throat tightening. "How do you know?"

"Everybody knew." He was just around the bend.

Her eyes were adjusting to the blackness, and she decided to go as far as the first window. "But you knew more than everybody else, didn't you?"

"Maybe." The lone word hung in the air, a soft, struck bell.

Oh yes, he knew. The world shifted; in the space of four steps, they were deep in the terrain of the past, the illusive, sought-after past. "Please . . . tell me, then. Tell me."

"I don't think you really want to know."

The chill of the stone worked down her throat, clogging her vocal cords.

"Do you? Want to know?" he goaded.

"Yes." A whisper.

"Come up then." She heard his footfalls, heading up.

The darkness coiled on the steps of the tower, blocking her progress. But she would climb just to the next window, the next glaring hole of light. When she reached it, she saw the far buttes swallowing the sun. She turned to the upward-winding staircase. "Lobo?"

"Vittoria wasn't very nice to me," came his voice.

"Not . . . nice?"

"No."

"How wasn't she . . . nice?"

"With matches."

A pause to process, to hear again. "What?"

His voice drifted down like a wraith. "Not just once. Lots of times."

"Matches?" Abbey leaned against the stone wall for support.

"She liked to hurt me. And others. She hurt them too."

Abbey's voice squeaked past the ice in her throat, just barely. "Others?" Her brain was starting to shut down. What did he mean, matches, others, liked to hurt?

"She wanted me to hurt her back. But I couldn't. The Z-man did. He'd do it for her."

"Vitt?" She had to get it clear, were they talking about Vitt? The wind blew a hollow, shrill note against the window slits.

"Yes, sweet little Vitt! And then she got a hold of the mega-game. And she didn't need us anymore. But we watched. She was fucking crazy, you know, Mom?"

"No . . ." He was a lying animal, a vicious, lying pimp, painting Vitt in his own image.

"You want to see my burn marks?"

"No. I don't believe you."

"Course not. Precious Vitt, right?"

A narrow band of light sliced through the air and coalesced into a floating vid just ahead of her. Lobo was casting a holo scene from just around the bend in the stairs. In this scene, Lobo was seated in a wing-back chair. Behind him, a painting of an old woman standing on the porch of a grand white home.

In the scene, Lobo's face twitched, watching someone out of view. "You said it was the last time," his voice came, tinny and strained. "When we did it before."

Another voice: "Well, *this* is the last time."

Instantaneous, the voice recognition.

"Oh, man . . ." Lobo went on, "you just crazy, you know?"

"You want to leave, Lobo?" Vitt said. "You can leave."

"Go!" Lobo's face contorted as he contemplated his choices. He looked up as a woman drew near him. Seen from the back, still unmistakable. "You know I don't want to go."

"Well then." She took a drag on her cigarette.

"Please," he said. "I love you."

She spun around, rolling her eyes in impatience at the person recording this scene. Abbey was startled at Vitt's face. So hard, so confident. A grown woman stood before her, it seemed. A woman with holes for eyes. Not the Vitt she knew . . . and yet the Vitt whose fantasy it was to cut off her own breasts, to reshape herself into someone better, someone worthy. . . .

"Then pull back your sleeve. If you love me."

"And this is the last time?" Lobo's sweat-drenched face looked up at Vitt, pleading, entranced. He rolled up his sleeve as she touched the burning cigarette to his wrist.

"Stop it!" Abbey lunged forward, through the stream of light, scrambling up the stairs. The projection disappeared, and Lobo stood in the shadows against the tower wall.

"I loved her," he said, as the rising wind outside trilled at the windows.

"You killed her, didn't you Lobo?"

A moan escaped his lips and he staggered up into the darkness.

Abbey followed. In her mind, a spreading black stain. A tipped vial of all the released truths, seeping down into her thoughts, coloring her memories of Vitt. Creeping over the image of Vitt as a baby, cradled in her arms, the picture of little Vitt smiling, front tooth missing, all the images coated in tar. And then Abbey herself as a child, in sepia tones, looking up at Mom and Dad, waiting for them to see her. To protect her.

She followed Lobo upward, following the sound of his steps just to hear him say how Vitt died. How it was. This would be her punishment for seeking to know too much.

It had all been stored away as a mercy, in this tower, until now.

On and on she climbed. Now that she was hearing the blackest things, it no longer mattered how dark and cold the tower got, or how high. She trudged up the stairs, turning from the windows. Let there be darkness.

At last the stairs emerged into the circular room at the top of the tower. Six window cavities sliced the world into narrow-frame views of the darkening landscape. Lobo held a palm-sized viewer to his eyes, backing up, recording Abbey.

"Turn it off, Lobo." Her voice sounded like stones splitting. "Turn it off."

Meekly, he obeyed, shoving it into his hip pack. "Thought you might like to be in some of my home movies." He snorted at her mute presence and turned to seat himself in the deep reveal of one of the viewing ports.

From the openings, the sun threw pale strips of light across the room. Abbey chose a dark trench to stand in. She should argue with him, deny it all, make it go away. She waited for her heart to rally, but it beat only now and then, moving toward icy rest.

"Why? Do you know, Lobo, why?" she whispered.

"She enjoyed it."

"Did Nir drive her to it?"

"Get real! She was *like* that. OK, Nir . . . it was bad for her. Yeah, she got a beta version—the full-blast ride, right?"

"Full-blast?"

"Yeah, a real dose of mega-joy. An overdose, you might say. Nir wasn't supposed to go that far. The Z-man, he told the Nir people . . ."

"Nir people?"

"Some out-of-state company. So they fixed it. But too late for Vitt. It gave her a little nudge, maybe. Over the edge. So to speak." He chuckled, a noise that sounded like blood bubbling in his throat. "But man, you can't blame the game. That's how she *was*."

Yes. She was like that. Locking herself in her room.

Friends falling away, replaced by darker and darker ones. And Abbey—oh God—*Abbey not wanting to know*. Even after the diary, not really wanting to know. Tears started the long, slow path down her face.

"So, Ab. That how *you* are?"

"How I am?"

"You like to hurt people? Or be hurt?"

Abbey's breath had retreated underground. She stood stalk-still, trying to shut down. But no use. The brain was operating all on its own. *You like to be hurt?*

"Do you?" His voice, needling, casual.

She didn't answer this specter, this wolfish, wasted creature. But yes, her mind answered. Yes, yes. I chose it, chose the grey little store, the cramped little life, the men who winter over, and leave when spring comes, when the child comes. . . .

His voice came again, pecking at her. "You know how many windows there are up here?" When she didn't respond, Lobo supplied the answer. "Six. There's six."

He stood up in the window. The deep reveal offered a solid planting for his feet, while the arched stone top just cleared his head. He turned outward.

Abbey walked toward him, tentatively, nervously. "Lobo . . ."

He turned back. "Think I was going to jump?" He grinned at her. She read in that grin: pathetic woman. Misguided, deluded, pathetic mother. He had a right to think so. Even she thought so.

"You know how many letters there are in the alphabet?"

Abbey leaned against the railing heading the stairway. He was playing with her. But lead on, Lobo. If you know. "Twenty-six," she answered.

"Right! So you could figure out her game, if you were smart. She was smart, even if she was crazy." He looked around at the six windows. His face was shadowed, while his whole body was fiercely outlined against the window casement.

"It was like a roulette wheel that day," he said finally.

"You . . ." Abbey stumbled. "You . . . were here."

"Vittoria said, whoever gets Z, jumps."

The sun winked out behind the buttes, leaving the room darker.

"Then she says, 'You want to start, or me? We'll go A, B, C, like that.' " He pointed to the windows in succession. " 'You start,' I said, and she frowned, so I thought that was the wrong answer, so I said, 'No, I'll start.' "

He pointed to himself. "A." And then he pointed to the window next to him. "B." And then the next window, "C." And, "D, E, F, G . . ." His voice droned on, giving each window a letter, once around. And around again, finger jabbing at a window, filling each with a dreadful name, M . . . Q . . . T . . .

"Z," he said finally, pointing to the window where she'd stood, where the die had fallen on the roulette wheel.

"She smiled at me. 'Oh well,' she says, as casual as that. And then she just tipped back a little, as though the air would catch her, like falling onto a bed. And I leaned out my window. I reached for her. 'It was only a game!' I screamed. She fell away from me, arms outspread. But no wings. She fell straight down until she hit." He leaned his head against the stone reveal. His voice came out in a scrape: "It was only a game . . ." He turned his twisted face to look at Abbey. "A game."

Abbey stepped toward him, her heart swollen to bursting. "No. It wasn't a game. To her."

"Yes!" he said with great vehemence. "A game! An accident! She didn't mean to die!" And then softer, "I didn't mean for her to die."

The wind blew harder, streaming in through the west window, thickening her tears to ice.

He spoke in a low, almost inaudible voice: "You know what Nir brings to me, the dream it brings? Do you?"

Abbey nodded. Yes, she knew. "Saving Vittoria. You reach out, and you catch her." Because it was *her* vision, standing there, reaching out and snatching her back from the air, lunging for her, saving her.

"No. That's not it." His voice suddenly clear and steady.

Abbey cocked her head a moment. In an instant she knew Lobo's dream. "No! Lobo!" She staggered forward, arms outstretched. Too late.

"Z," he said. And stepped backward onto the wind.

Chapter 13

~1~

Flown the coop. The bird had flown the trap. Somewhere up by the dam, Abbey and company had disappeared like rainwater into a wheat field.

Zachariah pounded the steering wheel with his fist. So close! The dogs had tracked them and were closing in at the foot of the dam, and in that great dead-end canyon—they vanished. Unless they climbed the dam itself, or the ravine. No matter, now. They'd escaped. And all Lieutenant Dern had to show from his tip off was an old Indian with a surly disposition.

He drove into downtown Medicine Falls, thinking to stop by the police station to interview that old man one more time, when his attention was drawn to the sidewalk where knots of people stood talking . . . passing out something. . . .

Block after block. People carrying sacks, shopping bags, duffels. Handing out something familiar . . .

They were distributing packets, the small, fuzzy packets of Nir.

No money exchanged, no electronic mobe transactions! Just handing them out, as if they were religious pamphlets. Dozens and dozens of people in the eight-block stretch of downtown, all smiling . . . and passing out his game of glory! Driving down the price. Killing the price! Ordinary people, in business suits, jogging suits, casual tunics . . . and teenagers, should have been in school, but here they were stopping people on the street. He rolled down his window to hear a nearby street conversation.

"Free trial," they said. "Nir, the game that's sweeping the country. Here you go. . . ."

It was like driving through a custom-tailored nightmare. But they were all, all custom, weren't they? Nightmares. And the sweet dreams, too. Isn't that what Nir was all about? They said, Never play Nir. Maybe he didn't need to, to find out his personal nightmare. It was Lowell Street, right now.

Pulling to the curb, he stopped the car, gawking at the spectacle. His game! It was Zachariah who first brought this game, the ultimate game, to the street, who made a deal with the dogs of hell. And now the game flooded the street, washing away his future, his hopes. He held his head in his hands, feeling the blood surge in his temples.

When at last he looked up, he saw them. A group of Instituters, a tight knot of bright color. Yes, they were on the job, and maybe skimmed a little profit first, before . . . before *this* started. He'd take the money, take it and run. Furiously, he punched in Megan's number, but no answer, no answer. . . .

His hand hurt. Why? He'd been hitting the dash, fist bashing it over and over. He made a supreme effort to breathe deeply, each breath pushing the fear and pain further down into his chest, adding to the deep, sedimentary layers laid down all these years. He couldn't leave Medicine Falls a poor man. Lonnie needed special care, didn't she? What would she say if they left town poor as the day they got here? Now that was dirt poor. We'll never be poor again, Lonnie.

Will we? He leaned into the dash, arms folded, and cradled his head.

When at last he looked up, a concerned-looking young woman was peering in the window at him. He waved her away and started the engine, but she stepped out into the street, blocking his way.

She said, "Are you OK?"

OK? Did he fragging look OK? But he stopped to really look at her. She was dressed in pink tunic and tights, with hair to match. One of his people. He rolled down the window.

"Because if you're not OK, I can help." She brought a small bundle into view. The sun sparkled off the fuzz that comprised that unusual fabric of the Nir assemblage, promising glamour within.

"How much?" he asked.

She smiled a wide smile of food-encrusted teeth. "Free trial. How many adults in your family?" She began digging in her tote.

Zachariah was out of the car before he even decided to move. The door swiped against her, sending her sprawling to the street. "Thief! You cheating thief!" Jerking her satchel away from her, he threw it behind him, hoarding at least that many packets, then lunged for her, dragging the girl to her feet. "Who told you *free trial*? These are mine! All of them, mine. And *they're—not—free*," he said, carving out each word.

The next thing he felt was his arm jerked fiercely backward, and his body swinging in a fast arc against the side of the car, where he came face-to-face with the beefy visage of a towering, enraged teenaged boy.

"I'm gonna make spaghetti sauce out of your face, mister." A huge, flat fist slammed into his nose and ground it into a mass of pain.

He slid down the side of the car, waiting for the next blow. Blood ran into his mouth, causing him to turn to the side to spit. There he caught a glimpse of many feet, and heard a scuffle. Looking up, he saw that three Instituters were attempting to restrain the giant.

"They're not free," he said under his breath, no longer caring about retaliation. "I'm Zachariah. They're not free."

Someone said, "That puny guy is Zachariah?"

"Shut up and leave him alone."

And then he *was* alone. The melting snow of the street soaked through his slacks, and passing cars spattered him with slush. He rested against the side of the car and watched the cars rolling by, the silver hubcaps, great silver dollars rolling by, an unending, relentless caravan. . . .

Who was this pathetic loser sitting in the street, face full of blood? This puny guy was not Zachariah. It was some delusional character who thought he owned a magic game. He watched himself sitting in the street. Here was some failed version of the self that dwelled within the layers of his body.

It was a version, merely. One that failed, failed, failed.

Then pink lady was standing in front of him again, and he raised the face of the failed version to whatever blows might come. She knelt down beside him and gently pressed a fuzzy packet into his lap.

"Be calm," she said in a sweet, soft voice. "It's what you always taught. Only this really works." Then she was gone.

After that he didn't remember how he got back into the car and managed to drive. It wasn't Zachariah who drove, it was that loser who'd let a pimply-faced teenager smash his face, who'd let his fortune and his future slip from his grasp.

The midmorning sun shone through the car window, drying the blood on his face. Outside, the warmth melted the last remaining clumps of snow on the sides of the streets, releasing rivers of water to surge over the gutters. The snow was abandoning its claim on winter, a claim that had seemed, even as recently as last week, to be cruel and sure. Now, all feeble and nearly gone.

At Harvest Home, the manager looked at him in alarm as he burst into the lobby. Zachariah ignored him, making his way to Lonnie's room, where he found her lying quietly, hooked in to Nir, a gentle smile on her lips.

Booger rested at the foot of her bed, off his air cushion, a half-dozen yellow lights blinking on his face screen, in energy-saving mode, a forlorn picture of a servant no longer needed but with enough loyalty to stand by.

The manager appeared in the doorway. "We tried to take the visor off her. That mech of hers won't let us near her." As if in response, several of Booger's lights shifted to a flickering green, but, in lackluster fashion, quickly resumed their yellow phase.

"It's Lonnie's game," Zachariah said, sifting through his numbness for some anger.

The manager shook his head. "She is old. Time now for others to have her place."

Zachariah let these words register for a moment. Then he turned to the mech: "Booger, this man is trying to hurt Lonnie."

The mech whirred and rose a fraction into the air, seeming to lock gazes with the manager.

After a moment, the manager turned on his heel and left, slamming the door behind him.

Sitting next to Lonnie's bed, Zachariah held his mother's hand.

Lonnie was dying.

Just a few days ago, so vigorous. And yes, demanding, castigating, dictating. That was Lonnie, brutal at times, a little girl at times, but always alive and fully—Lonnie. Now she lay in a fool's dream, sapped of strength. Nir had killed her. He knew this simply and surely.

He also knew that whatever dreams we have, we are never meant to realize them.

He'd named the game Nir. Nirvana, a blissful state beyond the ordinary round of days. Because, the Hhso told him, it gave people their dreams. Whether for evil or good, Nir delivered it, heightened and lifelike—and never mind *how* it did. Zachariah didn't have the slightest idea. He did know, however, that people would come back to play, time and again. And so they did.

But it was wrong. It incapacitated. It killed. And now it

struck down Lonnie. Struck her down by sapping her dreams.

Dreams were made to haunt you. Dreams were what you couldn't have in waking life. And the rage against that deprivation kept you alive. Kept Lonnie alive. Kept Zachariah alive.

He released Lonnie's hand, put on the second set of shades, and jacked in to Lonnie's dream.

Honeysuckle drenched the warm breeze. Under the azure canopy of the sky, a patio of white bricks stoked a summer afternoon's heat, while a shimmering pool beckoned. Beyond, a golf course fairway stretched green and undulating into the distance. Lonnie sat in a gleaming multilounger next to the pool, her smooth, white skin shaded by an umbrella. As she worked at her keyboard, a diamond the size of a marble kept slipping to the side of her finger. It flattened and snugged up. Nothing could intrude on the enjoyment of the hour.

"Nope," Lonnie said. Responding, the screen removed a name.

Booger, stationed at her feet, let go with a few short bursts of electronic noise, its equivalent of laughter.

Zachariah watched his mother as a young woman. A delicate, round face, and lustrous brown hair with deep-trough waves that caught flashes of sunlight reflected from the pool. Her face was strong and ecstatic. He realized how Lonnie had been carved on by the years, how today the frowns and creases hid the lovely face of the real woman. In a rush, Lonnie's happiness engulfed him. It surged through him like the finest heroin, and he gave himself up to her pleasure.

Another name disappeared from the screen along with a photo. This person couldn't make the cut into Lonnie's personal country club, with the velvet green grass, with the greens marked with rippling flags; a club with a membership of one. But people would continue to apply, thinking themselves good enough. Forcing her to set them straight on that score.

A mech brought a cold drink on a tray. A shot of whiskey and a beer chaser. No prissy drinks at this club. "Up," Lonnie said, and the multilounger noiselessly brought her upright. She tossed off the whiskey.

In the chair opposite her sat a startlingly large mech comprised mostly of long, jointed arms and legs. A narrow yet human-like face perched atop the metal assemblage. Though distantly humanoid in form, to Zachariah it looked like a fleshless concoction of bones; a black horror.

To Lonnie it looked beautiful. Booger noticed her affectionate regard, whirring and flashing up a proposed game of checkers, causing her to chuckle. It was supremely comforting to have her attendants vie for her attention, and she basked in this.

But it was not enough, the fantasy could be even better.

It was not enough to be happy, to triumph, if no one witnessed it. She swung the chair 180 degrees to face the patio entrance, and waited, excitement cresting through her. Then her eyes flicked with recognition.

Zachariah's father stood at the edge of the patio. Dressed in coveralls and work boots, he looked decidedly out of place, but Lonnie would have it no other way. Uncharacteristically, his face looked tentative. He took a few steps onto the white bricks of Lonnie's domain.

"I come for you, Lonnie," he said. A boy of perhaps seven stood just behind him. Zachariah recognized that boy.

"I come to bring you home," Dad said again.

"You did, huh?"

"You don't belong here, Lonnie." His voice rang hollow against the hard edges of the patio and Lonnie's mood.

"Oh? Just where do you suppose I do belong?"

"Back to home. With me and the boy, here."

Zachariah looked into the child's spacious blue eyes, and knew that look, that gravitational longing. Mother, Zachariah thought.

She rose from her chair and closed half the distance

between them. "I ain't coming home. So I guess you
wasted a trip."

"Oh, you are. You just don't know it yet." Dad was
heating up, like he always did.

But instead of backing up, she moved a few steps
closer. "Nope," she said, tossing her head, feeling her hair
sway beguilingly.

Grabbing for her, he took hold of her arm, bringing
her close to his unshaven, ruddy face. He drew his hand
back. Then stopped. Behind Lonnie, Black Bones had
risen to its full height, moving swiftly to a point just in
back of her. The clicking of its joints, the flash of sun on
black metal, got Dad's attention. A segmented arm
flashed out and seized Dad's wrist, gently it seemed, but a
cry erupted from him.

"Like I said, I guess you wasted a trip."

Black Bones released his arm, leaving him standing
there, rubbing his wrist, his mouth gaping open. After
looking from the mech to Lonnie and back again, Dad
backed up a few steps.

"Please," he said.

Lonnie cocked her head. "What was that you said?"

Dad grimaced. "Please."

She pretended to consider for a moment, then said,
"Nope. Not coming home. Not now, not ever."

"What about the boy?" Dad was pleading now. That
seemed a bit much. He would never plead . . . but it was
her fantasy.

Lonnie turned a slicing look on the child. Zachariah
winced. "That snot-nosed brat? You think I want any of
your mewling monsters? He's yours. You feed him his
goddamn cereal in the morning and clean up his messes."
She smiled, an elastic stretch of one side of her mouth that
quickly snapped back into place. "That's your job now.
Dad."

Dad grabbed the boy by the scruff of the neck, hurling
him forward toward Lonnie, where he landed at the feet
of Black Bones. The segmented creature bent down, impossibly low, knees pointing backward, and the thin face

examining him like some loathsome specimen. Trembling,
he flattened himself against the floor.

Lonnie giggled. "Don't like my bodyguard?"

The youngster tried to scramble backward, still on his
hands and knees. Black Bones followed him, in slow mo-
tion, matching his progress, clicking, jangling, like a pock-
etful of loose change. "Dad . . ." the young Zachariah
pleaded. He looked behind him. Dad was gone. He swiv-
eled back to look at Lonnie for help. She cocked her head,
waiting for his next move, whether it would provoke
Black Bones or cause it to lose interest. The boy crept
backward, followed by clattering, lurching bones. As
Zachariah watched, he urged the child to rush into the
mech's crushing arms. Yes, he thought. Do it. . . . But
no.

This was Lonnie's game, Lonnie's fantasy. Under the
imperative of her stare, the boy turned and crawled away,
crawled across the hot white bricks, crawled over endless
white bricks, and out of Lonnie's sight.

Free at last, Lonnie thought. Feeling years younger, she
turned back to her companions.

A banging on the door. The manager was yelling outside the locked door, banging to be let in. Zachariah
could barely hear him above the sound of battering metal
and the scream of Booger's voice. Summoning the steel in
his muscles, Zachariah grabbed the hoverchair again and,
swinging it in a wide sweep, rammed it against Booger's
faceplate. One of the armpieces cracked off the chair, and
he used it to pound on the screaming mech, who now fled
into the corner of the room. Zachariah kicked Booger into
the wall with hammering blows, again and again.

Breathless, he stood looking down on the thing. His
rage dissipated, he watched as the mech lay on its side,
lights flashing red and green, red and red. The faceplate
flashed a checkerboard, in what seemed, for a moment, a
bravura gesture. Then the game board disappeared as
Booger issued a final buzzing whir.

Meanwhile, Lonnie lay breathing easily, in her harness of pleasure.

So quiet, Zachariah's ranch. As Zachariah stepped out of the car, it was as if the whole world were submerged in a great, silent ocean. No birds, no crickets, no wind. The intense quiet made it easier to concentrate. Now that there were two of him to keep track of.

Then he saw that something was different about the bunkhouse in the distance. It looked as though it had been painted yellow. Maybe, though, his eyes were playing tricks. He swung to look up at the great house, with its sweep of stairs, its proud pillars, the white haven of his former safety. Sticks. Sticks, was all it was, and plaster. All gone now. Gone to the bank. Gone to ruin. Gone to hell.

Yes! Things fall apart. Life's little game . . . you get close to your dreams, then watch them crumble. Not fast, but slowly, one stick at a time. Start with a visit by Abbey McCrae to the Institute those many weeks ago, probing and sneaking. Add the betrayals of all who leaned on him: Vittoria, Lobo, the Institute sheep, Megan, the Dogs of Hell . . . watch it crumble! Final thrust: Lonnie. The woman he tried to please for forty years, the woman who despised him for forty years. Dummy!

You finally get it?

He staggered against the car fender, turning this way and that, talking to the house, the trees, highway, the bunkhouse.

The bunkhouse. He felt himself propelled forward to Big Dog's headquarters. A pitiful, shaking, slobbering man. The version that was above all this, that version watched in neutral mode. This puny man would confront the guests, and have it out. That might not be such a good idea, given that they didn't much like to be criticized.

As he walked closer, he saw that the bunkhouse had changed color. It was backlit from the sun, now close to setting, making it hard to see clearly, but it appeared to be *encased* in a golden-yellow envelope—on the sides, and starting to jut onto the roof. He walked toward it as though in a trance, his feet sinking into muck up to his shoelaces. He slogged forward, not caring where he stepped, drawn by the transformed building. On closer inspection, he saw that the encasing was crusty and irregular, like barnacles on a ship's hull. Around the bunkhouse door the crust stopped, in a fair approximation of a rectangle.

A scraping noise. Zachariah looked up to the roof. The crust formed a hump over the gutters and stubby extrusions reached for the roof shingles, with a gentle crunching sound of small, erupting bubbles of rock. He watched as popcorn-sized spheres, spreading out like hardened soap foam, exploded softly, emitting a creamy substance that adhered to the shattered bubbles behind. The sound of the almost sub-hearing explosions set his teeth on edge. But the crust had one blessed quality. It emitted a salty, pervasive smell that somewhat masked the personal odors of his guests.

He opened the door. As the hinges gave way, the door fell, shattering like porcelain. In front of him, the setting sun blazed. The entire back wall of the bunkhouse was missing, presenting a view of the broad field, stubby with winter grass and occupied by fifteen or twenty cows—and the Hhso.

Inside, surrounded by the yellow-encrusted walls, the furniture was canted this way and that upon a sagging wood floor. Beyond, the Hhso mingled with the cows, unmindful, it seemed, of Zachariah's intrusion. The door to the bunkroom was wide open, and as he picked his way across the decaying floor and passed the room, he saw that the beds were empty, some slumped entirely into holes in the floor.

All gone to ruin.

He plodded onward like a sleepwalker, peaceful, unafraid. As he stepped out of the bunkhouse into the field, he saw the Hhso's tube-creature next to a large mass, in the general shape of a chair. From the being's mouth came a strand of whitish material like taffy, which the creature layered over the chair by moving its head from side to side.

Zachariah could see Big Dog seated there, nestled into his newly created throne. As Big Dog shifted his weight, the seat depressed and sprang back to support his weight.

The Hhso didn't need beds anymore, didn't need the bunkhouse, didn't need him. They were standing in the field, combing the cows with their extruded nails, or just petting them. One individual wore the sparkling helmet. They were getting stronger, yes, as Zachariah got weaker. They had stolen his energy as they had stolen his future.

Carelessly, he walked in front of Big Dog, forcing the creature to look at him. Meanwhile, part of him waited to see this foolish man struck down.

Little Dog approached him, carrying the slate. With great precision of movement, he bent low, and for a moment Zachariah thought he was bowing. But as he watched he saw that this was merely a time-consuming effort to place the slate on the ground for Zachariah to pick up. In a fury, Zachariah bent and snatched the slate up. Reacting, Little Dog thrust a finger of his hand into Zachariah's stomach, with a hard punch that nearly drove the wind from him. As he staggered backward, he saw that a fluid dripped from the end of the Hhso's finger. A small trickle edged down the front of Zachariah's jacket, but not penetrating the thick material. Little Dog had sent him a warning.

He faced Big Dog. The ruin of the bunkhouse lay behind, framing the creature and his tube-slave.

"What have you done to the bunkhouse?"

It becomes suitable.

appeared instantly on Zachariah's tablet.

"Suitable for what?"

No answer, not that he expected one.

A cow mooed behind him, and was answered by a susurrating noise from a Hhso.

He sneered at Big Dog. "Why do you like cows so much? You . . . mate with them, don't you?"

Cows are not suitable. They have smells of interest. They tell of the fields.

As Zachariah puzzled over this answer, the words appeared:

Where is the Abbey one? Here?

They expected him to serve them. Even now. "You betrayed me. Our agreement was, donations for Nir! Now, no one buys."

Free to all.

"Yes! Free, and I have nothing!" He had never raised his voice to the Hhso. They would kill him now. It didn't matter.

Donations now are not needed.

"But you needed them once. Why?"

Many samples are needed to perfect Nir. It is now perfect.

Zachariah looked up from the slate, frowning at Big Dog. "That's all we are to you, samples?"

Big Dog canted forward, with a withering stare.

"Kill me if you like, it doesn't matter! Like you killed Lonnie, lying in her hateful dream. She'll never wake up, will she?" He felt himself close to tears. Hateful! To cry in front of these devils. No! He pulled himself rigid, staring at the slate for an answer.

Some weak ones will die.

A stirring behind him. He turned to see something rise from the field. A Hhso standing up, rising higher. A huge individual stood in the middle of the group of cows, and began moving forward. Half again as large as the rest, unsteady on its feet, it lurched forward as the cows and the Hhso parted before it. It stood a few meters away from Zachariah, swaying, watching. The creature's mouth was open. Zachariah could hear it panting.

The sooh-an now has your smell. It is not permitting this one's smell.

The reddish hide rippled for an instant across the creature's shoulders and arms as though it shivered in revulsion at the sight of him.

"What *is* it?" Zachariah's mind spun in circles. It was huge, six feet at least, massively built. Now he would die. They would shove him forward and this being would crush him. He gripped the slate hard to keep it still. The words appeared:

The sooh-an. We prepare you to serve the sooh-an. She will bring many Hhso. You will see how many.

"More like you fat dogs?"

We migrate.

Zachariah paused a long moment. What was that he said? *"Migrate?* You mean to Medicine Falls, more fat bastards like you?"

All become the Hhso herd. All.

"Where else do you have . . . bunkhouses?" A long silence. Zachariah filled in that silence on his own. "You are taking everything. The world. You are taking it, aren't you?"

All.

Zachariah turned to the field behind him. In the glaring sunset, the great sooh-an's shadow stretched long, enveloping Zachariah as he stood there. Then, in his mind's eye, he saw the entire field packed with cows, greater and lesser Hhso, and placid, swaying humans, a myriad of them standing in rank upon rank. And there in the center, Zachariah himself, one of the herd. He threw back his head, staring at the heavens—which strangely seemed tinged by the faintest trace of yellow—and laughed a barking, explosive laugh. He watched as this dummy laughed at his common and sickening fate.

They were migrating. They'd used him for *this,* for invasion and domination. All his power, how could it matter? All his plans, canceled from the start. His dreams. Doomed from the beginning. He was just one of the sheep, one of millions. The failed version laughed harder and harder.

~ 2 ~

Abbey stirred in Simon's arms, eyelids fluttering, suffering her dreams. He watched her face as the early dawn moved into the bedroom at Rocky and Lydia's long-abandoned house. This deep sleep followed a long night of crying, raging, and recriminations, a storm that, passing through her, left her trampled and exhausted. When she slept at last, it was in his arms, where he held her all night, keeping watch, trying by force of will to keep the police at bay, her nightmares at bay. Being in this house brought his own brand of nightmare, but one of long acquaintance, not the sudden revelatory anguish of Abbey's hour in Vogel Tower.

Now she stirred again, crying out, and he cradled her shoulders, calming her, hoping she would find some peace in sleep, but fearing that in dreams she relived the ghastly scene in the tower: the revelation of Vittoria as sadist and as genuine, tragic suicide . . . falling from the tower by a mere shrug of her shoulders. Then witnessing the reenactment, with the character she called Lobo, bearing witness to it all, down to the holo proof. Down to the final act of despair. *"I have to know, Mr. Haskell,"* she'd said, *"so I can sleep."* Jesus.

A spike of pain shot through his injured leg, reminding him of the three-hundred-meter climb up the dam that just a few days ago he would have considered an act of lunacy.

Ah, lunacy . . . there was plenty, and to spare: the sabotage of Chief George Dam . . . the police ready to kill them on sight . . . slow-moving, bizarre creatures, possibly linked with a powerful, unknown technology

. . . and Jaguar saying, and Abbey *believing,* that all this
had to do with an alien intrusion. . . .

Goddamn, enough thinking. Carefully removing himself from the bed so as not to wake Abbey, he got up and
rummaged through the kitchen, finding a few canned
goods and a can opener. He set aside the canned fruit for
Abbey, and set to work on a tin of sardines, suddenly
famished.

Then, as a predawn light lent definition to the cabinets,
table, and chairs of Lydia's kitchen, Simon found himself
staring at the spot on the kitchen floor where he'd taken
aim, where his aim failed. . . . He shook his head clear of
this vision. He didn't need the damn kitchen to remind
him; the memory was portable. He scraped the chair back
from the table and went out the back door in search of a
container of snowmelt that might serve for a bathing job.
The neighboring houses were still dark, with only the
wash of a nearby streetlight to expose his presence.
Shapes and shadows clustered along the fence and Lydia's
detached garage, shapes that seemed to be a garbage can,
a bush, a wheelbarrow. . . . Simon made a quick pass
through the backyard, finding a pail of water with a crust
of ice. He retreated with it back to the kitchen, where he
pulled the curtains tight.

After a frigid once-over with a washcloth he dressed
again, then sat down at the kitchen table and waited until
eight, the start of the business day at the *Capital Tribune.*
At 8:05 he pulled up the cuff of his shirt where he now
wore Rocky's mobe.

The main desk at the *Tribune* put him through to an
old acquaintance, Phil Agnew. Life, it seemed, maintained
a semblance of normalcy outside of Medicine Falls, at
least in the state capital. People still cared to read the
news; reporters still cared enough to write it, to look for
it. Phil would not have to look far to find the news today.

"Phil, this is Simon Haskell."

"Simon! How the hell are you?" In the background,
Simon heard the buzz of conversation, the usual pande-
monium that surrounded Phil Agnew on the job. *Sounded*
normal enough.

"Not bad. What's new in the big city?"

"You haven't heard?"

Simon suspended breath. "No, been pretty busy, out of touch."

"Governor's called a special session to deal with the anti-air-tax faction. It's pulling the scabs off a lot of old wounds."

"That's a big one all right."

"How're things in the Falls?"

How indeed? But no time to consider the irony, just play your part, Haskell. "Well, it's what I called about, Phil."

"Can you speak up? Our connection's not great."

"Sorry." Simon spoke closer to the tiny receiver. "I'm using a mobe."

"Can you hold a moment?"

"Sure." The line went mute, and Simon was peppered with tiny, stinging doubts—doubts about calls traced, friends betrayed. But he held on.

A full minute later, Phil came back. "Sorry, Simon. Things are flying pretty fast around here. So what's up? You were saying?"

"I need anonymity on this, for starters. It could be big." Trying for realism, his words sounded trumped-up, false.

"You got it."

"There's a guy up in these parts, name of Zachariah Smith. He's a cult figure, runs a self-help institute that's got people giving him a lot of money to tell them about other dimensions, supposedly for personal growth. The usual crapola . . ."

Phil interrupted. "We might take a look at that next week, send somebody up to nose around."

"No, that's not the story."

"OK, what's the story?"

"Well, it's a zinger." Simon prepared to roll out his story, cleaned up a bit for general audiences. "I think this guy's ranch is the site of some illicit biological experimentation. People have been sighting—mutations."

A pause on the other end of the line. "What do you mean, mutations?"

"I mean human genetic experimentation." Simon winced, despite himself. Well, he was in the middle of it now. . . .

"On a ranch? Sounds pretty strange. You say people have seen evidence?"

"Yes. Some reliable witnesses have actually caught glimpses of people that are . . . radically deformed. I think he may be using some of his cult followers."

"Well, how do you mean, deformed?" Phil's voice had developed an edge of incredulity, the exact tone Simon's own voice would have taken on, were their roles reversed.

"Well, the accounts vary. But pretty bad, I gather."

"You're being vague, Simon. What've you got?"

"I think the genetic engineering is being done out in the middle of nowhere for secrecy. And it's experimentation gone wrong, terribly wrong. They've created some fairly ugly mistakes, and they're willing to stop at nothing to cover it up. It's dangerous. Fact is, I'm half-afraid to show my face around here."

"Jesus, Simon. So who are the witnesses? The cult followers?"

"A local woman here, for one thing. Runs an antique store. Others. Several others."

"Simon. This is a little out of my area. People see monsters, the idea catches on, pretty soon everybody's seeing them, especially if it can be blamed on an unpopular local weirdo."

Simon gritted his teeth. Here goes. "Phil. I've seen them myself."

A long pause. "These . . . mutants?"

"Yes."

"OK, describe one of 'em for me." His tone just slightly patronizing. Christ almighty.

"Well . . . they're short, for one thing."

"Short."

Simon was breaking into a sweat. "And their skin is all wrong . . . mottled, and their faces are deformed . . . large and misshapen. Pretty bad."

"Did you call the police?"

"They don't take it seriously."

"They don't."

"No." Simon knew how it sounded. Ridiculous. He wasn't buying it, not even a nibble.

"But you've seen—something. You're sure."

"I saw it, Phil. I didn't hallucinate."

A long sigh. "Genetic experimentation. Creating mutations. Well. You've got me at a loss here, Simon. Doesn't sound like the Medicine Falls I ever knew."

"I know it's hard to believe. I'm not asking you to believe it, just *investigate* for Christsakes."

"Hold on again. Sorry."

Abbey was standing in the doorway, looking alarmed. Simon whispered, "Don't worry, just calling the *Tribune*."

Phil was back. "I have to call you back, where are you?"

"No. I won't be available for a while, Phil. Just listen. In all my years, I've never seen anything this bad. There's something going on. I think people may have been murdered."

A pause. The connection wheezed and hissed, like an audience getting restless. "OK, I'll see what we can come up with."

"Phil . . ."

"Look, I'm swamped here. I really have to go." It was a brush-off.

"Phil, please. I'm begging you."

"Simon, are you OK?"

"Sure, I'm fine. Just . . . look into it. It makes the air tax look like a school bake sale. This is news, I promise you."

"Right. I'll talk to my editor. See what sticks to the wall, OK?"

Simon's heart plummeted. On impulse he asked, "By the way have you seen that new retina game, Nir I think it's called?"

"Are you kidding? Think I've got time?"

Simon let go of the breath he was holding.

"My wife plays it though. Why?"

"Oh, no reason. Never mind."

Phil's voice turned solicitous. "Things OK up there with you?"

"Just super."

"How's Rocky?"

"Rocky's . . . fine."

"You guys have been through a bunch. Say hello for me."

"I . . . I'll do that. Look, Phil . . ."

"Thanks for the tip, bud. We'll be seeing you, OK?"

As Simon shut the connection, he looked up at Abbey. "You're right," he said. "No one will believe us." He might as well have called Phil saying he'd seen Bigfoot. Even the watered-down version sounded like the ravings of a crackpot.

"Give me the mobe." Her hand was outstretched.

He unstrapped it and put it on the table.

Scooping it up, she started punching at the keypad.

"What's up?" He tried to read the mobe screen as she worked.

"Just a little all-points e-mail." She finished, and handed the mobe back to him. He scrolled the message: *Haven't heard from Medicine Falls lately? Check out Zachariah Smith's ranch. Go armed.*

He raised an eyebrow. "So who's it go to?"

"The biggest direct-mail joint promotional service in the state."

"Might not do much," he said. "But it can't hurt."

"Want to send it?"

He shrugged. "Why not?" He looked for the Send button.

Abbey leaned over him and jabbed it. The message flew.

"It's not just Medicine Falls," he told her. "Phil Agnew's wife has it."

Abbey blinked. "Yeah. It's trickling out. Jaguar said."

He shook his head, and began pawing through the stack of canned goods, looking for something Abbey might like. "Pears?" he asked. "Fruit cocktail?"

She was hugging her arms against her sides. "It's cold in here."

"Electricity's shut off. No water either. Except for that pail over there; I saved most of it for you, if you want to wash up. I wouldn't drink it." She sat down at the table, apparently unable to decide between a frigid bath and a canned meal. "Abbey, you should eat."

She nodded, unmoving, so he chose a can of pears for her and watched her while she ate. Not tasting, not caring.

"How are you feeling?"

"Pretty good." He caught her eye, and made her smile. "OK, terrible."

"Anything I can do?"

"I wish there was. I wish like crazy it would all be different. I've been so full of wishes. Look where it got me." She stood up and took the bucket, heading for the bathroom, then turned back. "When I woke up this morning, for a moment I thought it was all a dream—that it was only a nightmare. It *is* a nightmare. Only it's really happening." She looked at him, with flat, cool eyes. Then she headed down the hall with the bucket.

"I'll bet there's some of Lydia's clean clothes still in the drawers," he called after her. "They'd fit you, I think."

Dawn leaked in through the kitchen curtains, revealing all the signs of the house's abandonment. The mildewed wood cabinets, rusted door hinges, years of dust, and on the far wall, a deep stain from a long-neglected roof leak. Memories of this kitchen in happier days flitted through Simon's mind: the true ghosts of the world, trapped in human memory. . . . Like Vitt for Abbey, like Lydia for him.

When Abbey returned, the improvement was stunning. Her scrubbed face sported a healthy flush next to Lydia's green turtleneck sweater. She'd combed her hair and pulled it back from her face with a flowered bandanna, making her look about twenty-five.

"You look terrific."

"Don't smell too good, though."

"In the condition I'm in, can't tell anyhow."

A flicker of a smile, quickly fled.

"We can't stay here," he said, plunging into it. "Someone may connect me to this house. I know some back roads out of town. We should leave."

"You think they'll just let us leave?"

"They don't know what car we're driving. I think we could make it."

"To where? It's spreading, Simon." She fingered her locket, absently looking toward the kitchen window. "I don't have the energy to run. I'm tired."

He took in a breath to argue, then reminded himself to take it slow. "I know you are." He reached for her hand, lying limp on the table. "Just don't give up, Abbey."

She looked at him, smiling an unpleasant, crooked smile. "Why not?"

"Because your life's at stake, that's why."

"My life."

"Yes, your life!"

She looked back up at the kitchen window, as though she could see through those curtains, as though she could see her life hovering out there. A bird beating itself against the glass.

He knew she was tired. He knew she was shattered and bleeding. But he had to get her attention, for just a few more hours, then she could rest, rest and heal. "Abbey," he said. "I'm going to pack up the car. Then we're going to leave this place. Do you hear?"

She shook her head. "I'm not running, Simon. I need to sleep. If they find me, I really don't care."

"No, goddamn it!" He slammed his fist on the table, jolting her in surprise. "You're not giving up!" He paced to the other end of the kitchen and back. "I know you've had a hard knock." At the look on her face, he said: "All right, you've had a load of them! But you're not throwing everything away. Life is still worth it, Abbey. Maybe I couldn't have told you why, a month ago; maybe I didn't think it *was,* a month ago. Today, I know that it's worth it. You're worth it."

Her response came back instantly. "Ask Vitt. Ask Vitt

if I'm worth it." She stared straight into him, venom in her eyes.

"Oh, Vitt, let's ask Vitt shall we?" Let me tell you something: Vitt made her choice. Should she have gotten help? Yes, certainly. Would I have helped her if I'd known? Yes. Would you? Of course. But it was *her* choice. Don't let her make your choice, Abbey."

She turned away, sitting crosswise on her chair.

Simon charged around to stand in front of her. He grabbed her hand as she reached for her locket. "Leave it *be,* for Christsakes! You've got enough guilt without carrying it around your neck!"

She shoved his hand away, sliding back the chair as she rose. "I'm responsible! Don't you see? I was her mother, I should have protected her!"

"From what? From evil? From Nir? From her own goddamned life?"

"Yes!" she screamed. "Yes!"

For an instant he weighed the merits of just shutting up. Nope, couldn't do it. There was something that needed saying, and it was forming behind his clenched teeth. The damned truth.

She stood in front of him clutching her locket, the life fled from her eyes. "Go without me, Simon. Go."

"You need a bigger locket, Abbey," he said. "Big enough to stuff everybody inside it: Vitt, your girlfriend Myra, your bastard of an uncle, everybody who's screwed up because of you."

She spun around, stalking to the window, but he caught up with her, turning her around to face him, the words spilling out of him, though he tried to stop: "Better yet, make it a wheelbarrow. Go ahead, push it around every damn day of your life. Or if it gets too heavy, make it a grave, where everybody can fit in. Then you can step in after them."

He didn't mean for it to come out like that. He gazed at her helplessly, trying to pull the words back out of the air.

She responded in a spooky, soft voice: "Sometimes guilty is the right way to feel."

"Jesus, Abbey . . ."

"No. Don't try to make it all go away. I've pushed it away all these years, I don't need any help. I *taught* her, Simon. I taught her to despise herself." She shook her head at his looming denial. "Because that's what *I* was taught." She looked at him steady, out of reach. "She got hand-me-down woes. I collected them. And passed them on."

The easy responses were to absolve and comfort her, and he wanted to, desperately. But she had her truth, awful as it was. Who was he to take it from her? He reached out to embrace her, to give her strength. But she backed away, hands held up, pushing him away. "Leave me alone, Simon."

She walked out of the kitchen into the living room, leaving him drained and heartsick. He leaned his forehead against the refrigerator. Haskell, you damn idiot, you really blew it this time. The conversation had gone all wrong; he'd driven her away. He was standing there, shaking his head, when he heard:

"Simon." She was calling him from the other room, her voice flat and chill. Then again: "Simon."

When he walked into the living room he saw that she was peeking out the front window, pulling back the drapes a notch.

She turned to face him. "They're going door-to-door."

"Who? The police?"

"No, ordinary people. Just knocking on every door. There must be dozens of them, both sides of the street."

She stepped away from the window, and Simon took her place, looking out. Two people were on the porch across the street, talking with someone in the doorway. By twos they were canvassing the entire street, and a young man and his older companion were just now looking up at their hideaway, perhaps judging whether it was abandoned or not.

"Don't answer the door," Abbey whispered.

"We have to, otherwise they may search." After a moment's thought he said, "You get in bed, like you're sick, pull your hair around your face. I'll answer the door.

With a few days' growth of beard, I don't fit any description they might have."

She grabbed his arm as a knock sounded at the door. "Simon," she hissed. "Act passive and confused. Talk about Nir."

He shooed her from the room. Waited a few beats. The knock came again.

When he opened the door he came face-to-face with a young man wearing a bright blue tunic and tights and an older woman in a jogging suit. Heeding Abbey's advice, he waited for them to speak first.

"Hi, neighbor," the young man said.

"Hello," he answered, hoping his voice sounded calmer than he felt.

"We're helping the police in a neighborhood search." The young man pulled out a strip of plastic and unfolded it into a square, like a picture frame. Within the frame, an image of him and Abbey appeared. It looked like maybe their driver's license photos, his own an unflattering image of middle-aged blandness. But the man standing in front of them at this moment could not look much like that Simon in the photo, like Simon before he was in love.

"You seen either of these people?" Blue-man smiled, narrowing his eyes. "Or both of them?"

The woman was standing on tiptoe, looking past Simon, into the house.

"I don't get out much."

"But have you seen them? Or know where they are? They're wanted by the police. Very dangerous."

Simon looked at the composite holo again. "No." He shook his head slowly. "I don't get out much."

"Live here alone, do you?" The man folded the frame back up and tucked it into the patch pocket on his tunic.

"My wife. She's sick in bed. We play Nir. Do you?"

"You do, do you?" came the response. "That why you don't cut your grass?"

"Grass? Don't have time. The neighbors complaining about me?" he asked, nodding his head across the street. "They making trouble for me?"

The young man put his hands up, defensively. "Don't worry. We don't care about the grass."

"How old's your wife?" the woman asked, speaking for the first time.

This question startled him.

"Could we see her?" She kept looking beyond his shoulder.

From behind him, Simon heard: "Who you talkin' to?"

Heart sinking, he turned to find that Abbey had come to stand next to him. Her face was ghostly pale, and dark circles formed hollows under her eyes. Her hair, cut short, stood out in spikes on her head. She stayed slightly behind him, pulling a bathrobe closely around her. Oh shit, the pair of them standing here, to match the photo . . .

The older woman scrutinized her. Then, without a comment, she turned and walked down the porch steps. After hesitating a moment, the man in blue followed her, to Simon's enormous relief. But he turned on the top stair, pulling out the closed, pencil-thin frame, gesturing with it. "If you see them, call the police."

Simon nodded. "We'll call."

He closed the door, leaning against it and let out a long, slow breath. "Jesus." He took a closer look at Abbey. "What happened to you?"

"Found the scissors."

Simon put his hand to her face, wiping off a heavy dose of powder on her cheek.

"Used a little of her makeup."

Damn, but she was resourceful. Damn if she hadn't just saved their hides. This time he succeeded for a moment in pulling her into his arms. He noticed he was shaking. The boy in blue had given him the creeps, him and his quiet companion. There was something about them; their self-assurance, perhaps; their single-mindedness, the slow progress of the patrol down the street, two by two, house by house. Simon's heart was sliding down a slope. He kept trying not to think, *mind control,* he kept trying not to think, *the Hhso have them.* And he kept thinking it.

They sat on the couch, huddled in each others' arms. As relief mixed with dread in a fine stew in his mind, he stroked Abbey's ruined hair, wanting more than ever to run, but not able to bring himself to fight with her again. They sat silently for a long while, and after a time, in sheer exhaustion, he drifted into sleep.

He awoke with a start. Abbey was standing in the middle of the living room. All around her, a field of wavering colors stretched from one wall to the other. A bird flew across the room, its long yellow fur rippling behind it like silken scarves. It disappeared into the wall.

Abbey turned to face the couch where he sat transfixed. "The pendant," she said. "It's making pictures."

~ 3 ~

After Simon's call, Phil Agnew tried and failed to dismiss Simon's story from his mind. If Simon—one of the steadiest men he'd ever met—was that edgy, maybe he had reason. Maybe something to the genetic-experimentation stuff—and if not, when, in the last thirty years of working the newsroom, was Phil Agnew above a wildgoose chase on the chance of a scoop? On instinct, he headed over to Riva Statten's office.

He was due at the legislature first thing in the morning; Riva had made that clear. When Riva Statten raised her left eyebrow, it meant you asked no questions. She'd done that, looking over her fashionable bifocals when she assigned him the story, so his priorities were clear. But he could be up to the Falls and back again in an afternoon, and it might be worth it.

He knocked on Riva's door and poked his head in. "Got a sec?"

She was busy scribbling something with an ordinary yellow pencil. Why Riva Statten, the hottest daily editor in the state, wrote with pencils, Phil had no idea.

"If I had a sec, my door would've been open."

He took that for a go-ahead, and sidled in. "Like to check out a story up-valley. Can you spare me for the afternoon?"

"No." Still writing. That was Riva, always doing two things at once. Always brief on the verbiage.

"I got a tip on some shenanigans. Like to check it out, Riva. Impeccable source. Feels like a story."

"We *got* shenanigans. The pres is going to have the gov's head on a platter. Got it straight from Phil Agnew." She looked at him deadpan over the glasses perched on her nose. A few wisps of grey framed her face like steel shavings.

He knew better than to argue. A bald plead was often best. "Please, Riva. I'll be back tonight."

"So where's this?"

"Medicine Falls. A cult group up there and a few of them maybe dead."

"Christ on a crutch. Medicine Falls? Last piece you did on the Falls was the hockey team. A yawner, Phil. Skip it."

He hesitated.

Riva stared at him, pencil still poised over the yellow legal pad, left eyebrow raised.

Phil bobbed his head. "Yeah. Right." He gently closed the door. *Heil Riva.* He sighed and went back to the growing mound of paper that seemed to be propagating on his desk.

Riva Statten took off her glasses and rubbed her eyes. Ye gods, Medicine Falls. Don't touch that one with a ten-foot pole. Keep 'em busy on the air tax. Last thing this paper needs is Medicine Falls, for godsakes. It was an enclave, a pulse-point. Soon the whole valley would look northward to the herding grounds. But not yet. So *no*, Phil. We won't do a story on Medicine Falls. We won't check out the *shenanigans*. We'll leave them the fuck alone, you aging, worthless has-been. When I need *ideas*, I'll let you *know*. The pencil snapped in her hand.

She got up from her chair and used the electric pencil sharpener on both pieces of the broken pencil, swung past the door, locked it, and resumed her seat, and her visor, and her interview with the Hhso.

A wordless interview. An inquiry would arise in her mind and then knowledge would seep in, replacing ignorance. She found that lately she experienced less of her little fantasy and more of these—communions. And that they were flooding her with similar pleasure. She saw, or daydreamed, scenes of o-ghan, thousands of them, and humans, thousands too. And the sooh-an mistresses of herds, powerful, supremely focused, objects of reverence and tribute. The gatekeepers, metering out o-ghan favors to worthy males. Knowing each and all strictly by smell, and their lineage and their health, but for humans, all looking alike, with their gibberish smells, human herd mistresses were required. Such females would know and translate human needs, lest this herd sicken and die, lest it fail to thrive, fail to bear young. So the Riva one would see to their thriving, and become strong and receive tribute also.

An image of singular, powerful, interconnected women flooded her mind: her sisters-in-rank, at many herd enclaves on countless plains. With them Riva would in Nir share an overlay of knowledge even beyond the collective sharing of the herd. Riva felt the rush of emotions grip her body, feelings of loyalty and compassion. Here were the sooh-an mistresses, desperate beings. Riva could feel the anguish of the sooh-an as they watched the o-ghan crowded onto diminishing plains. And then the pain was tempered by a surge of hope for the succoring fields of the new home.

Chapter 14

~1~

Max Cobb was worried. He leaned against a tree in the Town Commons and tried to gather his thoughts. A noon sun glittered off the shopwindows surrounding the little park, and drew a few people to sit on benches to enjoy the touch of warmth. But Max was too agitated to sit.

After crashing at the Salvation Army last night along with a roomful of outers and drunks, Max was ready to get out of town. But they weren't selling tickets. The TraveLink system wasn't accepting reservations for the intercity bus, though he'd tried four different times, at three different LinkStop terminals. You couldn't leave town, not by bus. He could understand a bus being full. But TraveLink said they were full tomorrow too. And all this week, and the next.

Max's plan had been to take the bus to Colson, where his nephew lived, the only one of the family who ever visited him. If he showed up on Nigel's front step, his nephew couldn't very well turn him away; and he'd listen about this Nir game, Nigel more than anyone.

If he could get there. Maybe he was just a crazy old man. They say that when you're crazy, you're the last one to know. But Max was not a man to dwell too long on self-doubt. He leaned against the tree, thinking through his options, and surveyed the park.

The little square, dotted here and there with twiggy winter trees, was faced by small shops, including Peavy's Drugs, with one of the last true lunch counters in the valley. But for such a nice day, the Commons was surprisingly empty. Often, on a sunny day and especially at noon, the place was filled with office workers enjoying a sandwich, and parents with strollers. Not today. In the whole park, only five people. Just over there, across from Peavy's, a young couple sat holding each other, sweetly, insipidly in love. A teenager with his back to Max sat on a newspaper and an old woman sat next to the fountain, eating something out of a bag.

Then he saw it. A bus humming down the street, and slowing to a stop by Peavy's. The intercity, by damn. Max hurried down the sidewalk and then across the street, ducking a few cars, and waving at the bus. Slow down, pal, he told himself. Heart getting a little workout.

The bus doors swooshed open and discharged a woman and a little girl with satchels. After letting them pass, he clambered in. "The LinkStop said you're full. But I see you're not," Max gasped to the driver. Indeed, the bus was empty.

The driver looked down on Max from his seat. "Will be," he replied.

"Will be what?"

"Full."

"You're not going to be anywhere near full!" Max pointed angrily down the aisle. "Every damn seat is empty!"

"Do you have a ticket . . . *sir*?"

"No, I don't have a ticket, I . . ."

"No ticket, no travel."

"But you . . ."

"But nothing." The driver and he locked eyes until Max relented and stepped back down to the street. The door pinched shut, almost taking his nose as a trophy.

The woman with the little girl looked at him pityingly, then took her child firmly by the hand and walked away. Max's face flushed. I look like a crazy old man.

But sane enough to notice they're lettin' folks *in* to Medicine Falls, if not out.

Taking up his post against the tree once more, Max tried to calm himself, closing his eyes, letting the sun warm them. He breathed deeply, smelling the musky odor of the thawing leaves. Need to avoid stress, Doc Harris said. But you needed a *little* stimulation, just to stay in the game, to bother to show up every day. And for all the stress and aggravation of running away from the home, he had to admit that this was about as alive as he'd felt for years. Like a hibernating animal, he'd been in that home, with most systems shut down, operating on minimal brain cells, letting the days count themselves off, letting his heart have its last few thousand ticks. Now, leaning against this tree, he thought of the old days when he had work to do, and the world noticed if it didn't get done.

The world of insurance claims adjustment was an exciting one. People in trouble; and sometimes out to milk everything they could from the little event that landed in their lives. Sometimes folks even staged the whole mishap themselves for personal profit, times when it was Max's special joy to expose them. So he had a nose for the phony, the doesn't-add-up, the slick performance. Case in point: the TraveLink system with its full but empty intercity buses.

The boy sitting in the grass in front of him stirred, shifting his position. From the side, Max could see he wore sunglasses, a bit of an overreaction to the first sunshine of the year. Then, Max saw what he really wore. A visor, a little blue-black visor like the kind Ms. Aziz used. Plugged into a hip pack.

A chill shimmied down Max's spine, and he pulled away from the tree. At that moment, he looked over to see the old woman near the fountain looking at him and smiling.

Now, it is one thing to smile at someone as you pass them on the street, but a good deal different if the smile comes from forty meters away. Typically such smiles came from salespeople, preachers, and nutcases, but Max found himself walking in her general direction anyhow, with no better destination in the offering.

She wasn't exactly old. Matter of fact, she looked to be a little younger than he was, which meant she wasn't old from his standpoint. She wore a pair of slacks and a high-buttoned blue wool coat, with her hair cut very short around a pleasant face and eyes with a knack for snagging at a distance. Around her feet were scattered pieces of popcorn. As he drew near, her smile broadened.

"Nice day," she said, innocuously enough.

He stopped in front of her. "I suppose it is."

Holding her bag of popcorn, and looking out into the sky, she said, "No pigeons today."

He looked around. That was true; no birds at all, in fact.

"I come here almost every day," she said. "I like to share my popcorn, but today I guess I have to eat it all myself. Would you like some?" She held out the bag.

Her eyes held a friendly look, but at the same time, the kind of wariness he'd seen in the eyes of people with something to hide. But he looked down at the bag, deciding it was time for a little human contact—a *reality check,* for Godsakes.

"Thank you." He dug into the small bag and took some popcorn. The butter and salt, two forbidden things on his diet, were wonderful. "Delicious," he said. When she offered again, he gratefully accepted.

"Too bad the birds aren't back," she said wistfully. "Do birds hibernate? I never thought they did, but then where have they gone to?"

"A damn good question." He plunged on, grabbing her lead. "Lots of questions could be asked. About lots of things." He pretended to examine the rust stains in the fountain, staying casual. "But no, birds don't hibernate."

"I didn't think so. Sometimes, at my age I start to wonder what I know, and what I've made up." She picked out and ate a few pieces of popcorn, but absently, as though she weren't tasting them.

"I know what you mean." *Like the park being deserted,* he started to say, then held back. Don't expose what you know; let her hang herself with what she says, if she's going to. In the claims business, he'd found that being silent would often draw people out to say things they wouldn't say if you asked them directly. They mistakenly thought that a quiet investigator was a satisfied one, and it put them at ease so they kept talking, adding to his store of details that might later fail to match up.

Then the woman did something unexpected. She turned to look at him, a direct, sudden and disarming gaze. "You're not one of them, are you?"

For a moment, Max wondered what she meant. She turned and looked over at the young man with the visor.

He wasn't sure who *they* were, but he answered, in spite of that: "No, I'm not."

"I didn't think so. I can usually tell," she said.

"Do a lot of people . . . wear those visors?"

She looked at him ironically. "Where've you been, if you don't know that?"

Sheepish, Max said, "Busy."

"You have to be pretty busy, then."

He gave up on pretense. Hell, what did he care what she thought of him? "I live over at Harvest Home. It's a nursing home." After a moment he added, "Minimum care."

"Oh. Well then, you might not know."

"Know what?"

"Know . . . how popular Nir is. The game."

"Some game!" Max snorted. "Our manager, she was totally addicted to it."

"Hush!" she said. She leaned closer to him, looking out on the Commons. "They might hear you."

Max was both intrigued and repelled. Miss Marple here might just be a little loopy, but if so, it was a winning loopiness. "Who's *they?*"

"I wish I knew. But they're making sure everyone plugs in. Except for old people like us; maybe we don't much matter to them. At least for now."

"And I thought *I* was paranoid." He said it nice, but it had to be said.

"I know how it sounds." Her voice was patient and sure. "You've noticed, though, that nobody can leave town."

Involuntarily, Max glanced over at the LinkStop. "You've been watching me."

"I'm sorry. I sit here a lot. And not much goes on."

Max shifted uneasily on the bench, a little farther away from her.

"You see," she went on, "I live just down the street. In a condo with my son." A soft, longing quality threaded its way into her voice. "He plays that game all the day long. Lately, he won't even come to the table for meals."

Her sincerity touched him. At the same time a pang of excitement rippled through him as he considered whether there could be a sinister connection between phony buses and addictive VR games. "What the hell is going on in this town?" he asked.

"Brainwashing's what it is. Turns people into Lost Ones, I call them. And some folks, well, they just go off the deep end."

"But who would try to brainwash a whole town?"

She nodded. "I let that stop me for a long while. No motive. But don't let it blind you to what's going on." She leaned in close, and whispered. "I think even the police play the game. They act real funny when you call them."

Max clicked on that one. That disengaged way they talked the time he reported Mrs. Anderson's death, yes it *could* be a connection, a lead.

"Kevin's a good boy," she was saying. "Divorced and all alone, except for me. . . ." She took a tissue out of her pocket and dabbed at her eyes.

"I'm sorry," he said. "It must be hard."

She smiled and perked back up. "Oh, sometimes, you've got to let the tears out. Lets me know I'm still alive. Not like one of them."

He nodded. "By the way. I'm Max Cobb."

"Gilda Tupper." She wiped her hand on her coat and offered it. "It's funny," she said. "This was my last morning in the park. I was going to leave today. Well, still am, actually."

"Leave?"

"Yes. And I planned to leave alone. Now . . . well, you wouldn't be interested in coming with me, would you?"

"You have a car?"

"Oh, a car won't do. But I have a better idea." She looked up at him. "By the way, how's your night vision?" Then she snapped alert, looking over to the west end of the Commons. "Oh dear. Here they come. The bully brigade."

Max followed her gaze. Several dozen people dressed in garishly bright colors were fanning across the Commons. They surged toward the young couple on the bench, who, oblivious, didn't look up until the group began to surround them.

Gilda sighed. "I hate to watch this."

Someone raised his voice, and a scuffle ensued, ending with the young man on his knees.

As Max started to rise, Gilda put her arm on his. "Don't. It won't do any good."

Several people in their bright costumes pulled the young woman along, obviously against her will, while her boyfriend was restrained by several others.

Max watched uneasily as two men crowded onto the bench, with the young man in the middle, and handed him a small package of something.

"That'll be his copy of Nir," Gilda said in disdain.

Max ran his hands over his face. My God, what was going on? He experienced a sudden, instinctive urge to get as far away from here as possible. Over among the bully brigade, the young man had donned a visor.

"It's like a drug, isn't it?"

"I wish it were a drug," Gilda responded. "You wouldn't catch respectable people shooting up or sniffing powders. But nearly everyone plays video games, and retina games are just the next step. So it's crept in among us." She looked him in the eye. "And it's killing us."

"How bad . . . has it got?"

She smiled. "Yes, that's the question, isn't it?" She crumpled her popcorn bag into a tight little ball. "I figure it's just about got everybody in the Falls now. Outside—I don't know. The bus drivers out of Colson are all Lost, and my sister in Two Harbors. I have a few friends in Minneapolis and Chicago. None of them has heard of it. So I think it starts in smaller places, and spreads."

Max tried to digest this information. It was slow going. But he asked: "So you've got some secret way out of Medicine Falls?"

She smiled a pert smile. "Maybe I do."

"Don't tell me you'd trust the first man you meet that doesn't wear sunglasses?"

"Oh, not the first. Not the first by any means."

Now he got the picture. "You've interviewed a bunch of people, haven't you, sitting here on this bench with your lure of popcorn and your little story of the missing pigeons?"

"Exactly."

He nodded in appreciation, coming to a sudden decision. "Ms. Tupper, I'd be honored to accompany you. If you'll have me?"

She looked at him with a cheerful, but shrewd eye: "Oh, you'll do."

~ 2 ~

From the tiled diamond in the lobby floor, a locator sprang to visual.

"Simon Haskell's office," Zachariah said. The woman's eyes scanned him with icy disdain, this ill-dressed, penniless loser. He would have taught her some respect, but she was a waste of time. He had to hurry before the world ended.

"Three-oh-seven," she said. "Unfortunately, the elevator is temporarily out of service. The stairs are to your right. Further assis . . ." The voice degraded into static as her form snapped into a thin line and disappeared, snatching the bright holo light away and leaving him in the murky foyer lit only by the windows fronting the street. A wisp of burnt plastic and silicon, the smell of electronic death, hit his nostrils.

Here was what folks thought was a smart building. Now fallen apart, dumb as a cow.

The stairway door yielded to him, swinging open to reveal a well of darkness. For reassurance he reached into his jacket pocket, touching the squirting packet, its silken hairs tickling his skin.

Zachariah watched this part of himself, this coward, with detached humor: afraid of the dark. Pathetic.

Groping for the stair railing, he ascended, thinking, thinking. . . . She had evaded them all: Hhso, police, townspeople, Zachariah too. But that was before he took time, concentrated time, to focus on her. Now she had his full attention. He climbed the stairs, seeing her before him, seeing her look down on him, sneering at his stupidity. From the beginning it was ruin she wanted. His ruin. Oh, it was all ruin, he knew that. The Hhso were coming, the Hhso were coming, the Hhso . . . but she *wanted* ruin. She was an agent of slumping decay, a virus to hunt down the structure of his happiness. He moaned. The stairwell moaned. Who was moaning?

He turned his head, listening. Buildings creaked, they settled, but even so, he drew out and fondled the soft packet. Maybe not as slick as shooting it out your finger like the Hell Dogs, but a nice little weapon, all the same. Just a squeeze would freeze!

At the third floor landing, he fumbled along the wall for the door.

A voice crackled: "Turn right down the hall for Simon Haskell's office."

The failed version staggered backward, nearly dropping the packet in his hand. He pivoted to face this attack.

A locator, *dummy*. The building power was cut off, but running sporadically on some emergency source.

"Simon Haskell is not in," the locator said.

Not in! Of course he's not in, you stupid mass of chips! He opened the hallway door. Overhead, clerestory windows lit the hallway, which was littered with papers and shattered glass. Maybe the place had been vandalized. Even in this extreme circumstance, crime still thrived. He felt a momentary affinity for anyone who still cared enough to steal. Here was venality you could understand: common human evil. Oh, bring it back, back. Perhaps some powerful few could yet strike out against the Hhso. A few good men: the vicious, psychotic, amoral.

How would the Hhso deal with all the evil humanity could muster?

As he walked down the hall, glass from the smashed office doors crunched under his feet, recalling that other recent sound of pulverizing, growing stone.

. . . the yellow, barnacled bunkhouse . . . Little Dog placing the tablet on the ground . . . the hulking monster, taller than the Hhso . . . the migration . . . many will come . . . you will see how many . . .

Lonnie, Mother, Lonnie, make it go away. Make it be different. Make the world as you do, as you always do. . . .

Behind him. Yes! Someone following. He ducked into an office where the door had been kicked in and flattened himself against the wall, gripping the freeze sack. The stairwell door closing, heavy, definitive. Someone standing there, smelling him out . . . Simon Haskell, Abbey's bodyguard . . . or . . . Hhso, out in the open.

The crunching of glass, stopping near his door.

Someone walked farther down the hall, passing him. He inched toward the door and peered out, holding the sack, ready to squirt.

He saw a diminutive man picking his way through the glass shards, arms full of something. Likely stealing things. He watched him try to open a locked door. He went on to the next. This thief wanted easy pickings.

Just above Zachariah's head an office voice intoned, "Mr. Ogden is not in. Please leave a message."

At this, the thief swirled, scattering what he carried in his arms, and Zachariah was out the door and after him, to bring him down before he called to his fellows. Glass flew out as his feet pounded down the hall, gaining, gaining. With a quick turn his prey vanished into an office, slamming the door behind him, but Zachariah's foot was already bashing into the door, gaining an opening. Then, with shoulder pressed against the frame, he came crashing through.

The man shrank against the wall, eyes popping wide.

In an instant, Zachariah could see he was a sheep. And more. Cheap, wrinkled suit, disheveled hair, simple fear radiating from a sallow face. Here was a man not yet seduced by Nir, hiding, stripping the offices little by little.

The sheep cowered before him, before his total control, before his force of personality. Before the true Zachariah.

The man rolled his eyes in the direction of Zachariah's outstretched hand, which held the freeze packet as though it were a gun. Zachariah feinted toward him, and the sheep flinched. It was like holding the strings of a marionette.

"Who are you?"

A tatter of a voice answered: "Roland Waler. I play Nir."

Zachariah snorted. The creature would say anything to please him. *I play Nir* did not please him, lie though it was. "You want to live? Or is it all the same to you?"

The Waler-sheep blinked. "Live."

"Have you seen Simon Haskell?"

Waler's face twitched to the side from time to time in an annoying tick that was worth shooting off a squeeze right there.

"Seen him?" He licked his lips. "Who's seen anyone here for weeks?"

Zachariah moved a step closer, leading with his fist. "You know what this is?" He held the packet up. "Poison and death. In a squeeze."

"Haskell," Waler squeaked, in response. "No, he's gone."

"Know where?"

Waler shrugged.

"Is that a no?" Zachariah was ready to put him down just for shrugging. It was rude.

"I haven't seen Haskell for weeks, or his partner." He gestured down the hall. "His office is right down there. He's a shifty son of a bitch. Keeps to himself." He began talking faster, spilling out words, watching Zachariah for some reaction. "I've got food, canned and vacuum-packed. I know where people keep things. I could help you. A man like me makes a good associate. Confidential."

"Shut up."

A twitch to the left, mouth snapping closed.

"Let's go visit Haskell's office."

Waler led the way, scuttling sideways, looking back now and then, focusing on Zachariah's balled-up fist.

Simon Haskell's door was knocked in, off one hinge. The entire room was torn apart, with desk drawers pulled out onto the floor, lamps overturned, computer cords yanked and scattered. Afternoon light slid through the two windows in shafts of dust-mote-ridden light.

Waler was a black silhouette. "They were here. The police."

"They find anything?"

"Find anything? Who knows?" Startled at Zachariah's expression, he added quickly, "I couldn't hear them talk. They were here a long time, took the computers. One thing the police didn't figure on, though," Waler said slyly. He waited a few moments, making Zachariah ask:

"Oh, what was that?"

"The comps. They were Rocky's. Not Haskell's." He smiled, showing brackish teeth. "Haskell was a bad fit with the twenty-first century."

Zachariah cocked his head.

"Paper, see?"

Zachariah stepped forward and slapped him on the side of the head, sending Waler to his knees. "Fast, tell me fast, or you're a dead man!"

Waler covered the side of his head with his hand. With his other hand, he pointed to a strange, black plastic item on the floor. Under the thing, small, oblong cards spilled.

"Rolodex," he said. "Haskell kept all his addresses on little white cards."

Zachariah glanced down at the contraption. "What addresses? Where might he be going, if say, he was going to hide?"

"I don't know! Maybe he'd go to Rocky's apartment?"

Dead end, police had searched there.

"Where else?"

Waler leaned against the desk, and pulled himself up. "Well, maybe Rocky's wife's house. I offered to buy it, as crummy as it was. Pretty good offer, but . . ." He shrank back at the look on Zachariah's face.

"What was her name, her maiden name?"

"Name?" He swallowed, twitching his last, annoying jerk to the side. "Paige. Lydia Paige. But then when she married Rocky . . ."

Zachariah smiled. "That's all, Roland Waler."

"That's all?" the sheep bleated.

"Yes." He sprayed him in the face with a few pumps on the little furry bag, and as Waler swayed, he kicked him backward so he wouldn't fall on the Rolodex.

~ 3 ~

Under a stiff breeze, in the middle of Lydia's living room, coppery grasses bent, glinting in a harsh sun. A tundra of burnished grasses shimmered into the far distance, beyond which the room's wallpaper formed an obscure, flowered backdrop.

Abbey heard Simon whisper from behind her, "What the hell is this?"

"Pictures," Abbey said. "The pendant is giving us pictures." She held Jaguar's medallion, which had altered from its cloudy appearance to a deep, translucent purple. The spiral in its midst glowed molten yellow.

Wind whipped the grass strands against the flanks of bloated, low-slung, four-legged alien creatures. Hundreds of them dotted the grassland. With slow tugs of their long necks, they dragged clumps of grass up by the roots and slowly masticated them. Off to the side, by the TV set, one of the grazers was giving birth. Out of a short tube in the back of the creature, a glistening sac bulged. Methodically, the creature detached from it by plodding forward a few steps.

The sac squirmed and trembled until at last a small, cylindrical foot emerged, with pearlescent toenails.

The mother—like all the grazers—was covered with a deep golden and short-napped hide, into which elaborate tattoos appeared to be etched. She turned around to inspect her issuance. Her head, protruding from the end of her neck, consisted of a tooth-encircled orifice over which a fold of skin was just now descending. Using this softened set of—lips—the creature nudged the pulsing sac, inducing a frenzy of jostling. Another foot emerged from the birth sac. The mother hissed soothingly, a sound that melded into the hissing of the other grazers.

Near and far, the birthing scene was repeated and repeated.

Simon put his arm around Abbey as she sat down next to him. "What in the world . . ."

The scene faded, to be replaced by a landscape of brown, undulating hills where patches of the orangey grass sprouted along channels running with water. A group of burly-armed individuals were cultivating the soil with short hoes. One of the diggers looked up, revealing a small face dominated by a great, hinged mandible which opened once and closed.

"Jesus," Simon whispered. "What *is* that?"

In the scene, the creature raised a thick hand, wiping it across its brow in an immemorial gesture of fatigue. Just above the heads of the workers, a network of fiery lines appeared for a moment, then disappeared, as though an invisible tent with thousands of struts covered the scene.

"What *is* this?" Simon repeated under his breath.

"I think they're worlds, Simon. Different worlds than ours, and different creatures." Her hand trembled, holding the pendant. It wasn't like a vid, or a computer simulation. These were, she felt sure, real scenes, real places, with the feel of actual wind, the sounds of the grazers, the musky smell of birth . . .

"How did it start? Did you push something?" Simon glanced at the square in her hand.

"No. It just started. I was asleep."

Another landscape infused the living room. A city of towers loomed up, far above the ceiling, with spires stabbing at high, cumulus clouds. Dust blew in rippling patterns down the narrow, abandoned streets, accumulating in great drifts against the towers and scouring into surrounding coppery fields that flowed to the horizon. Out from one of the towers a being emerged, shaped like a cone and rolling upon an unseen mechanism. Jutting from a topmost nodule, a spray of cilia fluttered in the wind, just above a circlet of metal within which a drill of light pulsed.

And everywhere, the copper grasses.

"What do you . . . want?" Abbey found herself saying, speaking to the cone-creature, or the towers, or the projection itself. Perhaps there was a message here, something she was supposed to understand. . . .

A piercing sound invaded the room. At first high-pitched, then zooming down into a soprano range, it warbled, half like a bird.

Abbey felt Simon's grip around her shoulders tighten. "It's responding!" he said. Then louder, "Who are you?" The tower-scene wavered, clouding into an opaque, watery blue. Through this liquid mass the living room furniture stretched and contorted as though seen in a funhouse mirror. Abbey swiped her hand through it, seeing her hand turn grey, and reemerge, leaving no trace behind. She held her breath, waiting.

"What . . ." she began.

"Wha . . ." a sound echoed. Before them lay a mass of thick blue jelly. In its depths, tiny sparks of light erupted in random progressions.

A tremor crawled down the back of her neck. "What do you want?" she whispered.

From the gelatinous blue came: "Do you want?" The words sang out, high and sharp.

"What are these scenes?" Simon ventured.

The jelly lay still. Deep inside, a pinprick of light sparked and dimmed, leaving the mass cool and dark for a time.

Abbey jumped up. "Maybe it only responds to me." She swallowed hard, trying to locate her voice, which seemed to have fled down her throat. "What . . . do you . . . want?"

Then, in an uncanny near-human voice, the word came: "Select."

Abbey turned to Simon, questioning. He looked at her, frowning, struggling.

She turned back to the projection. "How? How do I select?"

"How do you select?" The voice became female, oddly like Abbey's own voice, with a sharp harmonic at the edge. "Choose."

Abbey rummaged through her mind, wondering what she was supposed to choose.

"Shall we have a name?" the mass prompted.

She turned back to Simon, who pressed on her arm. "Jesus, Abbey," he said, "*talk* to it."

"Who needs a name?" Abbey asked.

A pause. "I do."

"Who are you?"

"I am gel. Shall I have a name?"

Simon nudged Abbey impatiently. "How about Fred?"

"Are you human?" Abbey asked.

"No."

She paused. "Your name could be Lucy. Is that OK?"

"Yes."

"*Lucy* for Godsakes?" Simon said in exasperation.

"Lucy in the sky with diamonds. The way the blue gel is sparkling with light." She looked at his confused face. "Never mind."

"Ask it why it's talking to us."

"What do you want from us?" Abbey asked.

The gel remained silent, the shards of light surging now and then.

"Ask it what it's showing us," he suggested.

"What are these pictures of—Lucy?"

"These are the herd worlds controlled by Hhra." The voice settled into a natural and familiar tone, as though Abbey were having an ordinary, pleasant conversation with . . . herself.

"Hurrah?" Abbey said, attempting the strange word.

The word *Hhra* appeared just to her side. Experimentally, Abbey reached out to touch it. The letters glowed for a second, undulating on the wavering gel.

Lucy corrected: "Hhra," making a guttural sound of the H as Jaguar had done with Hhso. "The herd worlds of Hhra are as follows: the Kezzri, the Lallu-Quostian, the Ne, the Jartreal, the M'tori . . ." Each word appeared on her right, stacking above the first.

As the names stacked higher, Simon reached out and touched the word *Hhra*.

"Hhra," Lucy said. "The Hhso origination world." Before them, an orange planet hung in star-strewn space. From the vicinity of the kitchen an enormous object—a moon—came barreling, slipping past Abbey and Simon even as they staggered backward. A series of numbers and descriptors offered themselves on Abbey's right, where the stack of names had been a moment before.

"Hhra is massive compared to your world." By way of explanation, a projection of Earth's blue orb appeared in the center of the orange planet, dwarfed by the great mass of Hhra.

This image vanished to be replaced by a skimming aerial view above a sea of long-necked grazers, placidly making their way through bright grasses. In the distance, and rapidly approaching, lay a sparkling compound of low, round, and deeply golden-red constructs that appeared to be made of crystal. Then, beyond the compound, another field crowded with birthing, chewing creatures.

"What are these animals, Lucy?"

"These are the o-ghan." The word appeared as Lucy continued: "O-ghan are Hhso breeder-constructs. Hhso measure personal value by size of their individual o-ghan herds. The size of each herd indicates sexual prowess and wealth. The vast and multiplying o-ghan herds require constant Hhso migration," the voice went on, assuming a lecture tone.

"They keep their females like cows," Simon said in disgust.

"Despite superb technological achievements and scientific grounding the Hhso are firmly tied to the millennia-long traditions of the herd. They are unable to break with this tradition. Therefore, overpopulation, war, and conquest are the chronic conditions of Hhso society."

As Lucy spoke, scenes of the herds followed one another in close succession, along with views of Hhso warriors massing on bare plains, and finally a mighty armada of spaceships.

"Their women are slaves?" Abbey asked, still troubled by earlier scenes.

The view resolved into a display of a crystal compound where a Hhso of a different sort was seen moving among the o-ghan. "No," Lucy responded. "Hhso females are of two types. Minor females are warriors. Females of note are called sooh-an. The large individual you see here is a sooh-an."

The female Hhso appeared identical to the male standing beside her, except she was larger by half.

"The sooh-an female controls a personal herd of o-ghan, including all sexual access to that herd. Female status is determined by the number of o-ghan." From the sooh-an's fingers dripped a yellow, viscous liquid. "This sooh-an is angry. She has rejected the appeasement brought by this male. He will not mate with this sooh-an's herd.

"All construct breeders are controlled by females. This distributes power between females of note and the males of note, the chho-u. Chho-u are prime male leaders in technology and war. Minor males are drones and warriors. The o-ghan breeders free the Hhso females from the rigors of bearing. O-ghan are without higher intelligence, yet they are treated with great care, including compulsive grooming and birthing rewards. Sexual transmission is accomplished with the left hand of the male Hhso. . . ."

"Please, spare me." Simon growled.

"Show us something else, Lucy."

A scene appeared of a herd of o-ghan over which stretched a complex web of light strands not far over their backs. A legless, pasty-white creature extended one of four appendages, contacting one of the light strands, and skimmed over the backs of the o-ghan to a point far out into the field, where it lowered itself and disconnected. "This is the I-haar, a genetically bred servant of the Hhso." Lucy was providing a closer view of the creature that rode the light threads.

"Ask it about the Leap Point," Simon urged.

"Lucy, tell us what the Leap Point is."

The scene faded, replaced by the shimmering gel, which Abbey took for its version of "File not found."

"You know, Lucy," she urged. "The way Hhso got to Earth. The way Jaguar travels."

Instantly, Lucy projected the flash of a Leap Point and an emerging warrior-Hhso. Abbey recoiled a moment, then shook it off. Just a projection.

"The psionic jump"—the phrase formed at her side—"is controlled technology. It is the macroscopic application of the subatomic quantum jump. The Galaxion does not permit nonmember worlds, including expansionist species, to construct Leap Point platforms and use the psionic jump. The Hhso are in noncompliance."

"Goddamn right they're in noncompliance!" Simon gestured at the air in front of him. "Tell Ms. Lucy they're about to turn Earth into a cow pasture!" He paused. "And what the hell is the Galaxion?"

When Abbey asked, Lucy responded, "They are the admitted worlds. Linked with Leap Points, they form a network of worlds."

"Who is the Regent?"

"The Regents of the Galaxion oversee admissions."

"What admissions?"

"Candidate worlds require screening for potential contributions to the Galaxion. Those deemed contributing may be admitted, if resources to fuel psionic jump for interaction and communication are commensurate with the candidate contribution."

"What do the candidates contribute?"

"Science. Art. Technology."

"We have those things. Earth does." Abbey hesitated. "Don't we?"

"The requirements have long since been set. They are specific, measurable, unalterable over the millennia. Entire systems for performing sociocultural analysis exist to interpret and defend the requirements. Wars and religions have altered but not destroyed it. It endures."

"Are we—is Earth—a candidate?"

"Yes."

"Will we pass?"

"In marginal cases like yours, the Regent has authority to decide. You are marginal. Like the Hhso, you are an imitative species."

"We're nothing like the Hhso!"

"You are like the Hhso in being imitative. Unlike them in your caution. Being cautious and imitative, yours is a habitual culture. A drain on the Galaxion, and therefore likely to be excluded, like the Hhso."

"That's not fair. We've invented fabulous things. Created wonders."

"Some few of you invent and create, this has been noted."

Abbey looked to Simon for him to summon argument, but he stood oddly quiet.

After a long, silent pause he said: "Ask it why Earth hasn't been visited before."

"Lucy, why all of a sudden is Earth being visited? Where have all the aliens been, if the universe is so full of them?"

"Earth has been visited many times. For millions of years you have been visited, while your life-forms developed. Also during that time the Galaxion was maturing, and growing old. For the last few thousand years you have been watched and protected from techno-shock, and to preserve your future contribution."

Simon growled: "Decent of them."

"But why?" Abbey continued.

"The Galaxion desires to avoid stagnation. Worlds, especially younger worlds such as yours, provide cultural and intellectual renewal."

"But now they're just going to give up on us?"

"The Regent will decide."

Simon touched her arm, saying, "Ask it who Jaguar is."

Abbey turned back to face the projection. "Who is Jaguar?"

The blue sea pulsed for a moment before them. Lights flickered far into the shaded depths as though the gel stretched on and on.

Reformatting the query, Abbey asked, "Who is the person who uses a Leap Point on Earth besides the Hhso?"

From the gel, came: "This individual tries to save his people."

"Why does he need me? Why doesn't he do it himself?"

"You are of Earth."

"Jaguar is not of Earth?"

"He is, and is not."

"Lucy, show me where Jaguar is from."

From deep in the gel, a shape was emerging: a figure, running. A young boy.

Then there appeared a tumult of people racing through narrow streets of mud huts. The young boy, barefoot, his coal-black hair drawn into a short topknot, shouted exuberantly and looked back as he ran. His bronze-skinned playmates scattered as a phalanx of richly dressed officials ran forward, breaking open a wide corridor for the slower-moving knot of attendants, behind.

Beneath the cacophony of the crowd came a thumping, clattering sound: ka-thump, ka-thump, as the bulky form of a great machine lumbered forward, atop which stood a man in an ornamental cape and headdress, with red, pink, and yellow colors flashing in the sun.

Women, many adorned with elaborate, carved green earrings, emerged from doorways to stare. They clutched babies or flowed into the hurrying crowd.

A great steam-spewing engine clattered down the

street, bearing the resplendent figure. Simple iron-rimmed
wooden wheels carried a square platform, the sides of
which were densely scrolled with flowing designs, curling
and massing into a bewildering montage of half-hidden
monsters and the unmistakable progressions of hiero-
glyphs.

A driver sat low and almost obscured in the front of the
machine, steering with a large wheel set parallel to the
base. The only other occupant stood at stiff attention, his
arm linked around a colorless tube embedded in the platform. Aside from a towering headdress of animal-like de-
sign, he wore a loincloth and stiff cape painted with
fantastic shapes and relentless strings of runes.

"This is the ahau," Lucy said. "The lord."

"They look like Aztecs," Abbey whispered to Simon.

"I don't think so . . ." he mumbled.

The machine spewed gouts of white steam in pulses as
the engine cycled and thumped, finally lurching to the
base of a large stone monument in the shape of a T lying
flat, with the stem of the T a long staircase leading up past
a midpoint plaza and on to a flat dais on top where towering transparent tubes—four of them—stood embedded in
the stone. The lord descended from the engine, his dark
face dominated by a pronounced hook nose and a full
lower lip, pierced with a thin black shard of stone. The lip
bled, dripping onto the lord's bare chest, where the cape
was tied with a woven sash.

Nearby, a great bonfire belched smoke into the main
plaza, where people were rushing from all sides to con-
verge on the temple. As the lord stepped down, he raised
his hand to his mouth, spattering a fistful of paper strips
with his blood. Striding to the fire, and flanked on either
side by attendants draped in animal skins and painted
leather, the lord cast the papers into the fire. A deep-
throated roar went up from the crowd. As the lord turned
to ascend the steps, he exposed the back of his cape,
where, coiling from around the front, was the depiction of
a huge snake, lavishly painted, with scales composed of
calligraphic runes. From the gaping mouth of the serpent
emerged a lord-figure, with his headdress erupting in

feathers, and his front tooth inlaid with a sparkling green stone. . . .

"Not Aztec," Simon muttered. He nodded at the cape. "Maya. That snake, it's a Mayan symbol of some sort. And the glyphs. I knew I'd seen that sort before. Mayan."

"With steam engines?"

Simon's expression turned wry. "Well, maybe Lucy's getting her Earth history a little muddled."

The scene began to grow smaller, as Lucy shifted the perspective to high over the monument. On every side, a great press of trees . . . rank on rank of translucent, column-like trees with a slight cast of lavender, and with fretworks of lacy white branches spraying out at the tops.

"I don't think that's Mexico, Simon."

He ran his hand through his hair, his face catching a sickly cast from the lavender shadows.

As the scene faded, Simon prompted, "Ask it what Nir is."

"What is the Nir game that is hurting people of Earth?"

"The neuronic bond. The neuronic bond sedates and controls, delivering pleasure and loyalty. It interfaces with the mind and retrieves the deepest desire, providing a trade: happiness for volition. The bond also provides Hhso indoctrination." A Hhso appeared before them wearing a complicated-looking piece of metal headgear. "This individual helps to monitor the neuronic bond. However, this technology is not permitted by the Galaxion. . . ."

Behind Abbey, Simon's profound snort.

A montage of scenes paraded before them, creatures upon creatures, subjugated, working, waiting, dying. All had a device attached, to head or neck. "The neuronic bond," Lucy said, "can be fatal. For the psychotic, or any other mentally ill individual, a neuronic surge executes. By this means the Hhso cull out the defective."

Simon sat back down on the couch, head in his hands, rubbing his eyes. "Christ," he mumbled. His voice came very quiet: "Turn the damn thing off, can you?"

"Just one more thing, Lucy."

Lucy went to blue. The gel settled into a thick, deep soup where only an occasional burst of light could be seen.

"Why doesn't the Galaxion help us?"

The living room was a deep pond of pure liquid. The light from the curtained windows didn't penetrate, but bounced back upon the window edges as though they were rimmed with fire. In the dining room and the kitchen beyond, intermittent sparks receded like beacons on sailing vessels fleeing a port.

"Why don't they help us?" Abbey repeated.

Finally, Lucy responded, "Some wish not to."

"Jesus, why not!" Simon blurted out.

"Why not?" Abbey relayed to the fading light.

The room darkened. "Too tired . . ." Lucy's voice grew faint. "Too tired . . ."

"What do you want us to do?" Abbey finally asked the question that had been lurking in the back of her mind.

But Lucy did not speak again. The gel began to dry up and separate into cavities which ballooned in size until only strands of viscous gel remained. Then this remnant snapped out of sight altogether, sucking out the remaining warmth of the room.

Simon looked up at Abbey, his face swept clear of his usual expressions. He looked strangely lost. "What the hell *is* all this?" he whispered.

She walked slowly to the couch, sinking down next to him.

He shook his head. "They think they can take us without a fight," he said. "And maybe they're right."

"No. They're not."

Simon tried to smile, failed.

"Simon . . ." she began. There was just one more thing she had to know. Otherwise it was all explained, or as much as she needed for what she planned to do. "When Lucy said, 'Too tired,' did she mean the program was tired, or losing energy, or whatever, or that the Galaxion was too tired . . . to help us?"

"If you ask me," he said, "I think we're on our own."

Drained, she leaned against him. "Simon, hold me."

His arms circled around her, blanking out everything. She lost herself in the exquisite comfort of his embrace. Then, after a moment, shivering with cold, they helped each other walk to the bedroom, each one steadying the other, and piled all the blankets from the spare bedroom on their bed and climbed under them.

They lay holding each other a moment, tangled in clothes and sheets. Then Abbey said: "Do you mind if I take my clothes off?"

A longish pause, and she was starting to regret the words. But he said, "Will it be up to me to keep you warm?"

"Yes."

"Then I insist."

She got out of bed and took her clothes off, burrowing under the frigid covers. Simon followed her lead, undressing and climbing in beside her.

For a while it was impossible to move, with the sheets like flaps of ice around them, but gradually they warmed each other, lying spoon-fashion, Simon's body wrapped around her. She heard him whisper: "I love you, Abbey."

"Shhh. You don't have to say that."

He gently pulled her onto her back and braced himself on one elbow. She could see him so clearly in the afternoon light, every nick and crease of his face, every corner of his heart.

"I know I don't have to say it. But it's true. It's always been true."

A smile welled up. Still, she asked, "Why?"

He smiled back, pushing strands of hair from her forehead, tracing her face with his fingertips. "Damned if I know." He bent down to kiss her throat, as he whispered, "But you do make me crazy." She opened her mouth to say something, but he touched his finger to her lips, silencing her. "I'm just stupidly, desperately in love with you. So you can do with me pretty much as you like."

He kissed her sweetly, then urgently, as Abbey gave herself up to it, to Simon, to a surge of unaccustomed arousal. She closed her eyes to savor this man, who loved her for no good reason, and whom she loved also, without reason. She whispered, "What will become of us, Simon?"

"Maybe we'll start over," he said, his voice gravelly. "How would that be?"

She clung to him. "So you'll stick around?"

"Try and get rid of me," he said, and he became insistent, and she gave up on words at last, and they gave up on the blankets, and tossed them back.

As the afternoon deepened, and the bedroom warmed considerably, Abbey learned that indeed, Simon was not a man who gave up too soon.

Chapter 15

~1~

Getting out of Medicine Falls was going to be a tricky enterprise, Max realized. First, they had to check out a co-op car—with a trailer hitch—from Gilda's downtown condo. That much had been easy. Nobody else was using the shared cars today, which in itself was a little fishy, lending more credence to Gilda's Nir conspiracy, that everyone was tuning in, turning on, and dropping out. Next, they needed to unobtrusively retrieve Gilda's plane from her sister's barn and hope nobody would notice that they were towing a collapsed ultralight airplane with a thirty-five-foot wingspan. Finally, and most improbable, they had to fly the damn thing—which on first glance appeared to be little more than a tandem lawn chair with wings.

Folded up on the lowboy trailer, the ultralight rattled behind them as they drove along the rough dirt road. With each wing jointed and folded in the middle, the plane was still a fifteen-foot-long advertisement that they were decamping Medicine Falls, and at dusk, no less, when they'd have some light to see by, but not *be* seen.

It wasn't that Max was becoming paranoid. No, he had begun this investigation fair and square, just digging for information, picking up stones to see what wiggled. But the facts, as he used to say, had reached critical mass. What tipped it over was the unpleasant little interview with Gilda's sister Lynn, who, wearing a flannel nightgown—no robe, mind you—and lug-soled boots, had keen misgivings about their taking the plane out for a spin. It gave him the willies to remember her shifty eyes and the hard set of her mouth.

"Can't you hurry?" Max felt decidedly uneasy, wondering just how fast Lynn had gotten to the phone after they left.

Gilda speeded up, leaning forward and squinting over the steering wheel, as they plunged into a depression in the road and flew out the other side, connecting with the road in a heart-stopping explosion of dust and Plexiglas followed a microsecond later by the ultralight's clattering protest on the trailer bed.

"My night vision isn't what it used to be," Gilda apologized. She was dressed in a paperish thermal suit with a few tears mended with tape, and goggles perched on her head. Amid the jolts, the earflaps of her leather helmet flapped like dog ears. At last she pulled into the scruff on the side of the road and stopped.

They stood on the windy flats of the southern edge of Medicine Ridge. Six hundred meters away, the ridge fell away to the valley floor. Not a good spot for a takeoff, in his opinion—but what he knew about flying would make light reading indeed. "I need the updraft" was all Gilda would say.

Max pulled out the gym bag stuffed with a few of Gilda's essentials: makeup bag, address book, clean blouse, change of shoes, bag of potato chips, a wrench, and a large roll of duct tape. When he'd raised an eyebrow over the tape, she'd said, "Most of my minor crashes, I can fix with duct tape."

As she lowered the back end of the trailer toward the

ground, she said, "Don't worry, an ultralight is hard to crash." She nodded at the little two-cylinder motor attached to the nose of the craft. "For go-power we have a good little Rotax engine that'll probably still be chugging along when I'm not."

While she unfastened the anchoring bungee cords on her side, Max followed suit on the other side, and they guided the craft on its wheel assembly down onto the dirt road. From the way it glided effortlessly, Max estimated it weighed no more than three hundred pounds, and most of that was probably the engine. Gilda unfolded the wings, securing them in place to reveal an expanse of rip-stop nylon over an airframe as light as sparrow bones. The cantilevered wings were supported by aluminum struts bolted into a go-cart-like cockpit that held two seats, one in back of the other, behind which a short tail group jutted. The passenger end of the cockpit had no floor, aside from two forlorn-looking metal stirrups.

Gilda stood back a moment to admire the plane. "Might be kit-built, but it's beautiful to its mother." From her flightsuit came a small mirror and a tube of lipstick. She pressed her lips together and grimaced into the mirror, then dumped the stuff back in her pocket. "It's been a while since it carried two people, though," she said wickedly. Then she scrambled into the pilot's seat, turning the engine over, twice, while Max ducked under the wings and managed to lower himself into the hard plastic seat behind her, slipping his feet into the stirrups and resolving not to look down past his knees.

She handed him a ski hat and gloves. "It'll be cold," she said, revving the engine. A cloud of white smoke belched out, sliced into ribbons by the propellers. And then she added: "You're going to be my eyes."

"Your *what*?"

"Eyes. Never flown at night before. Can't see in the dark too well. Ready?" A sustained clatter erupted from the engine as the ultralight began a slow roll. "Seat belt!" she shouted over her shoulder.

He found it flapping at the sides, and managed to clamp it tight around his midriff. As the craft picked up speed, Max pressed his hand against his chest, needful, since he was sure his heart was just then planning a jump out of his chest. The plane skipped over the bumpy field and with a final, paper-thin boost, laid itself on the mercy of the presumed updraft.

Hit by a surge of air roaring up the wall of the ridge, the plane bounded upward. Then it seemed to be treading air for a moment before it tipped to the side just enough so that Max could see the tiny conifers on which he would be impaled, below. Righting itself, the craft puttered forward, sailing into the icy, blue evening.

Tucked behind Gilda and the windshield, he found himself relatively protected from the wind, but he was still grateful for the wool cap and gloves. If he looked straight ahead, he could convince himself they were in a real airplane, and not this loose concoction of tubes and chairs. As they climbed, they burst into the sun's last rays, for a reprise of the sunset. Max's spirits soared.

Gilda's scarf was whipping backward like a flag, bravely slapping about in the wind. "You OK?" she said, looking over her shoulder.

Max grinned, giving her a thumbs-up. If only Doc Harris could see him now.

Down on the left, the lights of Medicine Falls were just emerging in the falling dusk. It was, all in all, a small place, with a fierce glow of commerce at the center, quickly falling off to the dark fields pressing in from every side. How small and brave it looked, and how vulnerable, seen from the eagle point of view.

He leaned forward to shout in Gilda's ear: "What am I supposed to be looking for?"

"The highway. We'll stay to the south of it, but keep it in view!"

As he looked down, he noticed a cluster of lights at a point on the highway, and in the next instant, he heard a series of sounds—thrup, thrup, thrup as a row of holes appeared in the nylon wing covering. Then a bright light flooded over them from below, and the right-hand wing strut cracked in two.

His torso yanked inward a moment, realizing, an instant before his brain, that someone was shooting at them.

"Gunfire!" he shouted. "We're hit!"

Gilda looked back in alarm at the aluminum tubing, now broken in two and flapping wildly under the right wing. More gunfire, which Max now realized was tearing through the nylon wing covers, passing through cleanly leaving only small, dark holes.

Gilda veered off at an angle to the highway, shouting, "Duct tape that strut!"

Fumbling at the bag with his hands muffled in thick gloves, Max tried and failed to yank on the zipper, and finally tore off the gloves, losing them overboard, but at least getting the case open. Duct tape in hand, he looked over at the separated tubing that would require him to lean far over into the wind, if he could even grab the damn things that fluttered in the wind, still precariously held by their respective bolts on wing and cockpit.

They were losing altitude.

"We took a hit in the engine!" Gilda hollered.

As Max looked down, he saw that a platoon of cars was speeding along the highway in their direction. "Get away from the road," he shouted back.

"Leave the flying to me and fix the darn strut before we lose the wing!"

He tore off a piece of tape and looked for something to hold on to, choosing the main strut running down the spine of the plane. Loosening his seat belt and hoisting himself into a crouch, he held on with his left hand as he leaned to the right, stretching forward to slap the tape on the upper fragment of the strut. The tape folded uselessly in on itself, forcing him to sit back down, pull off another length of tape, and swing back out to snag the fragment again and grab on to the other half of it, squeezing it together in a miserable approximation of a patch.

He collapsed back into the seat, swearing like he hadn't in years.

Gilda was turned around, looking behind them. A shot ripped through somewhere close to Max's head.

The ultralight was now in a steep descent, and caught

in the harsh beam of light from their pursuers on the ground.

"Turn right!" Max hollered.

She banked the plane, turning parallel to the path of the oncoming cars, and presenting, for the moment, the full length of the plane for a target. Just ahead was a farm building with a stand of poplars. Max shouted out course corrections, with Gilda responding, swerving in a drunken dance toward's Max's target. Shots erupted constantly now from the oncoming cars, as Max hunkered down as far as he could, clutching the role of tape, and wondering if they'd be using it for bandages in a moment, or if this damn toy would simply sink like a deflated balloon and set them down in the arms of the gun-happy crew below.

With Max's eyes and Gilda's piloting, they managed to strand the cars back on the road, as Gilda slipped the plane behind the trees, lightly brushing one wing tip along the wall of jutting branches. For a moment the gunfire stopped. When they emerged out the other side, Gilda managed to coax the plane into a climb. Skimming into the night sky and leaving the searchlight behind, they pulled the darkness around them like foxes slipping into a thicket.

Eventually they found the highway again, not venturing close, but with Max keeping it in sight, at least. He hunkered down in his seat, thoroughly chilled and shaking hard.

"How're you doing?" Gilda called back.

"Great!" he answered. Actually, now that it was over, he was scared to death. His heart was battering against his chest like a puppy struggling in a gunnysack, and at the same time his muscles were weak from exertion. But he was smiling. After all, he had just leaned out of an airborne hammock at fifty miles per hour and fixed a broken wing strut; and the best part of it was, this gutsy woman in front of him had fully expected that he would pull it off.

And he had.

• • • •

They landed in Nigel's not inconsiderable front yard, after circling with the last thimblefulls of their fuel as Max tried to locate his nephew's estate from the air—and *at night*, yet.

Gilda was looking up at the tiers of porches that comprised the front of Nigel's fortresslike mansion. "Oh my Looord," she said. "What does this nephew of yours *do*, for heaven's sake?"

It was always a tough question. "Sometimes he's a stock trader. Right now he's into Net music. But usually it's deengineering."

A light flashed on, submerging them in a traveling spotlight. When Gilda jumped, Max took her arm, saying, "Nigel's Seeing Eyes." He pointed above them, where, hovering about ten meters off the ground, a globe tracked them as they walked to the front porch. "Hey, Nigel, it's Max. Shut off the damn secret police, will ya?" Several Eyes were clustered around the visitors as they reached the front door, and in unison their lights winked out.

"Nigel regrets being unable to come to the door," the house informed them. "He invites you to join him in Mission Control." Max heard the door unlock, and he stepped forward to open it for Gilda.

As they made their way through the foyer, Max saw that not much had changed in the three years since he'd visited. Nigel still had the stuffed ocelot with the eyes that followed you and the enormous model-train platform shaped like a mountain and looped with track running over bridges and mountainside towns, carrying Nigel's prize Santa Fe Super Chief and twenty cars. The display was still in the middle of the living room, where, Nigel told his soon-to-be-ex-wife, it would stay until hell froze over. The walls were chock-full of a ludicrous variety of paintings, nestled among Nigel's collection of exotic and mind-numbing impulse purchases. It was a very large house. And it was full.

Three mismatched brocade chairs were lined up along the wall and Gilda sank into one of them. Putting her hand to her brow, she closed her eyes a moment. Max sat down next to her, watching her carefully.

"Max," she said. "Those people shooting at us. They were our *neighbors*. And they would have killed us."

He took her hand. "Well, we got out. We're safe."

She looked at him with those shrewd eyes.

He glanced down the hall toward the front door. Fact was, he had to wonder how far and deep this matter went, when the bad guys were willing to resort to murder. But for now he took a lighter tone. "There's one thing they didn't count on when they mixed it up with you and me," he told her. When she finished dabbing at her eyes and looked at him, he said: "Duct tape."

That got a smile, and he helped Gilda to her feet. At the end of the hallway an open spiral staircase led down to Nigel's inner sanctum: den, hobby center, bachelor pad, and business center.

The fluorescent-lit, windowless room was filled, deck upon deck, with screens and an elaborate array of computer appliances. Wires coiled and massed, disappearing into a central cable that ran along the middle of the floor like an anaconda that wouldn't be hungry for a while. From this electronic kingdom, Nigel touched the world—without having to touch it. And most everything he touched turned to gold. Even so, he still had the manners to stand up and shake Gilda's hand. Every once in a while Nigel surprised him.

Nigel Cobb was in his thirties, that era of energetic self-involvement that hardly had time for an elderly uncle, much less the wife he no longer had. But they'd kept in touch since his brother's death, and he hoped some of their old rapport would still be there. They'd need it. Max's nephew was prematurely bald, but he compensated with a misshapen beard that at one time had been clipped—perhaps last month—into a goatee.

"You finally break out of that cell up there?"

Max decided on the simple answer. "Yes."

A flat silence extended a little longer than it should have, and for a moment Max felt uneasy, remembering the conversation with Gilda's sister. He scanned the counter tops for any sign of visors or little fuzzy packets. But though there was a bewildering array of other VR and retina paraphernalia, no sign of Nir.

"Take the shuttle bus, did you?" Nigel asked.

"Flew."

A frown sliced down between Nigel's eyes. "I get the feeling something's up. Did somebody die?"

Max found himself groping for a handhold on his subject.

Gilda jumped in. "You've got the state of the art here, you think?" She was eyeing him like she did when she already knew the answer to something.

"Well," he began, looking over at his toys . . . his attention shifted back to her as he noticed that she was handing him something.

"No, Nigel," she said. "I don't think you do." She had pulled out the Nir assemblage that she'd confiscated from her son.

He took the little glasses and mass of wires from her, examining them closely. Then, in a Nigel-like gesture, bit into one end of the visor. "Feels like metal, but doesn't taste like it. Interesting." He smiled an I-give-up kind of smile. "Who puts it out?"

"That's the jackpot question, Nigel," she said. "We've no idea."

He raised his eyebrows. "Ah. A mystery." He sat back down in his multilounger and slipped the game tab into a port in the chair arm. "Mind?"

"Go for it," she answered. She grabbed an extra chair and sat down. "Only, do you have any food?"

Several ham sandwiches later, Nigel finally pulled the visor off. He had the slightly stunned look of a man who has forgotten what floor of the parking garage he left his car on. "Where the hell did you get this thing?" He looked from Max to Gilda. "I was going to say it's far and away the best raw graphics performance I've ever seen. But that's not what makes it strange. It's the *content*. Jesus, Max, the content. You played this game?"

"No. I'm afraid to."

Nigel's eyes narrowed. But letting that pass, he went

on: "See, this thing doesn't present like a standard synthetic environment. It's more like . . . memory. Like I'm recalling the scene, and then this Nir game displays on my retina—superbly enhanced." He shrugged. "But that's impossible." He waited for one of them to say something, while the whirr of numerous backup systems filled the air.

He shook his head slowly. "Oh shit," he said finally. "You think it's possible." He flashed a toothy smile. "Come on, guys."

"We don't know *what's* possible," Gilda said. "That's why we're here."

He absorbed that for a moment. Then, holding up the larger of the visors, he asked, "Second player?"

Gilda nodded. "It—tailors—the experience to one person at a time. But a second player can watch."

"Why would a second player want to—just watch?"

"Voyeurism?" she suggested.

Nigel laughed. "Guys, guys. You've been spending too much time playing gin rummy up there." He waved them off and punched at the keypad. "Let's just see what the architecture looks like." The port containing the tab hummed for a moment. "What did you say this game's called?"

"Nir."

Nigel stopped a moment. "Oh, yeah. Nir. I heard of that."

He shrugged, punching the keypad again, bringing up the coded program of Nir on the screen. "Yeah. As of yesterday, in fact. Going to be offered as an introductory free download on the Net beginning Saturday. It's going global."

"Oh dear," Gilda said as Max let out a long, slow breath.

Nigel's fingers skittered over the keyboard, communicating to his favorite listener: a computer. He squinted at the screen as a four-digit code scrolled and scrolled. "Oh, they really don't want you touring their program, do they?" He tried a few more maneuvers, his frown deepening. He was frozen out.

"Okaaaaay." For the next half-hour Nigel leaned back

in his chair and played Catch Me with Nir. The four-digit code returned again and again. At last the screen went to black. With a quizzical expression, he said: "Oh."

Gilda and Max both repeated, "Oh?"

"Yeah. I'm in."

"And?" Gilda prodded.

"Nothing to it."

Max cocked his head. "That easy?" The screen was filled with a repetitive code that meant nothing to Max but obviously meant something to his nephew.

"No. It was damn hard. It's just that there's nothing there."

The chair straightened up and he pulled the tab from the slot, fingering it like a trick playing card. "It's blank." He looked up at them, saying quietly, "The game isn't on the tab. The tab is just for show, I think." He sat quietly for a few moments, staring at the rest of the Nir assemblage on his desk as though it had bitten him. "It's all in the visor. It's as though they set this up to look like a conventional game. To hide the technology."

He picked up the small, blue-black glasses, grinning. "OK, Max, what's going on? This the first nanocomputer in these shades, or what?" He looked from him to Gilda and back again, turning the visor over and over in his hands.

"Go ahead," she said, "see how you like Nir the second time around."

He hesitated, perhaps sensing the irony in her voice. Then he slipped the shades back on, and the tab into the port.

Max had a pang of conscience about his nephew plugging into the device again, but Gilda patted his arm:

"Don't worry, twice won't hurt him. It takes days to blow a gasket."

Smiling halfheartedly, Max sat down in a high-backed chair and closed his eyes for a little catnap, until Gilda nudged him awake.

Nigel had taken off the glasses. Sweat beaded his forehead, his face gleaming bluish-silver in the computer display lights.

Gilda leaned forward and took the visor from him. He started to reach for it, then slowly withdrew his hand.

"That's the last time you should play the game, Nigel."

He swiveled the multilounger around to face them. "OK, you two," he said. "Now I want the whole story."

Gilda slowly lowered herself into a chair opposite him. She looked up at Max, who spread a hand out as though to say, *After you*.

"Things aren't quite right in Medicine Falls," she began.

~ 2 ~

Simon backed the car out of the carport onto a street at least temporarily clear of the door-to-door gestapo. It might have been Sunday morning, by the quiet sleepiness of the neighborhood, but it was Thursday afternoon. Simon figured that now the Nir priesthood had passed through handing out their wafers of communion, folks hereabouts were deeply reclined into their multiloungers, surfing their pleasure nodes.

Abbey had applied heavy eye makeup, smudging it enough to look well-used, over a face powdered deathly white and topped off with her now short, greasy hair. She looked both awful and wonderful, a fair approximation of how he entirely felt—the result of being hopelessly in love at the world's end. His own disguise consisted of Rocky's old blue knit hat and a baggy brown jacket.

Wearing Rocky's clothes, and last night, lying in his bed, rapturously in love, Simon felt that he had, in an unsettling way, become his old friend. He felt Rocky's presence keenly. Not condemning, but urging him on. Cheering him on.

On the corner stood a woman dressed in a sequined party dress, her jeweled purse dragging by its strap in the mushy snow. She looked up at them as they passed, raising a hand in a limp wave, and then scowling at them, as though changing her mind. Simon drove slowly on, creeping out of Rocky's old neighborhood, and turning onto

Penburton, thinking to use a busier street where they might find anonymity in numbers.

He grasped Abbey's hand, and she squeezed back, making his heart swell like a bellows. Things he wanted to say to her, that maybe he'd said last night, and maybe hadn't, but no time now, just keep driving . . . Still, the words formed just behind his lips. Hallmark sentiments, from a man unused to courting; words like devotion, forever, sweetheart, love . . . silly words that couldn't hold the weight asked of them. He shook his head.

"What?" Abbey whispered, her face tight with tension.

"I'm just speechless, that's all." He smiled over at her. "Not a condition I'm used to."

She smiled back, radiantly, with full frontal eye contact. Yeah, he was nuts about her.

As they moved into the downtown area, commerce had stopped. Cars were abandoned all down the street, forcing Simon to weave in and out, as a few other cars were doing. A group of teenagers jaywalked in front of him, a cluster of pasty-faced, hulking youngsters, plugged into hip packs, their glasses glinting in the sun like insect eyes. . . . It was a view he'd long held of teenagers anyway, but today, it had a new cast of meaning. A few other pedestrians meandered on their unknowable errands, some loaded down with bulky sacks.

Near the Commons, city workers in orange vests waved them around a burned-out car, still smoking. An accident, or a hopeful act of sabotage? It could have been a normal day, Simon told himself, with it taking a dozen government workers to flag cars around a traffic snarl.

"Simon," Abbey said. "I think we're being followed."

He looked in the rearview mirror. A white, older Toyota followed a half-block back. He turned the corner, and the Toyota turned as well. Simon pulled over to the curb, waiting for the car to pass.

"Don't turn toward the window," he told Abbey.

As the car came even with them, he saw a man with a hat pulled low, his face instantly familiar. . . .

And then the car halted there, in the middle of the street, as the man slowly turned toward them.

"Let's go!" Simon grabbed Abbey's hand, pulling her across the seat and out the sidewalk side of the car. They ran down a walkway between two office buildings where, in back, a small, deserted plaza lay at the hub of several routes of escape. Simon chose the alley to their right, and they raced over to it. "In here," he urged, as he spied a recess. They slammed into the alcove and pressed themselves flat.

Abbey leaned out just far enough to peer back down the alley. "It's Zachariah," she whispered. "But he's alone."

Simon traded places with her and peeked out. Zachariah stood in the center of the plaza. The sun, slanting in between the office buildings, caught his curly hair in a bright infusion, a parody of a halo on this man who helped to sell humanity to the highest bidder. *Come on, you bastard,* Simon found himself hoping. *Just choose my alley. Give me another go at you.* But then with a pang of relief he saw Zachariah hurry off in the wrong direction.

After a few moments Simon and Abbey crept out of their hiding spot and ran down the alley, only slowing to a Nir-like walk when they'd put several blocks behind them.

Zachariah might have been alerted by that door-to-door pair, and been following them since Lydia's house. Or he might just have got lucky. Well, given a clear opportunity, Simon would kill him. He realized this with a little spike of shock. It had come to this, that he would kill a man who got in the way of what must be done. What Must Be Done. He was not quite prepared to say, *save the world,* much less *get a message to the Regent,* but he would stand by Abbey, if that's what she would have him do.

The Comic Universe was metamorphosing. The familiar, prosaic universe, that used to chuckle at the occasional crossed paths of indifferent fate and human hope— that universe was changing. Now it seemed to him that it was full of meaning and drama. The strivings and passions on the small blue marble of planet Earth were not unique, remote, and petty. In fact, the universe was filled with like-minded creatures. It was all the same, every-where: evil, cowardice, despair, conquest, hope, love, and striving. The Galaxion, the Hhso, those poor droids the Hhso exploited, all were part of the common cloth of sentience. These galactic players were perhaps not much different than say, he and Abbey, here in this alley, where he gripped her hand like the end of a rope out of a very deep cave.

Abbey was pulling him toward two large glass doors recessed under an awning. "In here," she said.

There were at a side entrance of Maurice's department store. Though lights were blazing and the doors were un-locked, it looked deserted. "Shopping?" he asked. "Or shop*lifting*?"

"Shoplifting. We need different clothes. Grab some-thing." She bustled off into Women's Casual, shoving him in the direction of Men's Furnishings. He expected at any moment for a store clerk to step out and confront him . . . but no one—perhaps no one in all of Medicine Falls—was minding the store. He hurried past the jewelry counter, noting that the watches and jeweled bracelets lay untouched, proof positive that people were a little bonkers. Hhso, he had no doubt, would deal harshly with looters. The Big Looters would keep the Little Looters in check.

He ransacked a few clothing rounds, selecting a hooded green parka, then scanned quickly and in vain for a smoke shop, that endangered species of specialty store, catering to independent thinkers. Walking through Men's Shoes, he took the opportunity to ditch his old shoes, sopping wet from the Chief George hike, and select an expensive-looking pair of hiking boots. Then, from across the store, Abbey motioned to him and he followed her, disguised now in a black coat and snug felt hat.

They stood under the store awning looking out on a silent streetscape—without traffic, without pedestrians. The signal at the intersection flashed yellow in a slow, monotonous pulse. "Now what?" Abbey asked.

"We walk." It was at least two miles down-valley to the ranch. Maybe they could find a car, but for now they were on foot. After several blocks they saw a few people up ahead, all headed in one direction, walking purposefully south along Harris Avenue. Abbey and Simon blended into the ragtag stream, keeping their heads down.

He noticed that Abbey had drawn out the medallion and its little, ominous clip from inside her sweater and was holding it to her chest. She caught his eye, smiling weakly. He thought of the dam, miles up-valley past the reservation, surely too far for some weak radio signal to actually detonate charges.

Around them, walking silently except for the thudding of feet, people dressed every which way—in business suits and dresses, jeans, sweatshirts and glow-slick raincoats— looking as though they had been suddenly plucked from their individual pursuits to join this procession. A few were arrayed in flamboyantly colored tunics and tights, clear escapees from the nutcase institute.

They left the business district behind, walking through a neighborhood of used-car dealers and fast-food joints, finally turning onto the Valley Highway.

Simon tried not to stare. Everywhere, along the pasture fences, hundreds of people were milling, engaged in some kind of work, clustering around trucks parked every few hundred meters.

"Simon . . ." Abbey said under her breath, "what's going on?"

"I don't know." All he did know was that not all the good folks of Medicine Falls were playing retina games. Some of them, lots of them, were carrying objects out of trucks and lining up along the fields to . . . what? As they moved forward among their little group of latecomers, they saw people setting things out on the ground, only to stomp and kick at them.

"Let's get out of here—cut across the field," Abbey whispered.

"We'll be too obvious, out in that field. We've got to walk the road." Then he gently pulled his hand out of hers, and she looked at him with a moment of surprise, as though she were falling. "Better not hold hands." He glanced at the clumps of people up ahead who might take the holding of hands as an act of treason. She nodded then, and they walked on toward the gathering, under a towering, sunny sky that seemed to press all the valley flat under its blue fathoms. The rubble of last autumn's harvest carpeted the land in a spiky yellow mat, peaking here and there through the last crusts of snow.

Over this familiar landscape, a foreign thing crept.

Orange-colored smoke massed along the fences where the townspeople worked. As Simon watched, the ground-hugging gas poured slowly over the fields. A moment later he saw that the gruel-like ink was emitted from the small, round pouches people were pressing open with their feet.

Simon and Abbey walked on, stopping now and then to mingle with knots of people who watched as the alien paste rolled over the fields.

A woman turned to look directly into Simon's face. "Lord, but it's slow, Simon."

It was Linda Parker, a client for godsakes.

"Slow," he repeated, as his heart doubled its beat. Abbey's hand gripped his arm. What was the business he'd done for this woman . . . an asset investigation of her deadbeat partner who left her with three kids. . . .

"You press and press," she said, "and still it just comes out like molasses in January." She stepped back to show him, bringing her boot off a furry ball with a slit in the side like the frazzled lips of a sea creature. It was still ejecting its contents, salmon-colored and sour-smelling.

Abbey jabbed him, and he said, "Well, it gets the job done." What job, he had no damn idea.

"Oh, eventually. But the new fields need higher nitrogen than grass, so the whole process of reorientation toward an atmospheric nitrogen assimilation will take weeks. Lord, the poor o-ghan!" She winked at him. "But, by and by."

"Yes, by and by," he repeated. Then, "Good luck," he thought to say, as he started backing up, heading back to the asphalt of the road.

"Luck?" she said, startled. She looked at Abbey, then back at him. "Luck?"

"You got to press hard on those things to get it going,"

he said, floundering. She continued to frown as Simon turned away, trying to escape the sticky tape of the conversation. He nodded to her, and pulled Abbey into a quicker pace. "Jesus," he said under his breath.

"Don't let's stop anymore," Abbey said, voice grim, hand locked on the little pendant around her neck.

Good enough advice, not to stop, since they were the black ants in the red ants' hive, with no clue what was going on, no idea what words were fine and which were not. Add to that, seems his disguise couldn't fool a muzzy-headed woman he'd last seen three years ago.

Abbey was mumbling something. He turned to her, and heard her saying to herself, "It's starting, it's starting," her voice sounding like a tolling bell.

Farther down the road, folks were done stomping on the pus balls. They stood quietly, admiring their work: fields covered in a foot-high coating of curdled orange smoke. "Stinks, by damn," he heard someone say. Some stood among their neighbors with deep frowns, sober and fascinated at the same time, as though they might still possess at least a bit of that morbid human fascination for tragedy. Simon watched too, but concentrated on the backs of neighbors, acquaintances, and friends, praying not to see them turn, eyes flickering with recognition.

Just up ahead was Fiffer Road, the cutoff to Zachariah's ranch.

Together they put one foot in front of the other, each step a dispensation, a chance at deliverance. The highway stretched taut and thin ahead of them all the way to Colson and, beyond, the state capital, where Phil Agnew labored over his air-tax story and the governor sweated the next election, and where people might be just now settling back into their multiloungers with a cheap, new ret game. . . .

At last they found themselves far enough down Fiffer Road and away from the highway, where Simon could stop worrying about being recognized and concentrate instead on the blisters on his feet from the damn new hiking boots. They made their way into a thicket, where he pulled them off and massaged his feet.

"They're turning the meadowland into something," Abbey said, her voice quiet and flat, looking back toward the highway, just visible through the bare trees.

"Pastureland," Simon said. He couldn't bring himself to say, *o-ghan. O-ghan breeder pastureland.* She nodded. The closer to the ranch they got, the less they spoke, communicating instead with looks and the smallest of gestures. Their allotment of words. Running out.

But still, Zachariah must have heard them.

The crack of branches, and Simon cursed himself for zoning out . . . and Zachariah stood before them pointing the poison bag once again.

Simon was on his feet in an instant.

"Oh, Simon," Abbey moaned.

"Stop," Zachariah said. He turned his hand to one side, where a small, fuzzy packet was visible. "It kills, Mr. Haskell." He pointed his fist at Abbey. "Want a demonstration?"

"No," Simon answered, castigating himself for a damn fool, caught with his shoes off, and might as well be his pants down. He looked over at Abbey, and her stricken look spoke for both of them. Simon turned to face Zachariah, watching for an opening. Spring-loaded.

This close to the man, he could see large, purplish bruises welling around his nose and left eye. That, and his ripped tunic and slight growth of beard, gave him a rougher, meaner look.

As he glanced over to Abbey, he noted her hand slowly moving up to the pendant, and the small, metal clip that Rose had fastened there. Instead of the fear that he expected to show, her face was hard, almost predatory.

Simon's heart felt like it had fallen into a well. The smell of milk gone bad wafted over them. The smell of life gone bad. Maybe she was thinking the same thing. Maybe that was what made her do it, the smell.

She pressed the clip in the smallest of finger movements, pinching the two ends together.

"What is that?" Zachariah asked, reaching for the medallion. "Give it here."

Abbey was looking over his shoulder as though at something far away.

A rumble began, a ripping sound that could only come from the mouth of deeply buried rock. Abbey slowly pulled the cord from around her neck, handing it to him. The medallion hung down like a plumb line, pointing to the earth and swaying back and forth in a hypnotic motion.

"Give it here," Zachariah repeated. As he reached for it, he looked over his shoulder, perhaps wondering at the distant booming sound, far away, like the report of a distant war.

In another moment Simon felt the earth tremble beneath his feet. *It's happening,* he thought. *Sweet Jesus.*

Abbey was looking up-valley, toward Medicine Ridge, toward the disintegrating dam seven miles away. Lost in the distant roar would be the higher pitches of people screaming, of trees crashing. These would be lost like snowballs in an avalanche. Lost in the downward plunge of Medicine Lake.

Then it was quiet. They looked around, and all was as it had been, the stand of trees, the cold blue sky, Simon's boots lying side by side.

"What is this, how did you get this?" Zachariah asked.

"It's a necklace that I wear."

Still holding the pendant loosely in his left hand, he shook his head, incredulously. "I gave up on you. I was going home." As though speaking to himself, he said, "It never occurred to me you'd be going to my house." He seemed bemused, a man stunned by sudden good fortune.

Then he focused on them again and started backing up. "Let's go. Out to the road." As Abbey approached, he grabbed her, forcing her arm in back of her, and pushing his fist into the small of her neck. "See, if I squeeze it right here," he said to Simon, "she'll die fast. Not slow, like your friend Rocky."

"You son of a bitch." Simon followed, watching for his chance.

"Not far off the mark, actually," Zachariah said.

They stood on the dirt road. Zachariah's white Toyota

was parked on the shoulder. In the distance they could see the highway, with its milling crowds of people.

"They'll take you," he said to Abbey. "I'd kill you myself, but I'd rather watch them take you." He turned to Simon. "Did you ever think how many people she's ruined? You, your partner, her own daughter. Me." He turned his gaze back to Abbey. Yanking her hat off, he pulled on her hair, jerking her around to face him. He waved the little furry mass back and forth in front of her face, as she backed up slowly. "You know what it feels like when it goes straight into the eyes?"

Energy collected in Simon's muscles like a lightning charge, waiting, waiting. The bastard was loopy; he was going to make a mistake. Simon would be ready.

Chapter 16

~1~

Verna stood on a promontory looking out over the valley. The ground rumbled under her feet. In the hazy distance to the east lay the white man's town, just out of sight but never far out of mind. They controlled the valley, the jobs, the culture, everything. Until now. They were about to learn how hard the hand of the old pent-up river could strike.

If she put her ear to the hump of rock she stood on, as she did now, she could hear the water come, like a locomotive off its tracks. Come to reclaim its old route.

She stood up again, and looked down the ridge. Hidden beneath the trees at the foot of the ridge lay the reservation, which controlled nothing, hardly even itself. Its people would also learn the lessons of the medicine waters. But for them, hunkering up here in the Pine Wood caves, the river would not strike like a phantom, out of nowhere. The river was always in their hearts, buried deep—buried beyond memory, maybe, but never gone. When she and Mae and her daughter had gone through the reservation saying *the river is coming,* the old people nodded like she had announced an uncle coming to visit. The young people narrowed their eyes and looked beyond her to the cliff, as though they could already see the falls thundering. Before long everyone was trudging up the ridge to the caves. The hard way.

From her perch by the caves, she heard the Chief George canyon echo with the charging lake, louder and louder. She looked off to the left, where the tops of trees could be seen keeling over along the line of the as-yet-invisible flood. The scouring, thundering sound came from all sides at once: from the old riverbed, from the caves in back, from the sky in front—all rang with a warrior's yell.

Then she saw the giant pulse of churning water erupt into view below her, heading for the precipice. It emerged from the cover of the trees with a cloud of white fury, and then, snatching a few last trees for trophies, the waters plunged over the ridge, becoming Medicine Falls once again. The water thundered down, rescouring the old groove, then smashed into the village, shoveling everything before it.

Mae Two Hawks had come to stand by her side. She shook her head over and over.

Verna put an arm around Mae's shoulders. "The rez needed a good cleaning out, anyways," she said.

In a cleaning frenzy, the medicine waters rushed on.

Megan locked the Institute doors, and smoothed her red skirt around her. People were letting themselves go, lately. Just because there was work to be done didn't mean you should let yourself go to seed. Now, what was the work to be done?

She looked down at the sack lying on the steps, where she'd put it. Oh yes. She had such trouble remembering things lately. She put her hand to her eyes and rubbed them. Something was wrong, desperately wrong. Wasn't it?

That sound, for one thing. Like bass drums, like the ripping of the world.

Megan looked up to see, about three blocks away, what looked like an explosion of water heading for the steps where she stood. A roaring mass of water, trapped between the office buildings of Lowell Street, swept toward her with furious speed, carrying, she noticed, a telephone pole like a baton on parade.

Where in the world might so much water be coming from, was her first thought. Her second, and last, thought was to consider the keys in her hand, the keys to the great doors of Grummel High that she had just locked.

When the deluge hit her, it seemed like the first clear feeling she'd had in days.

Cherilyn Hoyle was rummaging in the hospital basement, in the empty kitchen. She was practically dizzy from lack of food and, she supposed, all those pills she'd taken in her aborted suicide attempt. She found a loaf of bread and commercial-sized toaster, and made herself a piece of marmalade toast. Where was everybody, anyway? You wake up with an IV in your arm and the hospital practically empty . . . her eyes flicked up to the windows where, she could have sworn, a gentle lap of water was sloshing against the glass. She put down the toast and stared. Within seconds the water rose to cover the daylight basement windows, and the lights went out. When the water broke through, Cherilyn was already racing for the stairs.

Kristin, the communications operator at the police station, took off her earpiece and looked up at him. Some days she came in to work, and other days didn't even bother to call in. Fading in and out, was how Lieutenant Dern described it to himself. The town was fading in and out. Like the demon in his brain. At times he devoutly wished for the new order of things. At other times he grieved for the utter irrelevance of law enforcement in a world without deviance, without crime.

Kristin looked up at him and blinked. "Lieutenant, they said the dam broke."

They stared at each other as though they'd just been given a major clue to a criminal case, but they couldn't quite remember *which* case.

"The dam," he repeated.

"Yes. It's gone." She began clearing her desktop. Then she remembered to say, "The lake is heading into town."

Dern went to the fourth-story window of the police station, and looked up the street toward Chief George Dam. Nothing.

"Are you sure?"

Kristin put her earpiece back on. "I'll ask."

Bill Petey, a rookie who still made it to work—but, unaccountably, in his Little League uniform—poked his head in the door. "The dam's busted," he said. "Blown to smithereens, and everyone's dead."

Dern nodded. "Thanks."

"You betcha." Bill nodded, and went back to his desk.

A thought bloomed in Lieutenant Dern's mind. It wasn't so much a thought as an image, an image of washing away, and the cleansing that comes with cold, clean waters. His gun still lay in the middle of his desk. In all his years on the force, he'd never once used it, and the fact was, he was afraid to put it to his head and pull the trigger. He never knew himself for a coward, but that was the truth of it. It made him sad to acknowledge this, and confirmed his fear that his personality was sifting out of him through a small hole, like sand.

He left the gun on the desk and walked through the precinct offices and down four flights of stairs, not trusting the elevators right now, now that the cleansing waters were coming.

Out in the bright sun of this April day, Dern looked up into the sky for a reflection of what the earth was bearing, but the few bright clouds kept their distance from the town's disaster. He could feel it under his feet, though. A hard tremor. Up ahead a flash of searing light.

The sun glinting off water.

He stood in the middle of the street, and turned his back to the approaching rampage. The sound was the worst of it, the tearing, roaring, impossible bellow. And it was also the best of it, as he planted his feet and bore that sound, as no coward would.

Sooze looked up the gritty sides of the Dumpster, planning her ascent.

A head popped up from inside, startling her so badly she jumped backward. "Hipe! This here's mine." It was her alley, and her find. The Dumpster had the best kick for blocks, and no way was Hipe going to crash in.

"Usetabe." His head disappeared again. Then, from deep in the bin, she heard: "Totally meg! I got one of them LazerRazors."

She scuttled up the sides and dropped over onto the fragrant mass of garbage. Hipe swung around, scowling. Sooze sized up her chances. He wasn't too smart, and she could probably talk him out of it, but he had a temper, for real. Wasn't called Hipe for nothing. She went for compromise. "Halves," she offered, leaning in a casual, friendly fashion against the metal sides.

His scowl edged deeper, registering what passed for thought with Hipe. "But I get first kick on anything you find."

"*Half* of first kick." A tickle needled her arm, like it had fallen asleep. The sensation crept up from her hand to her elbow. She turned and gripped the side of the Dumpster with both hands, feeling a tremor, and deciding it was a large truck rumbling down the street. "Shit. Here comes the garbage truck. We better hurry."

They culled through the top layer, tossing plastic bags aside and looking for the least rotten prospects for dinner, while the mound beneath them began to hum with a sound like the mumbles of previous lives. Sooze pulled herself up to the top of the Dumpster, and looked toward the street, eyes narrowed. This was no regular truck. She swooped over the side and down to the cobblestones, where she could feel her feet ring like struck gongs.

Then, out in the street, a gaggle of St. Croix kids pelted down the side street past the alley entrance. One of them, Pong, turned to shout at her, "Dam's crashed!"

Sooze jammed hard out of the alley and onto Defoe Street to catch up with the others. "Where you goin'?"

Pong turned to her as they ran, his face lit with wonder: "To watch!"

"Watch what?"

"The flood! The whole town's blown away!"

Sooze looked ahead, but the street looked about the same as any other day, with its canyon of brick buildings and knots of old men staking out their stairwells. A pack of dogs rounded a corner and came tearing down the street, away from midtown, barking like crazy.

She stopped dead in her tracks, then turned around and walked back to where Hipe stood at the alley entrance, guarding his cache. "I don't see no flood," he said.

From one of the apartment stoops a woman in a bathrobe ran out into the street and gathered up a young girl sitting with a doll. She held the little girl and squinted toward the roaring that now issued from the downtown.

Sooze turned to Hipe. The fight peeled off his face like old plaster, revealing a scared eight-year-old underneath. "That sound," he said. "That the flood comin'?"

"Come on honey," she said. "We'll be OK in the boat."

His eyes looked like they saw the dam busting, and the water plunging. But for now, all they knew of the flood was the scream of sound down the street—and the zinging earth beneath their feet.

They sidled up the Dumpster and huddled together, covering their ears.

When the water pulsed down the alley it slapped up against the Dumpster, dislodging it out into the middle of the alley, spinning it around a few times, before the water sucked back out to join the surge in the street. Hipe buried his face in Sooze's neck as the sirens of Medicine Falls blared in the distance.

"Don't worry honey," she said, patting his trembling shoulders. "We got our lifeboat, don't we?"

Rose could feel the thundering of the waters. Her whole body reverberated to the many pounding feet of the lake as it charged to war.

She had been sitting on the steps of the Commerce Building spying on the police station across the street where they were keeping Jaguar, while chugalugging a bottle of Pepsi wrapped in a paper sack. As the waters bore down, she ran up the steps into the lobby, shouting, "Dam's blown, dam's blown! Flood's coming!"

A door or two opened. A woman wearing the Nir glasses pushed up on her head looked doubtfully at Rose. But who would believe a Sun Rock Indian woman holding a bottle in a paper sack? She threw the bottle down, still hollering, "Flood's coming!" Then she ran for the stairs. At the third floor she ran to the hallway window, which was jiggling in its frame as the mind-numbing roar bore down. No time to worry about Jaguar, no time to do more than hope he wasn't kept on the first floor.

She looked out. The mouth of the great waters screamed toward her, registering hard in her chest as deep, base vibrations. Even her heart beat a new beat: Thrruuuum, thrruuuum!

In a bizarre snapshot, she had time to note that in front of the police station, a lone man stood in the center of Lowell Street, back to the flood, arms raised slightly like one of her people might, in prayer.

Then the window in front of her flew inward, as the fist of the river plunged down the hall.

The plaque on the front of the building noted that, except for Grummel High School, the YWCA was the oldest building in Medicine Falls. It had withstood 112 years of drought, blizzards, downtown renewal, and the persistent advances of the termite labyrinth under its north wall. Just last year a cadre of civic-minded folks had begun the massive project of repainting the place, beginning with the frontage on Lowell Street, with plans to work back from there as time and funds permitted.

But time had run out for the old warren.

As the leading wall of water and debris blasted by, it peeled back the street-facing wall of the building like a Band-Aid. For a moment, the structure bent toward the rampage in a deep bow. Not content with this show of deference, the torrent licked the top floor off to join the downstream frenzy, and after that, the bottom floors gave up and sagged into the deluge.

In less than ten seconds the old YWCA was gone.

Eleven guests in their thirty-dollar rooms were swept away, along with everything they owned. Among the debris was the entire contents of the room still rented—but not recently occupied—by Abbey McCrae.

As the waters slowed and spread across the bottomland outside of town, a small, black diary with the initials VM swirled on the local eddies before disappearing in the foaming top of the flood.

Zachariah held the pendant loosely, the cord coiled a few times around his hand, gesturing at Abbey. Simon watched helplessly from the sidelines. "You were going to my house!" Zachariah exclaimed, shaking his head. "You have any idea what my house is right now? What my barn is, what my bunkhouse is?" He laughed in a way that was a half a sob. "They're taking it all!"

"I know," Abbey said.

That sobered him a moment. "You know?"

"Yes. The Hhso. They'll use us. They want everything, like they've already got Medicine Falls."

"Yes!" he sneered. "Work for them, bow to them, smell them—while they take it all! Even what they promised me."

"Well, maybe we better not let that happen."

"Better not!" He laughed bitterly, turning to point his

fist at Simon, then back at Abbey. "You've seen the alfalfa fields? You've seen the good folk of Medicine Falls? We're the only humans left!" He jerked up his head to look back to the highway. And did a double take.

As a mass, people were crossing the highway and pouring into the field on the other side. They began to run, abandoning the fence line, surging over the road and into a field still ordinary in its turned black furrows.

Simon knew what they ran from, and looking across to the distant low hills across the valley, gauged they wouldn't make it.

Confused, agitated, Zachariah swung on Simon. "I'm watching you!"

"You know what that explosion was?" Simon moved a little closer. "You know what those folks are running from? The dam is blown, the biggest flood this state's ever seen is going to pay us a little visit."

"Flood?"

"Chief George. It's blown to hell and gone."

A distant roaring, like wind, came from up-valley. In his mind, Simon could imagine the surge of the lake waters over Medicine Falls, smashing through the Sun Rock reservation like a fist through tar paper. Heading into town.

"You're crazy!"

"Listen." The roaring noise grew in a slow crescendo. The waters were still out of sight, but coming, coming, screaming in both joy and fury. *Free the river*, Rose had said. Well, it was free now, and bent on vengeance.

"Get in the car," Zachariah snarled at Abbey.

Then Simon saw it. Staring past Zachariah's shoulder, he glimpsed a wall of water boiling onto the plain and forming a broad, rolling lake, spreading out now into the wide embrace of the valley, but too fast to outrun.

In the split second that Zachariah saw it too, and registered plain-out stupefaction, Simon sprang for him, knocking him down. But a foot in Simon's stomach kicked the air out of him. As Simon crumpled, he flung himself on Zachariah's legs, yanking him backward as he tried to crawl away. Then it was within reach. He ripped the cord from Zachariah's hand, eliciting a scream as the thong cut along skin. As Zachariah winced, he dropped the little packet, sending it rolling out of reach. Zachariah scrambled after it, with Simon crawling after him, and the rush of water came closer, closer . . . And then the surge hit, and he saw Zachariah leap onto the hood of the car, and then nothing but water, water, yanking him into its down-valley plunge. A fence post swirled by, close enough to knock him senseless, and he was riding the flood, holding on to that post, calling Abbey, Abbey, as all around him tree trunks cracked and Medicine Lake swept him away in a wild riptide.

From her vantage point up Lester Road, Renalda watched as the valley floor disappeared under the spreading waters.

The flood had come billowing out of the main streets of town, spreading like microwaved butter in every direction, but mostly down-valley, carrying part of Medicine Falls with it: roofs and cars and trees, roots and all. She was glad she was up on a little rise, or she'd be in that tide of water, rushing toward Colson, or wherever it would finally give out.

At last a few people appeared in dinghies and rowboats, helping folks in. She could see best through the telescopic sight of her high-powered rifle, and she watched for a long while until she remembered that she was keeping guard on the road. She'd do what she had to. People weren't supposed to leave, didn't they know that?

She heard a sound off to the west, a car coming up the road toward the town. Her knee served as a brace as she propped up the rifle and peered through the sight.

Just around the bend, Nigel drove his Moonrover jeep in a silent funk, ferrying Max and Gilda back to Medicine Falls.

Max didn't really blame Nigel. He stayed in that fortress of his for months on end, making a virtue of nonmovement, and suddenly he was on a dirt road actually getting his 100k jeep dusty, and running after a cockeyed story dreamed up, it must seem, by two oldsters with macaroni and cheese for brains. If it hadn't been for the Net message that Nigel had managed to snag, Max was sure he wouldn't be here at all.

Heard from Medicine Falls lately? . . . go armed.

Max squeezed Gilda's hand as they neared the crest overlooking the town. She was quiet too, maybe wondering, as Max was, what in dickens they were doing sneaking back *in* to the strange psych ward that Medicine Falls had become.

But Nigel was their only chance to put the kibosh on Nir. Who else could they hope to influence or persuade? His nephew might think him a crazy old fart, but maybe he remembered the old days: fishing trips and chess games, back in the days when Max had been a real person, and not just an inmate of Harvest Home. And maybe for the sake of that, Nigel said he'd take a look-see, and if there was something afoot in Medicine Falls, he'd put out enough of a Net warning that half the civilized world would be looking up Zachariah Smith, if only because Nigel Cobb said so.

Nigel slammed on the brakes. Just ten or fifteen meters up the road a woman was pointing a rifle at them.

"What!" Nigel said under his breath. "What the hell is this? Is this a public road or what?"

The woman was walking toward them, rifle raised and ready to shoot. She motioned the window down.

"Uh-oh," Gilda was saying. "I'd floor it, if I were you."

The woman had long, matted black hair, and a feral look in her eyes.

"Is there some trouble here?" Nigel asked.

The woman stood, panning the rifle from Nigel to Max to Gilda. "You coming in?" she asked finally.

Max figured he knew the right answer to that question, so when Nigel hesitated, he leaned over and said, real friendly, "That's right. Coming in to town, if that's OK."

She appeared to think this over for a moment. "OK. As long as you're not trying to *leave* town."

"No, no. Trying to join you."

She nodded, slowly. "Well, then. All the roads are mostly gone, though."

Max looked sideways at Gilda. *Roads gone?* "That's fine, whatever you say. If we can go now?"

"You can go." Still pointing the rifle, though.

Nigel smiled a ghastly, toothy smile at the woman, and inched the jeep away. In a short distance they crested the hill.

Below them, a staggering prospect. Medicine Falls poked up through a lake the size of the valley. The sun glared off the calm, preposterous waters.

From the back seat, Max heard Gilda say, "Oh, dear God."

"It's a flood," Max said.

"No, the side of the road," she said in a whisper. "The side of the road."

As if the sight of the flooded valley were not enough to stop his heart, Max looked where Gilda was pointing, seeing at last the body of a man, shot through the chest. And, as they drove slowly and deliberately away from the riflewoman, they found the others, six in all, lying where the feral woman had shot them.

~ 2 ~

Zachariah watched Abbey as she stood gaping. "How do you like my bunkhouse?"

As they stood in Zachariah's driveway, she could see a sparkling yellow crust encasing the outbuilding and covering half the side of the barn as well. Sunlight splashed off the faceted surface in a profuse glow.

The sight of the encrusted bunkhouse and barn drove home the reality of the Hhso, the reality of her failure. They had begun to make over the world—beginning with these ranch buildings turning to glowing, crystalline structures.

And she had lost the one hope of her people: the pendant.

"How do you like it?" he repeated.

She answered flatly, refusing to show him her defeat. "What are they doing?"

"Taking. Taking. Pretty, isn't it?" His face was brightened with a pasted-over alertness. "He used to worry about that."

"He?"

"Zachariah." He flicked a clod of mud off his shoes, frowning distastefully, annoyed at having soiled shoes though both he and Abbey were covered with mud up to their knees from the aftermath of the receding flood.

The first surging wall of Medicine Lake had spun the Toyota around 360 degrees, throwing Abbey against the door. With her face pressed against the window, she looked out onto the vast moving lake, heading to take over the valley. As the car swirled on the current, Zachariah was holding on to the outside of the driver's-side car door, while, spinning and spinning, they were on course to collide with a stand of trees. Then she felt herself thrown backward by the slamming impact.

She scrambled to her knees to see that the front and rear bumpers were wedged against the gap teeth of two birches. As the water rushed by, at times frothing up against the windows, she frantically looked for Simon.

But after the surging crest of the water passed, only Zachariah and she remained.

The pendant. Where in all the wide valley with its morass of silt and debris was it? Where was her act of courage, the one thing she was going to do right? Since Vogel Tower, doing it right had been the thing she held on to. *Go where the Leap Point takes you, Abbey. Pay attention this time. For Vitt. For Earth. For yourself.* But it seemed that no matter how hard you *intended* to do the best thing, what *happened* was still and always a matter of what stuck to the tree branches as the flood rushed by.

She wanted to tell Simon this. To tell him that he was right about the locket and the grave. That guilt was the name you put on your determination to divert the flood.

But *intention* was the only thing that you could do all by yourself.

And to tell Vitt: I did love you. As much as I knew of love. And now, more than ever, now when I can no longer reach you . . .

Zachariah pushed her in the back, shoving her up the front stairs of the house. She turned around to look for Simon, a reflex now, but all was abandonment and mud. Zachariah was pushing her through the foyer and up the white-carpeted stairs, up to the second floor and its long white hallway, then up, up the far staircase. Up to the attic.

Every horror she had ever known was at the top of stairs. Tucked away under eaves, under roofs, in the dark storage rooms. He pushed her harshly; she was slow, slow to climb those last stairs. Slow approaches were the worst, when the door at the top of the stairs held back the thing you didn't want to see, held it back in a lying way. Because, when you got to the top, it always opened.

As he shoved open the attic door and turned on the light, she was everywhere.

Looking back at her from the walls: her face, but then, nearby, Vitt's face, and then, an amalgam of her and Vitt, a startling, blended ambiguity.

She yanked away from him and spun around toward the door, but he was fast, grabbing her arm, surprised—from his look—by her strength. He backed her against the closed attic door, bracing her with the weight of his body, and carefully squeezed out onto her left hand a cold pinprick from the poison bag. He slid to the floor with her, pressing her body against the white rug. Her breath escaped in a long groan.

"Just a tiny hit," he whispered to her. "To calm you."

She lay beneath him, gathering her wits. When he moved she would strike free, when he pulled the stone press off her. But she was wounded, her hand, growing icy, turning her fingers to sticks . . . and her thoughts, congealing . . .

He lay over her, his mouth next to her ear, whispering: "I won't let them take you. I'm done with their orders."

"Zachariah . . ." she began.

He lurched back. "Don't call me that!" He began pulling off her sodden coat. "He's a loser. A loser." As he hunted around the room for something, Abbey tried to move, succeeding in sitting up against the door. She wiped her hand on the rug, over and over, to warm it, to cleanse it.

Then he was standing over her with a looped and braided cord. He pulled her up and conducted her to a small overstuffed chair, where, with surprising gentleness, he helped her to sit. She watched stupidly as he bound her ankles.

"We can stop them," she said, trying to clear her head. "They're . . . the enemy. . . ." She tried to catch his eyes, but when she did, she saw herself reflected in them, as though she could see what he was seeing, a haggard woman, a creature dredged from the flood bottom.

"They're taking everything," he said. "If you could see the field!" He dropped a small, glistening visor into her lap. "But I'm keeping you. They want you." She watched him jack in the leads to a game appliance on the table. "*He* would have gone along with the herd. See," he pointed to the wall, in the direction of the bunkhouse, of the realm of the Hhso, "to them, we're all a *herd*, animals to be tended. And Lonnie, she was no different! He was just a *dog* to her. A *goat*, you see? She was never his mother." He stopped for a moment, collecting himself, then shrugged. "He was such a dummy."

She watched as he used a patch cord to connect her visor and his. His voice adopted its old tone, like a cascade of thick honey: "Ever play Nir?"

Abbey looked down at the small visor, perched amid the wires in her lap. "No."

He nodded, almost imperceptibly, and said so softly that the honey became a mere strand of gold: "Are you . . . like Vittoria?" He was kneeling in front of her, his hands on her knees.

She looked up to the wall where Vitt's eyes were bearing down on her, hard, while Vitt's lips curled in a wry smile. . . .

"Are you?"

A kind, pitying look nestled in his eyes. "No?"

She shook her head, unwilling for this creature to be her confessor. She whispered: "I don't want to play. Nir." She kept shaking her head as he calmly fixed the visor over her eyes.

"Yes, Abbey, play. Be like her, Mother."

His voice was so kind. He had bound her feet, but not her arms. Her eyes were clenched shut. She could pull the visor off with her one good hand. She could refuse this. Bound and free.

She opened her eyes to the light. A pinprick of light hovered for a moment, then rushed forward like a train, its headlight bearing down. She was frozen in its cone of light, like a fly in amber, and the light sped along the pathways, jumping the barriers, hunting, hunting. . . .

She was home. The smells said it first: Mother's fresh-baked rhubarb pie, the sun on the linoleum, and outside the open dining-room windows, the air as still as glass.

Moving into the kitchen—oh, it was all, all as it had been—the small, sugared strips of baked pie dough, the tidy counters and scrubbed linoleum floors!

Trapezoids of light on the floor squeezed narrower by the minute as the sun climbed to noon. If the house was silent and empty, and rhubarb pie was baked, then this would be Sunday, and they would be at church. A stifling quiet muffled around her ears, except for the creak on old floorboards of her eight-year-old feet.

And Richard's.

Her hand reached for the sugared crust. The baking sheet was still warm, the pie strip filled her mouth with a sharp, hot pleasure.

"Bring me one, too, Abbey."

Everything was peaceful and heavy, sleepy with summer ease. The kitchen stove still pumping heat from its slightly open door. She walked toward him.

She lifted her eyes to see, far down the hallway, the insubstantial form of a young girl. Her head hung to one

*side, impossibly far. Myra, standing perfectly still, wit-
nessing.*

Abbey drew in breath to speak. Couldn't.

"I'm waiting," he said, his belt buckle glistening.

Then, forcing the words up, up out of her swelling
throat:

"No."

A frown plowed across Richard's face.

She shook her head, slowly to the left and to the right.
No. Her throat, now sewn closed.

"It's too late for no." He looked down on her, from a
great height. "If you didn't like it, you would have said no
already. But you didn't, did you."

His body was soft, rippled with fat, but strong fat,
enough to hold her still when need be. His belt buckle
gleamed in the light from the kitchen windows. It's too
late for no, too late . . .

The belt buckle started to move toward her.

"Noooo!" she screamed, tearing the stitches, ripping
them from the soft tissues of her throat.

He put his hands palms out, saying, "Quiet,
quiet . . ."

"Done with . . . done with that." Backing up, she felt
the refrigerator handle in her shoulder blades. This was as
far as she could retreat. She turned. Placing her hand on
the silver lever of the door, she opened it and her fingers
latched around a glass-necked bottle. Then the bottle was
sailing across the room, just missing Richard's head. The
bottle shattered against the wall over the kitchen table,
ketchup erupting everywhere, followed by pickle jars,
tubs of leftovers, salad dressing, prune juice. All colliding
with Richard, the wall, the sideboard with the pie crust,
the toaster, the teakettle, the hanging plate from the
World's Fair.

Richard's arms were crossed in front of his face, warding off, but it was not truly Uncle Richard she aimed for,
it was the kitchen itself, the beige walls, the order of
things, its lying cleanliness.

Shards of glass, lumps of food, ruptured containers,

pools of fluid, pieces of crushed fruit lay everywhere, dripping, oozing, puddling.

Abbey surveyed the remains of Mother's clean kitchen.

"This," she said, voice shaking, "this is what it looks like."

Richard was backing up. "You'll have to clean this all up," he said. "Before your parents come home."

"This is for them. Just like this."

He backed into the hallway, becoming obscure in the shadows. "They'll be angry with you."

She followed him a few steps, holding on to half a grapefruit.

"That's OK," she said. Myra turned and walked away down the blocks-long, the years-long hallway. Head lying to one side, she walked on, until she vanished in the distance.

A disembodied voice came to her ears: "Look at the mess you've made."

She hurled the grapefruit squarely into the rhubarb pie, which exploded in chunks of red fruit, over and over again, drenching the counter and wall with rosy, permanent stains.

"You used to be such a good girl," came the whisper.

She rubbed her arm, sore from the force of her pitching.

"Not anymore, I'm not."

With her good hand she ripped the visor off. "Not anymore," she said again, her throat swollen and hot.

Zachariah slowly removed his own glasses.

"Your turn," Abbey hissed at him. She waved the small visor at him. "Isn't it . . . your turn . . . Zachariah?"

He cowered in his chair, shrinking away from her, away from the proffered glasses.

She thrust them closer.

"I'm not supposed to," he said, his voice a whispered falsetto.

He was strangely fearful and passive; now was the time to challenge him, to lure him to Nir, if he could be lured.

"You still . . . take their orders?" she said, mimicking his wheedling, velvet voice.

He paused, weighing this. He looked past her, up to his wall where the holos flickered, where his interchangeable McCraes cast a wan light on his face.

"You let the Hhso tell you what to do?" she pressed.

He looked back at her with his face relaxing, all the old expressions slumping away, like old snow. "Not anymore," he said. He looked at her with a sudden and boyish hopefulness. "Watch?"

She nodded, exchanging visors with him.

A cacophony of voices descended, trapped voices that had massed at the roof of his skull. They flocked down, fighting for his attention . . . and then a woman's face emerged, hovering over, looking down, as mothers do, at their children at bedtime. Through the dusky evening air, he could just make out her lovely blond hair, with that wave in the side, slightly covering one eye. Her eyes were that good, she only needed one.

She was smiling, as mothers do. "Don't want a story tonight, Zacky?"

"No, not tonight," he said. It was enough just to feel the bed dip under her weight, as she sat beside him, warding off the powers of night.

The bed began to rotate. As it did, he noticed that his little night-light flashed with each rotation. The eruptions of light highlighted one side of mother's face, one side of the room, making him nauseated. He wished it would stop, because, except for this, everything was as perfect as it had ever been, or ever would be.

"No story tonight?" she asked again, disappointed.

He reached for her hand. She grasped it firmly.

The bed turned faster, with the night-light flashing like a lighthouse beacon. He had to hold on tight to her hand, but as long as he held that hand, he would be safe. His head felt like it was bulging on one side. All the memories of a future he never had, thrown there by centrifugal force: the family Sunday drives, the picnics, the laughing in front of the TV, Mom and Dad together and happy, faster and faster, the bed spinning, Lonnie holding his hand, smiling . . .

"What's happening, Mother?"

"Going to sleep, is all. Going to sleep."

But the bedroom swooshed by in a senseless, twisting blur . . . and his head swelled like a balloon, collecting all those hopes and throwing them to the side . . . he and Lonnie, he and Lonnie, happy together . . .

"Anything at all, Zacky?"

He squeezed her hand. "What's wrong, Mother?"

"Oh honey, you're going to sleep, is all."

"I'm afraid." *The wind howled as the bed frame clattered in its awful dance.*

"It's all right. Mother's right here."

And then, in a sickening burst, all the contents of his mind flung out into the room, scattering through endless black space, leaving through his ears, his eyes, his mouth. . . .

From far away came her soothing voice, "No story tonight, Zacky?"

The sheets were fluttering as the bed spun, but she gripped his hand tighter and tighter. He looked up at her, and though her hair now whipped around her face, wilder and wilder, he could still see her smile, until he had to close his eyes.

He screamed, oh the pain in his head, oh Lonnie, it's . . . killing . . . me. Don't leave, don't leave . . . I'm . . . leaving now . . . Mother . . . and everything was flying apart, and he was crying out in a long, animal wail that ramped up to fill the room and then leaked away to silence.

Abbey tore at the visor, but her hand didn't obey. She was locked in endless black, still spinning, spinning, screaming . . . Zachariah screaming . . .

After a few minutes she slowly pulled her visor off and looked at Zachariah. His mouth gaped open and his body was splayed out in the chair. He was dead.

With her good arm, she reached over and took the tiny visor off his face. He didn't need ecstasy any more.

But she did.

She was so tired, yet so hungry, for more. Nir could choose from a wide palette of her desires . . . a last goodbye to Myra . . . a last challenge to Uncle Richard . . . She put on the glasses and the light hurtled forward into her eyes.

And the thought bloomed: *the Zachariah one is dead.* Around her swirled an eddy of consciousness, the suggestion of a powerful being. It was intensely female, one who protected the young. One who would teach her to protect the young.

And then there was a deserted ocean shore, scoured by a thunderous surf. In the far distance was a figure. It began walking toward her. At the same time the intention, the brooding, of the Hhso crashed forward into her awareness with the rhythm and inevitability of the ocean breakers. It frightened her, that roaring surf. And comforted her at the same time. And the one called the soohan spoke with the voice of the great ocean, giving her to know that she could be among those who served this being, since all would serve one way or another, and all would link powerfully in Nir, and Earth would evolve past failure and ignorance.

And above all the young would thrive. The young would receive the best, not the discards. Not the hand-me-downs.

Abbey retreated from the water's surging edge, backing up a few steps. The price was submission. Slavery. Hhso killed the imperfect.

A pulse of anger. The ocean turned steely grey, white crests curling down, dashing themselves. Abbey saw images of humanity's treatment of the imperfect, humanity's enslavement of one another, a roiling mass of misery and starvation, poverty and the trivial distractions of the wealthy few.

Yes, distractions like Nir, she thought.

The figure down the beach continued to walk slowly forward, appearing now clearly human.

The deafening presence of the sea spoke to her of the true power of the neuronic bond, with its instant links to unlimited knowing, to wonders, and clarity and the unfolding of the small and large mysteries of being and reality. These were not mere facts, but connected, integrated, meaningful knowing.

But the Galaxion might also offer knowledge. . . .

Dripping contempt wrenched through her body. An impression of worn-down, infinitely weary allies of little worth. These beings held themselves absurdly aloof with their archaic screening of worlds, of species. Fatally biased and discredited theories.

A graph with two axes occurred to her, its coordinates labeled:

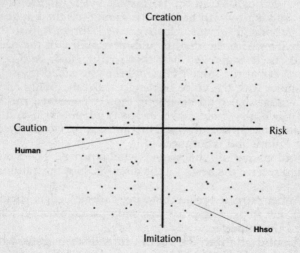

The essence of their system of values was a continuum representing the relative presence of creativity, in which the expressed opposite was imitation. All that species and cultures produced and manifested was catalogued and measured and weighed and folded into a highly complex evaluative system. The y axis represented the driving set of factors, although the range from caution to risk also carried value-laden meaning and helped to place all worlds in functional relation.

And although the matrix was merely a simplistic expression of the highly empirical metric of the Galaxion, it was clear that worlds and species were, to the Galaxion, only a series of coordinates. Dots on a diagram. Those above the y axis, admitted. Those below, excluded. The Creation Matrix. It destroyed. It cut the galaxy in two, severing the body of sentient life.

The ocean was composed of fathoms of bitterness, its frothing crests only a small hint of the frenzy below.

The graph appeared again, full of worlds:

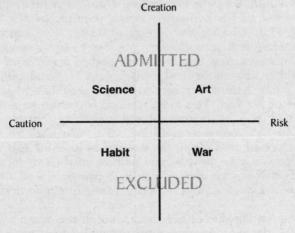

They would plot the Earth just there, a measured outcome between dulling caution and crass imitation, among the Habit Makers. Excluded. The Hhso, plotted also, in relation to risk and imitation, judged War Makers. Excluded. By the Galaxion's metric, both would ever be outcasts. But inclusion was only in the Hhso gathering, in neuronic connection with the other excluded worlds.

The concept *excluded* stirred righteous indignation, primal rage. And the placement of humanity and Hhso, in excluded quadrants. The swell of anger rumbled on the shore in an immemorial lashing surf.

The figure stood, facing away from Abbey, a few paces away. It was time to leave. There could be no purpose in bargaining with the Hhso. Abbey would remove the visor . . .

The figure turned. It was Vittoria.

She cocked her head, and squinted at Abbey, a fleeting ripple of astonishment registering on her face. *Mother?* Tentatively, she walked closer.

Abbey stood frozen on the shore.

And the words came flooding: *In Nir, no one ever dies, ever is lost. We have her forever. Duplicated utterly, her every reaction is known by neural imprint. In Nir, she lives. How stinging the outrage of death, how unnecessary. How shall a mother say goodbye to her young?*

Vitt's eyes grew luminous with unshed tears. *Mother?*

Abbey stepped forward, reaching out her hand, pulling Vitt's hair behind her ear, so that it wouldn't blow in front of her face. Her face! She had forgotten so much. She had thought she remembered everything, but no, no.

You will commune with her, as we do with all our transformed ones, dead, but not lost to us. And also you will groom your people, you will be mistress of human herds, and we will reward you with influence, and a network of knowing. And with this young one who lives in Nir.

She felt the skin of her cheek, cool in the ocean wind. *In Nir, she lives.* As Vitt's mouth trembled for a moment, Abbey took her daughter in her arms, holding her with all her strength. Her heart swelled to fill her chest.

Where are you? The query echoed down the beach. A strange question.

She held Vittoria, who clung to her with increasing abandon, now sobbing. A fleeting stab of fear: in an instant Abbey realized her peril. She jerked her body away from Vitt, staggering backward . . . Vitt reached out for her, her face shattered with pain . . .

Abbey pulled off the visor, hands trembling and cold.

The Hhso didn't know where she was.

But they wished that they did. They cloaked their intention . . . but they would not truly allow her to choose. . . .

She heard calling from deep in the house. Voices, human voices. Abbey sprang up, falling over her bound feet, crashing onto the floor.

"Up here!" she heard someone shout from the hallway.

She lay crumpled on the floor, clutching the glasses, as the image of the ocean receded in her memory, but the vision of her daughter lingered. *Vitt, Vitt, oh Vitt.* By the time she was able to sit upright again, an old man was gently shaking her by the shoulders, saying, "It's OK, it's OK."

He was untying her ankles. Someone was standing beside him.

"He's dead." It was an older woman with a kindly but grim expression. "This dreadful game," she said.

A man stood behind her, young, with a goatee. "My God, the game *killed* him?"

"Culled him out," Abbey murmured.

The old man pulled closer, looking at her with concern. "What's that you said?"

"Culled him out of the herd."

He looked up at his companions. "Let's get her out of here."

They helped her to her feet. "How did you . . . get here, find me?"

"That's a long story," the old man said.

"We heard someone screaming. We were just breaking in downstairs," the woman said. "I'm Gilda, and this is Max and Nigel. Don't worry, hon. It's over now." She took Abbey's other arm, looking keenly into her eyes. "That was Zachariah Smith, wasn't it?"

Abbey nodded. She bent down to retrieve the visor from the floor. Inside it was a piece of her daughter—a piece that contained all, more indeed, than she had had of Vitt in life. . . .

The old woman gently withdrew the glasses from Abbey's grasp. "No. We'll just leave this here." She fixed Abbey with a friendly yet steely gaze.

Abbey allowed the woman to take the visor and steer her toward the door. Yes. We'll just leave it here. Tears streamed down her face, accompanied by a growing fury. That the Hhso could . . . offer her . . . that. Their hideous bribe.

They descended the steps, Max supporting her on one side, Gilda on the other. Behind them, she heard the younger man, the one called Nigel, still repeating, "The game *killed* him?"

Abbey looked into the old man's face. He was perspiring, with droplets of water trickling down his hairline, his skin pale as bone. "It's not over," she told him.

With a trembling hand, he patted her arm. "I know."

Out on the porch Gilda put a sweater around her shoulders, a welcome wrap in the crisp spring air. Abbey made her way over to one of the porch pillars and sat down, leaning against it.

"I don't mean to rush you," Gilda said. "But if you know what's going on in Medicine Falls, tell us. Nigel Cobb here is a very influential man. He can call in help."

A groan behind them.

"Max!" Gilda sprang up.

The old man had fallen to his knees. He crumpled to his side as though his bones had turned to sand. "Oh God. Jesus, it . . . hurts." The last word came out as a whisper.

Gilda was at his side. "Max, Max!" She rifled through his pockets, finding a vial of pills. "Water!" she told Nigel, who disappeared into the house on a dead run.

Abbey crawled to him. He was panting, his mouth slack, his eyes clenched shut and squeezing tighter in a rhythmic pulse, the tracing of pain on the slate of his skin. "Hurts . . ." he whispered.

"His heart," Gilda said, looking up at Abbey, then back at Max, wincing as he winced, holding his hand to her chest, as though to teach his heart a steady beat.

Nigel was back with the water.

As Abbey held Max's head up so he could drink, she

saw out of the corner of her eye, someone standing in the driveway. She turned her head to look.

Simon.

He was about twenty meters away, standing there, watching. He began walking slowly toward the porch steps. Stopped. "Abbey," he said. He looked then, over toward the bunkhouse, then back at her.

Her eyes filled with tears. "It's started," she said. The end of the world. But Simon was here, and that was something to hang on to. It was everything to hang on to. A man like Simon didn't give up, didn't leave in the spring with a "thank you ma'am," didn't let the flood hold him back. He was here.

Still weak, she made her way to the head of the stairs and slumped against the pillar again. "Zachariah's dead, Simon. Nir culled him out. These people helped me."

He nodded, coming closer. "Abbey. I came as fast as I could. I've been crazy . . . so afraid . . . that you . . ." Moving up the stairs and kneeling in front of her, he touched her cheek with a soft, slow caress. She moved into his arms, shaking now, but holding him with all her strength.

At last he stood up. Looking again at the remains of the bunkhouse, he said: "Rose called me on the mobe."

"She did?" Abbey could feel it, something coming. There was more, always more.

"He left, Abbey."

"Who?"

He paused, holding her gaze. "The Regent. He gave up."

She sat stupidly, trying to process, or maybe trying not to. "They've abandoned us?"

He looked off toward the shattered light of the encrusted bunkhouse. "I think they need a little wake-up call." As he fished in his pocket, all at once she knew. Knew that he had the pendant. Jaguar's words circled back around her. *If the Regent is gone, you will end in fire.*

She struggled to rise.

He didn't help her.

Her plea came out in a deep shudder: "Please, oh please no, Simon."

Backing down the stairs, he stood, finally, at the bottom, in the mud of the driveway, looking up at her. "My love." Then he turned and walked toward the barn.

Behind her, Max groaned. Gilda dabbed at his face with a scarf, looking up from time to time at Abbey. "Who is that?" she asked.

Abbey staggered down the steps, woozy. Then turned to face Gilda and Nigel. "For the love of God, can one of you help me?"

Nigel got a nod from Gilda, and he hurried to Abbey's side.

"The barn!" she whispered, and they started forward. The mud sucked at their feet, conspiring, with Zachariah's poison, to keep her from her job. "Oh please," she said, over and over.

"What's in the barn?" Nigel asked, his voice nearly as shaky as hers, sounding like a man way over his head.

"My . . . job," she said.

The front side of the barn was still a natural, weathered red, not yet turned to stone, or whatever was happening to the rest of it. Through the wide-open barn door a shaft of light reached in vain for the deeply dark stalls and soaring rafters. The aroma of hay and silage lapped up to their faces as Nigel and Abbey staggered into the cool gloom.

Just past the terminator line between day and night lay the burned circle that had taken Rocky. Simon was standing next to it. "Don't move, Abbey," he said.

"The destination's gone," she said. "It ends in fire." He remembered that part, didn't he? That it ended in fire?

He nodded.

Of course he remembered. How slim are the threads we hold on to, when so much is at stake. He knew, and it made no difference.

"Maybe our galactic neighbors need a little call to arms," he said, in a chilling, steady voice. He put the pendant around his neck.

"Simon, oh please, let me do this. It's mine to do," she said. "From the beginning, it was mine to do. Please . . ."

"What kind of a man would I be, to let you do this?"

She shook her head, slowly, helplessly. "Simon, that's a crazy way to think."

"Why?"

"It's so old-fashioned!"

"That's me. Always was."

"No, it's not being old-fashioned, it's being controlling, taking what's mine!"

"OK, it's being controlling."

"Jaguar gave this to *me* to do."

"Maybe he thought you were the only one who cared enough. And maybe he was right, a few weeks ago. Not anymore. I love you, Abbey."

She shook her head, not to say that he didn't, but just trying to say, *don't let me kill you too.*

"You're still young, you can still find someone Abbey, someone worthy of you. Promise me he'll be worthy of you this time."

"I don't want anyone else. . . ."

His mouth hardened, and she knew mere words would not sway him. She started toward him, but he put out his hand, palm up.

"What's going ON?" Nigel asked, looking from one of them to the other in high frustration.

With her eyes still on Simon, she said: "We're saying goodbye."

"I love you, Abbey."

"Let me go too." It was for the best, it would cancel the pain, it would . . .

He shook his head, looking at her with great tenderness. "My love, this is my gift to you. Let me give it. Please." He gazed at her another moment, across that gulf of distance between them.

Her voice rose from her throat like water drawn from a deep well. "I love you, Simon." she said. "I always will."

Simon turned and entered the Leap Point circle. In his

hand he grasped the medallion hanging around his neck. In a heartbeat, a crisscrossed web began climbing up from the circle to form a cylinder of cracked light around him, from the floor to high in the barn rafters. His eyes appeared closed as he stood there, relaxed and tall, until the interior of the cylinder clouded, obscuring his form.

A deep ringing sound invaded the barn, as the vase of light appeared to solidify. She clung to Nigel, and he to her, as the ringing escalated to a reverberating gong. As the sound grew deafening, the column shriveled, collapsing the image of the man who stood there, until only a thin line stretched from floor to ceiling. It shifted, becoming a plane, like a giant wall. Then, rotating, it was a line again. Then a wall.

For a brief moment a scene appeared on that wall. A creature—it took her a moment to see that it *was* a creature—faced away from her. A narrow head and pear-shaped body resting on two great haunches. Covered with a grey, velvety fuzz, with ridges running and branching through it, in what might have been external blood vessels. In front of this creature extended a horizontal bar, a pipe sparkling with nodes of light. She saw a short arm reach out and a pincer clutch the bar, indenting it, and causing a few facets to glow brighter. Then, slowly the creature turned . . . a delicate, very narrow face with two double-irised eyes . . . *the Regent,* Abbey thought. It seemed to frown, or squint. At last it looked right into Abbey's own eyes, and it lifted its long chin in what she would have said was a look of dumbfounded surprise. At the same moment it squeezed the bar again, eliciting a frenetic light show. . . .

"Yes!" Abbey shouted. "We are Earth. We exist! How dare you say we aren't worth it!"

The wall turned, shrank to a two-dimensional line. The vision was gone. Then, as the clanging noise sheered up in pitch to the uppermost reaches of their hearing, the line exploded, sending a shock wave that threw Abbey and Nigel flat on the ground and took out the front wall of the barn, sending debris flying across the barnyard.

For several minutes Abbey lay stunned in Nigel's arms.

She lost consciousness, thinking, *I'm dying, I'm dying. Simon, wait for me.* But before long, she heard her name called. Nigel was kneeling beside her, his beard singed heavily on one side.

"What, what the hell is happening around this place!" Nigel was shaking his head as though the explosion had occurred inside it.

As Abbey looked up at him, her attenion shifted to the barnyard behind him. She had to pull some words out. She grabbed at words and they came loose, like rotting weeds. "Nigel," she said hoarsely, "do you know how to be very, very, quiet?"

He nodded. "Why?"

She grasped his arm, and pulled him backward with her as she crawled into the ragged corner of the barn.

In a moment Nigel found his voice, such as it was. "Oh, sweet Jesus."

Several Hhso stood at the entrance, not five meters from them, looking silently at the steaming circle of blackened earth.

Abbey gripped Nigel's arm, hard, trying to maintain silence. Sensibly, he said no more.

Another Hhso walked slowly around from the side path, pivoting for a moment to look, apparently, at Gilda and Max, still on the house porch, then rotating back to resume his course to the barn door. Behind him, several more. Perhaps, Abbey thought, Simon's passage had sent alarms through their midst. Their numbers grew until a small gathering stood. Their smell lay pungent in the swath of afternoon sun pressing into the barn. Occasionally a susurrating vocalization would pass among them.

One stepped forward. It had a great splotch on its beefy upper arm where the hide bore some violent mark. This one turned to look on Abbey with a steady gaze, aiming straight at her quivering stomach, bringing to mind, *if looks could kill. . . .* But she met him, glare for glare, while holding on to Nigel's trembling arm.

The scarred one turned away. Something else was approaching. Something massive, slow-moving. The group of Hhso parted, and from their midst emerged a hulking

individual, identical to the other Hhso except for towering a full head and more above them. It emerged from the
huddled group to stand in the gaping opening of the barn.

Nigel shrank against Abbey's side, drawing the attention of the creature. Its head swiveled to gaze at them, and
its mouth parted in an enormous, slotted grin. A panting
noise emerged. Nigel backed up, crawling farther into the
corner of the barn.

Abbey held the being's stare. The leader, clearly. Perhaps even the one who spoke to her in Nir, who offered
her shadow-Vitt. Abbey faced off with this creature, unwilling to flinch, to be the first to break eye contact. *She
doesn't live in Nir. Nothing lives in Nir. We live while we
live, and when it's time, we die. And if I'm going to die
now, let's not pretend it's something else. Whether you
are the high-and-mighty sooh-an, or only a pitiful female
frantic to breed: let's call things like they* are.

The creature turned away, pivoting back to stare at the
steaming circle. It appeared stunned, if its reactions could
be gauged at all. Then, it lumbered forward and entered
the circle, and was instantly encased in a maze of webbed
lines within which its form wavered. Behind Abbey, she
heard Nigel whimper. She quieted him with a hand gesture, all the while watching as the creature became at last
a spun ring of light.

Two Hhso stood together, watching this scene. Abbey
waited for them to turn on her, to take their revenge. She
was preternaturally calm. Then, a noise filtered into her
consciousness. From a remaining shred of the barn frontage, a plank of wood hung down, swinging in the slight
breeze and squeaking from the top where it hung from a
nail. The squeaking set Abbey's teeth on edge, even amid
the bizarre scene playing out before her.

It may have been a universally annoying sound.

In a spasm of violence, the foremost Hhso grabbed the
plank, yanking it loose. Then it stopped dead and closed
its eyes, holding the plank above its head. Something
stirred amid the crowd; a creature, pale and tubelike, with
four arms—the being Lucy called an *I-haar*—chose an unfortunate moment to enter the barn. Swinging around,

and bringing the plank around with him in a vicious sweep, the Hhso caught the I-haar in the side with a hammering blow. Again and again the Hhso smashed the board against flesh until the creature lay immobile at its attacker's heavy feet.

All was still as stone. The gathered Hhso watched and waited.

Another plank-length distance from the chief, the second Hhso stood rigidly, with, Abbey thought, a look of terror on its face. But the first individual wasn't looking for another victim. He faced into the barn, arms at his side, as though seeing beyond the end wall, where a yellow gleam shone through a knothole in the wood like their hopes for a new creche, for the fields of Earth.

After a moment the board dropped from his hand to the floor. With a slow-motion, measured step, the first Hhso walked to the circle and entered it.

No sooner did an aura surround him than his lieutenant walked like one hypnotized toward him and stepped in also, as a core of light pulsed hotter and they coexisted in the same space, or alternated, first leader, then subordinate. Whatever havoc Simon had produced with his destructive act, it appeared that these creatures were in a hurry to leave. One by one they walked swiftly into the light stream, clutching, all clutching something suspended from the leather breastplates they wore. Their beacons, perhaps. Oh, they would know their way home, would leave the back door open in case Earth repulsed them, would leave this herd behind, seeking other, easier stock. Would bow to the superior force of one man who with his body blocked their advance. Exposed their stealth. With a shout loud enough for the galaxy to hear.

Oh, Simon. Your wake-up call. I believe, Simon. Believe it was heard . . .

The line of Hhso advanced, going home. Abbey watched, transfixed and numb, watched as they stepped over the body of the I-haar where it lay in a pool of pale fluid.

They were gone.

A tumble of dust from the rafters announced a hole in

the barn roof, in the exact shape of a circle. Dust motes swam in the core of sunlight, a core that held steady as Abbey walked to the circle, passing her hand through the shaft of light.

"Don't!" Nigel said.

Abbey stood in the exact center of the shaft. "It's just sunlight," she said, though she felt Simon everywhere, in her very marrow. "It's over. The Leap Point is gone."

Chapter 17

~1~

Grummel High School had taken a beating on the Lowell Street side, with missing windows and decimated landscaping, but the basic structure had withstood the deluge with stone, mortar, and sheer irascibility. This town landmark had become the disaster relief center where now about two hundred people were being treated for major and minor injuries on the gymnasium floor, among them Max Cobb. To Gilda's eye he looked pale, but not that awful fish-belly white when the heart attack took him down. To her relief, Max was getting sharper by the hour. Sharp enough that Nigel was able to go back to Colson, driving that all-terrain thing he called a car, and wearing a decidedly stunned expression. Gilda doubted he would ever leave his electronic fortress again, but then, maybe she underestimated the lad.

The doctor looked down at Max with a worried frown. "Care for a cup of tea?"

Gilda paused a beat, trying to make eye contact with the man. Eye contact was important. Once you got the Nir folks to really look at you, *focus* on you, they tended to have more of their wits. "He's not supposed to drink right now," she said.

"Not thirsty?"

"The nurse said, if he loses consciousness, he shouldn't have anything in his stomach."

"Oh. Right. Heart, was it?"

"That's right," she said, as though speaking to a bright six-year-old. "His heart."

As the doctor continued his rounds, Max groused: "That youngster will kill me yet."

"Maxwell, that youngster is at least thirty. And he's doing the best he can."

"He's no more than a teenager," Max insisted.

"At our age, everyone looks at least fifty years younger than us."

She looked at him, smiling, as they intoned together, "Because they *are* fifty years younger than us." She wondered how she was going to break it to her son that, at forty-one, he was old enough to find his own apartment, and that no, at sixty-eight, she was not too old to take a lover.

Mrs. Lydell, the retired main-branch librarian, approached carrying a stack of blankets, handing one to Gilda, who unfolded it and tucked it around Max's shoulders. Given the state of the few befuddled doctors and nurses, older people were the only ones you could depend on. An energetic group of elderly women had taken over the cafeteria, creating a soup kitchen of the first order, while work crews of grey-haired stalwarts were busy cleaning up a few of the main streets to allow at least a minimal passage of traffic.

Gilda sighed. It was a mess. But it was a comforting mess. Comforting that a few medical types had summoned their wits and showed up to help, comforting that politicians and bureaucrats still believed that government was possible, comforting not to cringe anymore at youngsters in sunglasses.

Not that folks were Strictly Normal, mind you. Those gripped by Nir—the Lost Ones—were still fading in and out. Like radio signals from a distant town, people were tethered to reality by a fairly tenuous link. One moment they were staring around themselves as though they'd forgotten what they were just that moment up to, and the next, discussing the Hhso as if they were last week's infestation of grasshoppers.

Hhso was the name they gave the visitors, the purveyors of Nir. Pronounced it with a funny up-front sound like a soft cough. Gilda had seen them herself, these reddish dwarf-creatures, had watched them disappear into the barn, but never knew their names until she overheard Mayor Hodges tell Mrs. Lydell that the Hhso thought Earth was more trouble than it was worth.

"Once the Leap Point blew," the mayor said, between mouthfuls of tuna sandwich from the piled-high serving tray in the Grummel cafeteria, "it rightly put us on the map. A few more days, and they'd of been here in force. Might've been hard then, to get rid of 'em."

Mrs. Lydell had nodded, a little worry wrinkle between her eyes. Gilda herself might have been the only person over sixty who figured the alien-invasion theory was more than a pervasive rumor. But rumor wasn't the word for it. To hear the Nir folks talk, it was more like a conviction, or a shared memory—like the memory of a near-death experience . . . as indeed, it could well have been.

Gilda made her way to the list of the dead. The latest update still didn't show her son. In her heart, she knew he was still alive, and by force of will she would continue to think so, rather than hang out by this damn list. The toll had soared to 108—sadly, many of them her friends and acquaintances. It didn't say how they died, swept away by Medicine Lake—or Nir.

The sound of helicopters trickled through to her hearing. The outside world. Taking notice, folks said, of Zachariah Smith's crystalline bunkhouse and its unique inhabitants. But the connection between the barn, Zachariah Smith, the game of Nir, the creatures—wherever they came from—and the nice young woman who seemed so upset at the ranch, all that was on a back burner in Gilda's mind. In due time it would sort through; in due time.

Nir, for instance, had lost its hold on the town. Discarded, abandoned, littered on the street. Cast aside as easily—as old people, it occurred to her.

Another helicopter rattled overhead. The U.S. Army, a day late and a dollar short, but dear God, how she loved them. The sound fairly thundered outside, that unmistakable rattling of big chopper blades. She hurried across the gym, and joined several others in climbing the folded bleachers to stand on tiptoe to peer through the windows set high in the gym walls.

A line of helicopters stretched north into the distance, toward Zachariah's ranch, thumping the air in a satisfying turbulence, the growl of the U.S. Army, on the move at last and maybe just a tad pissed off.

Far out, she whispered. Her spine tingled with excitement. By damn, it would be fun to fly one of those things.

~ 2 ~

Colonel Ishida stood slowly, stretching his arms as far as the biosafety suit allowed. He had been sitting, watching the alien form laid out on the surgery table, for what seemed like hours, and his back felt like it had a boomerang embedded it in. As he reached toward the ceiling of the refitted jet, he pressed his hands firmly against the bulkhead panels, allowing the craft's rumble to gently vibrate through his body.

When he looked back down, the creature was stirring.

"*Colonel . . .*" Major Dunning warned him through the headset.

Ishida saw from the corner of his eye an army guard move a step closer, spray adhesive at the ready. No guns aboard ship. If the creature became violent they had more sensible ways of subduing it. The colonel eyed the guard back into place. "Easy, now," he said into his suit mike. "Slow and easy, patient gaining consciousness. Time is eighteen hundred hours." The scanner above the table shifted lenses with a soft clicking noise.

The patient recoiled. Then a spasm took the battered, segmented body and bent it into a high arch, giving it the appearance of a dog-sized caterpillar moving into a humping forward walk. The four arms—each ending in fleshy disks—flailed like feathers in a high wind. As the center of the creature arched upward in a fair approximation of a bell curve, the pale skin stretched and thinned, giving Ishida a glimpse of a shadowy form the size of a fist moving underneath the skin.

"Discrete, subcutaneous object appearing in specimen's medial section, moving slowly. Purpose unknown."

Whether the moving object was a mobile internal organ or the creature's last meal, Ishida had no idea. Possibly the subject was pregnant, or about to reproduce asexually, or getting ready to defecate. My God, they were starting from nothing, absolute zero. All that he was sure of at this point was that it was alive, and a creature totally unknown to science . . . with a strong presumption it was not a terrestrial being, in which case even its chemical makeup and respiratory requirements were also uncertain.

To his great relief, the spasm subsided—if a spasm it was.

The subject had been found in a barn on the outskirts of a nondescript Midwest city in the aftermath of a devastating flood. No one knew—or they weren't telling *him*— the connection between the apparent sabotage of Chief George Dam and the discovery, by a team of medics on a heart-attack call, of this mutilated, unidentified creature. If there were others, none had been found so far. The colossal responsibility of keeping this specimen alive long enough to maximize their understanding of it was almost paralyzing. Anything he might do—or not do—could be critical to the subject's survival. And to aid him, he had what? Thirty years' experience in . . . clinical practice and surgery. Along with plenty of unsolicited and often irrelevant advice from the gaggle of observers outside the isolation chamber.

The creature was badly torn. Hunks of pale flesh lay open, seeping a glutinous, cloudy fluid. Exposed tissues appeared as marble-sized globules suspended in the viscous solution. A circulatory system could not be discerned, nor any external indicators of organs. The head—in his judgment, it *did* have a head—was devoid of eyes or nose, but in the center was situated an ovoid, flaccid opening, possibly a mouth, the size of a Johnson dollar. The most bizarre of the myriad bizarre features of this specimen was that it had no visible means of locomotion. It did have what appeared to be four manipulating limbs, none of which looked to be adapted for propelling the creature. Perhaps, then, it was a stationary life-form, a vegetable-like form, or quasi-animal, like a sea cucumber. . . .

"Ishida, what the hell is going on?" Colin Fletcher had been fidgeting outside the quarantine bag for hours now, along with another bigwig from CDC, trying to peer through the imperfect plastic tent, advising from the outside mike when he wasn't pacing and muttering. Ishida had known Fletcher for years, and never could adjust to his frenetic energy, even if it did come packaged with the foremost biological scientist in the western hemisphere.

"It doesn't need a *doctor*," Fletcher groused for the hundredth time, "it needs close observation!"

"I am *observing* it, Fletcher, every damn move, if you didn't notice."

The sensor whirred a few centimeters down its track as another violent spasm shook the creature.

"Deactivate overhead scanner," Ishida told Major Dunning. "The sound may trigger the seizure activity."

"Colonel." Major Dunning's helmeted face hove into view. "We need the record."

"Then hook the damn thing up somewhere else. The *record* isn't worth killing the specimen." Ishida narrowed his eyes at the major, waiting for another volley of protest. None came. At last another suited guard came in to help Dunning set up the camera at the posterior end of the table.

"Ishida," Fletcher said. "It's dying. Let me help you."

The colonel swiveled to regard Fletcher impatiently. He was about to say, *It would help immensely if everyone would just keep quiet so I can think.* But, as much as he disliked Colin Fletcher personally, and as much as he desperately wanted to do the right thing and perhaps single-handedly succeed in this assignment, it was—it *undeniably* was—more than one man could do. It might be more than all of medical science could do, to attend, soothe, heal, and save the first extraterrestrial being ever to appear on humanity's doorstep.

The creature jerked, limbs flailing. This time a high-pitched, staccato mewl came from the orifice in its head. Then, abruptly, it ceased. From its side, liquid extruded in a lumpy gruel.

"All right, Fletcher, suit up."

The biologist exchanged places with Major Dunning, keeping to a minimum the number of bodies crushed into the quarantine room. When he came through the air lock he stayed just inside the chamber opening for a moment.

"Come on, Fletcher, the thing's helpless."

"Not the point, Doctor. Less confusion." He began circling the table, keeping to the perimeter, scrutinizing the figure, now gently trembling along every limb and body segment. "Turn the lights down."

"The lights?"

"Yes, let's try damping down all stimulation. It's too bright in here. See, the creature may be oversensitive to stimulation—sounds, lights, voices . . . Maybe it has a distributed sensory system, on its skin, even. Moving the camera didn't help. I'd get rid of it and dim the lights. For starters." Slowly, Fletcher pulled a stool up to the gurney and sat on it. "Pull up a chair, Doctor. We must look like giants to this fellow."

Ishida hesitated a moment. Then, making a voice record of his decision, he deactivated the camera and turned down the lights.

Fletcher scrutinized the top segment of the creature. "What was the temperature of the environment where he was found?"

"I don't know."

"I suggest we *find out*?"

Ishida gave an order for someone to do just that. When the answer came back from the cockpit, where they were still in touch with the ground quarantine mission, he ordered the thermostat down to forty degrees. Then he pulled up a stool next to Fletcher and sat waiting, as the jet sped onward to Andrews Air Force Base and a permanent observation theater. In the twilight of the now-darkened cubicle, the creature's skin took on a pearlescent gleam, as though a remote flame of life had been fanned for a moment, deep within this prostrate body. Ishida wondered how far that flame had come in such a fragile vessel of tissue. Not for the first time in his medical career, he was struck by the ineffable quality of sentient, viable life, which could be aided and coaxed, but which could also drain away as irreparably as rain through a sieve. In the cool, humming, and silent chamber, he felt an impulse—instantly dismissed—to grasp the creature's hand and urge it to hold on.

The patient's single orifice was twitching. Ishida stared as it opened slowly to a diameter of about six centimeters. From this cavity a pinkish tendril emerged, waving slightly as though searching the air, and then extended half the length of the body, inserting its leading point into the largest wound, and extruding pale matter similar in texture to the creature's skin. The new material cohered readily to the ragged flesh, smoothing out the ruptures.

Ishida watched in fascination as this process continued for every major wound on its body, while the patient lay unmoving in any other respect. At last the tendril retracted and the orifice contracted.

Incredible. The rapidity of the tissue repair was astonishing, as though it were a liquid skin. His further musings were interrupted by a yet more amazing display.

The creature was speaking.

"Nkkk" was what Ishida heard. And then again, the aperture puckering with the effort, it enunciated, "Nkk."

Ishida and Fletcher stared.

"Kkkkinkkk. Inkkk."

The voice sounded like a squeak of chalk on a board.

But it had said—for a moment Ishida *imagined* that it
said—an English word:

Ink.

Fletcher turned slowly to make eye contact with Ishida,
then jerked back to look down on the gurney as:

"SSSSS . . . ink," the creature enunciated.

"Maybe it's choking on something," Ishida offered,
not wanting to be the first to say what they must both be
thinking.

But Fletcher was less constrained. "I don't think so,"
he said, in a hushed voice.

Again, the chamber filled with the same, high-pitched
vocalization.

Ishida took the leap: "It's saying . . . *sink?*"

Fletcher looked into his eyes. Nodded—as slow a
movement as Ishida had ever seen him make. "I wonder,"
Fletcher said, "if what it wants is *water?*"

Ishida considered this. Then he followed Fletcher's
gaze to the lab sink in the rear of the chamber. For all that
the creature had no apparent eyes, and seemed to be only
half-conscious, it was possible that it was aware of the
room's source of water. He thought for a moment about
the advisability of giving this gravely injured individual
something to drink. Finally he rose, and following his in-
tuition, he went to the utility sink and brought a paper
cup full of water, hesitating about how to administer the
fluid.

Fletcher took the cup of water and held it on the table
next to the creature.

The mouth opened. A tendril emerged and waved in
the air for a moment before arching over the body and
diving unerringly into the cup. Rapidly, the water disappeared. The tendril snapped out of the cup, waving with
somewhat more energy.

Fletcher turned to Ishida with a slightly stunned expression. "I think it wants more."

Nine cups of water later, the tube shrank back into the
mouth, where a border of flesh that might serve as lips
had now become engorged and smooth.

The being was speaking again. ". . . aaaam," it said.

A clicking sound preceded this word, a sequence it repeated two times more.

The biologist stroked his chin. ". . . come?"

Lying there in perfect stillness, the patient appeared exhausted.

"Calm?" Ishida offered.

"KKKK . . . aaam," it said, somewhat louder.

Fletcher released the cup to the being's grip. "Maybe," he said, "it's his way of saying he's content."

From the disk at the end of the creature's closest arm, four digits emerged to cradle the cup, dimpling the sides of the cup with a tenacious and gentle force.

Chapter 18

~1~

A thin dawn light seeped through the windows, revealing the wreckage of the Haskell and Ginestra agency. Every drawer lay open and gutted, with papers strewn, and Rocky's desk was stripped bare of electronics, with a few cords and cables lying about like severed limbs. Amid all this, Simon's swivel chair was pushed against the wall and facing the window, as though he might have—moments before—been sitting there, watching for someone.

Abbey stood in the exact spot where she had stood aeons ago, asking him not to turn her away, to help her discover Vitt's fate. As indeed he had. And she would have gone back and reversed it all in a moment. *Just walk away, Simon. Not your case, remember?*

Her arm ached with the Hhso poison. She held it against her body, keeping it immobile. The long walk from Zachariah's ranch last night had sapped her strength and brought on a cold delirium by the time she reached the town. She'd left Nigel and Gilda tending to the old man who'd collapsed on Zachariah's porch. With their attention focused there, Abbey had slipped away, numb with shock and needing—desperately needing—time alone. She could have slept anywhere, in department stores, abandoned houses . . . but she pressed on, no destination in mind, until, at last, she found herself in Simon's office, where she collapsed in a nest of strewn papers and spiraled into sleep.

She turned back to Simon's chair. In her mind's eye she saw him so clearly, this man she had loved only a few days—in return for his loving her always, from the first moment, he said, and now, fatally proven, to his last. A poor exchange, her love for his. As she looked back on his illness at Verna's, their hike with Rose to the dam, their time together at Lydia's house, all those moments became part of their love story, however brief. But, a poor exchange. Except, what did he tell her when they were sitting in the car waiting for Renalda, that moment before consciousness lapsed? *It was worth it, you see? It was all worth it, no matter what happens* . . . He *would* leave her that. It was so like him, to absolve her from the very beginning. With her left arm feeling like a piece of driftwood, she slowly raised her hands to find the clasp to her locket. The little clasp proved maddeningly elusive, but finally she managed to unhook it, removing the locket from around her neck and letting it fall onto Simon's desk.

As the day poked between the remains of downtown Medicine Falls, a glint of light bounced off the floor. A framed picture lay there, its glass broken. She knew which picture. Crouching down, she turned it over and carefully removed the backing, slipping out the old photo.

She took it over to Simon's chair near the window and sat with it as the day bloomed. They looked so young, he and Rocky. Slim, young, and happy, with their arms around each other's shoulders. The faces were too small to wring out all the details she hungered for, but it was enough to hold her through the morning.

•   •   •

A door slammed down the hallway. People's voices. A crew of people could be heard going from office to office, stopping at last at Simon's. A slightly stooped, bald man stood in the doorway, wearing a yellow plaid jacket and workman's boots.

"I was just leaving." She rose from the chair.

"We found a body in here yesterday," he said. "You know anything about that?"

She shook her head.

"Name of Roland Waler?"

"I met him once."

The workman regarded her another moment. "Well, we're keeping everyone out of this building because of structural problems. It could collapse. If you want to help, the women got a first-aid center down to the old high school."

She made her way down the stairwell as the building manager system sputtered in and out of life, mostly warning against using the elevator, but throwing in an occasional regret for various absent tenants, and fruitless calls for maintenance personnel to clean the lobby, which now sported a gaping hole instead of a door and four inches of mud for a carpet.

Out on the street, a warm breeze carried the stench of sewage and rotting garbage, as the temperature soared into the fifties. Beyond the wasteland of Lowell Street itself—with its mud dunes and upended tree trunks—Abbey noticed first of all a soup line threading out of the Salvation Army outlet just up the street. Blessedly, the line was short at this hour of the morning, and she hunkered down at one of the tables with vegetable soup and a large slice of bread, which, though stale, was achingly delicious sopped up with soup broth.

When she emerged back into the street, more people were out, avoiding the center section, where Medicine River had cut a two-meter ravine through the mud, and was gushing along in a cheery spring torrent. A brigade of older men and women were digging cars out of the mud, and a fire truck, planted at Lowell and Defoe, blasted the main intersection with water. Everywhere Abbey could see the tiny discarded visors, like some twiggy extension of the Hhso themselves. She wondered if they still worked—and had a fleeting urge to tuck one in her coat pocket. The urge quickly subsided.

In the distance what looked like army trucks were just entering down Fourth Avenue. National Guard, most likely, come to help with the cleanup. Or arrest the town for collusion with the enemy. Anything could happen. Anything had already happened. All she was sure of for now was that she had nothing to tell them. She barely had her own tenuous understanding, much less words to explain, much less anything resembling proof. If they wanted explanations, maybe the people who'd fallen victim to Nir could tell the real story.

If they remembered.

A crowd of people had gathered to watch the fire truck hose down the street. They were a passive, quiet bunch who looked as though they had been awakened in the middle of the night. As she walked past the crowd, she caught snippets of conversation that began to weave a ragged tapestry of the day's news: the great dam's annihilation, the flood, the army's arrival, and here and there, a comment on Zachariah Smith's ranch, the stony scabs on the buildings—as though they'd *seen* it—and strangest of all, a matter-of-fact reference to the Hhso. They even pronounced it right, like Jaguar did. And some called them "those creatures." And from the prosaic demeanor of the townsfolk, it seemed clear that everyone knew, *really knew,* that they were gone.

"Abbey."

At the voice, she turned to see Rose picking her way across the street, jumping over the stream. Abbey strode forward to meet her and gave her a long hug. "Rose!"

"You cut your hair," Rose said.

Abbey combed her hand through the remnants of her hair, the least of her losses. Tears filled her eyes, as she gazed at Rose, the first friendly face she'd seen in a long while.

Rose nodded solemnly. "You should be very proud of Simon."

Abbey bit her lip. So Rose knew.

They walked together for a few minutes as Abbey struggled to hold back tears. God, but it was foolish after all that she'd been through, to cry now. But being with a friend was like that, releasing gates, opening doors.

"Simon did a very brave thing, Abbey. My people believe that through sacrifice comes renewal. It will all be renewed. You'll see."

An army half-track plowed down Lowell Street, GIs hanging on to the sides, eyeing everyone warily. Armed. Abbey watched as it ground over a small, glistening visor set.

"Everyone has thrown the game away."

"Some may keep them. But without the Hhso influence, most folks will come to their senses."

"The Hhso are gone," Abbey said. Partly a statement. Partly a question.

"Yes. They're gone."

"Because of Simon . . ."

"Yes. He created a psionic tremor when his journey dead-ended and blew up. No one has ever done that before. You probably got the Galaxion's attention, big-time. Now they'll realize the Hhso were using a Leap Point. They're not supposed to." She picked her way around a shattered billboard, layers of ads peeling back in a collage of merchandising. "The Hhso want easy pickings. With the Galaxion alerted, they'll back off. They're like hyenas against a lion pack; they'll avoid outright confrontation."

Abbey watched as the half-track receded, tracks churning mud behind it. "They sure left in a hurry."

Rose nodded. "The Leap Point was faltering . . . and they wanted to get home before it collapsed."

It seemed funny that the Hhso had a *home*. But she guessed it must be true that everyone has a home. Some things are the same everywhere. And then, for the first time, Abbey took the time to think of what must have happened to Rose's home.

In answer to her question, Rose said, "It's gone. But

it'll be back before long. This place"—here she looked around at collapsed storefronts and the detritus of Medicine Falls poking through the mud—"will take a long time to rebuild. You folks sure need a lot of stuff to survive."

"And Verna and Jaguar?"

"They're OK." She stopped in front of a small diner. "This will do." She tried the door and, finding it open, went in. Abbey followed her.

"I'll make you some tea. You look terrible." Rose dug in the fanny pack she carried, pulling out packets of herbs, and bustled around behind the deli counter. There was no electricity, so she found some bottled water and made Abbey a weak infusion of herbs, with the unmistakable aroma of the recuperation days at Verna's.

As she sipped, Abbey tried to fill in the missing pieces of her saga. "If the Regent hadn't left, where would Simon have ended up? Where was the Regent?"

Rose was silent for a long while. Finally: "You ask a lot of questions."

No. This stuff wasn't going to fly. "Rose," she said, "we risked everything. Simon's gone. And I damn well deserve to know!"

Another long pause, as Rose pursed her lips. "A near-Earth asteroid. Hollowed out, from what I hear. I've never been there. But it's gone now, blown to bits, when Simon tried his leap. The explosion worked its way back upstream and ruptured the Hhso Leap Point too."

"Will the Galaxion deal with us now, then?"

Rose spoke in a soft voice: "It's complicated. Some predators make the Hhso look like small potatoes. We've been at war with these—not the Hhso, they're just scavengers. Our enemies have retreated, but we are tired and drained. The Leap Points are expensive. They're the only good way to travel, and to communicate. Everything else is too slow. But the Leap Points need a tremendous amount of energy, at least for galactic distances. That's why to be a member, you have to convince them that you can contribute something worthwhile."

"You have to measure up on the Creation Matrix."

Rose looked at her. "How do you know about that?"

"I had a chat with a sooh-an."

"You spoke to a sooh-an? In Nir?"

"Yeah. The big cheese herself. She offered an alternative to the Galaxion. Among other things."

"Maybe you know more than I do, then."

Abbey sipped her tea, assessing how pitifully little she did know. "The Hhso have their take on things. They think they got a raw deal from the Galaxion. And I think *Earth* is getting one."

"Well, maybe that will change now. You know," Rose went on, "you've done something no other species has ever done—driven off the Hhso. And it wasn't Simon alone. It was you, and the way the flood mobilized outsiders, and it was also old people, lots of old people." At Abbey's inquiring look, Rose said, "The Hhso misjudged the elders. They figured they were irrelevant, and easy to control. Turns out, they made a lot of trouble for the Hhso, everywhere that Nir had spread."

"But you weren't sure I had it in me, were you? So you used the medallion to show me the Hhso threat. To convince me."

"No. It was Simon that Jaguar worried about. Jaguar thought he might pull you off course, to protect you. He didn't want to interfere, but when he realized the Regent was packing up, he activated the program."

Abbey shook her head. "Rose," she said, placing her cup on the floor, "who *are* you? It's time for me to know."

Rose stood, brushing off her jeans. "Ask Jaguar these things."

"I'm asking *you*. He doesn't answer questions, you know that!"

"He couldn't before. I think he will now. Let's go ask him."

Leaving the deli, they made their way toward the Commons, as a TV helicopter circled overhead. The world was taking notice of Medicine Falls. Perhaps even the Galaxion was taking notice of Medicine Falls. And even so, she found herself returning to the loose ends of her own life. "Rose," she said as they walked, "aside from breaking

our will, do you think that Nir . . . could drive people to
. . . abnormal actions—things they would never nor-
mally do?"

Rose was silent for so long Abbey thought she might
not answer. Finally she said, "Usually the Hhso start too
strong with the neuronic bond and then step it back. And
sometimes they start out by directly activating the pleasure centers of the brain. Then the small thing you desire
becomes the thing you must have. The early beta versions,
they became too addictive, and the Hhso modified them."

Rose looked sideways at her, sighing, as though she
knew why Abbey asked. But she let it go. And Abbey was
going to press further, but then she found herself letting it
go. It was good practice, and it felt right.

As they passed Peavy's Drugstore, Abbey could just
make out Jaguar's unmistakable presence on a park
bench. He was feeding bread crumbs to pigeons. Though
he ignored them, Abbey felt sure that he was aware of
their approach.

She and Rose stood beside the bench, waiting to be
noticed.

Finally he said, not looking at her and tossing a few
crumbs at the birds: "You did a pretty good job."

She stared at him, deflated. But what was he going to
say? Thanks for saving the world? "It would have been a
lot easier if you'd just told me what it was all about in the
first place."

His quick glance sliced through her. "And you
wouldn't have run?"

Abbey opened her mouth, then closed it. Who knows
what she would have done? It was all so long ago.

"It was important for it to look like you took the initia-
tive." He tossed the last of the crumbs to the birds. Abbey
noticed now that there *were,* in fact, birds. "Without too
much prodding," he added.

Damn, but he could be galling. The cavalier attitude,
the assumption of superiority. Abbey locked on to him
with a knowing gaze. "You've manipulated everyone,
haven't you? Even the Galaxion."

The first smile she'd ever seen on him crinkled across

his face. "It was their turn," he said from deep in his belly, from some enormous fount of enjoyment. "They have manipulated my people for a thousand years. Their turn, this time."

"What kind of game *is* this? We pretend that Earth people are smarter than they are so your high-and-mighty exclusive club can decide who's worthy of membership?"

Jaguar crumpled the empty bag of crumbs and watched her, scowling.

"Hundreds of people are dead. Simon's dead! And you just throw me these . . ." She jerked her head at the crumbled bag in his hands. ". . . *crumbs* of information and expect me to accept it—to accept everything!" She stopped to catch her breath. "And you know something? I think you enjoy watching me squirm. Watching me beg for information."

His face grew darker—if that was possible—but he remained silent.

Now that the words were pouring out, she let them. Let them flood. "You never cared about Vittoria. You used my vulnerability, used Vitt's connection to Zachariah to hook me into your schemes." Rose's hand was on her elbow to restrain her, but Abbey shook it off. "You lied to suit yourself, didn't you?"

Jaguar rose slowly from his seat. It was a movement designed to intimidate, that rising like a leviathan from the deep. She held her ground. Too much of being passive, obedient. That stuff's over now.

"I am finished with you." He turned and walked away, scattering the pigeons as he cut a swath through them.

Her feet were locked in place, as though the mud were cement. She tried to summon movement, words, a bolt to strike him dead. But finally she was hurrying after him, Rose trailing.

She would make him take notice of her, of Simon.

"I'll tell them!" she screamed at him, matching his stride as he hurried from the park. "I'll tell them you conspired! I'll find a way, so help me God I will, to communicate with your honcho with the wires or whatever they are under his skin . . ."

He slowed, eyeing Rose darkly.

Rose frowned and shook her head.

"Oh yes, I've seen him," Abbey went on. "There's lots I've seen, and I'll use it all, just like you used me and Simon! Who knows, maybe they'll include us in the Galaxion, and the whole story will come out, because they'll set up their damn Leap Point and we'll be talking every day like e-mail!"

They were crossing the street, walking around a Volkswagen buried in mud halfway up its tires.

"If you were not a small, pathetic woman," he said, "I would turn my attention to this matter. As it is, I am in a hurry." Indeed, he seemed intent on getting somewhere, and his short legs carried him surprisingly quickly without actually breaking into a run.

"I'll find a way," Abbey said. Her voice deep and sure. She had done harder things: Nir in the attic, for one. And at that moment, she was convinced she would succeed.

He slowed his walk, sneaking a side look at her. Maybe it was the tone of voice. The weaker you appeared before Jaguar, the less he respected you. They were headed south on Third Avenue, where the flood had barely touched, into the warehouse district.

"I will tell you," he said simply. "You will listen." Still walking, but slower, he summoned his story for a few moments. "No questions, you understand?"

Abbey held her tongue for now, and he seemed to take her silence for acquiescence.

He began: "Long ago, my people were dying. The Galaxion watched Homo sapiens, waiting for the unfolding of your culture. Your people spent much time in war, wasting time, wasting each other. As did my people in the southern lands, but we took time to create architecture, literature, science, and art. The Galaxion took an *interest*, you comprehend? We had a unique culture, while your people were still forging swords from iron."

"Your people? The Maya?"

He squinted, and clammed up.

Abbey took a deep breath, summoning patience.

"It was the finest creation this world had accomplished, but our warring kingdoms and finally the incursion of the white conquerors sapped our strength. As a mighty people, we would disappear forever. Perhaps it would have been for the best. But the Regent . . . interfered."

A line of helicopters flew low over the tops of buildings, heralding a further buildup of army.

Rose looked up as Abbey did. "They found the I-haar," Rose said. "It was still alive."

"That ought to get the Galaxion's interest up," Abbey said. "It certainly has got the U.S. army's attention. Hey, Jaguar, we're in the game, whether you guys want us or not. You can't keep us down on the farm forever."

Ignoring this, Jaguar said to Rose: "The funds transfer is complete."

Rose nodded.

"What funds?" Abbey asked.

He turned into a cobblestoned alley off Dellacourt Avenue. The sun, now at its highest point, painted a swath of sunlight down the middle of the narrow lane. He walked in silence now, quickening his step.

Rose said, "Zachariah's estate. There wasn't a whole bunch left, but what there was got transferred to the reservation. An electronic bequest."

"I interfered a little bit," Jaguar admitted, "with Zachariah's bank account. I worry about interfering."

Sure you do, Abbey thought.

"We could give it back," Rose offered.

"I'm not *that* worried."

After a moment, he continued: "The Regent Komen-Ar was in charge when it happened."

He had switched topics again, casually expecting Abbey to accept his meanderings. She bit her tongue.

"He interfered. He was a putterer, a collector—but what else did he have to do, thrust away in the great rock, with only a few servants? His preoccupation was culture—as is the Galaxion's. They are fools! Dilettantes!" He glared at a stray dog who stopped digging at a sack of garbage to stare at them. "He lusted after what you people call *artifacts*. Do you know what an artifact is? It is a piece of our body, the spirit brought into form: sacred. But to you people—to him—it was an *artifact*." As he said this word his lips coiled like a snake. "My people were his especial favorite. So he saved a remnant, a community of three thousand individuals. They passed out of the Earth through the Leap Point and into the Galaxion, but did he truly save them?" He snorted. "It was like placing a flower in the snow. First, because we were cut off from our world and our ancestors. And next, because of the infection of technology. Though isolated, we spied out technology, beginning with the Leap Point, and other mistakes. Therefore the Galaxion took extreme measures to prevent cultural contamination, relocating us in a great jungle on a far-off world."

He stopped in front of great warehouse doors, and swiped a card through the lock panel until it blinked green. They passed through to an empty two-story garage. To one side, a blackened circle announced its purpose.

"Komen-Ar was disgraced, and he was removed from his post. The fate of my village was uncertain for many decades. But listen: my people were inventive and strong. To explain the experience and to cushion the extreme shock, they incorporated into their mythology all that was incomprehensible. Intrusions of technology became the icons of evil spirits, and as such, we could deal with them, keeping them taboo while acknowledging their presence in our midst. Over time, we invented our own versions of what we had observed, but slowly, organically. Our culture and religion make all things in relation, even the dreadful and dark things. In our cosmos everything is imbued with meaning—all places, all times in the calendar, all is sacred." His mouth curled in a lush sneer. "You have no culture. That is why your people are so crazy."

He paused. "Even you fit in, with your chosen Net name, Venus. Sacred star to my people."

"That was just a whim, that name."

"A whim." His expression flickered only slightly. "I must leave before you make me crazy."

"Yes, hurry," Rose urged.

"Another crisis. A techno leak. Someone is tinkering

again—some in the Galaxion believe they can sneak up on my village and observe us. They think we are *children*." He set his mouth, hard. "I must return. Soon my people will weave the Galaxion and all its toys into a modern cosmology. Little by little. The groundwork is laid. A few more years, when the great cycle of time will return us to power. Rose's children will see this."

He turned to face Abbey. "I must leave now. But I will tell you who I am, though you have not earned it."

"I am Toc-Xul, ancestor of the great king Kan-Jenebe of the trading center of Ahlobque. It was this village that the Regent tricked into immigrating. Afterward, to propitiate the gods, my ancestor Kan-Jenebe sacrificed himself for the restoration of his village, its return home. Still, the gods did not listen. But even so, my people have begun to flourish, after a fashion. I am their shaman. That is who I am."

He nodded, in a movement slow as transfigured stone. He moved to the circle. "Goodbye, Abbey McCrae. Keep my secrets."

"Tell her the rest!" Rose said, raising her voice so that it echoed in the cavernous room.

"The rest?" He stopped just at the circumference of the blackened floorboards. He sighed, scowling. "Words, everyone wants words." He raised his chin and looked down his formidable nose at the two of them. "I move between the worlds. I minister to the Maya remnants in the southern lands, where Mayan things still underlie white man's ideas. I move between the southern lands and the new Maya, appearing and disappearing. I am a shaman. They accept this. The Leap Point is my due, a concession from the Galaxion." He shrugged. "They're not all bad."

"How did you know the Hhso were invading Earth?" Softly, he said: "I was paying attention."

Rose stepped forward. "He was visiting *me*." Looking nervously sideways at Jaguar, Rose continued: "He detected the presence of the other Leap Point. I am his apprentice."

Abbey watched as Jaguar's chest slowly expanded, producing a long, almost indulgent, sigh. "She is young, but I do my best. You see how she repays me, by giving up secrets."

"One of you could have alerted the Regent. Why me? Why us?"

Rose waved her hands. "No. It had to come from one of you. You are representative of Earth. We are not."

Abbey stood in the cold, musty air of the warehouse, while her anger faded, and her confusion dimmed somewhat. This man Jaguar, he was so much more, and so much less, than she ever knew. Like most people, she supposed.

"Jaguar," she said, feeling a surge of emotion, "I wish you well. Speak for us . . . if you can. So it will all be worth it . . ."

His hand shot out, finger pointing at her. "Understand this. I did not do this for you. I did it for my people, my remnant in the old villages, the southern hills. Your ancestors are paltry, weak, and cowardly, and I soil my name to be the white man's savior."

Abbey lobbed her best parting shot. "Then, in a sense, Simon and I were *your* saviors."

As he stepped into the circle, Abbey thought she saw the slightest twitch of a smile at the side of Jaguar's mouth. He looked up at the rafters, his hand cradling a medallion around his neck. A razor line of fire raced, buzzing, around the circle's perimeter. As she'd seen in the barn, the Leap Point seemed to grow from this molten ring, like volcanic fissures appearing in a seemingly cool crust. The filaments shot upward in branching veins until they flared for an instant, turning dark. Jaguar's image was obscured by what appeared to be a glassy liquid. In an incandescent snap of light, the Leap Point compressed into a rotating plate that spun, accelerating, until the molten matter in the disk migrated to the edges, creating a glowing hoop.

He was gone. The two women stood for a moment, while bright circles floated on their retinas. The warehouse cooled into shadow.

Rose's soft voice broke the silence. "When we leave

this building," she said, "I won't know you." Her face crumpled into a rueful half-smile. "Sorry. It's that I'm the only one, the only apprentice. I protect my identity, like Jaguar does. The Galaxion allows one shaman to interact with them, and use the Leap Point. And one apprentice, to keep the unbroken line of knowledge of my people."

"Then you're not from Sun Rock."

She smiled.

In the dark warehouse, Rose's form looked as insubstantial as a ghost. As though she was already fading from Abbey's world. Fading from the regular life that Abbey must now return to. If anything would ever be *regular* again. Abbey put out her hand and Rose took it, grasping it with great delicacy.

It seemed to be the end. It had all happened, it had all been told, or most of it. She formed her last question. "Will we ever join the Galaxion, do you think?"

Rose shrugged, reminiscent of her teacher. "Stranger things have happened," she said.

~ 2 ~

By the end of the second day after the flood, Fiffer Road leading to Zachariah Smith's farm was closed to traffic and serving as a staging area for army, FBI, and local law-enforcement operations. A security cordon encircled the ranch house, the ruined barn, and what officials surmised was the remnants of some kind of outbuilding, perhaps an old bunkhouse.

It was hard to tell just what it was. It looked like a geode turned inside out. In the eyes of the soldiers assigned closest guard duty, it looked *wrong,* for sure. The cheerful, sparkling yellow of the stuff did little to disperse the unease among them, particularly as all of them knew there was an alien creature somewhere in all of this— supposed to be secret, but even a grunt could pick up the innuendo. Or maybe the growing yellow rock *was* the alien, like in that movie. . . . Anyway, you had to admit it was damn strange that what started out as disaster assistance was turning into the guarding of a barn.

The other part of this that didn't add up was their orders to watch for any funny business from the local civilians. *Trust no one,* the briefings went. *Report any unusual circumstances.* . . . What the hell did that mean, "circumstances"? Why the hell didn't they say what to watch for, instead of leaving everything to the imagination?

Word was that a Red Cross helicopter flying over caught sight of some old woman waving a white towel in the front yard here. Her husband had gone down from a heart attack and as they packed him up, one of the copter crew checked out the ruined barn.

Whatever he saw, he called his supervisor.

When their army unit arrived, a makeshift tent stood cloaking a portion of the ruined wall of the barn, and though they had taken the—discovery—away, the plastic sheeting and poles remained to mark the spot.

"That crystal monster, man," Corporal Hamula said to his partner.

"That what it was?" Private Eckles asked. "The thing they dragged out of there?"

"Yeah, I think so. . . ."

The captain stopped as he passed them, and their conversation paused in freeze-frame. He eyeballed them. "You got orders to think?"

"No sir."

He nodded. "That's right, you don't. Turns out we found a bomb, not . . . anything else." When they didn't catch that as an order, his eyebrow went up.

"Yes, sir." He watched them for another second, then walked off, leaving them to their for once fertile imaginations.

That night as a new patrol kept watch, the sounds of the alien bubbles spreading over the barn cracked like teeth bearing down on rock.

•   •   •

Phil Agnew wasn't the first reporter to tear into Medicine Falls after the flood, but he was the first to write the real story. While others were interviewing the flood victims and the Red Cross field director, Phil was checking out the extraordinary army interest in the Zachariah Smith property.

He got as far as the entrance to the Smith driveway, when the army checked *him* out.

He managed to play dumb and get out of the interview after a half-hour of paranoid questions and a phony briefing on a bomb blast that looked to have taken off the front half of a large red barn. Dutifully, he took notes on the army's cover story. After which he hitched a ride back into town in a Red Cross van and started talking to folks who told a different version of the trouble at Zachariah Smith's ranch.

The trouble, it seemed, was that Zachariah Smith was playing host to a group of individuals known as the *Hhso*. Short—as Simon Haskell had said—and broad, with a close-cropped, napped hide. From the planet Hhra.

Phil got the impression that many people were just plain dazed, that parts of them were shut down as they tried to make sense of the last month out of their lives. But even the most bewildered seemed willing to talk. Everyone was talking. To him, to each other—as though getting it all out was important, perhaps therapeutic.

His interviewees looked him in the eye, and didn't justify or overexplain. Phil took furious notes. All the while, thinking, *Jesus H. Christ, is this the biggest story of my life, or am I going as nutty as the rest of Medicine Falls?* And: *Sorry, Simon. I owe you one, that I do.*

People milled everywhere outside, bundled up in the cool breeze, talking, comparing notes, and helping each other with the numerous practical details of food and shelter. And before long, people recongnized Phil and would come up to him to add in another detail they remembered, seeming to take satisfaction in watching as he scribbled it all down in his notebook.

Although the stories were varied, and laced with personal anecdotes of all that Medicine Falls had gone through, one thing everyone agreed on: The Hhso—pronounced with a decidedly un-English guttural sound—were all gone now. And good riddance. Except for the I-haar, the genetic-construct assistant of the Hhso. One of *those* didn't go home, but was hurt pretty bad, and most folks hoped he'd be all right. Asked to draw both the Hhso and the I-haar, people in Medicine Falls produced perfectly consistent sketches.

Strangely, after all they'd been through, the residual emotion people expressed was not one of fear, but closer to bemusement. They had all experienced a sense of each other *as a whole*. A whole that, briefly in Nir, was both intimate and energizing. Phil kept trying to find a term for it, for his story. He tried *sense of community, patriotism, town spirit,* but people frowned, shaking their heads. No, it was more like *gathering* or maybe *unity*.

Then did they miss Nir?

He only asked that question once.

Older folks were a different matter. Most he'd questioned seemed puzzled by what they considered rumors of aliens. They preferred to talk about the flood instead and the retina game—Nir—that had come close to shutting down the town for a while. But mostly, the elderly were too busy to talk for long. They were the only ones running the place, aside from the now steady stream of outside volunteers come to provide flood aid.

After searching in vain for Simon Haskell and Rocky Ginestra, Phil sat down in a diner on the edge of town, ordered a large plate of bacon and eggs, and wrote the most bizarre story of his career. The story of a town with a nearly univeral experience of alien intrusion and deliverance; and the story of the Nir possession, the game that delivered your deepest fantasy. For just a small price. When he finished, Phil Agnew had no idea what to make of what had happened in Medicine Falls between Palm Sunday and May Day, but he did know what nearly everyone in Medicine Falls *thought* had happened.

And that was story enough.

He e-mailed it out to the *Capital Tribune* and the Associated Press . . . and every reporter in his journalistic address file, a network of contacts and close friends from thirty years in the news field. Then he found a tavern called the Purple Haze, and ordered a stiff drink, thinking about Simon Haskell and the phone call when he'd taken a rain check on the story of the millennium.

While network TV was dutifully discussing the crackpot rumors of aliens, and allotting Phil Agnew's version only minor exposure, Net users were hungrily interviewing thousands of Medicine Falls residents who matter-of-factly told what they knew, and then listened with uncommon curiosity to what everyone else thought.

A week after the flood, with Philip Agnew's story circulating as fast as the spring flu, the FBI and the army finally abandoned efforts at a wholesale cover-up. It was becoming clear, as the Net conversations proliferated, that it wasn't just a case of mass hallucination in Medicine Falls. . . . True, it was the only place people claimed to have *seen* the aliens in the flesh, but the evidence was widespread: the little visors with their incomprehensible technology had infiltrated across the American Midwest and even beyond, sprouting up as far away as Darwin, Australia, and the Hupeh province of China.

On a more personal level, Phil continued his search for Simon Haskell. He never found Simon or Rocky, or any clue what might have happened to them. The only connection he might have made—a business card Simon left with Renalda Delacruz at the apartment she shared with Abbey McCrae—got thrown out with the trash when Renalda finally dumped her fantasy lover and decided to do some spring housecleaning instead.

Spring housecleaning was on the minds of many people in Medicine Falls that day.

Cherilyn Hoyle stood on her front porch in a filthy bathrobe, watching as some of her neighbors, armed with shovels, climbed into a flatbed truck to join a bevy of cleanup volunteers. Even blocks away from the main channel of the flood, mud covered the streets and sidewalks in sporadic washes of brown silt. No sign of winter snows remained, a combination of the great waters and the second day in a row of temperatures in the fifties. Rivulets of melt-off now traced their way through the silty residue, fingering down-valley like channels in a delta.

It would take a shovel just to clean the *inside* of her house, Cherilyn thought, never mind the outside. Wandering into the front hall, she spied a box with a warm meal that her sister had left, along with a note saying she'd be back to check on her. But who could eat in a house this filthy? Picking up a dirty coffee cup, an armload of newspapers, her big fuzzy sweater, and several pairs of socks, she stood listlessly for a moment wondering where to put things. Wondering how she had come to the point of playing that foolish game all the day long, and capping it off by swallowing two bottles of aspirin.

Her glance fell on a clipboard on the top of a stack of papers on the coffee table.

Squinting to see the small print, Cherilyn fumbled in her pockets for her glasses, finding them at last on top of her head. "Citizen Petition," it read, "for the Preservation of the Historic Name of Medicine Falls." Here were the names of friends and neighbors: James Caldren, Nikki Scott, Brian Gallagher, Robert Myhr, John Lindall, Billy Clifton, Ross Parish, Loretta Z. Posy. Cherilyn had cared once, about what the town was called . . . and now Loretta's name jarred her thoughts. Such a good friend, Loretta, and how many weeks had it been, since she got her to sign the petition? And how had the flood treated Loretta? And old Robert Myhr, and Nikki Scott . . .

She leaned heavily on the coffee table and struggled to her feet. Out of shape, by God. The clipboard was still in her hand, and she regarded it critically. By now those Medicine *Flats* people would be out in force, despite the undeniable fact of the flood and the grand cascade of Medicine River over the bluff, proving to all but the worst blockheads that we had, by God, a *falls*.

She headed upstairs to shower and change. And wait for the next truck ride to town.

~ 3 ~

The herd mistress didn't come around anymore, in Nir.

Riva Statten took off the visor and rubbed her eyes, vaguely dissatisfied with this Nir session and its alter-world of sweet—and cloying—pleasures. It was pleasant enough, but without the communion of the Hhso, something was missing. . . .

She twirled the goggles in her hand, absently. She felt strangely blank, unable to come to grips with anything: with this Nir game; with her odd fascination with the sooh-an; or with her disintegrating ties to the office that had once been her life. Every time she summoned her rational mind to inquire, she fuzzed over, thoughts scattering like spilled ball bearings. And underneath her mental confusion was a growing feeling of *flatness* or *restlessness*. She sighed deeply and pushed herself out of her chair, stretching her cramped legs and shoulders. Opening her office door, she surveyed the newsroom, mostly empty, with a dozen people up at the Falls covering the flood.

She circled back around to her chair and sat staring through the door at the newsroom staff, typing at computers, or playing Nir. . . . For a moment she stood there frowning, trying to connect with something. Then she started slowly walking into the newsroom, pausing at the first desk, where one of her people had decided to hook into Nir at ten o'clock in the morning. She reached down and plucked the goggles off his face.

He blinked, startled.

"Get rid of it, Dan," she said.

"Huh?"

She shook her head and disconnected the visor from his computer, confiscating the glasses. Then she did the same thing with the four other reporters who had no business forgetting the business they were in.

She spun around and stalked back to her office, gripping the mass of visors and cords in one fist. She thought she knew, now, what that pervasive feeling of restlessness was.

Boredom.

She turned at her office doorway and faced the bemused group. All eyes were on her. They seemed to be waiting for something. "OK, everybody," she said with a hint of the old Riva Statten. "Game's over. Back to work."

~ 4 ~

Abbey closed the black leather satchel, pulling on the silver-tipped straps to secure it. Half the bag was filled with warm clothes, the other half with shorts and tees; she wasn't sure just how far south she'd go, and best to be prepared for anything. She sat on Renalda's neatly made bed and pulled on her reconditioned red leather boots— still a little stiff from their mud soaking, but sure to soften up on the road. The cutaway flower designs had turned a deep burnished brown, proving that some things, like blue jeans and leather boots, did indeed improve with age. Then she undid the satchel again and stuffed in another pair of wool socks. In the last two days she'd learned— among much else—the supreme importance of warm feet.

The stunning array of possibilities stopped her for a moment. She could go anywhere; it was her first vacation in years, and she'd planned nothing except the direction— *south,* make no mistake—and anything could happen along the way. She hoped she'd have some company riding along; but that remained to be seen.

Hefting the satchel over her shoulder, Abbey went into the living room, easing the pack onto the couch. Somebody had been cleaning up the apartment, at least at the edges. In the kitchen, the empty refrigerator had been scrubbed inside within an inch of its life, and the overflowing garbage can was secured in a big plastic bag. Here in the living room a freshly potted plant sat on the windowsill, sucking up the pool of sunlight arming its way through the big oak tree outside. On the top shelf of the bookcase, amid a small bunch of dried roses, Renalda had laid out Harley's chain-link collar, its circle describing the general dimensions of his neck and absence.

It was time to go. But there was one thing she needed to do, and she'd left it for last, knowing it would be tough.

She sat down at the kitchen table to leave a note for Renalda. Grabbing an envelope and a stubby pencil, she began, *Dear Renalda . . .*

The face of her glassy-eyed roommate about to sink a kitchen knife in her chest came to mind . . . Harley's body, stiff and matted in the trunk of Renalda's car . . . Abbey looked over at the apartment door, wondering when Renalda would return. She took up the pencil again. *Dear Renalda, hope you're OK, after all the disaster and everything. . . . We'll have a long talk when I get back but . . .*

Abbey crumpled the envelope up and started on a new envelope, *Dear Renalda . . .* but five minutes later she had gotten no further.

She heard the muted slam of the front shop door, and then the sounds of Renalda's feet on the stairs. Rising from the table, she walked to the kitchen door and saw her old roommate with two bags of groceries in her arms just closing the front door, and then turning around to see Abbey.

"Abbey!" she screamed. Her hair was artfully cascading down one side of her head, pinned back with a sparkling pin. "Abbey, my God in heaven." Renalda rushed forward, crushing Abbey between the celery and a dizzyingly fresh loaf of french bread. Abbey hugged back, fiercely, not caring—or not much—about the fate of the bread. Amid the groceries, she noticed that her roommate was about fifteen pounds lighter, thin as a stick.

Renalda released her and strode forward to plant the grocery bags on the kitchen counter. She swiveled expertly on her four-inch spike heels, spreading her arms in happy exasperation. "My God, where have you been!" She scanned Abbey's head, noting the do-it-yourself haircut. The look on her face was beyond disdain.

"Honey," Abbey said, "I thought you were . . . a goner."

They hugged again. Renalda's face was painted on with exquisite care, but couldn't quite hide the pallor. Her earrings flashed with a sexual scene so complex, Abbey couldn't quite tell who was doing what to whom.

"You're not gonna *believe* this! I slept through it!" She strode over to the kitchen window and yanked on the blinds, pointing out to the mess in the streets. "I've been *real* sick." Here she rolled her eyes. "You don't know how sick—and when I got out of bed," she pointed out the window, "Medicine River had come and gone."

Renalda was back. With only a few weeks missing from her life . . . "I was worried about you," Abbey managed to say.

"Me? *Me?* Jesus, God, and Mary, what about *you?*" Her cheerful voice cushioned the blame Abbey could see coming a mile away. "Who knew where you were? You could have been killed by an axe-murderer."

Abbey stared at her blankly, only recovering herself when Renalda turned her back to dig in one of the bags.

"Look for the chip dip, will you?" she said, as she pulled out Fiesta Fire Potato Chips and ripped them open. As Abbey pawed through the other bag, Renalda went on: "Last I heard, you were going to be gone a little while. *A little while,*" she said, turning and eyeballing her. "Three—count 'em—*three* weeks later, and the Chief George blows a gasket, and not even a phone call!" She turned, and with a mouthful of potato chips asked, "So how *are* you. Tell me everything."

She hadn't planned what to say. Didn't know what could be said, what condition Renalda would be in, how much she'd even want to say. So she was plenty surprised when what came out, did. "It was a guy."

Renalda's face sprouted a knowing smile. She struck her forehead in mock dismay. "I should have known! My God, cooped up for months—if not years—in this dump and suddenly Mr. Right comes along, and you're oughta here, phttt . . . gone!"

It was the perfect answer. She fell for it, hook, line, and

sinker. It was the perfect out, and it felt lousy, but no turning back now.

Renalda put the perishables away, leaving the half-full grocery bags on the counter, as Abbey dug into the potato chips. Her roommate raised an eyebrow. "You, eating potato chips?"

"Yeah. Why not?"

Renalda smirked with one of her *Okaaaay* kind of smiles and plunked herself down at the kitchen table, scooping up a gob of dip on a potato chip. Mouth full, she waved her arm impatiently. "So tell me everything, who is he? No, wait. What kind of car does he drive? How tall is he?" She stopped in mid-chew, and looked carefully at Abbey's face.

Abbey was suddenly unable to continue the charade. She felt her throat constrict.

After a pause Renalda said, hopefully: "He's a wonderful lover, right?" Then, watching Abbey's face, her smile retracted in a long, slow slide.

She reached across the table grabbing Abbey's hands. "Jesus, I'm such a fool." Her eyes, doe-like. "It didn't work out?"

Abbey stood up, moving away and brushing the crumbs off her jeans. "It worked out," she said softly. "It just didn't last long."

At this revelation, this exquisitely familiar territory, Renalda audibly sighed. "You're shook up, aren't you? This guy must have really been something. . . ."

She faced Renalda, suddenly unable to say more, unwilling to share what was left of Simon, her memories, unwilling to give them word shapes and watch them float away like helium balloons, into a sky too big to care.

"Look," Abbey said, "I'm off to pick up a friend of mine. . . ."

"A friend? Another friend?"

"Yes, and I'm going on a little trip." She escaped into the living room, retrieving the silver-studded knapsack.

One of Renalda's Revlon eyebrows arched at the sight of the showy black case.

Abbey shrugged. "I bought a motorcycle." She paused. "A Harley."

Renalda's jaw was locked in the position of a cruising trout.

"Can you watch the shop for a couple weeks?"

"Sure . . " Renalda grew quiet.

"I need to get away for a while."

"Where are you going?"

"A little road trip. Be back in a few weeks." At Renalda's expression, she added, "Promise."

As she turned to go, Renalda grasped her arm, and they faced each other again. "Abbey, about Harley . . ." A look of anxiety crouched in her face. "He ran away. I looked everywhere for him. Maybe he'll wander back, after the town settles down. . . ." After another moment she said, "I've been sick, you know? Delirious, I think."

Abbey gave her a quick hug and, grabbing her satchel, headed out the door and down the stairs.

"Hey! Wait a minute," Renalda shouted after her, "did you hear that everyone thinks the Hhso are like, *aliens,* or something?" In the quality of her voice, it was as though Renalda had said, *"Did you know the rent is due again?"*

Abbey froze at the head of the stairs. Taking a moment to process this statement, she turned slowly around, looking at her roommate, who stood in the doorway with a bemused expression on her face. "Yeah, I heard that."

"Well, what do you think?"

Abbey gazed at Renalda another beat, and then said, "I think we kicked their ass out of Medicine Falls. And if they ever come back, we'll do it again."

At the bottom of the stairs Renalda's voice reached her with one last jolt of conversation.

"I guess the I-haar survived."

Abbey hiked the satchel up to a better perch on her shoulder. "Take care, Renalda. It's great to see you back to your old self."

The used XL 1200C Sportster was waiting for her outside, its pockmocked chrome still gleaming after three decades. The Pidduck Brothers New and Used actually carried a loan for her, and threw in a cutaway helmet with the gold "live to ride" trim on a concord blue background. If she hadn't known Jason Pidduck for twenty years, Abbey would have thought this transaction enough reason to believe in alien possession.

She donned her fringed leather gloves and started the engine, that deep-throated rumble going po-ta-to-po-ta-to, and eased into the street, finding her balance after several motorcycle-less years. The polycarbonate tinted windshield kept her snug enough as she pushed the motorcycle up to a modest speed, maneuvering around obstacles in the road with mud spitting out behind in great fantails as she took the corners. The plastic bag holding the size-six leather jacket fluttered against the bungee cords holding it onto the rack behind her.

Vitt's father had taught her to ride his Kawasaki years ago, and time had not diluted the sheer joy of riding free with the sun glinting off the buckhorn handlebars and the tach face. Once, when Vitt was about twelve, she had put Vitt on the back and the two of them had cruised down to Bison Caves in cutoffs and biker boots, with the hot breath of the August day streaming over them. When they discovered they'd forgotten the sandwiches, Abbey sprang for a fancy meal at the Valley Inn, where people stared at their bare legs and leather jackets, and where she'd let Vitt eat her piece of cherry pie *before* the meal. . . .

She swerved to miss a rolled-up sleeping bag half submerged in a drift of mud, and then a shattered ceramic pot. . . . You had to keep your eyes peeled, or anything might reach out and grab those tires. All the bits and pieces of Medicine Falls not securely tied down had found themselves cast up on the beach after the tide of events. Already, folks were picking through the flotsam, searching for what was theirs, or what could become theirs. Some looked up as Abbey rumbled by, waving, like they used to do in the time before. All, or almost all, faces she knew, by sight or name, or reputation . . . the people she had gone to the barn to redeem, the people she had used the dam to destroy. Like Jaguar they were both more and less than what she supposed, but each of them was known to her, and knew her in turn. They had all witnessed each other's lives, even Vitt's, for as long as it lasted. Jaguar's words ran a continuous loop in her mind: *who are your people, Abbey, who are your people?* She figured, now, that she knew.

She'd be back to help clean up Medicine Falls. This road trip was just to blow the carbon out and get a head start on healing. To be ready for what came next. And if it was to be a social call from Earth's galactic neighbors, then she was going to have something to say. And it didn't matter that she was just a small-town antique dealer without a college education. She was plugged into the Net, and she knew things people would listen to: The Galaxion wants something from us. They want contact with our vibrancy, our youth. Because they're past their prime and scared of dying. So if we ever get the great privilege of haggling over the price of admission, we want credit for what we bring to the table. We want respect. And we want our own damn Leap Point.

The day was clear, with a towering blue sky presiding over the scenes of wreckage in the city streets. She rode on, turning onto SW Defoe. The afternoon sun cooked up a fine stew of supersaturated aroma from rotting garbage, overrun sewers, and dead fish carried down from Medicine Lake. It was wonderful. *Smell that, Vitt? It's just normal human stuff, bad enough, but sweet too.* The plastic bag flapped in answer, fibrillating like some living thing. But Vitt's answer never came.

She brought the Harley to a roaring pause in front of the St. Croix apartments. There was still time to move on, go solo, the familiar pattern that had always worked so well. But she found herself flipping the ignition switch off, and sitting there in the settling, pregnant quiet.

Faces pressed against occluded windows, at the heights of children from seven, maybe, to seventeen. One of them could have been Vitt, could have been Abbey herself, as the old brownstone hoarded its secret tenants, kept them alive and peering from windows like all the children who ever lived, like your heart kept all the children you ever were.

From the group crowded just outside the front door, and spilling down the steps, the little girl Abbey had come for stepped forward, her yellow ponytail perched high on her head and swinging as she jumped down to the sidewalk. "That yours?" She eyed the motorcycle with wonder.

"Sure is." Abbey swung off the motorcycle and removed her helmet, running her fingers through the remains of her hair. "I'm going on a road trip," she said. "You could come with me, if you want."

The youngster looked at her with calculating, narrow eyes.

Abbey nodded. "I'm saying I'll take care of you. It means minding me and taking baths, and sometimes, it means a long motorcycle trip where we don't care what happens."

"You're the lady who came to see Lobo," the girl said. Her face fell into a doubting shadow. "The one who said we'd all have to go to school."

"Yup, that's part of the deal." Unhooking the plastic bag, she pulled out the small leather jacket and shook it out. "I used to have a little girl. We had lots of good times."

Sooze was eyeing the jacket. Abbey thrust it out to her. "Want to try it on?"

Without a moment's hesitation, the girl stepped forward and touched the leather sleeve of the jacket. She rolled the material under her fingertips, as though she'd never seen leather before.

Abbey helped her into it. The zipper didn't quite work, so Abbey secured the leather jacket belt in a tight cinch, and pulled the ponytail free. "What's your name?"

"Sooze." Sooze hugged the bulk of the jacket against her, a smile tugging at her mouth, but not quite making it out.

"Well, Sooze, you coming?"

She nodded, solemnly.

Abbey swung her leg over the seat, and fired the bike up, then reached over to help Sooze onto the back.

The girl leaned forward from her perch: "Can you really drive this thing?"

They eased off from the curb and headed south, down SW Defoe and out toward the down-valley highway. "Just hang on tight," Abbey said, "and let's find out."

About the Author

KAY KENYON, the author of *The Seeds of Time*, has worked as a radio and TV actor and copywriter, and in a Cousin Reality as a bureaucrat. She was raised in Duluth, Minnesota, and now shares a vintage old house near Puget Sound with her husband, who is also an avid reader of science fiction. Between them they have four sons and a very large cat.